LOOKED DOWN UPON

THE EXILED KIN

JORDAN LOPEZ

To my Grammy, Debbie Sacherek.
You were one of the first readers of this book and believed in me until the very end. Through good times and bad, you never failed to make me smile. I hope that I keep making you proud. May your soul rest in eternal peace and remain "Forever Young." This book is dedicated to you. Love you always, your grandson, "JoJo."

LOOKED DOWN UPON

THE EXILED KIN

JORDAN LOPEZ

1

ORDEAL OF FAITH

Mowing the lawn on a beautiful yet scorching hot day in the town of Blackroot, Tennessee, Lucas "Luke" Ramirez is drenched in sweat. His brown skin tans in the summer sun, and as he inhales deeply, the pleasant but sharp scent of freshly cut grass attacks his nostrils.

The neglected garden has grown into a lush jungle, resisting the outdated mower. The more Luke pushes forward, the more the grass fights back. Its contents tangle within the blades, overwhelming the mower. The motor comes to a full stop halfway through. Luke falls to his knees and rests his eyes, deciding to take a break. I should've mowed it last week like mom asked, Luke thinks to himself.

His mind wanders off until a whisper in the wind falls upon his ear, and Luke stops. Gazing up, he sees a shadow across the street. It darts away before his eyes can focus. Luke shrugs his shoulders and flinches as the handle scorches his hands. A figure arrives in front of him, grabbing him by the throat and burning it. Luke shudders, recognizing the man in his black mask. He's haunted his dreams for a while now. Luke attempts to pry the arms off his throat, but his attempts are in vain. The Masked Haunter's gnarled hand launches toward Luke's face, and he closes his eyes.

"Luke?! Luke! *Nieto!*" A distant voice calls out.

Luke gasps and looks around, no sign of any shadows or monsters. His hands are still on the mower, but the motor has shut off. He glances back at the porch, seeing his grandmother.

"Is everything all right, dearie? You've been standing there staring off into space for a minute or two now."

Luke smacks his head and violently shakes the cobwebs out, sweeping his textured, dark hair out of his earthy brown eyes. The sixteen-year-old will be starting his sophomore year of high school in two days.

"Yeah, Bela, I'm okay. I . . . I just think the heat is getting to me."

His grandmother rolls her eyes and gingerly walks away, mumbling under her breath, "Silly boy, forgetting to drink in the heat."

Luke pulls the ripcord and continues his chore. The tiny lawn usually only takes about ten minutes, but today it took Luke almost thirty. He glances back where his grandmother beckons and kindly offers him a refreshing glass of lemonade. After a big gulp of sweet lemon goodness, Luke shatters the peaceful silence.

"Shouldn't Mom be home by now? It's nearly half past six. It's time for dinner."

"I'm sure she's on her way, dearie," Sophie says.

Sophie is small, but she has a fiery spirit at seventy-two years old. Her dark, wavy hair with gray streaks reveals her age. A Puerto Rican flag hangs proudly beside the front door. The red, white, and blue pops against the neutral-colored siding of the house.

Sophie smiles proudly at it and back at her grandson, wrinkles surrounding her tired eyes.

Minutes later, the red station wagon belonging to Luke's mother pulls in, and an exasperated Courtney exits her vehicle with bags of groceries in hand. The sun's rays reflect off her caramel skin. Thirty- seven years old, dark circles surround her eyes. Courtney's personality and looks resemble Sophie.

Luke takes no time to berate his mother's tardiness.

"Where have you been? It was time to eat twenty minutes ago," Luke says, putting his hands on his hips.

"I'm sorry, Luke, I got stuck in traffic. I know how important routine is to you. Can you please help me with the bags, honey?" Courtney asks.

Luke carelessly seizes two handfuls of groceries. Sophie lumbers to the dining room, the weight around her middle slowing her steps. As her son sprints for the kitchen, Courtney follows closely behind. Luke nearly knocks over his grandmother, passing her in the narrow hallway.

"Lucas, be careful!" Sophie yells.

"Sorry, Bela," Luke says, still full steam ahead to his destination.

"This is why you should stay in your wheelchair, Mama," Courtney says, holding Sophie up.

For the past two years, Sophie has battled liver cancer, and for the last three months COPD—a disease that affects her lungs and requires her to breathe through an oxygen tank throughout the day. Despite being ill, she still fights to live as normally as she can.

As for her grandson, he might never live a fully normal life. Luke has autism, albeit on the high-functioning end of the spectrum. It's still a challenge, as he has difficulty making friends and coping with change.

The Ramirez family lives in an old, small cottage. Courtney is a nurse at the hospital across town. She works long shifts to provide for her family so they can have a roof over their heads.

Luke sets the bags on the floor. Right away he hears the

pitter patter of paws trotting across the floor. He turns around and a mass of brown fur jumps on top of him, bombarding him with wet kisses.

"Pedro, down boy," Luke says, petting the dog's forehead.

The loyal German Shepherd obeys and backs down. He acts as a shadow, following Luke, who loves Pedro like the brother he never had.

The family is not a wealthy one, but when it comes to love, there is plenty to go around.

The creaking of the chairs echoes in the dining room as the Ramirez family takes their seats at the table. Due to Luke's hatred of taking pictures and Courtney's frugality, there are no family photos, paintings, or even a chandelier in the room. The only other décor is a small cabinet where they store plates, a grandfather clock, and an old crucifix that has been passed down for generations. It looms over the room like an owl, Jesus's absent pupils seemingly following one around the room.

As per family tradition, the Ramirez family says grace, but it is to Luke's annoyance since he never understands the purpose of thanking God before a meal when they could simply say thanks after the food is in their bellies.

"Why do we have to say grace before every meal?" Luke asks.

"Luke, I thought you love repetitiveness? Also, we're Catholics. It's a wonderful gift to thank God for the food on our plate," Courtney says.

"Also, I'll throw my shoe at you if you ever ask that question again, *comprende*?" Sophie says as she points her fork at Luke.

"Yes, I understand, Bela, but still, if God loves us so much, then why did he give me autism? Why did he give Bela cancer? And why did he kill Dad?!" Luke shouts.

Both Courtney and Sophie exchange surprised looks and nod. They know how to diffuse the situation. This comes up from time to time when Luke thinks of his deceased father and becomes aggravated—he sometimes has difficulty controlling his emotions.

"Honey, God doesn't give us more than we can handle," Courtney says. "Look at you, you're doing much better than any of your elementary school teachers thought you would. I mean, you're doing great in regular classes. Your abuela here is spending quality time with her family. She is the toughest fighter I know. Her love, faith, and perseverance keep her strong. As for your dad, it simply was his time. We never know the day our time comes, and everything happens for a reason, honey. Now, please finish your supper."

"Listen to your mother, dearie," Sophie says.

Luke has struggled with his faith as of late, as he's found it extremely difficult to believe in something he can't see, hear, smell, touch, or even taste. It wasn't long ago that a Sunday consisted of their family going to church, but with his mother having to work more hours, his grandmother being sick and already receiving the Sacrament of Anointing of the Sick last year, and Luke being a teenager who wants to hang out with his friends, it's been phased out of the equation. The fact that the family has little money to spare for the church didn't help its cause either. Luke refuses to argue any further. He doesn't want to get a shoe thrown at him—again.

Luke cleans his plate within ten minutes of the food being served. He remembers that he wanted to ask his mother if he could spend the last day of summer vacation with his best friends.

"Mom, is it fine if I hang out with Drew and Bonnie tomorrow?" Luke asks.

"Okay, but just make sure you're home before curfew. It's the first day of school the day after. I want you to be well rested," Courtney says.

Curfew is at nine o'clock, as it's always been during summer vacation. Luke's mother worries about him on a daily basis, so she requires a curfew to make sure he is always in bed by dark.

"That's plenty of time. Thank you, Mom. Have a good night," Luke says as he drops his dirty dishes into the sink.

Luke has no memories or recollection of his father because he passed away in a car accident when Luke was only three years old. He apparently loved Luke unconditionally, or so his mother tells him. He often gave him piggyback rides and took him to the park to play on the swings. His mother speaks really highly of him.

Courtney told her son that his father's name was Benjamin Miller and that he was a successful mechanic. She met him in middle school, and they got married right after graduating high school. They had Luke after three years of marriage. Luke had always wondered what his father looked like, but his mother said he wasn't big on taking pictures, so there weren't any photos of him in the house. Luke is curious what they would have had in common if he were alive today.

Luke washes his plate before running upstairs and taking a well-deserved shower. He always takes steaming showers, having never liked the cold. He enjoys the feeling of his drenched hair, the texture of it when he runs his fingers through like wet pasta being drained into a colander. After drying off and putting on his pajamas, Luke returns to the bathroom to brush his teeth. He dislikes the aftertaste of toothpaste. The lingering flavor of mint is an annoyance to him, but he holds hygiene to a higher degree than his comfort.

Luke's bedroom is relatively small. He doesn't have a TV since his family could only afford one, and it is located in the living room downstairs. In his bedroom, the space consists of a twin bed, a nightstand, a medium-size dresser, and an old toy chest which is stashed in his tiny closet. There is also a window, which has a view of the entire street. On some nights, Luke gazes at the moon until he becomes lost in thought.

Luke kneels down, the beige woolen carpet grating against his knees. He brings his hands together and closes his eyes, taking a deep breath in to recite a brief prayer.

"Dear Heavenly Father, I ask that you please look after my friends and me. Amen."

With his nightly routine finished, Luke lies in his bed and closes his eyes before finally drifting off to sleep. Luke dreams that his grandmother is healthy and happy. His dad is alive, and he and his mom hug and kiss. Luke and his friends are celebrating that the school bully, Rob Jones, has been expelled from school. Luke is surrounded by loved ones, and all is peachy.

Suddenly, the sky turns to an eerie darkness. Luke's family and friends have caught on fire, but for some reason, Luke is spared. He just sits there, infinitely stunned at what he has just witnessed. Then Luke sees a silhouette of a man who seems to have horns and flames engulfing him, yet he doesn't seem fazed. Luke walks closer to make sure his eyes aren't playing tricks on him. The crackling inferno and heat become more intense the closer he gets. As Luke walks behind him, the man turns around, and Luke sees that he has no pupils, just empty, soulless balls of white. There are no other visible facial features beyond those, as if a dark mask is embedded upon his face. He is also wearing some kind of robe that conceals his whole body. Without so much as a warning, he lunges toward the boy, and Luke screams. Just as Luke thinks he is done for, he wakes up, shivering like a leaf.

Perspiration drips down his nose, onto his covers. His entire body trembles in cold sweat. Luke runs his fingers through his thick brown hair and can feel the humidity. These nightmares only happen occasionally, but Luke can't help but think they have a deeper meaning. Who is the Masked Haunter? The Devil trying to play mind games on him? To trick him into doing something he shouldn't? Was it God trying to warn him of his impending doom? Or was it just that: a nightmare? Luke comes to the conclusion it is best not to give it any more thought, as it will lead to nothing except exhaustion. Luke rubs his eyes and glances at his alarm clock—it is 1:22 in the morning. He sighs and decides to go back to sleep, hoping for a more blissful slumber so he will be fully ready for the next day.

2

A BOND NEVER BROKEN

At ten o'clock in the morning, Luke dresses and embarks on a five- minute stroll to meet his friends. As he approaches the park, he sees flashes of red contrasting against the dilapidated basketball court. Drew Thompson shoots hoops in his trademark Michael Jordan jersey. Wisps of dirt kick up with every movement Drew makes, and the cracks in the faded paint seem to expand with each bounce of the ball. He drives to the basket, his large, wooly afro towering above the rim as he dunks the ball. He's seventeen years old, with bold lips and skin as dark as coal. He is the starting shooting guard for Princeton County High School's basketball team. Drew came from Baltimore, Maryland, when he was in third grade (his family wanted a quieter and better life) and was the first student to treat Luke as his equal.

Drew said, "I know what it's like to be treated differently. I have your back if you have mine." Luke proceeded to reach for Drew's back, initially thinking Drew meant it literally, not knowing what a figure of speech was until Bonnie taught him a year later. With Drew being the only African American in their grade and Luke having autism, they have stuck by each other's sides. Drew might be a positive guy, but he can scrap when he has to. Luke remembers in third grade when Rob Jones pushed him down in the hall. Drew came out of nowhere and socked him in the mouth. Seeing Rob burst into tears was one of the most memorable moments of Luke's life. Rob always picks on Luke because of his disability.

"Yo, *Luke!* What's up my brotha from anotha motha?" Drew says when he notices Luke walking toward him.

Luke laughs so hard that his side aches, causing him to reach for his ribcage. Once Luke reaches the basketball court, he and Drew perform their iconic fist bump as usual per greeting and farewell. Drew dwarfs Luke, at nearly half a foot taller, his hair adding an extra few inches on top.

"Nothing really. I've just been mowing the lawn, doing chores, and taking care of Bela. What about you?" Luke asks.

"I got a job. No biggie," Drew answers, shrugging his shoulders.

"Really? Where?" Luke asks as his voice rises to a higher pitch.

"At the burger joint, on Main Street. It's not much but it gets my Pops off my back," Drew says.

"Well, congratulations on the employment."

"Thanks, homie. Anyways, wanna have a dunking contest? While we wait for Bonnie?" Drew asks while dribbling his basketball.

"Come on, man, I'm only five foot seven with no vertical. It's highly unlikely that I beat you," Luke says.

"You'll never know 'til you try, Luke. I'll go easy on you," Drew says.

"You know I hate when people hold back against me," Luke says.

"Well, you're gonna get owned then. I'm boutta go all Jordan up in here," Drew says as he confidently spins the basketball on his finger.

"I don't want to," Luke says, shaking his head.

"Oh, you missed your shot, champ. Look who's here," Drew says, pointing behind Luke.

Luke turns his head to his left, spotting a familiar face out the corner of his eye. His face brightens upon recognizing the golden braids he'd know from anywhere. He cups his hands to his mouth and calls out to the blonde girl by name.

"Hey, Bonnie. Over here!"

Bonnie's wandering gaze shifts to the call's origin. She waves emphatically and hastily makes her way to the basketball court. As she runs, her two braids spring up and down her shoulders like two live snakes. Her blue overalls, now long faded, conflict with her pale skin and blonde hair. Bonnie is sixteen years old and a self-admitted tomboy. She wears overalls nearly all the time since she lives on a ranch about a mile out of town. Bonnie can fight with the best of them. She never shies away from standing up for herself, and especially her friends. Bonnie usually carries a notepad consisting of poetry, homework, and a planner with her daily schedule. She is the only person who loves organization more than Luke.

Luke met Bonnie in fourth grade, a year after he met Drew. When Drew was sick with the flu, Rob was being an antagonizing idiot again, when this girl intervened and told Rob to leave Luke alone. Bonnie stood face to face with Rob, who towered a head and a half above her, firmly holding her ground, and Rob decided that Luke "wasn't worth it." The rest is history, though to this day Luke still doesn't know why she hangs out with the likes of Drew and him—as she's one of the smartest people in the class—and why she seems to get flushed after spending long periods of time near Luke. Drew had told Luke a long time ago that "women are confusing—nice but confusing."

"Hello boys, playing your juvenile sports again, I assume?" Bonnie asks.

"Hey, you won't think I'm juvenile when I get paid millions just for doing this," Drew says as he swishes the ball through the partially torn net.

"I just got here a minute ago, when Drew saw you coming. How have you been?" Luke asks.

"You know, just helping around the ranch, milking cows, cleaning the stables, and lugging hay bales in the blistering heat. In my spare time I've decided to apply at a university in New York to become a lawyer," Bonnie says.

"A lawyer? So, you wanna go from shoveling shit to spewing it? I thought you wanted to become the next Oprah Winfrey," Drew says, spiraling into laughter.

Luke barely manages to contain his laugh as Bonnie punches Drew in the shoulder for his snarky comment. Luke is proud of Bonnie, but now he can't help but ask himself, *Where will he go and what will he do after high school?* Just the thought of college makes his stomach turn and palms shake, so he thinks of something else to take his mind off it.

"So, what should we do today, before we go back to school?" Luke asks.

Bonnie suggests the ice cream parlor, and Drew suggests the movies. Luke has the deciding vote, but he feels like doing both since there's plenty of time. Plus, Luke isn't in the mood to deal with one of his friends pouting all day because he decided to do what the other wanted.

"Great, we can do both," Luke says as he sticks his hands out.

"That's what I'm talking about," Drew says as he high-fives Luke's hand.

"Sounds fair," Bonnie says.

The three of them head down to Main Street—the lengthy block has all of the small town's attractions and main buildings. The public library, post office, sheriff's department, and city hall can be found here, as well as souvenir shops, restaurants, and a motel. Any tourists or people making pit stops come to Main Street, one of the few areas in Blackroot that looks like a city. Beyond this street lies almost entirely suburban neighborhoods or rural farms.

Halfway down the block, the teenagers arrive at the local theater, located in the center of town. It is relatively small but serves its purpose. The corroded letters on the Now Playing sign appear as though they could fall at any moment. The downside is that this theater doesn't feature any great recent films, so moviegoers have to watch older or bad movies. One of their friendly classmates, Ryan O'Connell, is the ticket taker. His employee cap struggles to contain his frizzy, strawberry blonde hair. As they approach the booth, Luke notices grease smeared on Ryan's glasses, which clouds his blue eyes.

"Hey, guys, what movie would you like to see?" Ryan asks in his nasally voice.

"Three for *Terminator* 2, please," Bonnie says as she holds up three fingers.

"Ah, it's quite the blockbuster. Enjoy the movie," Ryan says as he hands over the tickets, showing his braces.

Luke, Bonnie, and Drew grab three buckets of popcorn and watch *Terminator* 2; it is one of their favorite films. Despite the fact it came out six years ago, it is arguably the most well-known film playing today. Then again, Luke never understood why robots would betray their creators or who would repair them when they had damages or needed to charge their batteries. His two friends tell him it's not meant to be taken literally, so he sits back and enjoys it as best he can.

In the afternoon, the three of them go to the small ice cream parlor, which is run by the greasy-haired, cigar-smoking, and hot- tempered Italian, Giuseppe Ricci. If you're caught loitering on the property, and he sees your face, you won't be served there again. So, it's best not to get on his bad side. Many had unfortunately already learned that the hard way.

They enter the small parlor, and Giuseppe greets them kindly since they are some of his most loyal customers. Drew orders chocolate with nuts, Bonnie picks strawberry with sprinkles, and Luke chooses mint chocolate chip. As they wait, Luke's gaze falls to the old-school black-and-white tiled floor. One by one, Giuseppe serves each of them their desserts. Luke nearly drops his cone when Bonnie yells out in anger at the TV as the news anchor announces that the allegations surrounding Bill Clinton would not yet result in congress demanding an impeachment inquiry.

"I thought you dug Bill Clinton, Bonnie?" Drew says.

"I thought I did until I found out he's an adulterer and took advantage of his underage secretary," Bonnie says, grinding her teeth.

"Wait, what's an adulterer?" Luke asks.

"It's when you sleep with someone who isn't your husband or wife. So, you cheat on your spouse."

"Oh, so Drew is an adulterer? Because he's kissed girls he wasn't in a relationship with?" Luke asks.

"Whoa! Luke, easy there. I didn't cheat on any of those girls. I just kissed some without telling them about the other girls. You're supposed to be on my side, man," Drew says, raising his hands to face level in a defensive pose.

"I'm just being honest," Luke says.

"Drew isn't an adulterer. He's definitely a pig, but not an adulterer, Luke."

"Don't hold back on me now, Bonnie," Drew says.

"I think I have a firm grasp on the word now," Luke says.

The three of them decide to spend the evening hanging out at Drew's place, which is about three blocks from Luke's house. Drew lives with his father, Stephen, his mother, Tiffany, and his younger brother, Elijah, who is nine years old.

The friends pass the time playing Nintendo. Drew plugs in his only game that all three can play at the same time, *Mario*

Kart. They grip their controllers, understanding glory is on the line. Drew leads for most of the race, flexing his muscles toward Bonnie after making her spin out on a banana peel. Silently, Luke sneaks up and launches a shell right at Drew, who curses under his breath. The three go back and forth on the final lap, with Drew again leading after getting mushroom turbo boosts. Drew laughs as he's seconds away from the finish line, until Bonnie lets out a giggle and lightning strikes him. Luke passes him and raises his hands in victory. Drew smacks the carpet as Bonnie smiles and points at him before flexing her arms, getting the last laugh.

Drew and Bonnie settle their rivalry with a game of *Donkey Kong* while Luke takes a bathroom break. Luke arrives back to them at the loading screen. After many intense rounds, it ends in a stalemate, with neither able to conquer the ape as they are repeatedly crushed underneath barrels.

"I'm just going to write some poetry and study. Enjoy your games, boys. Extended periods of playing video games are not good for the brain," Bonnie says.

"Whatever you say, nerd," Drew says, inspiring Bonnie to hurl a book at the back of his head.

The video games remind Luke of a couple months ago, when his mother brought him to a hangout with other teenagers his age with autism. The other teenagers were obsessed with this show called *Pokémon* that aired last year. It has a TV series, trading cards, and is coming out with games soon. Luke doesn't find it all that fascinating, just some creatures that "evolved" into stronger creatures. At the very least it wasn't worth hours of repeating conversation—Luke had no playing cards and little knowledge on the subject. Luke felt like the odd man out, so he didn't return. Even among other teenagers on the autism spectrum, he still feels like he doesn't belong.

After about two hours, Luke yawns, glancing at the clock

through half-open eyes. Realizing that he can't read the hands clearly, he rubs his eyes, and once they adjust, he sees it is already 8:30 p.m. They turn off the game and agree it's time to call it a night.

"See you at prison tomorrow, guys," Drew says.

"Oh, come on, do you hate learning that much?" Bonnie asks.

"Yeah, I do," Drew says with no hesitation.

"Luke, is it really all that bad?" Bonnie asks.

"I mean, the people there are that bad; the learning isn't," Luke says.

"You boys are overdramatic," Bonnie says, rolling her eyes.

Drew fist-bumps both of his friends goodbye. As they're on their way out, they notice Tiffany Thompson in her chair, reading a magazine.

"Can I give you kids a ride home?"

Luke gazes back at Bonnie before turning and nodding at Mrs. Thompson, powerless to reject such a genuine gesture of kindness.

"That would be mighty kind of you, Mrs. Thompson," Bonnie says.

Tiffany rises and throws her hair into a tight but messy bun and traipses out the door. Her large hoop earrings clink in the wind. The teenagers get into Mrs. Thompson's car, and they all drive off into the night. She is a strict yet fair woman, taking no nonsense from anyone, especially her own children. She is a receptionist for an insurance company but also provides for her two kids; balancing work with family is one of her special skills. Stephen Thompson, Drew's father, works long hours and is seldom home during the day. So, Drew and Elijah rely mainly on their mother to take care of them.

As they arrive at Luke's address, Luke reaches for the door, but Bonnie hugs him. Luke sinks back; Bonnie's arms feel like he is being hugged by a roasted marshmallow. Luke hates being touched by anyone besides his mother, grandmother, and Bonnie. When he's in their arms, all his woes fade away in an instant. The car door lock next to him clicks, and Mrs. Thompson clears her throat. Taking that as his cue to leave, Bonnie releases Luke, and he gets out of the car. Turning back, he waves goodbye to his friend. While entering his home and locking the door behind him, Luke's stomach knots up at the thought of tomorrow's unknowns.

3

WORLDS COLLIDE

Luke wakes up at 6:35 in the morning. He gets dressed and has some toast that his mother left for him. His grandmother is still fast asleep, so he walks off to school. It takes almost half an hour to walk to the neighboring town of Jasper Hills, as there are no schools in Blackroot.

Luke refuses to take the city bus for two reasons: the crowds of people and the cost of taking it daily. Luke doesn't mind the journey, as he gets to witness the beautiful country between the towns. The green fields, the lush woods, and the fresh air are just a few solaces Luke finds here. On the way, Luke sees a few of the isolated farms randomly spread outside of town; some are tobacco farms, others are cotton farms, but like Bonnie's farm, most are ranches. Drew and Bonnie usually arrive at school before Luke does since Drew's father drives him on the way to work and Bonnie wakes up before sunrise.

Princeton County High School is an old three-story building that houses roughly seven hundred students and ninety faculty. It's a small school, not budgeted very well, and quite overcrowded with students—the only high school in all of Princeton County. Luke always questions the reasoning behind this, and Bonnie replies that most public schools don't have a great budget in America's public education system. The school has no air conditioning, which makes it unbearable during the first few weeks of school.

"Hey, Bonnie and Drew! You ready?!" Luke calls out as he jogs toward the school entrance.

"Luke, ain't you excited for school?" Bonnie asks, as she puts her journal back in her backpack.

"Weirdos. We still got a few minutes to kill," Drew says, leaning back and shutting his eyes.

They sit on the concrete steps for a couple more minutes, and then head in. Walking inside, the dreariness of the gray lockers and beige walls momentarily suck the life out of the group. After a quick recovery, Drew high-fives Luke before departing upstairs for his morning class, leaving him and Bonnie by themselves.

"Let's go, Luke. Drew's a big boy, he'll be fine. We'll see him in second period," Bonnie says.

"I suppose you're right, let's get to English class," Luke says.

First period happens to be with Luke's favorite teacher, Mr. Alterman. He endures constant harassment from students and even some of his peers due to his religious beliefs, but he ignores the ignorant comments and acts professionally. Mr. Alterman teaches English; he got Luke into writing and even said that he has great potential. So, as a result, English became Luke's favorite subject.

Luke dabbles in poetry, Bonnie helped get him into it. Luke finds that rhyming words into beautifully structured messages with deep meaning is an enjoyable pastime.

Luke knocks on his teacher's desk, which Mr. Alterman initially tweaks his nose at, but that quickly changes to a faint smile upon seeing Luke.

"I think the only way I would dislike you, Mr. Alterman, was if you were a math teacher, because you're just the best."

"Well, I am honored to have chosen an area of teaching that is to your liking, Lucas," Mr. Alterman says.

Allen Alterman is the only Jewish person who works in the building. His full beard is complemented by short but thick hair. He is a plumpish man, but his eccentric button-up shirts distract most from his weight. He also has a thick pair of glasses that make his blue eyes brighten up the room.

Unfortunately, Drew didn't earn a high-enough grade last year to take accelerated English 2 with Bonnie and Luke. They told him they would meet him in second period, which is American History. Luke feels sympathetic toward Drew; he is all alone to deal with Rob and his two goons, Travis and Brandon. Luke remembers spotting the three of them together during the summer. Rob finally has himself a crew. Luke figures that he probably wants to become the "Prince of Princeton" again and required some reinforcements.

In the middle of class, someone catches Luke's attention out of the corner of his eye. A girl with lovely brown hair, sparkling dark eyes, and a skin complexion somewhat similar to his own is sitting to the right of him. She is something else; Luke can't figure out the words to express it. He begins to sweat, feeling flustered. He elbows Bonnie's arm to get her attention.

"Bonnie, who is that girl? I don't recognize her," Luke whispers as he nods his head in the girl's direction.

"Oh, her? That's Natalie Brown, a new student. I saw her walk in before you showed up," Bonnie says.

"Oh no, she's in trouble. It's important that we introduce ourselves to her," Luke says, beating his hands on his desk like a drum.

"Why?" Bonnie asks.

"Well, I think Rob will target her, and also . . ."

"Is that the only reason, or you just want to talk to her?"

Bonnie is right; Luke does want to talk to her. He still isn't sure the reason why. Luke usually keeps to himself at school.

Most of his classmates think that he is weird and unapproachable. Other than Bonnie, Luke doesn't really talk to girls. However, he has a unique sensation around this girl. He feels drawn to her, like a moth to a bright flame.

"Bonnie, what are you implying exactly? I just don't want her to get hurt. Not because I think she's pretty," Luke says.

Luke gasps, realizing what has slipped out, but there is no taking it back now. Bonnie opens her mouth for a split second but bites her tongue. As class goes by, he notices her dark freckles disappear as her cheeks turn rosy pink. Her button nose twitches when looking at Natalie, but her eyes retreat whenever Luke glances back her way. The bell rings and Bonnie gets up from her desk first. She dashes out of there as fast as she can. Luke stares at the door opening, thinking about how peculiar it is that she left in a hurry. Luke severely wants to speak with the new girl, but he doesn't have the confidence to make the first move. As soon as he is ready to cut his losses and go to history, he hears a feminine voice behind him.

"Excuse me, do you know where the math classrooms are?" Natalie asks.

Luke stops in his tracks. A part of him wishes she is talking to him, but another wishes she is asking another student. Luke slowly turns around to face the new girl. He looks around; the classroom is entirely empty besides himself, Natalie, and Mr. Alterman. Luke stands with a lump in his throat. He swallows and feels the saliva fall to the pit of his stomach. He tries but cannot gather words to form a sentence.

"Oh, sorry, how rude of me. I'm Natalie Brown. I'm kinda new around here. Do you mind directing me to the math classes?" Natalie asks.

It is now or never, Luke thinks to himself. The perfect opportunity to introduce himself to her has presented itself. He shakes off the cold feet and forces himself to approach Natalie but bangs his hip on the desk walking over to her. He desperately hopes she didn't notice as he rapidly shakes off the stinging pain.

"H-hey, I'm Lucas Ramirez, but you can call me Luke," Luke says.

"Hi, Luke. Look, I have to get to class, but maybe we could have lunch and talk?" Natalie says, shrugging her shoulders.

"I-I, okay, sure, I'll meet you there. Oh, right, the math classes are upstairs and to the left," Luke says, trying not to stutter over his words.

"Thank you, I look forward to seeing you at lunch," Natalie says as she walks past Luke and out of the classroom.

The last time Luke had so many butterflies in his stomach he was playing in the playoffs for league baseball in seventh grade. The bases were loaded, and all he needed to do was not strike out. His knees were weak; he felt the weight of the world was on his shoulders. All he had to do was not strike out, but the ball came in fast like a speeding bullet. Luke swung as hard as he could, and when he heard the crack of the bat and the crowd roar with excitement, he knew he had hit it. He hit a triple, and in the end, his team won.

Next period is history with Mr. Calhoun, and Bonnie sits on the opposite side of her two friends. Luke's mouth gapes as Bonnie walks past her usual seat. Drew sits to Luke's left, glancing back and forth between Drew and Bonnie, curious to know why they aren't all sitting together.

"What's up with her?" Drew asks Luke, cutting his eyes at Bonnie.

"Not sure. I just asked her if we could introduce ourselves to the new girl in class, and she just got kind of quiet after that," Luke says, shrugging his shoulders.

Drew has never been one for a committed relationship. In the past, he always broke things off when the girl wanted to get more serious. Once Bonnie told Luke that Drew is insecure and just covers it up with his moxie, which Drew firmly denied.

Luke feels Drew's eyes on him. Despite his failures with them, Drew still occasionally gives him advice on girls.

"A new girl? Well, go on, man, don't leave me hanging," Drew says as he smirks with excitement.

"I told her that I think the new girl is pretty, and I think she's upset. I'm not sure why; it's strange," Luke says.

Drew rubs the back of his head and his gaze retreats to the side. He mutters something out of the corner of his mouth.

"Drew? Is everything okay?" Luke asks.

"Oh . . . um, yeah, she's being weird dude. Don't worry about it," Drew says. "So, did you talk to the new girl?"

"Yep, told her my name, and she asked me to meet her for lunch."

"Oh, snap my main boy, asking out girls. I'm so proud," Drew says with enthusiasm.

"I'd hardly call it a date. It's just an opportunity for two people to get to know one another."

"Listen, man, girls never just want to talk. They want to—"

"Silence! Mr. Ramirez and Mr. Thompson, this is history, not public speaking," Mr. Calhoun yells.

"Apologies, Mr. Calhoun," Luke says.

"Sorry, Mr. C," Drew says.

Mr. Calhoun is one of the worst teachers anybody has the displeasure of meeting. He is forty-five years old, bald, chubby, and gets angry so often that his fat face seems stuck in a permanent tint of pink. He has a thick Southern accent and male pattern baldness, which left remnants of whatever hair he had just at the back of his head. His thick, graying mustache attempts to compensate for the lack of hair on top of his head.

While many found his appearance revolting, what disturbs people further is the pride in his family history. His grandfather was a high-ranking member of the notorious Ku Klux Klan, and despite complaints from the faculty, Mr. Calhoun continues to brazenly fly a Confederate flag on the back of his pickup truck.

His disregard for Rob's bullying makes History comparable to getting teeth pulled at the dentist for the other students in his class. All because Rob's uncle is a good friend of Mr. Calhoun, so he treats Rob like a prized pupil.

Mr. Calhoun is Principal Jackson's worst critic, as he was supposed to be the next principal, according to seniority. Then the more qualified Olivia Jackson came along and "stole the job from him." This made him even more bitter than he was before. Students and some staff have tried to get him fired, but to no avail. It is rumored he has friends on the board who protect him from his own heinous actions.

Rob, Travis, and Brandon snicker in the background at Drew and Luke's embarrassment. Bonnie just gives them a nasty glare. Halfway through class, Luke feels something damp and wet pelt the back of his head. Drew glances back and catches a spitball right to the face. The bullies in the back keep firing spitballs at Drew and Luke for several minutes. They growl at Rob, Travis, and Brandon in frustration and disgust. Rob smiles, exposing his yellow teeth, before flipping off both of them. As soon as the bell rings, Drew and Luke get out as fast as they humanly can. Bonnie leaves quickly too, even though she still doesn't say a word to Luke.

4

CALM BEFORE THE STORM

For lunch today, the choices include chicken nuggets, salad, quesadilla, and deli sandwiches. The generic options disappoint Luke, but when his stomach growls, he is reminded that at the end of the day, food is food. Luke and Drew contemplate the selections before choosing their meals.

"Think I'll go with chicken nuggets; it's my personal favorite," Luke tells Drew.

"I know, Luke, you've told me a hundred times before," Drew says.

"Oh, sorry, I'm feeling a little forgetful. Guess I'm nervous for my meeting with Natalie."

"Man, just relax and be yourself. If that girl doesn't dig you, she's not worth the time and effort," Drew says, placing his hands out.

Luke thinks about this advice. It seems like something his therapist would say if he brought up the subject of dating. The only difference would be the choice of words.

"Anyways, I'm going with the quesadilla. Remember, don't panic. See you after lunch. Good luck, brother," Drew says before walking to the quesadilla line.

While waiting in line, Luke catches a glimpse of both Bonnie and Natalie getting salads, just a couple spots in line separating the two of them. He notices Bonnie staring a hole into the back of Natalie's head, as if she has something to say to her, but Bonnie bites her tongue. Bonnie sighs and shakes her head side to side at Luke, as if he had stabbed her in the back. Luke sucks in some air and raises his finger, ready to retort. However, both girls disappear from sight into the kitchen as their line moves along.

"What did I do to her? I sure hope she doesn't tell her anything that'll jeopardize this lunch," Luke says to himself.

When it is Luke's turn to be served, the lunch lady deals him six chicken nuggets, fries, a fruit cup, and a small chocolate milk carton. Luke tends to gobble his food down, but he doesn't want to gross Natalie out, so he reminds himself to eat slowly. Luke scouts the cafeteria and passes Drew and Bonnie sitting at their usual table.

"Good luck," Drew whispers, giving Luke a wink and thumbs up.

"Break a leg, I guess," Bonnie mumbles out of the corner of her mouth.

"Thank you, guys, I promise I'll do my best," Luke says to his supportive friends.

Four tables away, Natalie is waiting. She waves Luke over in her direction. She is sitting by herself. Luke assumes he has been the first student to introduce himself to her.

"Glad you came to sit with me. I'm sorry, what was your name again? I was in such a rush earlier," Natalie says.

"Lucas Ramirez, but I prefer Luke."

"So, Luke, what made you want to talk to me?" Natalie asks. "Well, you're new here. I just wanted you to have a friend," Luke says.

"That's very kind of you, but are you saying I can't make friends?" Natalie asks.

"What? No! I wasn't implying—"

"Luke, relax, I was only joking."

"Oh, you made a joke? Well, haha, it was funny," Luke says as he runs his fingers through his thick hair.

Luke tenses up, his shoulders rise, and his muscles stiffen. This happens whenever he is stressed or anxious. He attempts some relaxing breathing techniques Dr. Washington taught him when he was a young boy. He breathes smoothly to calm himself down. This will help him stay focused on the conversation, so it doesn't appear like he is ignoring Natalie.

"So, would you like to tell me a little about yourself?" Natalie asks.

"Um, how about you start off first, Ms. Jokester?"

"Okay, my name is Natalie Brown, I was born in Oklahoma, and I love animals. My favorite color is green. I aspire to be a biologist. When I grow up, I want to help save the environment."

Natalie tosses her coarse hair back behind her bony shoulders, revealing a pendant around her neck. It looks simple yet exquisite at the same time. A black cord leads to some kind of circular web with three bird feathers hanging off it, nothing like the jewelry Luke has ever seen.

"What kind of symbol is that?"

"It's a dreamcatcher. If you couldn't tell already, I'm Native American. It's one of the few things I have left from my tribe. Oh, um . . . anyway, tell me about you."

Luke smacks his lips and hums, wondering what happened in Natalie's past. He quickly forgets about this. His eyes dart around the cafeteria until his rehearsed introduction remanifests itself.

"My name is Luke Ramirez. I was born and raised in Blackroot. I am half Puerto Rican and half white. My favorite color is blue. I'm not sure what I want to be yet, but I love writing; some even say I have a talent for it."

"Maybe you should be a writer," Natalie says.

"Eh, it seems kind of risky; there's no guarantee that anything I would write would get published."

"There's a risk in every job field, Luke; you can't succeed without taking risks." If you play it safe, it's impossible to amount to anything.

"Maybe you're right, but—"

"Hey, those boys, do you know them? They're coming this way," Natalie says, pointing behind Luke.

Luke turns around so fast that he cranks his neck. Just as he fears, Rob, Travis, and Brandon are heading in their direction, with gigantic smirks of arrogance and glee written all over their faces. You can't miss the three of them. Rob has dark hair with a faux-hawk hairstyle and a soul patch; he's roughly the same height and build as Drew and has a gap in his teeth. Travis is even taller, with long light brown hair, the smartest amongst them (which isn't saying much)—he lacks the superb physique that Rob has. Brandon is the shortest, dumbest, and fattest of the group. He has a dirty blonde mullet and pale skin.

"Well, well, well, what do we have here? Fresh meat!" Rob says, taking an exaggerated whiff of air.

"Hey, Pocahontas, why you talking to this slow idiot?" Travis says as he grins pridefully.

Brandon nearly burst into tears, howling with laughter. Rob slaps the table and doubles over with mirth. Natalie pinches her nose and shakes her head. Luke feels like prey as a pack of laughing hyenas encircle him, each one salivating to get the first bite as they close in.

Refusing to lay down quietly, Luke musters his nerve and leers directly at Rob. Rob returns the stare, but as the discomfort becomes too much to bear, Luke's gaze retreats to the floor.

"What do you mean by that . . . um . . ." Natalie asks, turning her gaze toward Luke.

"Rob Jones, also known as the school fool," Luke mumbles.

"That's the school king, you spaz! And didn't he tell you, girlie?" Rob says. "Oh, Luke, I thought you were always honest."

"Tell me what?" Natalie asks.

"I-I am being honest, leave us alone!" Luke says, swallowing his saliva.

"Or what? You'll have a breakdown again?" Rob says, getting right in Luke's face.

Bonnie looks up, hearing some commotion. As she sips some water to moisten her dry throat, she sees Rob hounding Luke through her water bottle. When she finally notices Luke's predicament, her eyes bulge and she nearly chokes on water while quickly swallowing it. Bonnie taps Drew on the back to get his attention. Drew looks at Bonnie with raised eyebrows, and Bonnie points in Luke's direction. Once Drew sees Luke and Rob, he quickly swallows the food he was chewing, almost choking on it. They both get up and start making their way to Luke's defense.

"What is he talking about, Luke?" Natalie asks.

"Well, I'm . . . I have . . ."

"He's autistic," Rob says. "A full blown re—"

"Shut it, Rob. Before I shut it for you," Bonnie says.

"Yeah, we'll mess you and ya boys up," Drew says, throwing his fists up.

"Oh, ho, ho—the dork brigade is here," Rob says.

Luke's head spins in circles. His eyes shift from his friends to Natalie, and to the bullies. As Rob, Travis, and Brandon stare down Drew and Bonnie, who are not backing down, Luke bites his lip. Luke doesn't want conflict, he absolutely loathes violence, but the only thing he hates more than fighting is standing idly by and watching someone else get hurt because of his complacency. Natalie is someone who is in danger of getting hurt. Luke doesn't want that to happen. He digs deep to light the fire in his belly and clenches his fists, ready to make a stand against Rob.

"What about you, Mute Luke? Have anything to say?" Rob asks, getting in Luke's face.

"Actually, I do. Why don't you, Dumb, and Dumber get out of here before we have to kick your butt again, like we did back in middle school?" Luke says, pushing Rob away.

"I don't think so, losers, not a chance," Rob says.

Luke, Bonnie, and Drew can feel the intensity in the air. Students aren't eating their lunches anymore; they are staring at the seven of them, some of them even chanting, "Fight!" Natalie's hand spreads across her chest. This certainly isn't what she expected when she invited Luke to lunch. He just hopes she can forgive him. Luke didn't think Rob would do this on the first day.

"What is going on here?!" Principal Jackson asks as she storms toward the students.

Principal Jackson has purple glasses, shoulder-length hair, and skin like copper. She is the first African American principal in Princeton County High School's history—a fair but disciplinary leader who has the respect of most of the faculty. Her straightened hair swings side to side as she drives her arms back and forth, picking up speed as she plans to discipline the seven students involved in the conflict.

"I'll ask once more, what is going on here?!"

"We were just minding our own business when the little turd wanted to start a fight," Rob says, thrusting his hands into his pockets.

Travis and Brandon nod in mutual agreement as Principal Jackson moves her eyes toward them intently. Before Drew, Bonnie, or Luke can even attempt to attest to their innocence, Natalie speaks up.

"That is simply not true, Principal Jackson. Luke and I were peacefully eating lunch when these three started antagonizing Luke and me. His two friends here were just defending him."

Principal Jackson knows all too well about Rob's reprehensible history from reading his permanent record. She understands the truth in a matter of seconds.

"Mr. Jones, Mr. Williams, and Mr. Taylor, go to my office now. Your parents will certainly be receiving calls today for your shenanigans."

"You're all dead meat," Rob whispers as he walks past.

As Rob lags behind Principal Jackson, he makes one final threatening gesture at Luke before turning the corner.

Luke brushes it off and approaches Natalie. "Thank you, Natalie, for sticking up for me. You didn't need to do that."

"No problem. I don't like bullies; I've dealt with them in the past. Luke, listen, I know you can't control what they do, but promise me that you won't fight them. Find a teacher, walk away, or ignore them if they bother you. I wanna get to know you better, but I just . . . can't get into trouble right now. I'm new here, understand?" Natalie asks.

"I understand. It's no problem at all. I promise," Luke says. "Thank you. Maybe we can try talking again tomorrow?"

"What about my autism?" Luke asks dispiritedly as he slouches over.

"What about it? Your disability doesn't define you, your character does. With friends like these two, you have to be a good guy."

"Thanks," Drew says.

"Appreciate the compliment," Bonnie says.

"Thank you," Luke says.

This girl just learned that Luke has autism, and yet she still wants to talk to him. Luke almost can't believe it. He thought Rob had ruined the moment for her. Rob failed to, just like he failed to bully Luke into submission all these years. Natalie's eyes are gleaming, like the sunlight hitting a diamond. The sight is borderline mesmerizing, one that Luke could spend hours admiring.

"Will I see you tomorrow?" Natalie asks.

"Absolutely. See you tomorrow, Natalie," Luke says, nodding his head wildly.

The rest of the day goes by painlessly. Biology and PE are Luke's two afternoon classes. Thankfully, Bonnie and Drew are in both of these classes, so he isn't worried about being alone. After school ends, Luke ponders the day and how south it could have gone. Once at home, he avoids speaking to his family, only going downstairs to eat dinner. While at the dining table, Luke shoves the food in his mouth, drawing glances from his mother and grandmother. He cleans his dirty plate and dashes upstairs, deciding to go to bed early, unable to stop thinking about Natalie no matter how tightly he closes his eyes. An hour passes before the toll of sleeplessness overtakes him.

5

YOUNG LOVE

Luke dreams of his conversation with Natalie earlier in the day. Nothing seems out of the ordinary—Luke makes full eye contact with Natalie as they get to know one another. As Luke is about to utter something, Natalie points at something behind him. Luke looks over his shoulder, expecting it to be Rob once again. Yet, no one is there. A howl in the wind hits his ears. Luke's eyes land forward again, his mouth gaping as Natalie and everyone around have vanished. Luke turns his head back and forth, another gust arrives, and the Masked Haunter sits across from Luke. He stares right through the teenager's soul with his white, empty eye sockets. A chill travels up and down Luke's spine as he fruitlessly attempts to pull himself out of the chair. The frozen teenager tries to talk, but a short squeak is all he can muster. The Masked Haunter pounces across the table onto Luke, the creature's chilling hand enfolding his throat, choking the teenager as he fails to pry the hand off of him.

"Ahh!!!" Luke screams.

Luke looks out the window—the moon glows in the starlit sky, and the crickets chirp in the night. The Masked Haunter has continued appearing relentlessly these past few weeks—

just the thought of him makes Luke's blood run cold. He attempts to put the recurring nightmare to the back of his mind and returns to bed. He thinks blissful thoughts, such as spending time with his friends and his date with Natalie. Soon enough, this strategy returns him back to a slumber.

The next few days seem almost too quiet. Luke and his friends learn that Principal Jackson sentenced Rob, Travis, and Brandon to after-school detention for three days. However, they haven't been showing up to their classes since. Rob can't have many chances left before the school considers suspension or even expulsion. Please, God, let him be expelled, Luke thinks. after what Natalie did for them, Bonnie now holds some respect for her and is on speaking terms with Luke again.

"Man, I can't believe we might not have to deal with Rob anymore very soon," Luke says, smiling widely at his friends.

"Trust me, that buffoon won't go quietly," Bonnie says.

"There's no way that stupid gorilla would try to fight all of us in broad daylight. Even with Brandon, the hyena, and Travis, the string bean. They're all talk, no action," Drew says, puffing out his chest.

"Guys, we should probably get to class. I'm gonna go find Natalie. I'll meet you in English, Bonnie," Luke says.

"Sure thing, Luke," Bonnie says, waving without looking at him.

Luke walks down the hall and catches Natalie talking to Patricia Roberts and Sandra Wilson, two bleach-blonde popular girls from Jasper Hills, the much larger town across the county. Bonnie had mentioned that both have grown close with Rob, Travis, and Brandon.

"Hey, Nat!" Luke shouts from down the hallway.

Natalie looks over her shoulder, letting out a small gasp as she places a hand on her chest. As Natalie looks over her shoulder, she sighs in relief.

"Oh, Luke, hi," Natalie says, waving as she glances back at the two girls.

Patricia and Sandy walk away, giggling at one another. Both girls abhor Luke, Drew, and most of all, Bonnie. Since elementary school they have despised her for numerous reasons, from the fact that Bonnie was from Blackroot instead of Jasper Hills to the way she dressed. They even got most of the other girls to exclude Bonnie from their activities. One time, when the girls were playing double Dutch, and it was Bonnie's turn to play, Sandy shouted, "No boys allowed." Bonnie followed that insult by punching Sandy in the face. She got detention as a result and refused to participate in activities with the girls for the rest of the year. She had preferred hanging out with Luke and Drew ever since.

"May I walk with you to class?" Luke asks Natalie.

"Absolutely. I thought you'd never ask," Natalie says.

Luke has his mind in the clouds, thinking about the test in third period for science today, when he feels something soft and warm touch his hand. Luke pulls away from it and looks to see Natalie with her hand out and her head tilted to the side.

"What were you doing?" Luke asks.

"I was just trying to hold your hand, Luke, is that okay?" Natalie asks.

Luke remembers hearing Drew say that holding hands means your relationship is solidified. Well, his exact words were "on lock," but the point still stood. Luke's palms feel clammy from the potential realization that he could have his first girlfriend. He quickly wipes his hands on his shirt to dry them off so Natalie won't be put off.

"S-sure, that'd be excellent," Luke says.

Luke's quivering and clammy hand slowly reaches toward Natalie's. Their palms meet. Natalie's hands are soft and well-moisturized, like a newborn. The only other girl's hands he's felt are Bonnie's, and her hands are scarred and calloused from years of manual labor like building fences, carrying hay bales, and fixing the tractor.

They stride together across the hallway, met with glances from other students. When the pair arrive at English class, Bonnie catches a brief glimpse. Luke rips his hand away from Natalie's grip so fast that a couple drops of sweat hit the floor. Luke paces away from Natalie in a hurry. While Natalie still has her feet planted in the same spot, she has one eye raised and lifts both hands momentarily before they swiftly fall to her hips with a smack. Luke takes a seat next to Bonnie, bracing himself for a scolding. He widens his eyes, but Bonnie merely scoffs and turns the other way, flipping her braid in Luke's direction.

"Why can't you just be happy for me, Bonnie?"

"I think she's very nice. I'm just concerned is all," Bonnie says.

"Why would you have any reason to be concerned?"

"Well, sometimes, Luke, people are only out for themselves. She could just be using you."

Luke tilts his head sideways and bites his bottom lip, not saying anything.

"Natalie knows you have autism. Maybe she's taking advantage of that to do something bad to you," Bonnie says.

Luke leans back and throws his hands in the air. He cannot stand when people other than his therapist bring up his disability. He rarely advocates for himself, despite strong recommendations from his therapist, teachers, and mother to embrace his true self. However, Luke sees his "true self" as something rather shameful. In his mind, whoever knew about his autism would treat him differently, like he was inferior.

"Are you saying I'm gullible? Like she's playing me like a musical instrument?" Luke asks.

Bonnie's jaw drops, and she frantically shakes her head. She drops her blue pen and reaches out her hand.

"Luke, you know that's not what I meant. Look, I'm sorry. It's just —you've known this girl for all of four days. I just think you're moving too fast."

"It was just a little hand holding. Then again, Drew once said it makes a relationship official," Luke says, tapping his chin.

"Please don't ever take dating advice from Drew. There's a reason his longest relationship lasted only two weeks," Bonnie says.

"That's actually a good point, Bonnie," Luke says, stroking his chin.

"Okay, class, today I want you to write a poem. Its theme can be romantic, inspirational, or expressive. With your imagination, pen, and paper at your disposal, the world is your oyster," Mr. Alterman says.

Luke has a poem he wrote weeks ago in his backpack. It is about the hardships that come with his disability. Dr. Washington recommended that he write it to raise his low self-esteem. As a kid, Luke struggled learning basic skills that many considered to be "easy," such as tying his shoes and reading. Through patience, help, and will, he has overcome these problems. However, Luke still feels alienated by most of his teachers and peers. He doesn't see how a poem is going to change that.

"Come on, where is it?" Luke asks himself as he rummages through his backpack.

When he showed it to his mother and grandmother last month after family dinner, they sat on the living room couch with broad smiles. Luke tugged the collar of his shirt and gulped. Unconvinced that it was as fantastic as he initially thought, he slowly handed his mother the poem. She placed one half in his grandmother's bony hand, so they could read it at the same time. When Luke saw their eyes move across the page, and their mouths silently uttering the words, he clasped his hands together, covering his mouth and nose. As they got deeper into the poem, Courtney put her free hand over her mouth, and Sophie's eyes started shining, and a single tear flowed down her cheek. When they finished reading, Luke crossed his fingers, hoping they liked it. Courtney and Sophie wrapped their arms around Luke, hearing his voice quake. They pleaded with Luke to show Mr. Alterman when the time came. He agreed, and now is as appropriate a time as any to share it.

Luke pulls out his poem. He reads it over, but feels it's missing something. So, he places his old poem on his desk and rewrites it with a couple last-minute revisions. He presses his pencil against the paper and starts jotting down the words of deep, powerful meaning or, as Mr. Alterman would say, "words of art."

"God created me as I am
Please do not feel pity
This was all according to plan
Please do not feel pity
For I am no different from you
Society has your thoughts on me skewed
I also want a girl to hold and love
And elevate myself to the heavens above
Please do not feel pity
Everything is how it should be."
~L.R.

Luke puts down his pencil and blows the eraser shavings off his paper. He closes his eyes and takes a deep breath in and blows warm air out. He compares the original with the revised version until deciding that the latter is superior. Just moments later, Mr. Alterman collects the students' poems, and then slowly falls back into his chair to grade them.

The majority of students take advantage of the free time to

pass notes around and gossip to one another. Luke leans forward, staring at the chalkboard. Bonnie knocks on Luke's desk, catching his attention before handing him two notes. Luke unfolds one, revealing a hand-drawn smiley face with the initials B.D. at the bottom. Luke glances up to Bonnie smiling; she mouths the words, *You're a great writer.* As he breathes a sigh of relief, he opens the second note, which is scribbled over. Luke narrows his eyes and can just make out the initials N.B. in the corner. Turning around in his seat, Luke raises his eyebrow at Natalie. She nods and gives him a thumbs up. Luke notices the original words on Natalie's note are in black ink, while the scrawls are in blue. He glances back at Bonnie, who had handed him both notes. She shrugs her shoulders as he shows her the unreadable note. He stares at the note for a few more seconds before stuffing both papers inside his pockets.

Luke watches Mr. Alterman set his red pen aside and arrange the stack of papers in front of him. The teacher sifts through the poems and grabs one of them. Mr. Alterman adjusts his glasses, his mouth moving along with the words as he reads. His blue eyes seem captivated by whatever is written on the paper; he doesn't take his eyes off the poem. His fingers caress his thick beard. The teacher's eyes scan the top of the poem, and a genuine grin spreads across his face. Mr. Alterman gingerly gets up and marches toward Luke, who stares up at him with wide eyes.

"Luke, this poem is quite phenomenal. May I please share it with the class?" Mr. Alterman asks.

"Oh . . . I, um . . . don't know," Luke says as he shakes his head back and forth.

"Please don't make me beg now, Mr. Ramirez," Mr. Alterman says. "Sure, you may," Luke says, tapping his foot.

"Thank you, Luke, you have a gift. Your work must be shared," Mr. Alterman whispers.

Luke never likes to brag about his work, yet he allows Mr.

Alterman to share his deepest personal thoughts with the class. He also struggles to say no sometimes, and he almost immediately regrets his decision. What if people hate the poem? Luke plays with his fingers as Mr. Alterman unfolds his poem. He stares as Mr. Alterman walks heavily to the front of the classroom, tugs on his suspenders, and clears his voice.

"Excuse me, class, may I have your full, undivided attention?"

The entire class stops chattering within seconds. It isn't fear that silences their voices but rather the mutual respect the students have for Mr. Alterman. They turn their heads forward, anticipating his next words.

"Mr. Ramirez has permitted me to share his masterpiece. Please listen and hold your applause," Mr. Alterman says as he adjusts his glasses.

As Mr. Alterman reads carefully, Luke slowly sinks his head down to his desk, dreading the class's reaction to his poem. After Mr. Alterman has finished reading the poem, there's a pause of silence. Luke expects nothing but cricket chirps. Luke doesn't look at anyone, not even Bonnie. He can't bear the thought of anyone throwing harsh criticism his way, but as the seconds pass, scattered applause is heard throughout the room. Luke glances around the classroom; many of the students are clapping, with Bonnie leading the charge.

"Great job, Luke. That was very exquisite," Bonnie says, still applauding with all her effort.

The cheering swiftly dies down, but Luke catches Natalie out of the corner of his eye. She is clapping her hands as a single tear runs down her face. Mr. Alterman looks at him with his soft blue eyes and a slight smile that says, *I told you so.* Bonnie is smiling from ear to ear and even stands up to give her friend a standing ovation. Luke has never had this much attention on him at once. He feels a chill go up his spine, but it's not from fear. He feels an exhilaration, like he could run through a brick wall.

"Thank—thank you everyone," Luke says.

After class ends and the students rush out the door, Luke hangs back and decides to speak with Mr. Alterman on the topic of women, since Mr. Alterman is married. Luke approaches Mr. Alterman as he organizes his lesson plans for his next class.

"Oh, Luke, you startled me a little. You know, I've never seen a poem get a reaction like that in my class before. If I read it to adults instead of high schoolers, I bet the whole room would shake. Most kids don't appreciate the craft yet, but it still got a very good ovation from them. Oh, is there something I can help you with?" Mr. Alterman asks as he sets his papers aside, clasping his hands together.

"Sorry, but yes, Mr. Alterman. How do you know if a girl is attracted to you?" Luke asks, disregarding the praise.

Mr. Alterman's eyes widen, and he tugs on his shirt collar. He takes a long sip of his coffee and wipes his beard with his sleeve. Mr. Alterman taps his thumbs together and tightens his lips.

"Oh, this is unexpected. Well, I met my wife, Freida, in the local synagogue when we were in adolescence. She was, and still is, the most beautiful person I've ever met."

"Is she a supermodel, Mr. Alterman?" Luke asks.

"No, she's a librarian. Beauty isn't simply just a pretty face, Luke. Looks fade, but the personality, what truly matters, doesn't," Mr. Alterman says.

"What do you mean?" Luke asks.

"I mean, some people that are beautiful on the outside are hideous on the inside."

"Thank you, Mr. Alterman, I should get to class," Luke says.

"Have a good one, Luke. Make sure you keep up the good writing," Mr. Alterman says as Luke leaves the classroom.

History with Mr. Calhoun is slightly more bearable for the teenagers without the bullies launching spitballs at them. The only downside is that Mr. Calhoun blows a fuse when Bonnie interrupts him during a lecture about Abraham Lincoln when he takes a jab at the former president for his actions against the South. He says, "Liberating the slaves was detrimental to the South's economy."

Bonnie slaps her desk and stands up, pointing her finger at Mr. Calhoun. She lists many of the president's accolades. "What about preserving the Union? The Gettysburg Address? And all his other accomplishments?"

Mr. Calhoun's face puffs up, and he sentences Bonnie to Principal Jackson's office, but she returns right before lunch without receiving detention.

At lunch, all four students opt to sit together, knowing it will be peaceful without Rob, Travis, and Brandon there to stir up trouble.

"Luke, thank you for the poem. That was simply beautiful," Natalie says.

"Oh, it was nothing."

"You're way too modest, Luke, it was outstanding!" Bonnie says.

"Wish I heard it," Drew says.

"Oh, Drew, you probably wouldn't have understood half of it," Bonnie says before giggling.

"I mean . . . you're probably not totally wrong, but you didn't need to do me like that," Drew says.

"Hey, are you a vegetarian?" Bonnie asks as her eyes land on Natalie's plate.

"Oh, yes, I love animals. The way they're treated in the meat industries makes my heart ache, and it should make anyone with a heart think twice about what they put in their mouth."

"Oh, no, a dirt eater," Drew whispers to Luke.

"I've wanted to be vegetarian, but my pa won't let me. Most of our food we grow, raise, and kill. I begged him, but he won't be reasoned with. So, here's the only place I can eat what I want," Bonnie says.

"Well, it's a shame your dad won't let you make that decision," Natalie says.

"Bonnie, maybe you could show Natalie around the ranch sometime," Luke says.

"Maybe, but the place is a mess right now," Bonnie says.

"It's a ranch, it's always a mess," Drew says with a mouthful of food.

"Yet I still have more manners than you. Don't talk with your mouth full, it's disgusting."

Drew mockingly sticks out his tongue with clumps of chewed food covering it, irritating both Luke and Bonnie, while Natalie covers her mouth, letting a minor chuckle escape.

Lunch ends as the bell rings. Unfortunately, Natalie doesn't share the same afternoon classes as the rest of her friends. Before clearing the table, Natalie leans forward and gives Luke a peck on the cheek. His face turns a rosy shade of pink, and he places his hand over the spot where Natalie's delicate lips made contact. He looks at Natalie wide-eyed and says, "Thank you." He waves as she stands to leave.

"I gotta get to class. See you guys tomorrow," Natalie says, waving goodbye.

Once Natalie is out of earshot, Drew gives Luke a thunderous high five that is heard across the entire cafeteria. Like Luke's, Bonnie's face is red, but Luke has an inclination she isn't feeling his same emotions. Bonnie ignores Luke throughout Science and PE, even when a rogue basketball nearly hits him in the head.

At the end of the day, Luke strides home alone, walking with a pep in his step, all the way to his front door. He gives his dog, Pedro, a gentle pat on the head and lets him out into the small backyard. Luke, at this point, is nearly jumping out of his shoes. He hastily grabs his mother's arm as she washes the dishes and leads her to the living room sofa. His grandmother is already in the living room watching cable news. Luke turns off the television, putting a frown on Sophie's face. Now that both his mother and grandmother are gathered in the living room, Luke can deliver the good news. Courtney's eyes squint and her mouth slightly opens as she settles onto the sofa. Sophie sits back on the couch. Her lips purse and her eyes narrow. Luke bites his lower lip, jumping up and down with excitement. With the suspense building, Courtney leans forward and tilts her head.

"I have a girlfriend!" Luke victoriously chants, raising his arms in the air.

"I've known Bonnie for years, honey," Courtney says.

Upon hearing Bonnie's name, Luke stops jumping and scratches his head. Courtney and Sophie look at one another briefly before returning their puzzled expressions to Luke.

"Huh? No, I mean I have an actual girlfriend. Her name is Natalie," Luke says.

"Well, I'll be, the kid's got your charm, Courtney," Sophie says. "So, when did you meet this girl, Luke?" Courtney asks.

"On the first day of school. She's a new student and knows I have autism," Luke says.

"Is she nice?" Courtney asks.

"Don't worry, Mom. She's amazing! She even gave me a kiss today."

"She did what?!" Courtney asks, pushing herself off the couch.

"Relax, Courtney, the boy is growing up. Let him be a man," Sophie says

"Ma, I'm sorry to be upset that a girl, who my son has known all of four days, is already kissing him."

"Well, if that's how you feel, how about you tell Luke about Mike?" Sophie asks.

Sophie quickly covers her mouth. She hadn't meant to say that out loud, but it is too late. Courtney freezes in shock, like a child who has just been caught doing something naughty.

"Who's Mike?" Luke asks, giving his mom a dazed look of bewilderment.

"Mike is your mother's boyfriend. He's a doctor at the hospital," Sophie says.

Luke's face drops, hoping he has misheard his grandmother. He shakes his head in denial. She can't be dating someone.

"Luke, he . . . we've been seeing each other for a few months. He works in the hospital's clinic," Courtney says as she reaches her hand out to comfort Luke.

"What? How come you didn't tell me?!" Luke asks.

"I thought you'd be upset if I moved on."

"Mom, even though Dad's been dead for over a decade, you can't just replace him with some random stranger! I can't believe you've done this."

Courtney takes a step toward Luke, but he retreats a step back himself. Her earthy brown eyes stare into his for just a brief moment.

"Luke, you have to understand—"

"Is that why you're sometimes late for dinner?"

Luke doesn't wait for his mother's answer. He believes she'll only offer some flimsy excuse as to why she didn't want to hurt him, but in his mind, she accomplished that feat regardless. Luke runs upstairs as fast as he can, covering his mouth to avoid weeping. When he reaches the second floor, he slams his door and throws himself onto his bed, crying into his pillow. Learning his mom has moved on, he thinks about his father and how he'll never meet him.

Dinner at the Ramirez house is silent and awkward, with

Courtney ignoring Sophie and Luke ignoring her. Besides saying grace and Pedro begging for scraps at the dinner table, there is absolute silence for the rest of the night.

6

LUKE'S FIRST DATE

Thursday is Luke's favorite day of the week because every Thursday he has his therapy session with Douglas Washington. Dr. Washington has been Luke's therapist since he was three years old, when he was diagnosed with autism. The therapist has been the closest thing to a father figure Luke has—he taught him correct pronunciations, how to tie his shoes, and even recommended Luke take karate lessons to defend himself against bullies.

Thursday is another quiet day with Rob, Travis, and Brandon still gone. The day goes smoothly, and Luke and his friends are on their way out the door after lunch.

"It feels good knowing the drool patrol isn't here today," Drew says.

"Ditto," Bonnie says.

Natalie is holding Luke's hand again while they're walking through the halls; for Luke it still doesn't feel real. Yet, it is. It feels as though they are a chain link. They are at their strongest when they are together.

"Aren't you worried he'll want revenge?" Natalie asks.

"Oh, we know he'll want revenge. Ever since Luke pushed

47

him into the sandbox in first grade, he wants nothing but that,"
Bonnie says.

"Wow, I didn't think you had it in you, Luke."

"The only reason I did that was because the opening presented itself, and he was picking on poor Ryan, calling him four eyes and all."

"I didn't think I would become his primary target for the past decade."

"Well, I still think you were very brave for doing that." Natalie kisses Luke on the cheek. Luke smiles as his cheeks turn rosy pink.

Bonnie folds her arms and grunts at Natalie, while Drew grins at Luke like a father witnessing his son play in his first baseball game.

"Oh, it was nothing, Natalie."

"Luke, would you like to hang out after school today?" Natalie asks.

Luke looks at Drew, puzzled, unsure what to say. Drew just motions his hand, signaling for a quick, smooth response. Luke quickly says the first thing that comes to mind.

"I . . . um sounds good. How does meeting at Giuseppe's Ice Cream Parlor around six sound?"

"Sounds amazing. I gotta get to class; see you then," Natalie says.

Natalie puts her hand on Luke's shoulder and kisses him on his forehead. She smiles at Luke before turning around and walking to her afternoon class. Stunned at what he has just gotten himself into, Luke almost doesn't respond to the peck on the forehead. Feeling like a lost child at the mall who cannot find his mother, he isn't sure exactly what to do next. As Natalie walks off to her class, Luke just stands in the middle of the hall, trying to pull himself together.

"Oh, snap, you're going on your first date," Drew says.

"Congrats. I hope you have a good time," Bonnie says.

"What do I do? I've never been on a date, and I only have an hour after therapy to get prepared."

"Why don't you just make the date the topic of the therapy session?" Bonnie says.

"Yeah, Washington has helped you through worse. I'm sure it will be groovy," Drew says.

"Okay, if you guys think he can be of service, I'll tell him."

Next period is biology class with Mrs. Green, who is short with curly brown hair and round spectacles. Her paleness makes it appear as though she hasn't been outside in a long time. Mrs. Green's laugh is eerily disturbing—it sounds like a witch cackling in the night.

Science is actually Luke's second-favorite subject, after English. Unlocking the secrets of what makes up the Earth, the universe, and human beings is interesting to Luke. Today, however, Luke is daydreaming throughout class about his date with Natalie, thinking of all the possible scenarios in which the date could end badly. Luke only has five hours until he has to meet her. *What will I do?* he asks himself.

"Luke? Lucas Ramirez!"

"What? I'm here," Luke says as he turns his head left and right, looking for who called his name.

"I see today's lesson is boring you. Would the principal's office be more arousing to you?" Mrs. Green asks.

"No, Mrs. Green. Sorry, I just got lost in thought," Luke says.

Today, students are observing bacteria through a microscope. Luke scouts around the classroom, noticing Harper Lavine in her element; biology is her favorite school subject. She is tall with thin brunette hair and a mole on her left cheek. With the exception of Bonnie, she is the only girl in the class that is not sickened by what she sees in the microscope. Back in middle school, Ryan told Luke he had a crush on Harper. They happen to be partnered together, and the way he glances at her tells the story that he still likes her.

"Those things are gross," Drew says, his upper lip pulling up.

"They're living creatures, not 'things'—you're almost as bad as the two princesses over there," Bonnie says as she sticks her thumb out in the direction of Patricia and Sandra.

Luke looks over to Sandy and Patricia's station. Bonnie is right; Sandy and Patricia appear to be gagging from the sight of what they have just witnessed in the microscope. Their faces twist like pretzels, slowly turning to a grotesque shade of green. Both girls place their hands over their mouths and dart out of class without asking, never returning.

Next period is PE with Howard Payne, a dirty blonde, fit, middle- aged man who played college football. He is more laidback than most teachers, which isn't a bad thing, but he doesn't push his students beyond their comfort zones. The musky scent of Mr. Payne is enough to burn one's nose. His unforgettable odor makes students believe that Mr. Payne sweats through four shirts a day. Very few doubted this rumor.

The class starts with running to practice for the mile run. Luke is alone with his thoughts, and Drew and Bonnie know that, so they leave him alone. Luckily, PE is a class where you don't have to worry about focusing on a lesson. Mr. Payne blows the whistle, which makes Luke jump as he is pulled out of his daydream.

The gym teacher allows the students to play a game of dodgeball where Drew and Luke are on a team with Harper Lavine, Patricia Roberts, and David Smith, a beady-eyed student who has only ever said a grand total of two words according to his peers. Bonnie is on the opposing team with Ryan O'Connell, Sandra Wilson, Justin Timmons, and Philip Johnson. Both Philip and Justin are on the basketball team with Drew. The game is brutal; dodgeballs are firing in all directions. Drew is a madman throughout the game, tagging both Justin and Philip out. Ryan and Patricia toss dodgeballs at each other and simultaneously eliminate the other. Sandy smiles gleefully as she hits Harper in the chest with a dodgeball; Harper's height makes her an easy target. Luke furrows his eyebrows, eliminating Sandy by hitting her in the leg. Bonnie is in a position to save her but opts not to. Bonnie knocks Drew out of the game by landing a blow on his abdomen. Luke has a chance to eliminate Bonnie, but for some inexplicable reason, he hesitates. Snapping out of it, he finally chucks the ball at Bonnie, but she catches it, knocking him out of the game. As Bonnie smirks at Luke shaking his head in disappointment, David, who hasn't even thrown a ball as of yet, quickly takes the opening and eliminates Bonnie, making Luke's team victorious with David as the sole survivor. Drew celebrates, but he is embarrassed that Bonnie knocked him out of the game. After gym class, the two get into a minor argument.

"I let you hit me," Drew says.

"Yeah, right. Maybe that hair of yours slowed you down," Bonnie says jokingly.

"What a day, see you guys tomorrow," Luke says.

"See you tomorrow, Luke. Good luck tonight," Bonnie says.

"See ya later, man. Don't mess this date up; I hope it's epic," Drew says as he slaps Luke's shoulder.

"I'll try not to," Luke says through chattering teeth.

As Luke is walking home, he decides he will not tell his mother or grandmother about his impending date with Natalie. Luke believes if he does, his mother will forbid him from seeing her again. He doesn't understand why his mother has such a problem with him dating. As he approaches his front door, he stands there with his feet planted and his eyes closed, thinking about what he'll tell his family. Luke opens his eyes and grimaces. As much as it pains Luke, he plans to lie and tell them that he will hang out at Drew's house tonight. He opens the door slowly and approaches Courtney and Sophie, who are on the couch talking.

"How was your day today, honey?" Courtney asks.

"Yeah, anything exciting?" Sophie asks.

"Oh, it was fine, learned a lot. Also, Drew wants me to hang out with him after therapy."

"Well, okay. Just as long as you're home before curfew," Courtney says.

"Thanks, Mom," Luke says as he turns to head upstairs.

"Oh Luke, I'm sorry about yesterday. I just think you should take your time. That way you're sure she's the right person for you," Courtney says as she looks up at Luke.

"Okay, thanks Mom, I'm sorry too for my outburst," Luke says before running up the stairs.

"I'm sorry too, *hija*. For, you know, spilling the beans about Mike," Sophie says.

"It's fine, Ma. He was gonna find out sooner or later."

"When you said 'right person,' I thought if he'd end up with anyone, it'd be that girl Bonnie," Sophie says.

"I did too," Courtney says.

Courtney and Sophie go back to watching television and talking about the events of their days. Luke lies on his bed and relaxes for an hour. When it is time for him to leave for therapy, he gets up and walks downstairs, noticing that his mother hasn't moved an inch. He hears the concentrator—the machine that connects to Sophie's oxygen mask to help her breathe while she is asleep—operating in the guestroom. Luke frowns. He's noticed that his grandmother has been falling asleep much earlier as of late.

"Have a wonderful time at therapy, sweetie," Courtney says.

"Don't worry, I will, Mom."

"Make sure you look both ways before crossing the street."

"Mom, I'm not a baby anymore," Luke says, somewhat annoyed with his mother.

"Just making sure you're being responsible."

The therapist's office is about six blocks from Luke's house.

Luke briskly walks toward his destination. Before crossing the busy road, he looks both ways. When he enters, Mae, the medical receptionist, is alone in the waiting area on her computer. She is always kind to Luke when he enters the facility on Thursdays, though her constant smile occasionally seems more petrifying than inviting.

"Luke, Dr. Washington is waiting for you," Mae says with a huge smile on her face, which is otherwise adorned with red glasses.

"Thank you, Mae."

"You're welcome, Luke—hope you have a productive session," Mae says, moving her light brown bangs before filing her nails.

Luke walks through the hallway and three doors down to the left. He approaches the wooden office door with the glass panel that reads, Dr. Douglas Washington, Psychiatrist. He knocks and the old but polite voice of Dr. Washington says, "Please, come in."

Dr. Washington is fifty-six-years old, with medium-length gray hair that splits down the middle, a noticeable scar above his left eyebrow, and square glasses. Douglas is an extremely private individual. The only things he had revealed about his personal life were that he was drafted to the Vietnam War when he turned eighteen and that he grew up in New York City. He wouldn't go into detail about his past unless it was necessary to do so. He has no children that Luke knows of, but he does possess a picture of himself as a young man with a gorgeous, young, blonde woman by his side. Luke didn't dare pry, as he was afraid that he would say that she had passed away or was deathly ill like his grandmother. One artifact that always catches Luke's eye is a framed painting of a puzzle piece. It proudly hangs above the couch on which Dr. Washington's clients sit. Luke was told long ago that it is a symbol of the autism community, though he didn't understand why people like himself were represented by something as dull as a puzzle piece.

"So, Lucas, how was your day?"

"It was pretty good, Dr. Washington, but can you please call me Luke?" Luke says.

Dr. Washington smiles and nods his head.

"Absolutely, I was just testing you on self-advocacy. So, what would you like to talk about today, Luke? Public speaking, job applying, maybe even registering for college, perhaps?"

There are multiple subjects that could be mentioned, such as his poem being shared with the class, but he wants to cut to the chase.

"Oh, all that sounds great, but today I would like to talk about . . . um, dating," Luke says, struggling to get the words out.

Dr. Washington's sunken, dark eyes expand and come to life. He takes off his glasses, huffs on the glass lenses, and cleans them with his sleeve. As Luke put his hands together with his thumbs pointed up, he taps them together repeatedly. His gaze shifts to the diamond pattern of Dr. Washington's sweater vest, eagerly waiting for his therapist to respond.

"Pardon me, maybe I am mistaken, but it sounds like you said 'dating,'" Dr. Washington says.

"That's correct, I did," Luke says.

Douglas Washington hums at this. He licks his pen before writing something on his clipboard and places it face down on his lap. After a few seconds, Dr. Washington looks back up at Luke and leans forward.

"Are you anxious to put yourself out there? Or . . ."

"No, Dr. Washington, I actually have a girlfriend right now."

"Oh, well, congratulations, Luke, that's phenomenal. I see you didn't need my assistance with this challenge."

"Yes, she knows I have autism and is very understanding.

Only problem is she asked me out on a date tonight, and I'm not quite sure what to do."

Dr. Washington blinks and raises the butt of his pen to his mouth. Another hum escapes his lips; his vacant gaze feels powerful enough to pierce through the wall. For moments the only noise is the clock's hand moving.

"Huh, I understand your dilemma. Unfortunately, there is only one solution to it."

"What would that be?"

"Just be yourself."

Luke lets out a deflated sigh.

"You sound just like Drew. What does 'being yourself' even mean? I don't even like the real me that much."

"First off, I don't ever want to hear that sentence come out of your mouth again. Secondly, if you're really meant to be, then she will love you for who you really are. Otherwise, I'm afraid you're just wasting precious time, Luke. Yours, hers, and mine."

"What if she finds me boring or weird?" Luke asks.

"Then it's simply not meant to be, Luke. If this girl likes you, she'll see the young man I see. Smart, funny, and kind," Dr. Washington says.

"Wow, I never quite thought of it like that."

"Not many do. Most try to make an incompatible relationship work," Dr. Washington says.

"Did you learn your dating advice in Vietnam? Is that how you got that scar above your eye?" Luke asks.

"Luke, how many times do I have to go over this? Unless it's completely necessary, I will not tell you stories about my past in Vietnam."

"One day I'll get answers, Dr. Washington."

"Maybe—I am getting up there in age after all."

Luke laughs so hard at Dr. Washington's response that he falls back in his chair. As Luke sits back up, Dr. Washington smiles and taps his pen on his clipboard. For the rest of their time together, Dr. Washington teaches Luke proper etiquette, preparing him for the date.

"Remember to compliment her outfit, show her that you're interested in learning about her, and what else?"

"Be myself?"

"Excellent! You're ready. I just hope the dating game hasn't changed too much in the last couple decades. Oh, don't forget to pay for her ice cream, Luke. Prove that chivalry isn't dead, young man."

"Chivalry? Oh, you mean be a gentleman, right? Yes, okay I can . . . I can do that."

Luke counts the lessons he's learned on his fingers and repeats each one to himself until committed to memory.

"It appears our session is just about over," Dr. Washington says, frowning as he checks his wristwatch.

"I really appreciate the advice, Dr. Washington."

"I'm serious about considering registering for college," Dr. Washington says, pointing the butt of his pen at Luke.

"What subject would I even major in?"

"Think about it. You're a brilliant writer and you care about justice. Maybe you could be a future journalist."

"You're quite hilarious, Dr. Washington."

"Not at all, Mr. Ramirez. Now, please show this girl a good time, and remember to maintain eye contact."

"I will, Dr. Washington, thank you."

Luke walks out of the therapist's office, giving Dr. Washington a slight grin before shutting the door on his way out. Luke can never get a read on Dr. Washington—not that reading people is his forte. He is relatively gullible, although people just tell him that he "sees the best in people" as an excuse for his foolishness. It just seems that Dr. Washington knows what Luke will say before he says it. Perhaps, decades of learning psychiatry gave him the perspective, or his fighting in Vietnam makes him immune to any surprises.

Luke readjusts his priorities, as it's nearly time for his date with Natalie. The sun reddening people's skin, reminds him that the summer season is still going strong. He sprints home and feels the sweat dripping from his forehead, down his neck, and onto his shirt. When he arrives home, he busts through the door and runs upstairs to his bedroom. Luke opens his closet door and intently stares at the neatly hung clothes. He decides on wearing his favorite pair of jeans, a black polo T-shirt, and a pair of white Nikes.

"Bye, Mom and Bela, see you later," Luke says as he descends the stairs.

Although Luke is still upset with his mother for not telling him about her new boyfriend, he still loves her with all his heart. As his mother waves goodbye to Luke, he gets an uneasy feeling in his stomach. Luke rarely lies in general, let alone to his own family.

"Have fun at Drew's house, and be safe," Courtney says.

"*Que guapo*. Make sure you give that boy some advice on talking to girls. He needs it more than you," Sophie says.

Courtney narrows her eyes at her mother while Luke chuckles nervously. As Luke turns toward the door, Pedro is in front of him, expecting a treat. Luke pets Pedro's head, telling him goodbye. The German Shepherd lifts his front legs up and presses his body weight against Luke, licking him repeatedly with his wet tongue.

"Now, be a good boy while I'm gone," Luke says as he scratches Pedro's ears.

He checks his watch. The time has come. Luke leaves his house and starts his journey to the ice cream parlor. While it is quite a stroll, this is a worthwhile trip. As the sun sets, he thinks in advance of all the things he should and shouldn't say while on the date.

During his journey, Luke ponders what Drew and Bonnie are doing. He pictures Drew at the burger joint, working behind the register. It's most likely a slow evening, and he's bored out of his mind. He imagines Drew leaning on the counter, staring at Giuseppe's parlor across the street, hoping to catch a glimpse of Luke on his first date while avoiding work duties.

As for Bonnie, he recalls her telling him she's got to clean the chicken coops when she gets home. Luke pictures Bonnie's overalls covered in feathers and chicken feces. While that would gross most girls out, Bonnie is an exception. By the time she's finished, it'll probably be dark and her navy-blue overalls will blend in perfectly with the night sky. Luke knows what Bonnie will do once she's done—she'll take a moment to gaze up at the crescent moon surrounded by the stars. She and Luke would always admire the night sky together whenever he went over to help, and then she'd write in her journal that he's not allowed to peek at. A small part of him wishes he could join her. It'd be more relaxing than going on a date.

At 5:55, Luke finally arrives at the ice cream parlor with five minutes to spare. Luke opens the glass door, and a bitter chill engulfs him. Goosebumps cover his arms. Behind the counter as always is Giuseppe, with the familiar trace of tobacco and ice cream filling the surrounding air. Shockingly, there are no customers. The parlor is as empty as a ghost town.

"Ciao, Lucas, what brings you here this evening? Where's Drew and Bonnie? Thought you three were inseparable," Giuseppe says.

Giuseppe is one of the few people Luke wouldn't correct when he called him Lucas. Giuseppe hates when people talk back to him, and besides, he has the best ice cream in town. Giuseppe's reasoning for calling Luke by his given name is that Lucas is more Italian than Luke, and Luke just rolls with it.

"Hi, Giuseppe, I have a date tonight, actually."

"Woah, we got a real man here. I knew you and Bonnie would happen sooner or later," Giuseppe says.

"No, not Bonnie. It's this pretty, new girl named Natalie. It's our first date together."

Luke doesn't understand why everyone is assuming his date is with Bonnie. Yes, she is the only girl he spoke to regularly before Natalie, but they're just friends, Luke thinks to himself.

"I see, my boy. Well, you came to the right place. Nothing says a first date quite like ice cream."

"I just hope tonight will go swell," Luke says.

"Say, you give a little somethin' somethin', and I'll treat you and the lady extra nice. If you catch my drift," Giuseppe says as he winks at Luke.

Luke reaches into his jeans pocket, and Giuseppe leans in close enough that his hooked nose threatens to poke Luke in the eye. Luke slips out a crisp ten-dollar bill and hands it to Giuseppe, who stuffs the bill in his apron pocket. At this point, Luke isn't taking any chances. If Giuseppe can help, and all it took was an extra ten dollars, he believes it is worth the expense.

"Magnificent! I promise my services will not disappoint you or the lady," Giuseppe says.

"That's great to hear. I'll have my usual, Giuseppe: mint chocolate chip with hot fudge and sprinkles."

"Excellent choice, my friend, and what flavor and toppings does the lady like?"

"I'm not sure. This is our first date."

"Ah, I remember my first date with my ex-wife before she ran off to be with a 'more' successful man. Yeah, she was like, 'Giuseppe, I can no longer be with a piss-poor ice cream man anymore.' I told her, 'But, Irene, I am a successful businessman. How dare you compare me to . . .'"

Luke is only paying half-attention to Giuseppe's ramble about his relationship with his ex-wife. Instead, he is occupied looking outside through the glass doors for Natalie. His eyes lock onto the person coming to the front door. It has to be her, Luke thinks to himself.

"Wait, I see her coming. Be cool," Luke says, raising his index finger to his lips.

"No problem, my friend," Giuseppe says.

Natalie enters wearing a blue-and-brown, splotchy dress. She looks elegant, like a peacock showing off its majestic feathers. Luke's jaw almost drops to the floor at the mere sight of her. He quickly gathers some confidence and prepares for the evening ahead as she sits down across from him.

"You look beautiful tonight, Natalie."

"Why thank you, Luke. You look handsome yourself."

Natalie rubs her bare arms with her hands and begins shivering. Luke clicks his tongue, wishing he had a coat or blanket to cover her up. Natalie and Luke exchange glances with each other, and Giuseppe, with little patience, interrupts and asks Natalie, "What would you like?"

"I'll have vanilla with M&M's and gummy bears," Natalie says.

"Great choice. I see you have great taste," Giuseppe says. As he turns around, he gives Luke an okay gesture with his hand.

Giuseppe is exceptionally fast—it only takes him a minute before both of their ice creams are ready.

"That'll be $11.99, kids," Giuseppe says.

Natalie lifts her small handbag over her naked shoulder and forages through its contents, pulling out a wrinkly twenty-dollar bill. She places it in the middle between the bowls and waves toward Giuseppe. Luke bites his lip, quickly digging into his pockets. He opens his mouth to protest Natalie's insistence to pay for them, but stops, realizing he only has five dollars left since he handed Giuseppe a tip earlier.

For the next few minutes, Luke and Natalie sit in silence as they eat their ice cream. Luke mistakenly takes a bigger bite than he had intended, and the brain freeze that follows feels like a massive blizzard in Antarctica going on in his head. Natalie notices this but waits for Luke to stop grabbing his head to start a conversation.

"So, how long have you known your friends?" Natalie asks as she tinkers with her necklace.

Luke looks up at Natalie; her hair is tied back into a single, long braid. He keeps reminding himself to maintain eye contact, which is sometimes difficult, especially around people he hasn't known for long. Luke slowly looks up from his ice cream and forces himself to lock eyes with Natalie as he starts to speak.

"Well, I first met Drew in third grade when he came from Baltimore, Maryland. He introduced himself to me. He said he couldn't stand people avoiding me because I was different. Bonnie, I met the year after. Drew was home sick, and Rob threw sand at me from behind. Bonnie stood up to Rob and then started spending time with us. We've been inseparable since."

"Wow, what a heroic story," Natalie says.

Suddenly, music plays in the room. Natalie gazes up at the speaker while Luke looks back. He sees Giuseppe in front of the blue jukebox. The owner grins, giving Luke a thumbs up before retreating back to the kitchen. Luke turns back toward Natalie, who taps her foot to the beat of the old rock song.

"Did you ask him to play music? How sweet of you," Natalie says, resting her chin in her palms.

"I guess I did. Anyways, what's your story, Natalie?" Luke asks, shrugging his shoulders.

"Well, I grew up in Choctaw Country, Oklahoma. My mom didn't want me to grow up on a reservation. My dad disagreed. He wanted me to stay and learn my culture, and they fought. She wanted me to learn English and make non-Native American friends. She told me that it would help me build a more successful life. My dad said that I belonged at the reservation. So, one day in the middle of the night, she took me with her and drove as far as she could from there," Natalie says, looking down at her dreamcatcher pendant.

"Oh, I'm very sorry about that. Why'd she take you here? Tennessee isn't exactly the most welcoming place toward . . . people that look different."

"You mean minorities? I gathered that. My mother couldn't afford to go as far as she wanted. Originally, she wanted to take me to Boston, but she didn't have enough money to buy a house in the Northeast. Believe it or not, some places are actually worse than this place. Trust me, I've seen them," Natalie says, fiddling with her pendant again.

"Yeah, Bonnie told me there are places where they kill folk on sight for looking at them the wrong way."

"That Bonnie, I don't think she likes me very much."

"She'll warm up to you, I guarantee it. She's a little rugged on the outside but sweet on the inside, at least she is with me."

"You really think so?" Natalie asks.

"I know so," Luke assures.

"On the house, courtesy of Romeo over here," Giuseppe says, placing two iced teas on their table.

Luke raises his glass to his mouth, the iced tea quickly curing his thirst. He believes the date is going great so far; time is accelerating with every moment. He didn't even need to pretend to use the bathroom in case the date was going horribly wrong. They exchange small talk and Luke enjoys learning more about Natalie. Before they know it, the sky has turned from a warm orange to a chilling black. Luke checks his watch to see how much time he has before he has to go home.

"Oh no, it's nearly 8:30. I have to get home," Luke says as he springs up out of his chair.

"I can take you home if you like," Natalie says.

"That'd be great."

Natalie throws her purse over her shoulder and pushes her chair in. They pass by Giuseppe wiping down the counters. He stops and waves goodbye as the teenagers exit his parlor.

"Have a good one," Giuseppe says.

Natalie is the only one of Luke's friends to have her driver's license. A thirty-minute walk turns into a ten-minute car ride in Natalie's blue Toyota Corolla. With their torsos, Natalie and Luke dance to the music on the radio the entire ride. As Natalie's car pulls into the driveway of the small cottage, Luke says, "Thank you so much, Natalie. I'll see you at school."

Natalie says nothing at first—she only gazes at Luke. Then she slowly leans forward and closes her eyes. She purses her lips and kisses Luke on the lips. She wraps her arm around the back of his head. Luke is caught off guard and nearly jerks back. His eyes swell up to the size of golf balls. Luke realizes this is a kiss, a showing of love, and he returns the favor. Her lips feel so soft, like a fluffed pillow. Her lipstick tastes like freshly picked strawberries. Luke is jumping for joy on the inside. He has finally kissed a girl that likes him for who he is.

"See you tomorrow, Luke," Natalie says.

"I'll see you soon," Luke says, waving goodbye.

Luke glances up at the moon, a beacon of light in the shroud of darkness. He opens the door to his cottage. As Luke enters the living room, he sees the glare from the television screen. His mother is waiting for him on the couch with Pedro sitting by her side watching TV.

"How was your evening?" Courtney asks.

"Good, but I'm tired," Luke says, stretching his arms.

"Well, you can tell me about your night tomorrow then. Goodnight honey, I'll see you in the morning."

"See you tomorrow, Mom."

Luke goes upstairs, yawning uncontrollably. He puts on his pajamas, turns off his light, and collapses into bed. After a short while, he lets the drowsiness take control over his body and he falls asleep.

Moments later, Luke is sitting at a table across from an empty chair. He peers under the table—nothing. His ears prick up when he hears the sound of someone clearing their throat, the kind to gather one's attention. He thrusts his head back above the table and sees Natalie. She smiles smoothly, as if their date had not occurred. She doesn't bother touching her ice cream. She simply rests her head in her hands with her elbows on the table, eyeing Luke. Luke says nothing. He puts his head down and looks at his feet.

Natalie reaches across and lifts up Luke's chin and purses her lips. Luke closes his eyes and leans in for the kiss. Seconds pass, but there is no softness, no strawberry scent, not even a sensation of warmth. Luke opens his eyes, and Natalie is gone. He forces himself up from his chair and turns around, calling out Natalie's name. He faces the table and almost falls back.

The Masked Haunter is sitting right where Natalie had sat. The bowl of ice cream is melting from the flames surrounding the table. Luke can't move; he is petrified, frozen with fear. What does he want with Luke? Luke begins quivering, sensing that death is near. The Masked Haunter looks like a cat about to pounce on its prey. The Masked Haunter leans in closer and says, "You're naïve to think anyone could ever love someone like you. Soon enough, you will learn that lesson."

"What do you mean? Who are you?" Luke asks as sweat drips down his forehead.

Luke's trembling hand reaches across the table for the Masked Haunter's mask. Before Luke can comprehend his sentence, the Masked Haunter lunges across the table at him again. The brief darkness is enough for him to wake up. Luke throws his blanket off and sits up. He can feel his short breaths begging for oxygen. It is 4:17 in the morning. Luke knows there is no chance of returning to sleep. His only option is to stare at the dark ceiling, waiting for the sun to rise.

7

A JUDAS AMONGST US

The following morning, while walking to school, Luke drags his feet across the dirt road. The soles of his shoes scrape against the terrain and kick up dust; his eyes are half-open. A strange combination of fatigue, anger, and happiness causes his sluggishness.

Luke had reconciled with his mother before she headed off to the hospital. He had begun to feel like a hypocrite for being upset with his mother while, at the same time, not telling her about Natalie.

Luke's heavy eyes stare blankly into the distance as he reflects on the sinister nightmare from last night. The Masked Haunter can't be right about Natalie, can it? Lost in thought, he continues to replay the events from last night, unaware he has entered the school grounds. Gradually, indistinguishable voices of other students infiltrate his mind, snapping him back into reality. He checks his watch and, despite being extremely tired, he has made it to school with some time to spare.

Luke spots Drew and Bonnie sitting on the front steps as usual, but Natalie is nowhere to be seen. He lets out a mighty yawn.

"Where's Natalie?" Luke asks while rubbing his eyes.

"Maybe she's sick . . . or she just ditched you and moved on," Drew says.

"Drew, how could you say such a thing?" Bonnie asks.

"She didn't. We had a fantastic time last night," Luke says.

"Bonnie, why do you even care? I thought you hated her guts anyway," Drew says.

Bonnie frowns and twirls her braid. "I most certainly don't," Bonnie says, clearing her throat. "I was just wary of a stranger, is all."

"Right . . ." Drew says, rolling his eyes.

"Do you guys see her anywhere?" Luke asks.

Luke, Bonnie, and Drew scan the school grounds. In the far distance, Luke's eyes land on Natalie first. He realizes, however, she's not alone; she is talking with Patricia and Sandy again. He taps Bonnie's knee and then Drew's shoulder, pointing the group out to them. Bonnie's eyebrows furrow, and she clenches her fists. Drew and Luke stand open-mouthed, both perplexed by the situation in front of them. Sandy and Patricia lead Natalie around the side of the school.

The three friends exchange looks with raised eyebrows. They nod at each other and begin making their way toward the three girls, hugging the wall. Luke, Bonnie, and Drew sneak in closer until they can make out the words just around the corner of the building. As Luke takes a step toward the open, Bonnie pulls him back against the brick wall.

"Wait, let's see if they're up to anything first," Bonnie says as she raises her finger to her mouth.

Drew nods with approval. Luke briefly clenches his jaw but exhales deeply. He reluctantly stays put and listens intently to Natalie's conversation.

"Anyways, my boyfriend, Rob, is coming back today. Did you know he's the starting quarterback for the team?" Sandy asks.

"Wow, I didn't, but he sure sounds like quite the hunk," Natalie says as she rolls her eyes.

"Very funny. Don't forget our agreement. You lure Luke to us, and we get out of your hair," Sandy says, chuckling.

"It was more of an ultimatum than an agreement," Natalie says as she folds her arms.

"Same difference. By the way, you came to us first. Remember?" Sandy asks.

"I've regretted it since," Natalie says.

"The sooner you do as you're told, the sooner it'll be over," Patricia says, hissing at Natalie.

"Anyways, here's the plan. We all go on a triple date tonight. Rob and me, Travis and Patricia, and you and Luke," Sandy says.

"We're gonna get them back so good. You kissed him; he's head over heels for you. He'll do anything you say," Patricia says, rubbing her hands.

A couple crunches of gravel behind her briefly grabs Natalie's attention. However, no one comes around the corner, and the sounds suddenly stop.

"Hellllooo?!" Sandy says, snapping her fingers.

"No. I'm not going to do that," Natalie says.

"Excuse me?!" Sandy exclaims, stomping her foot to the ground. "I will not feed him to the wolves. This, between us, is over," Natalie says.

"Why are you backing out? You don't even love him," Sandy says.

"Doesn't mean I want to hurt him. He's just a kid with autism—I'm not sure if he's even capable of a complex emotion such as love," Natalie says.

"You held his hand. You said you kissed," Patricia says.

"He doesn't even know what he wants to do with his life. I just played a part," Natalie says. Under her breath she adds, "Like I've done most of my life."

"I'll tell you what he'll do. Live with his mommy in his small, tacky cottage until she dies," Sandy says.

"Then they'll put him in a mental institution," Patricia says.

"Or a group home," Natalie says.

Patricia and Sandy roar with laughter at Luke's expense.

Infuriated by what he just heard, Luke slams his fist into the brick wall. He peeks his head around the corner, kicks up some gravel, and takes off. Drew reaches out to comfort him, but Luke is already halfway to the school at a full sprint. Luke tries his best not to bawl his eyes out, but his vision is already blurred from water forming in his tear ducts.

"Luke, wait up, it's OK. Shit happens!" Drew says as he chases after Luke.

Bonnie maintains her position, keeping her eyes focused on the three girls. In a silent rage, she clenches her fists and waits for an opening.

Natalie turns around; the rapid but fading thud of footsteps puts her in a fight-or-flight mode. Was that Drew's voice? Before she makes her way around the corner, she reluctantly turns back, marching briskly toward Sandy and Patricia.

"I'm done with this. Have fun executing your plan without me involved," Natalie says.

Mischievous grins spread across Sandy's and Patricia's faces. This causes Natalie to raise her eyebrow. How can they be happy? She thought. Sandy waves her finger to beckon Natalie, who inches closer to hear what Sandy has to say.

"Behind you," Sandy whispers.

Before Natalie has a chance to react to this statement, Bonnie taps on her shoulder and socks her in the nose, drawing blood. Sandy and Patricia pretend to gasp in fear when they see Bonnie punch Natalie to the ground.

"What the heck?!" Natalie exclaims.

A petrified Natalie looks up, realizing it is Bonnie who struck her. She must have heard the comment that Natalie just said. Bonnie looks as if she wants to hurt all three of them severely. She takes a sharp inhale and lowers her hands, apparently thinking better of it.

"Bon-Bonnie it's . . . n-not what it looks . . . like, I was just . . ." Natalie stumbles over her words, unable to justify herself.

"Making friends? At Luke's expense? You're a disgrace to women, but that I can tolerate. What I will *not* tolerate is you hurting my best friend by leading him on just to feed him to the wolves."

"Why do you always act like Luke's big sister?" Sandy asks. "What, he can't stand up for himself? What a loser."

"If you so much as *mention* his name again, no amount of makeup in the world will be able to cover up what I do to your face," Bonnie says.

"Sandy, let's get out of here. This farm trash ain't worth it," Patricia says, grabbing Sandy's wrist and walking her in the opposite direction.

"Bonnie, you have to understand. I was on their hit list, but I wouldn't—"

"So, you sold him out to save yourself. And for who? These fake bitches? You're nothing but a Judas."

"Bonnie—"

"Get out of my sight right now! If I see you *anywhere* near Luke, I don't care if I get expelled, I'll give you the beating of a lifetime. Are we clear?"

Natalie spits on the ground beside her. Blood drips down into her mouth, reddening her teeth.

"Crystal clear," Natalie says.

Inside the school, Luke is sprinting down the hallway. Along the way, he hears his science teacher, Mrs. Green, yell, "Luke, stop! No running in the halls."

Luke doesn't stop, and he has no intention to. He hopes to get as far from Natalie as possible, wanting to forget what he just saw. Luke needs advice and comfort from the school's custodian, Kai Yamamoto. He helps out students daily who are dealing with all kinds of issues about life, love, or bullies. Luke pounds on the closet door, and Mr. Yamamoto answers. "Yes? You may come in."

Luke forces his way into the small broom closet and collapses in the corner. Mr. Yamamoto is the only faculty member of Asian descent. He is fairly skinny, has nearly shoulder-length black hair, no facial hair, and a constant, emotionless expression on his face. He doesn't look a day over thirty even though he is in his late forties. The students had made up a rumor that he is a kung fu master and was even trained by the legendary Bruce Lee. Most rational students, however, seriously doubt these ridiculous and stereotypical rumors.

"Luke, what's wrong?" Kai asks.

"N-Nat-Natalie, she said something awful about me, and I thought we were solid," Luke says, nearly hyperventilating.

"Luke, deep breaths, deep breaths. Here, have some water," Kai says, handing Luke a paper cup of water.

Luke downs the entire cup, as if he has been deprived of water for days. He sighs in relief after finishing the drink. He viciously wipes the tear streaks off his face, unwilling to show Kai any weakness. Luke takes another deep breath, finally feeling refreshed enough to form coherent sentences.

"Now, slowly and calmly tell me what brings you to my office, Mr. Ramirez."

"I didn't hear everything, but I think she was using me. Maybe some sort of triple date—Sandy and Patricia are dating Rob and Travis. I'm confident Brandon would've tagged along. I'm sure they would've isolated me with Rob, and I can only imagine what he'd do to me after."

Even after taking in all that information, Mr. Yamamoto's expression doesn't change. He has arguably the best poker face in town. This reminds Luke of the time he was in the restroom, and he asked Mr. Yamamoto, as he was mopping, if he ever played poker. Mr. Yamamoto side-eyed him as though he had just been greatly insulted and said, "No, never."

"Luke, I'm sorry about your situation, but you are extremely lucky that you discovered this before it was too late. I already know how unpleasant those girls and boys can be. I know it feels like you'll never love again, but trust me, you will, and you shall be wiser next time."

"I was a fool, Mr. Yamamoto . . ."

"Please call me Kai, Luke. I'm not your teacher, I'm merely the janitor."

"Kai, I was a fool for thinking a girl that pretty could fall for a guy like me."

"Quite the contrary, Luke. She was the fool. She didn't expose you; she exposed herself. The universe will punish her for her betrayal, and you will be rewarded for your honesty. Luke, many students have come to me with problems. Some of them even involved life and death. Eight years ago, someone found out a male student fancied other boys. He was beaten, harassed, and abused. Even his own parents, who were Evangelicals, abandoned him. It got to the point where he was talking about taking his own life."

Kai becomes silent; he looks down at the floor. Luke notices a frown developing, and he decides to pry to learn the rest of the story.

"What happened to him?"

"I saw him in the hall, not doing anything. That's when things get scary—when you're going through tough times and you just . . . Anyhow, I brought him to my 'office' and gave him half my salary to pay for a therapist to talk to."

"Wow, and that saved him?"

"I don't know," Kai says, shrugging his shoulders.

"What do you mean?" Luke asks, dreading the answer.

"He stopped coming to school not long after, ran away from home, and sadly, we never heard from him again."

"I'm sorry that happened," Luke says.

"Me too. I just hope he's fine wherever he is. Another student from three years ago came from Iraq, Muslim girl, pretty and genuine. Until, one day, a girl ripped off her hijab in front of the whole class."

"What's a hijab?"

"It's a covering of the head, for women of the Muslim faith. Women usually don't show their hair in public; it's a sacred thing. She wasn't the same after that horrific experience. She barely came to school, had her house vandalized, and was eventually run out of town."

"What's the purpose of you telling me these stories, Kai?"

"To show you that you have a good thing going, Luke: a loving family, loyal friends, and untapped potential. You'll bounce back."

"Kai, I have a couple questions."

"Shoot," Kai says.

"If this place is so bad, how come you never left?"

Kai pauses for a moment, as if he has waited all his life for someone to ask this question. When Luke attempts to rush his answer, Kai raises his index finger, signaling Luke to be patient. Mr. Yamamoto takes a sip of his tea and closes his eyes, trying to savor the sweet taste, before answering. He opens his eyes and takes a deep breath, as this question requires a long story to answer.

"My father was born in San Francisco and dreamt of becoming an engineer. One day, Japan bombed Pearl Harbor. Then, this great country of ours determined that any and all Japanese Americans could be affiliated with the enemy. They rounded up any Japanese Americans from the West to the Midwest. For two years, they locked my father and his parents up in an internment camp for simply being of Japanese descent. His parents died there.

He didn't have money to go to school, so he just settled, becoming a waiter, living paycheck to paycheck. He met my mom in the camp, so at least something good came out of it. My father managed to get as far away from California as possible, and he wound up here. I was born here, and I will die here. Unlike my father, no one is taking me from my home. It doesn't matter how much people in Princeton County have beaten me, harassed me, and mocked me. I'm a proud American, no matter how much they try to dehumanize me."

Luke's jaw drops, and he claps his hands slowly, but Kai motions for him to stop.

"Wow, that's amazing."

"Grit, kid, it'll help in life," Kai says.

"Now, why didn't you become a teacher? You certainly have the intelligence for it."

"Maybe I'll tell you another time, Luke. I think I hear Drew calling for you now; you should get to class."

"Thank you, Mr. Ya—I mean, Kai."

"No trouble, kid. Stay safe now, both of you," Kai says.

8

BATTLE OF PRINCETON

Luke exits the janitor's closet and looks down the beige hallway. He hears his name once again and rushes around the corner. He witnesses Drew running around like a headless chicken, calling for him. Luke sees his afro from a mile away, checking every classroom within the hall for his friend's whereabouts.

"Drew, I'm over here!" Luke calls out.

Luke catches his attention, and Drew looks back. His eyes bulge and then he sprints toward Luke, his long stride helping him reach his friend within a few seconds. Drew gives him a pat on the back.

"It's all good bro, she wasn't worth your time," Drew says with his hands on his knees, trying to catch his breath.

"I understand that now. I talked to Mr. Yamamoto. He's the wisest person in the school."

Drew glances up with a dazed look and shrugs his shoulders.

"Yeah, it makes you wonder why he's just a janitor," Drew says.

"Boys!" A voice behind them shouts.

Luke and Drew see Bonnie jogging toward them. She is cradling her hand like a fragile newborn baby.

Once she reaches them, they all embrace in a lengthy group hug.

"Luke, everything's gonna be fine. I made sure things wouldn't escalate further," Bonnie says while supporting her hand.

"Bonnie, what did you do?" Luke asks.

"Is that blood on your hands?" Drew asks.

Bonnie looks down at the back of her hands. Dry blood is dispersed all across her knuckles from making contact with Natalie's face. The red splatters that were warm, wet, and sticky, have now become a glossy crust.

"Yeah," Bonnie says.

"Whose is it?" Luke asks.

"Natalie's."

"Why'd you go and do that?" Drew asks.

"After what she did to Luke, she should be happy I didn't do worse."

"Bonnie, you didn't have to do that; I should be able to fight my own battles," Luke says.

"Well, were you gonna punch her?" Bonnie asks.

Drew places his hands on his hips and looks to the side, biting his lip and shaking his head.

"Probably not. I wouldn't hit a girl," Luke answers.

"Then I had to fight this particular battle for you," Bonnie says.

Luke sighs and sags his shoulders, pacing down the hall toward Mr. Alterman's class. Bonnie takes a step to go after him, but Drew sticks his arm out in front of her.

"Any teachers see you? Did you get yourself suspended?" Drew asks.

"No teachers saw us, but I told Principal Jackson what I did.

She gave me a Saturday detention, but if I do anything like that again, it's suspension," Bonnie says.

"Listen, you gotta tell Luke how you feel before this thing gets even more out of hand. If you don't, I'll tell him myself," Drew says.

Bonnie had told Drew about her feelings for Luke in the sixth grade. She made him swear an oath never to tell Luke, who, to this day, is oblivious to her crush on him. Drew was hesitant at first since he has never been good at keeping secrets, but Bonnie convinced him to put an effort in for his friends. Drew has told Bonnie repeatedly that she and Luke are made for each other. "Just tell him," he'd said. "As long as I don't become the third wheel, I'd be happy for you two." Bonnie has never mustered the courage to tell Luke she likes him, but Drew has kept his word and never told Luke about Bonnie's fondness for him.

"We can't! He just got his heart broken. Luke's already been through enough with Rob and Natalie. He's barely keeping it together. We have to be there for him, but as friends, like always. If either of us tell him I like him, I don't know how he'll react."

"If you had told him like you told me in the sixth grade, this thing with Natalie doesn't happen," Drew says, pointing his finger.

"You don't know if he likes me back! If you say anything, I'll —" Bonnie says, getting in Drew's face.

"You'll what?" Drew asks, not backing down.

Bonnie exhales and takes a step back. She adjusts her overalls while Drew crosses his arms.

"I'm begging you, Drew. I will tell him, soon. I promise."

"Fine. Can't we just forget about all this and get through the day, please?" Drew whispers, peeking to the left then right.

"I won't forget what she did, but for you and Luke, I won't mention it," Bonnie says.

"No problem," Drew says.

After about half an hour of English, Natalie enters in with a nurse's pass and some tissue in her nose. No principal or teacher trails behind her. She sits on the opposite side of the class and doesn't acknowledge Luke or Bonnie's existence. In history, something seems amiss, but Mr. Calhoun is his usual unpleasant self. Lunch is more or less the same; Natalie briefly sits with Patricia and Sandy. At first glance, it appears like they've been friends for years; they appear angry with each other. Luke sees fingers being pointed, and moments later, Natalie slaps the table and gets up, sitting alone at the same empty table where he'd first spoken to her.

"Where's dumb, dumber, and dumbest? I ain't seen them all day," Drew says as he tilts his chin toward the corner of the cafeteria.

"They weren't at history class, either. Wasn't their punishment up today?" Luke asks.

"Maybe they forgot how long their punishment was," Bonnie says.

"I wouldn't put it past them," Luke says, scouting the entire room.

"My guess is they got suspended for skipping school and detention. It's not like they value education anyway. Don't worry about them. Rob won't be a problem soon," Bonnie says.

"I hope you're right," Luke says before taking a bite of his hot dog.

"Hey, if he has something up his sleeve, we'll be ready for them," Drew says.

Science is excruciatingly tedious today; the whole class consists of the students watching a documentary on fungi. In PE, Mr. Payne has the students run the first practice for the mile. Drew is one of the first to complete their laps in class. Once Luke finishes the mile run, he's reduced to breathing heavily with his hands on his knees. Bonnie finishes half a minute after Luke. She keeps her arms above her head to help her lungs take in air.

"Hey, Luke . . . you mind . . . if we walk you home . . . after class?" Bonnie asks, still struggling to catch her breath.

Typically, Luke, Bonnie, and Drew never walk home together since Drew normally takes the bus in the afternoon and Bonnie walks a different route.

"That would be excellent," Luke says.

* * *

At 47 Lincoln Avenue, Courtney gets out of the shower and blow- dries her thick, wavy hair. She picks out a gorgeous red dress to wear for her lunch date with Mike. Courtney's hands are trembling; she botches her makeup and washes it off to start over. She hasn't been on a real date in fourteen years. Sophie bursts into the bathroom unannounced, causing Courtney to jump back in surprise. Fortunately, Courtney has finished applying her makeup for the second time.

"Ma! You should know better than to barge in like that!"

"Oh my God, you look just like you did at the high school dance."

Courtney looks in the mirror, in awe that her hair isn't up in a clumsy ponytail. It is down, her natural curls reaching past her shoulders. Her red dress shows off her curvy frame, and she even wears high heels. She *does* look like she is going to a high school dance.

"I don't know about this, Ma. Maybe I should call Mike and cancel our plans."

"Hija, I know you're scared, but the way you speak of Mike, I can tell he's a good man. You can't let him slip through your fingers. I believe you'll do what's right. You can do it."

"Gracias, Ma. Well, I already bought and put on this dress

and put on all this makeup, so no sense in wasting it. All right, I'll do it."

"Have a good time. I'll be asleep when you come home."

"All right Ma, bye!"

Courtney walks downstairs slowly, almost tripping in her high heels. She grabs her purse, draping it over her bare shoulder, and walks out the door. While in her car, she looks at herself one last time before driving off to her destination with revamped spirit. She is about to have lunch with a handsome and good-hearted man. Seeing Mike for over a month now, she hopes that he is really in it for the long run.

* * *

After PE ends, nearly ten minutes pass before Bonnie, Drew, and Luke get out of their locker rooms, sweaty and exhausted from the physical activity. They exit the now-empty school and start walking through the back near the parking lot; it seems students and even a couple faculty members have left in a hurry. It isn't strange for a Friday, since most people want to go home and enjoy the weekend.

"I appreciate you guys immensely," Luke says to his friends.

"Hey, it's the least we could do, bro," Drew says.

"Yes, especially after the rough morning you had," Bonnie says. Despite exhaustion from the practice mile run and Luke's rough day, the trio of friends smile and laugh as they prepare to leave the school grounds and make their way across town.

"So, what should we do tomorrow?" Drew asks.

"Maybe we spend the day at my ranch," Bonnie says.

"Now I know you're just trying to get us to do your chores," Drew says. "Why on earth would Luke want to go to your stanky—"

"I'd love to," Luke says. "Some honest, hard work around the ranch will clear my mind of—"

It happens so fast. A thunderous punch hits Luke's ribs, bringing him to his knees. Luke looks up as he struggles to catch his breath. He sees Rob with a big smile on his face.

"So, I was told that your friends needed to walk you home today? Whatever, we'll kill three birds with one stone."

Rob places two fingers inside his mouth and whistles. Within seconds, Travis and Brandon appear slowly from around the corner of the school building, as Rob cracks his knuckles. Drew and Bonnie have already lifted Luke onto his feet. Bonnie rolls up her sleeves, prepared for a fight. Drew takes off his shirt, ready to brawl. Luke looks in all directions. He can't see a way to avoid this fight. He is already somewhat tired from the mile run; now Rob has just knocked the wind out of him. There is no way out of this. Nearly a decade of torture has led to this exact moment. Rob stops smiling and quickly barks orders at his minions.

"Brandon, you take farmer girl. Travis you take care of tall, dark, and ugly. Leave Luke to me. He is 'special' after all."

Brandon runs up to Bonnie and strikes first, punching Bonnie in the chest. He follows up by pulling on Bonnie's braids and putting her in a headlock.

"Come on, girlie, is this all you got?" Brandon says.

Travis connects with a left hook on Drew's cheek, dazing him and backing him up against the wall. Rob, who is just under six feet tall, has about five inches and fifty pounds on Luke. He picks Luke up and throws him back first at the brick wall of the school.

Luke cries out in pain and collapses to his hands and knees, wincing. His back feels like it has just been snapped in half. He shakes his legs and sighs in relief that he can still feel them. His thankfulness is short-lived as Rob kicks him in the sternum.

Bonnie squirms as her ears turn a shade of crimson from the pressure of being trapped between a forearm and chest. She cocks her elbow back and thrusts it into Brandon's stomach, causing him to grimace. His loosened grip allows Bonnie to escape the headlock. Brandon goes in for a punch, but Bonnie dodges and kicks him in the shin.

"Oof! Oh, so you wanna fight dirty, farm girl?" Brandon asks.

Bonnie punches Brandon in the jaw quickly after dodging another strike from him.

Drew grunts as he uses his superior strength to pry Travis's arm off his throat. Drew punches Travis in the kidney, in retaliation, momentarily stunning him. Drew commits to another shot but Travis blocks it, using his longer arms to his advantage and slamming Drew into the wall once again.

Brandon screams as Bonnie kicks him where no man wishes to be kicked. He drops immediately to the ground and violently retches. Within seconds, the puddle of vomit spreads to his hands. Bonnie takes advantage and kicks him across the face with all her might. Brandon rolls over and the force causes his head to bounce back against the pavement, rendering him unconscious, lying in a pool of his own vomit. Travis is choking Drew against the wall, grinning until he notices his fallen comrade. Travis releases Drew, who falls to his knees; his lungs surge for oxygen.

"You'll pay for that, bitch!" Travis yells as he charges at Bonnie.

Before Bonnie can turn around, Travis tackles her to the ground, and she yelps in pain as the pavement tears inches of skin off her arm. As the commotion distracts Rob, Luke stands up and punches him in the sternum as hard as possible.

"Oof . . . well, so you can fight back? Guess you're not a total wimp after all. I'm still gonna turn your brown ass black and blue," Rob says.

Rob pushes Luke to the ground, and the collision of pavement and flesh removes the skin from his elbows. Luke grimaces in pain as Rob advances toward his rival.

Drew regains his composure, and with all his might, punches Travis in the spine, making him tense up. Bonnie takes the opening to punch him in the stomach, knocking him off her. Together they kick him repeatedly.

Rob grabs Luke by the neck and lifts him to his feet and balls up his right fist. Luke hears the cracking sound of knuckles and waits. Rob swings but misses his target, as Luke ducks out of harm's way. Luke recovers and takes the opening to side kick the off-balance Rob in the stomach.

"You son of a—" Rob shouts as he winds up.

It hits Luke so fast he can't dodge it in time. Rob punches Luke in his left eye, knocking him to the wall, and Luke slowly slides back down to the earth. The pain is excruciating, and Luke immediately covers it. He already knows it will be black and blue within a matter of minutes. Rob steps forward, casting a shadow over the autistic boy. Luke is exhausted and beaten; he feels like there is no scenario where he can win.

"It's over, you autistic—"

"No, it's not, you piece of shit!" Bonnie bellows.

Rob looks back before he can finish Luke off. Bonnie jumps on his back and puts him in a headlock. Rob stumbles but regains his footing. To everyone's astonishment, Rob pulls Bonnie off and slams her face-first into the pavement. He stomps on the back of her leg.

"No, Bonnie!" Luke yells.

Drew catches his breath and spots Bonnie. He dashes over and punches Rob with enough force that a tooth is knocked out. Rob stumbles but is still on his feet. Travis regains his footing, sees Luke, and starts running full speed toward him. Luke quickly sidesteps

Travis. He runs face first into the brick wall, falling like a rag doll to the pavement, leaving behind a bloodstain on the building. Drew and Rob are practically dead even in terms of size, strength, and aggression. As Drew goes for another punch, Rob snatches his arm and twists it behind his back.

Drew yells out in pain.

"I'm gonna break your arm, boy, and you'll never play basketball again, shit stain," Rob screams at his victim.

Luke looks around for something that he can use as a weapon. His brows sweating, he wipes his forehead. His eyes stop when he sees a big rock that must've been a part of the asphalt at one point in time. He battles through the throbbing pain in his back and crawls to it and grabs it fast. Using the ground as leverage to lift himself up, Luke advances toward his attacker, screaming, "*Rob!*"

"Huh?"

Luke has Rob's full, undivided attention, and he slams the chunk of pavement with such force on the back of Rob's head that it crumbles to dust on impact. Luke's forward momentum causes him to fall back to the ground. Rob stumbles back against the wall, dazed and confused. Blood drips down his forehead. He uses the wall as leverage to pick himself up.

"Is your arm okay?" Luke asks Drew.

"I think it's sprained, but I can still move it."

Bonnie lifts her head off the ground; her right cheek is bloody and bruised from the impact. Luke quickly helps Bonnie to her feet. Miraculously, she is still conscious. Her fearlessness and tenacity made her no doubt the toughest person that Luke knew.

"Bonnie, are you okay?"

"Yeah, this ain't nothing," Bonnie says as she spits red saliva on the ground.

All three of them are still standing, but just barely. Rob is all alone, reeling, and just as battered as his three adversaries. His allies, Travis and Brandon, are down for the count. He continues to fiddle with his wound, the bloodied welt on his temple appearing to swell up by the second.

"Come on, let's finish this fool," Drew urges as he charges toward Rob.

"Drew, don't!" Bonnie says.

"Wait!" Luke yells.

The warning is too little, too late. Drew is already within Rob's reach. Rob smiles and swiftly takes something out of his pocket, slashing his arm across Drew's face.

Drew screams like a wounded animal. He stands frozen, stunned, and Rob kicks him all the way back to his friends. Drew now has a deep cut on the side of his face and is bleeding profusely. He reaches toward his wound and squints at Rob. Once Bonnie and Luke see Drew's face, they all look at what Rob has taken out of his pocket. They see it—a pocketknife, locked in a death grip in Rob's fist—and back up, as they look in horror at the sharp blade in Rob's hand.

"I would say that I didn't want it to come to this, but that'd be a goddamn lie. I told you assholes that you were dead meat," Rob says.

Rob inches forward with his arm extended, knife pointed at his three enemies, who are all covered in blood now. Luke and Bonnie struggle to lift Drew to his feet, but all they can do is hold their ground. None of them are foolish enough to charge at someone with a knife. Just as they think Rob has them right where he wants them, the four teenagers pause. A sound that was barely detectable moments ago echoes in the distance. Seconds pass by and the audio becomes louder steadily, getting closer and closer. It doesn't take long to figure out what the sound is—police sirens are heading in their direction.

"Oh, shit! The cops," Rob screams.

In that brief moment, something comes flooding back to Luke. The martial arts classes he took for years growing up prepared him for this very moment. While Rob is distracted, Luke takes the opportunity to hop in front of Rob and attempt to pry the knife from his grip. Only, his rust shows when he stumbles, reaching in, and Rob catches on. He slashes Luke's wrist, but Luke catches his hand just when the blade is inches from his face on the follow-up. Luke elbows Rob with his free arm, but he is unfazed. A crazed grin spreads across Rob's face, as a weakened Luke's hands begin to give under the bully's strength. Then, a high-pitched shriek emits from Rob, and he drops the knife. Bonnie has kicked him in the shin with her good leg before crumpling. Luke quickly punches him in the stomach and swiftly spears his hand underneath Rob's arm and throws him over his shoulder. Drew throws the discarded knife as far as he humanly can. As soon as Rob rolls onto his belly, Drew dives on top of him, smashing his face to the pavement until he is knocked out.

Practically leaning on one another for support, the trio of friends gawk at the fallout of the war. Brandon, Travis, and Rob all lie unconscious and no longer pose a threat to the three of them. They each collapse in agony and exhaustion but laugh weakly. Their heavy breathing is only drowned out by the sirens closing in.

With a little reprieve, they wince at the pain of moving their bodies. Luke has a black eye, and his back is mauled. Drew's cheek is gashed, and his shoulder is messed up. Bonnie's leg is bruised, along with scrapes all on her face, which includes a chipped tooth.

About a minute after the fight has ended, police arrive at the scene. Paul Berkowski, the fearless sheriff, gets out of his car and walks toward the scene. He looks like the epitome of a man—with broad shoulders, slicked-back, dirty-blonde hair, a full beard, and a misshapen nose that has been broken multiple times. He also wears dark shades that add to his already intimidating appearance.

"I hope you kids can explain yourselves. I got a call about a fight," Sheriff Berkowski says in his deep voice.

"We sure can, Sheriff," Bonnie says.

9

SHOCKING INTERRUPTION

On their day off, Courtney Ramirez and Mike Montgomery are enjoying late lunch at an upscale, local restaurant. Despite the early hour, the outdated décor makes the large dining hall appear dark and mysterious. Rich, brown paneling covers the walls, complemented by a deep red, luxurious carpet. The fragrance of onions sautéing wafts through the air while the sound of soft jazz fills the room. Courtney admires the giant chandelier above them and notices how the light shimmers off of Mike's parted brown hair like a diamond. As the couple opens their menus, Mike initiates the conversation at the table.

"You look beautiful today, Courtney," Mike says.

"Why, thank you, though I'm sure you would say that anyways. You've only seen me in scrubs and jeans before," Courtney says.

"Only because you are just as beautiful in scrubs."

"Oh, stop, you," Courtney says, blushing.

Mike stares intently into Courtney's brown eyes as she gazes back into his hazel eyes. Distracted, they don't notice the waitress with her notepad at their table until she clears her throat.

"Excuse me. May I take your order?"

"Yes, I'd like a steak, medium well, with white rice and cooked vegetables," Courtney says.

"Good, and what would you like to drink?"

"Um . . . water's good," Courtney says.

"And what would you like, sir?" the waitress asks.

Mike scratches his clean-shaven face; his eyes expand as he points to his order.

"I would like to try out the cooked salmon with a side of asparagus. With water too, please," Mike says.

"Thank you both. My name is Liz, and I'll be your waitress this afternoon. Let me know if there's anything else you need," Liz says in an inviting tone.

"We sure will," Mike says. "Have you ever been to this place, Courtney?"

"Not since I was with . . . you know."

"Sorry, I didn't mean to bring up bad memories."

"It's okay. I won't let him take away the marvelous time we're having. He's taken enough from me already," Courtney says.

"I'm proud of you. You're one of the strongest women I know. I hope your family knows that as well as I do."

"I'm sure they do. I'm glad I met you. You're the nicest man I've met in a long time. Also, the handsomest."

"Ah, shucks, you don't really mean that, do you?" Mike asks, raising his eyebrow.

"Wholeheartedly."

Courtney places her hand on Mike's. They smile softly at each other.

"So, Courtney, what do you think about today's entertainment?" Mike asks, gesturing toward the band.

"It's nice, a little . . . fancier than what I'm used to though," Courtney says laughing.

Mike smiles back at her, and then the conversation takes a serious turn.

"Courtney, we've been seeing each other for a couple of months now, but I feel like I barely know you. Is there a reason you seem to be keeping me at a distance?"

Courtney swallows. While they've been on countless dates now, it's still easier talking at work or getting coffee. She recalls intentionally choosing the movie theater first to keep the chatting minimal and then the bar to get Mike and herself drunk enough to loosen the nerves. She's been looking for red flags, but none have appeared yet. The walls have been lowered. When Mike suggested the restaurant yesterday, Courtney felt something fall to the pit of her stomach. This is the night that will determine the course of their relationship.

"Oh right, um, yeah. I forgot that that's sort of the purpose of a date. I apologize for making you question my intentions. As you already know, I've been through a difficult relationship and tend to keep my guard up, but we can talk about whatever you'd like. Is there anything in particular you want to know?" Courtney asks, leaning forward and cradling her chin in her hands.

"I remember you grew up in Houston, Texas, right? The dress makes it obvious that your favorite color is red. You haven't really talked to me about your family though," Mike says before taking a sip of water.

Courtney begins tapping her foot.

"I could say the same to you. I have a good memory too. You grew up in Frankfort, Kentucky, you're German, and your favorite color is orange."

"Do you remember why?"

"It was the color of some dinosaur toy you had as a kid. That's probably the most adorable story any man has ever told me."

Mike chuckles, running his hand through his gelled hair.

"About your son . . ."

Courtney swallows again and grips the dangling tablecloth.

"Yes."

"So, how's he doing? Have you told him about me? About us?" Mike asks, gesturing to himself and Courtney.

Courtney knew it was inevitable that the question would come up. Sadly, she was hoping to enjoy a few more minutes of small talk before the subject came up.

"Not exactly how I wanted to, but yes, he knows I'm seeing someone."

"So, he didn't take the news well, I assume," Mike says, looking down.

"No, he didn't take it great. But you know how teenagers get. I'm sure he'll adjust. It's my fault for not telling him months ago," Courtney says as she leans forward, clasping her hands on the tablecloth.

Mike takes a gulp of water, tugging on his shirt collar.

"I . . . overheard one of your nurse friends mentioning the other day that he has autism. Is that true? If so, why didn't you tell me?"

Courtney prepares herself to leave at that moment—not being accepting or accommodating of her kid is an automatic deal breaker. She doesn't care how handsome or kind he is to her—if he's not welcoming of her son, she wants nothing to do with him.

"He does. Is that going to be a problem?"

"Not in the slightest. I think special needs kids are gifts from God. We can learn so much from them, such as empathy, perspective, and kindness," Mike says.

Despite knowing he means well, when he says the phrase "special needs," Courtney squeezes the draping tablecloth. She always detests that phrase; her son's needs are the same as anyone else.

"I . . . thank you. Those words mean a lot to me. I know you didn't mean to offend, but please don't call my son 'special needs.'"

"Oh, sorry, it won't happen again. I'm sure your son is a fine young man."

Courtney hadn't expected that response. She wonders if he could be the one. No one except her mother had said anything that empathetic about her son, not even his own father.

"Thank you. I'm sorry for not telling you. I just assumed you wouldn't want to see me if you knew about his disability," Courtney says.

"You're welcome. It's annoying how idiotic some folk are toward people with disabilities. I can understand you not wanting to tell me," Mike says. "Oh, it looks like our food has arrived."

"Anything else you would like?" Liz the waitress asks.

"No, that will be all, thank you," Courtney says. "So, why are you still single? A man as sweet as yourself must've been with someone at some point," Courtney says as she cuts into her steak and takes a small bite.

Mike pauses, as though to gather himself for a tragic tale. He clears his throat and drops his silverware.

"It's a long story," Mike says before letting out a sigh.

"Sorry, I didn't mean to pry."

"My ex-wife . . . she was my high school sweetheart, and we were together for over ten years. One day I got home from work early, and I saw some stranger in bed with my wife," Mike says.

"Oh, I'm so—"

Mike cuts her off mid-sentence. He is so fixated on telling the complete story that he doesn't hear Courtney's sympathies.

"I kicked his ass right in front of her. She just stood there, watching. Looking at me like I was the monster, like I ruined our marriage. So, I packed whatever I could fit into my bag and left."

Courtney grips her thigh tightly, opening and closing her lips until her questions escape from her stammering tongue.

"Did . . . did you hurt her as well?"

Mike chokes on his water and punches his chest until he coughs a little. Under the table, his long legs accidentally clash into Courtney's. He takes a deep breath and looks straight into her eyes.

"I'd never lay a hand on a woman. Her or any other—because that would make me worse than her or any homewrecker," Mike says. "Why didn't you kick her out instead?" Courtney asks, propping her chin in the palm of her hand.

"I guess some small part of me still loved her. We were just talking about having kids a couple days before. That was eight years ago. So, anyways, that's why I moved to Princeton County. It's smaller, simpler." Mike exhales deeply.

"Where do you live?" Courtney asks.

"In a small apartment, down near Route 38. It ain't much, but it's a roof over my head. Better than nothing, I suppose. It's just a temporary thing. After the separation, I needed something quick and easy to get away. But I've been looking at some houses lately."

Mike sighs. Courtney understands what it's like after a divorce. She looks down at her half-eaten plate and back up at him.

"Why don't you . . . wait, hang on, someone's calling me," Courtney says, feeling a vibration in her purse.

"Oh, take the call, it could be important," Mike says.

"Hello, I'm busy right now could you . . ."

"Ms. Ramirez, we have your son and two of his friends down at the station for questioning, and he keeps asking for you," the operator says.

"I . . . what? Hang on, what happened?"

"He's fine, but meet us down at the sheriff's office, ma'am. The police have questions they need answered."

The operator hangs up. Courtney's hand covers her mouth,

and her eyes bulge out of their sockets. She's too frightened to scream. The fun they were having seems like a distant dream she's been ripped away from. She can hardly remember the purpose of the date, let alone wearing this dress she's wearing.

Mike can plainly see that something is wrong. "What's going on Courtney? Are you okay?" Mike asks.

"Um . . . I'm sorry. I gotta go. It's an emergency. Please send me the check."

"What about our—"

"It's Luke," Courtney says.

"Don't worry. I understand. I'll take care of it."

"Thank you so much, Mike. I'll talk to you tomorrow," Courtney says as she runs out of the restaurant.

"See you then, Courtney," Mike calls after her.

Courtney gets into her car, so worried that she drops her keys before they're in the ignition. What could've that boy done to get arrested? Or was he a victim? Her makeup begins to run from the sweat, and her eyes are watery thinking of all the worst-case scenarios. She needs to make sure he's safe. He must be shaking in his boots. The station is close by, only twenty minutes away.

"Hold on, Luke, I'm coming," Courtney says to herself.

Courtney takes the back roads to avoid getting stuck in traffic. She wants to get there before anything bad happens to the kids—if it hasn't already. She dials the number for Bonnie's parents first.

* * *

All six kids are in handcuffs. The groups are separated by two tables, with Sheriff Berkowski between them, pacing back and forth. The room is dim, with a single fixture as the only light source. Their injuries have been nursed, but they now have

93

bigger problems. It is only a matter of time before Sheriff Berkowski finds out who is responsible for the fight.

"I know one of you started this skirmish, so fess up, and maybe your punishment will be light. Luckily, five out of the six of you are minors, and no one was killed. So, just spill the damn beans, before it gets worse for you."

"We told you and your officers already, they started it," Luke says. "They hid around the corner and tried to kill us."

"He's lying, sir. They came out of nowhere and jumped me. My boys were just trying to help," Rob says, licking the gap in his mouth where a tooth used to be.

Rob has welts all over his face from Drew smashing his face into the asphalt but continues to trash talk despite losing the fight.

"Sheriff, please, you have to believe us, we—" Bonnie says, but Sheriff Berkowski blows a gasket.

"Enough! Frankly, I don't believe a single word any one of you are saying. Think you're feeding me bullshit. I know the people you run with, Jones. This ain't your first time in handcuffs. You're hardly innocent."

Rob grunts in frustration, but he stays quiet. Sheriff Berkowski leers at Rob before continuing his interrogation.

"Smart, using your right to remain silent, Jones. As for you three, you expect me to believe you three got jumped by these three, and not one of you were knocked out, but all three of them were? No offense, but doesn't seem likely," the sheriff says, sauntering down the line of suspects before stopping in front of Luke, Bonnie, and Drew with his arms crossed.

"They ain't as tough as they look, Sheriff," Drew says.

"Shut your damn mouth, Thompson," Brandon says.

"Make me, Taylor!" Drew barks back.

Sheriff Berkowski slams his hand on a metal table, making all the teenagers flinch. He slowly removes his shades, revealing his gray eyes.

"Shut up! So, I see I'm gonna need to bring in my witness to speed things along. When she confirms who's at fault, you're in a heap of trouble," Sheriff Berkowski says.

10

TURN OF EVENTS

Sheriff Berkowski and another deputy bring all six teenagers into the room where suspects usually lined up. The room has a white wall that measures height. Across the room there is a one-way window, so none of the teenagers can see the sheriff or the witness behind it.

"Who do you think the witness is, Bonnie?" Luke asks.

"I don't know, maybe Patricia or Sandy," Bonnie says.

"If that's the case, we're screwed," Drew says, palming his forehead.

Bonnie peers past Drew's tall frame and leers at Rob, noticing sweat dripping down his forehead.

"I don't think it is, boys, just look at those three," Bonnie says.

"They don't look like they had this planned. Rob was surprised when he heard the siren, and they've all been nervous since they woke up. Also, their alibis ain't convincing either."

"Whoever that witness is might be the only one who can save us now," Luke says.

"Or end us," Drew says.

* * *

In the room opposite the lined-up teenagers, the sheriff glares at the suspects as the witness taps her finger to her lip repeatedly, trying to remember the group that started it all. Protected by the one-sided window, the sheriff and the witness are in no danger of being seen by the suspects.

"So, who did you see attack first?" Sheriff Berkowski asks.

The witness's nose scrunches, able to smell remnants of cigarette ash in Sheriff Berkowksi's beard.

"I believe it was the three on the left: Rob, Travis, and Brandon."

"Are you absolutely positive?" Sheriff Berkowski asks, wanting no doubt in their mind.

"I'm sure of it. I remember now. They waited outside for Bonnie, Drew, and Luke, and then attacked them out of nowhere."

"Thank you for your assistance in the investigation, Ms. Brown. If you didn't call it in, it could've ended a lot worse than it did."

"It was my pleasure, Sheriff. I needed to do something about it. I heard a couple girls talking about some plan to beat up a student," Natalie says, rubbing her elbow with the opposite hand.

"You did the right thing, young lady," Sheriff Berkowski says.

"I hope so," Natalie says.

"Okay, let them out!" Sheriff Berkowski says.

The six suspected teenagers march out into the interrogation room with their heads down. All they can do now is anxiously wait on who the witness said was at fault.

Sheriff Berkowski and three deputies with handcuffs walk out of the room.

"Robert Jones, Travis Williams, and Brandon Taylor, you

boys are all under arrest for assault and attempted murder," Sheriff Berkowski says. "Williams and Taylor, you two might only have to serve a few years in juvenile detention since you're minors and didn't pull out a pocketknife against these kids. Robert Jones, you will be tried as an adult—that is, if you three want to press charges."

Luke, Bonnie, and Drew huddle together; they nod at one another. One by one, they step forward and utter the word.

"Yes."

"Now, there's one more option for you three. There's three victims, an eyewitness, and y'all three don't have the most reputable history. I'll just say this now. It's not looking too good for you boys if this gets settled in court. What I suggest is you cop a plea, and maybe, just maybe, you'll get a lighter sentence."

"I'll take the plea," Travis says.

"Fine, I'll do it too," Brandon says.

"Sure. Why the hell not?" Rob says.

"Good. Deputies, take these three to their new homes," Sheriff Berkowski says.

"You sons of bitches! You're all gonna pay for this!" Rob yells.

The officers escort the three bullies away from the teenagers, and they disappear around the corner. It's finally over; they all are going to be expelled, Luke realizes. He almost can't believe it, blinking rapidly to make sure he's not just dreaming. The physical pain didn't matter; it was irrelevant to the emotional trauma that pathetic excuse of a human being had caused throughout his childhood. From Rob putting a handful of sand down his pants to pushing Luke into the pool while fully clothed, and even throwing a cup of water at his crotch to make it look like he peed himself. Luke could barely get a moment to process everything before he heard his name.

"Lucas! Lucas! Where are you?"

Luke snaps out of his daydream, and his eyes bounce around the room. He recognizes the voice; it's his mother. She has finally arrived, but Luke isn't sure whether to hang his head in shame or smile at her presence.

"Mom! I'm in here," Luke howls.

A rhythmic clicking noise rushes toward the interrogation room. The deputy outside extends his arm out in front of him.

"Sorry, ma'am, we're not done with the interrogation yet," a deputy says.

"Let her through. We are just about done here. Remove their cuffs, Deputy Johnson, they're free to go," Berkowski says.

"Hey, you play ball with my kid, right?" Deputy Johnson asks Drew while stroking his goatee.

"Philip Johnson? Yeah."

Courtney is still wearing a bright red dress and heels. It has taken a moment for Luke to realize that this is his mother. She looks like a Hollywood actress in Luke's opinion. She runs toward Luke and wraps her arms around him. Luke feels his mother's makeup- streaked tears running down his shoulder. He has never seen his mom cry in front of him until this moment.

"Oh, my baby, I never want to let you go again. What happened to your eye?" Courtney asks as she examines his eye, patting the tender flesh surrounding it.

Luke's left eye is practically swollen shut from the heavy punch he absorbed earlier. He was so focused on his mom's outfit and her crying that he momentarily forgot about his injuries.

"I'm okay. It doesn't hurt as bad as it looks," Luke says, removing his mother's hands off his face.

"Bonnie?!" A female voice yells that Bonnie immediately recognizes.

The metal door barges open forcibly, and a stout woman steps into the room. It is Bonnie's mother, Laura Davis. Like her daughter, Laura has blonde hair and freckles. She is confined to doing chores in the farmhouse while her husband and daughter do the bulk of the field work. The stress of having to raise five kids, three daughters and two sons, has taken a toll on her health. Of her children, Bonnie is the youngest, the only one still living on the ranch. Laura has a good heart and has raised Bonnie into the fine young lady that she is.

"Oh, Bonnie, darling, your face, it's all scratched up," Laura says, pulling Bonnie into her soft frame with her large arms.

"Mom, I'm fine. I was just standing up to some jerks. You should see the other guys."

Ten minutes later, Stephen Thompson arrives. Drew's father looks like he just rushed from work, as he is still in uniform. His tie is crooked, and his armpits stained with sweat. Stephen is lean and clean shaven, with short hair. He works long hours as a construction worker. He looks like the older version of his son but without the oversized afro.

"Drew, how are you? You hurt?" Stephen Thompson asks, nearly out of breath.

"It's cool, Dad, they popped my shoulder back into place. I'll have a scar from the cut, but it will impress the ladies," Drew says, fondling the slash across his face like a mustache.

"Typical Drew. I can hear it already, 'I nearly died, but I didn't give up. I knocked the guy out in one punch,'" Bonnie says before scoffing. "Wouldn't be a complete lie, though," Luke says, shrugging his shoulders.

"Yeah, but it's still a half truth," Bonnie says.

Sheriff Berkowski opens the metal door, hands on his hips, and lowers his head.

"I'm sure y'all would've liked to meet the witness that saved you three. But, for their own safety, they have decided to remain anonymous."

The kids exchange looks with their parents as somber silence fills the room as if someone has just passed away. The officers, parents, and teenagers scratch their heads, waiting for someone to speak up. Courtney lets go of Luke and steps toward Sheriff Berkowski with her arms crossed.

"So, the person who rescued our kids isn't coming forward? Why?"

"Sorry, I can't disclose that," Sheriff Berkowski says.

The parents approach the sheriff and surround him, pleading to meet the witness, like the homeless begging for change on the street. The sheriff backs away, until eventually his broad back is against the wall.

"But I need to thank them for helping my darling Bonnie," Laura says, clasping her hands.

"My boy is alive because of that witness!" Stephen Thompson says.

A deputy steps forward to intervene, but Sheriff Berkowski puts two fingers in his mouth and whistles. Courtney, Laura, and Stephen immediately stand down and back away.

"Okay! How about we not do this in front of the kids? All right, well, I need y'all to fill out some paperwork anyway. Let's give them some room."

"But . . ." Courtney says, looking back at Luke.

"It's okay, Ms. Ramirez, we'll watch over him," Bonnie says as she supports Luke's shoulders.

Noticing Courtney's hesitance, Luke nods at his mother, trying to reassure her.

"Follow me, everyone," Sheriff Berkowski says as he gestures his hand in his direction.

The parents nod in agreement, and Sheriff Berkowski leads their parents out to the front desk. The heavy metal door echoes shut behind them. The teenagers realize it is just the three of them in the interrogation room all alone. Moments of quiet pass, but after a while, it feels like years. Luke hums loudly, hoping for someone to say something. Unable to take the silence any longer, he asks the question on all their minds.

"So, who do you think called the police?" Luke asks.

Drew folds his arms and Bonnie scratches the back of her head. Luke has a sneaking suspicion, prodding the inside of his head, but considers other possibilities.

"I ain't got a clue. Everybody hated Rob's guts. Could've been anybody," Drew says.

"But why not show their face to us?" Luke asks.

"Maybe they're scared that Rob would've seen them, or they just wanted to help and move on," Bonnie says, shrugging her shoulders.

Luke paces back and forth across the room; the buzzing of the light fixture starts giving him a headache. "What if it was Natalie? You don't think maybe..."

Bonnie clenches her fists and begins seething. She shakes her head.

"No way! Why would she help us after I punched her? After what she did to you, Luke?!"

As Luke lowers his head to the floor, Drew puts his arm in front of Bonnie.

"Bonnie, relax! Luke was just putting an idea out there."

Bonnie takes a long breath and unclenches her fists. Luke takes a seat on the cold concrete floor, cradling his knees to his chest. Bonnie lowers herself to the floor in front of him.

"I'm sorry, Luke. I didn't mean to yell, but there's no way Natalie would've helped us. You know that, right?"

"I'm with her. Why would she flip-flop like that?" Drew asks, nodding his head.

Luke struggles to keep his emotions in check. A tear drips down his cheek and drops onto his pant leg.

"A group home. Is that what people think of me?" Luke asks as he sniffles.

"Oh, Luke, no," Bonnie says, pulling Luke in for a hug.

Luke cries into Bonnie's shoulder, while Drew pats Luke's back. The weight of the day's events finally crushes his spirit.

He weeps as his blackened eye throbs from the tears. One day, he had a girlfriend, now he doesn't. Luke doesn't understand people. He rarely trusted strangers before today. Now he can't trust anyone that he doesn't know.

* * *

In the lobby, Sheriff Berkowski and the teenagers' parents are conversing. While Stephen and Laura fill out some forms at the desk, Courtney stands in front of Sheriff Berkowski, begging him to tell her who the witness is. The sheriff says nothing and slowly shakes his head. Courtney scowls until she notices a young lady exiting the witness room from behind the sheriff's broad frame. The girl takes a seat on a bench, crossing her legs while staring at the floor. She looks around the same age as the rest of their kids.

"Excuse me! Young lady," Courtney says, stepping past Sheriff Berkowski.

Natalie looks up and locks eyes with Courtney. She swiftly covers her head with her hoodie and looks down. Sheriff Berkowski turns around and scratches his beard. Stephen and Laura gaze up, with Stephen dropping his pen to the floor.

"Was it you?" Courtney asks.

Natalie gets up from the bench and glances at Sheriff Berkowski. Courtney, Laura, and Stephen step closer to her. The girl backs away toward the building's exit, hiding her face. Natalie stares blankly at the parents' feet; she rubs her shoulder and gulps.

"Yes," Natalie says.

"You did good, kid," the sheriff says, tipping his hat.

"Take your hood off, missy, I wanna see your face," Stephen says.

"Thank you for saving our babies! What's your name?" Laura asks.

"You're all too kind, but no," Natalie says before sprinting out of the building.

The tiny bell rings as the door flies open. Courtney chases after her, with Laura and Stephen following closely behind.

"Wait!" Courtney calls out.

* * *

Natalie closes her car door and steps on the gas pedal. She starts driving toward her house, wiping a tear out of the corner of her eye. If only those parents knew what kind of damage she had done. *I just wanted friends.* She looks back into her mirror to get one last look at the sheriff's office. She hates how Sandy and Patricia used her and tricked her into losing the only true friend she ever had. Her knuckles tighten on the steering wheel until they turn pale white. Natalie knows that one way or another, she has to atone for her sins.

11

BELA'S CONFESSION

Drew's and Bonnie's parents take them home. Courtney takes a little longer to speak with Sheriff Berkowski to learn any details she missed. As Courtney drives Luke home, he gets lost in his thoughts. He is positive that inevitably they will all be grounded. Still, that is preferable to the alternatives, which were jail or six feet under.

Courtney chews her son's ear off the whole car ride, but in the end, she's just glad Luke is fine. Luke is glad too that he'll never have to see Rob's dim-witted face again. Rob is in custody and will go to jail since he took the plea bargain. He'll be expelled. Luke actually hopes no one finds out what truly happened because they might treat him like he did something heroic. All Luke did was defend himself, while Drew and Bonnie had risked their lives for him. If anything, they are the heroes. He will never forget what they did for him today.

"Luke Ramirez, I was on a fabulous lunch date today, and then I get a call that you're down at the station as a suspect," Courtney says as she turns the rearview mirror toward him.

"Mom, I didn't have a choice. They snuck up on us; the fight was unavoidable. Besides, you know how miserable Rob made the lives of kids at school. He would've been locked up sooner or later."

"That's beside the point. That's not your call to make. Luke, you're grounded for two weeks," Courtney says.

"Two weeks?!"

"That's right. That means no hanging out with Drew, Bonnie, or your girlfriend after school or over the weekend."

Now that Luke has been punished, he supposes it is the right time to finally to get his secret off his chest.

"Mom, I have something to tell you. My girlfriend broke up with me."

"What? Why in God's name didn't you tell me?" Courtney asks, slapping the steering wheel.

"Well, you kept your relationship secret, so turnabout is fair play," Luke says.

"Luke, you're grounded for a month now. For lying and talking back to me."

After fifteen minutes of going back and forth bickering at each other, Courtney and Luke finally pull into their driveway. It is pitch black outside. Luke and Courtney can barely see the outline of their small cottage. Luke finds it difficult to believe today is at an end. This day might as well have been a year in Luke's book. Courtney clomps toward the front door barefooted, her high heels in her hand.

"I am your mother. If I don't tell you something, that means it's none of your concern," Courtney says.

"Do you really need to know every single detail of my social life? Some things that happen in my life aren't your business," Luke says.

"Why are you two yelling so late at night?!" Sophie demands, having been woken by her family's commotion.

"Ma, your grandson got into a fight today. Nearly got himself arrested," Courtney says as she crosses her arms.

"Why is he here then?" Sophie asks as she raises her eyebrows.

"Brought down for questioning. He's lucky some nice young lady called the police. I saw her face for a second, but she covered her head before Stephen or Laura could get a look. I wish I got her name," Courtney says as she places her hands on her hips.

"Me too," Luke mutters under his breath.

"Really? That's quite a shiner, sonny. Put a frozen steak on that eye of yours," Sophie says.

"Some ice will do just fine, Ma. Go to the freezer, Luke, and put some ice on that eye to make the swelling go down."

"Fine," Luke says.

"I don't understand why that boy is so stubborn," Courtney whispers, shaking her head.

"It's not the autism. Our whole family is stubborn. That's why I'm still kicking," Sophie says.

Luke slowly walks to the refrigerator and opens the freezer. The frigid air gives Luke goosebumps. He pulls out a few ice cubes, wraps some paper towels around the ice, and rests it against his throbbing eye. Luke applies pressure to relieve some of the pain and walks back to the living room, where his mother and grandmother are chatting about the rough situation he got into earlier.

"Luke, now go to your room, and remember you're grounded for a month," Courtney says.

"Yes, Mom. Goodnight," Luke says flatly.

"Wait. Courtney dear, can I have a talk with Luke before I go back to bed?"

"Of course, you can, Ma. Just don't take too long," Courtney says as she walks off to her bedroom.

Luke is so petrified that he almost drops his handmade ice pack. What would his grandmother want to talk about this late at night? Luke guesses that it must be about the fight and the sheriff's office. Was she going to give Luke another black eye? Yell at him? If Luke had the choice of fighting Rob again or Bela "disciplining" him, he would choose the former over the latter any day.

"Luke, come here!" Sophie yells.

"I'm coming, Bela, just need a few minutes to get ready for bed."

"Make it quick, dearie. You two woke me after all," Sophie says as Luke climbs the stairs.

After brushing his teeth, taking a brief, two-minute shower, and changing into his pajamas, Luke goes to the guest bedroom where his Bela has slept since moving in. As he opens the door, the room is pitch black. Sophie turns on her nightstand lamp, which dimly lights the bed area. She is waiting with her nasal cannula on, which is attached to an oxygen tank at her bedside.

"So, is it true?" Sophie asks.

"Is what true?" Luke asks, trying to stall.

"Don't play dumb now, dearie, you know what I mean," Sophie says, seeing through Luke's charade.

"Yes, Bela, my friends and I got into a fight. Well, it was more like defending ourselves against Rob and his thugs."

"Well in that case, there is only one thing I can think of to say at this moment," Sophie says.

"Wh-what Bela?"

"I am so proud of you."

Sophie yanks Luke in for a hug and kisses him repeatedly on his forehead. Luke is relieved but confused at the same time. Why was his grandmother not yelling at him for getting in trouble?

"Proud, why?"

"You finally stood up to your bully, and now he's in custody, right?"

"Yeah, since he's eighteen now, he will go to jail."

"How does that make you feel?"

"I don't know, relieved, I guess. I don't have to deal with Rob anymore."

"Thank God for that," Sophie says.

Luke had been thinking deeply while at the station. He questions the existence of God from time to time, but he believes everything that has happened this past week or so was no coincidence. As for the witness, all Luke knows is that it was a girl who called the police. Thanks to her, his bullies were vanquished, and now he is safe and sound with his family. Luke tries to believe in something larger than himself. He wants to—he just isn't sure—though he feels like a guardian angel is protecting him.

"Bela, how do I know God is with me?" Luke asks, hopeful for a positive answer.

Sophie smiles, to Luke's surprise. Luke thought she would be upset with him for simply asking a question like that. She reaches in for a hug, which Luke reciprocates.

"I've witnessed miracles, Luke. You being one of them. I should've been dead long ago. I was afraid, but now I'm not anymore. I think it's God's way of telling me that I'll be with him soon, and everything's going to be fine. Faith is a powerful thing, Luke," Sophie says.

"Amen, Bela," Luke says.

"Lucas, there's something I've wanted to tell you for a long time. I think it's time you knew the truth," Sophie says.

"About what?" Luke asks, turning his head sideways.

"Your father," Sophie says.

"He died in a car accident when I was three. What else is there to know?"

"Come and sit down," Sophie says.

"Your mother and your father met in middle school and stayed with each other throughout high school. I thought he was a handsome and kind man. Your dad was a mechanic, a great one at that. One day, he proposed to your mom, and they got married. Two years later, they decided to have a child. That's when you came along, and he loved you, almost as much as your mother did. Eventually, when you were three years old and in Pre-K, he received calls from the teachers that you weren't interacting with the other kids. You weren't doing as teachers told you, you didn't like being touched, and you would make 'weird noises' when it got too loud. He insisted that you were fine. Your mom, being a nurse, believed you had autism. So, she finally convinced him to take you to a specialist to diagnose you. The doctor's diagnosis concluded that you had autism and recommended Dr. Washington as your therapist. Your father didn't take it well; he believed you were broken. He started drinking, a lot. He lost his job when he dropped a car, almost crushing his coworker. He refused to look for another job. During this time, your mom became pregnant with your sister."

"What? I have a sister?"

Luke's mouth drops open slightly, in shock. Sophie's eyes are watering now. Luke feels his heart beating rapidly, but he needs to know the rest of the story.

"When he drank, your dad started taking out his anger on your mom. At first, he tried to strike you. You were at the age that you should've been talking. You weren't, and he would push you and squeeze your face. When your mom found out about the abuse, she slapped him. After that, she didn't leave you alone with him. She wouldn't let you get beat. She would bring you to the day care at the hospital. When Ben came to the hospital one day to look for you, she started having a friend watch you. Your mom tried to fix things. She became pregnant to calm Ben down. She hoped he'd stop drinking, but he didn't."

"No. That can't be. Is . . . is my dad alive?"

A queasy feeling surfaces in the pit of Luke's stomach. It is too much information for his mind to process all at once.

Sophie stops speaking, noticing his groaning. She waits for a few minutes before she waves her hand in front of Luke's face. He ceases making noises and acknowledges her by shaking his head, as if brought back to reality.

"Do you want me to stop?"

Luke shakes his head aggressively side to side, and Sophie coughs into her hand, clearing her throat.

"She put up with his behavior as long as she could. One day, Ben punched your mother so hard in the stomach that it caused a miscarriage after she was almost five months pregnant."

"What's a miscarriage?" Luke asks, picking at his fingernails.

Luke has a devastating feeling about the answer, even though he isn't completely sure what it is. Luke almost doesn't want this question answered. How could he not remember all this? He was five years old. He was sure that he had developed some memories when he was that age. His mind is drawing a blank. He doesn't remember seeing his mom get hit.

"Your dad punched your mother so hard, that . . . he killed your sister. I think he realized it when your mom was in terrible pain. She tried to reach for the phone, but he panicked. He knocked her out right in front of you. He took whatever he could fit in his hands and left the house. He never came back."

"Unbelievable," Luke says.

Luke can't muster any more words. He is almost speechless.

"I think you realized that your mom tried to call someone to help but couldn't. You must've picked up the phone and dialed 911. You remembered that even at five years old; you were so smart. The police showed up with an ambulance and saved your mother. You saved your mother's life."

"But I couldn't save my sister. In fact, my stupid autism is what got her killed."

Sophie closes her eyes and shakes her head side to side

insistently. She reaches for Luke's hands until their palms clutch one another's. Sophie's hands are cold and veiny, while Luke's are warm and soft. The frigidness bothers Luke until Sophie's hands warm up in his grasp. Luke avoids eye contact, staring at the wall to his left.

"No. Luke, look at me! Your father killed your sister because he was drunk and didn't know how to cope with your autism. That's on him, nobody else. It's not your mom's fault, your fault, or anyone else's," Sophie tells her grandson.

"Why didn't Mom, you know, try to find him and put him behind bars?"

"She was scared. Being beaten for over a year will do that to even the strongest people."

"Why didn't she tell me?"

"She was frightened of the possibility of having to face him again. Also ashamed of you finding out the truth; she was looking out for you."

"Is that why I didn't take Miller as my last name?"

"Exactly," Sophie says.

"Mom doesn't know you told me this, right?'

"No, dearie."

"Do you think I should go find him?"

"Listen, Luke, I'm at the end of my rope here. If I have one dying wish, it would be to see that man put behind bars. Give my daughter, you, and my granddaughter some justice and peace hopefully. I would die a smiling woman knowing that, but no I don't think you should."

"Oh, okay. Do you know where he went into hiding?"

"Maybe with his parents in the outskirts of Memphis. It's a few hours away."

"Bela, I . . . what do I do with this information?"

"I just thought you should know the truth, honey. Don't get any funny ideas now. Odds are your dad isn't even there anymore."

"Bela, I hope one day things are set right. For my mother, she didn't deserve that type of pain."

"God bless you, *nieto*. I'm sure one day they will one way or another."

"Thank you for telling me this, Bela."

Luke gets up from the bed. On his way out, he turns off the lamp before stopping at the doorframe.

"You're welcome. Take all the time you need, honey. I know it's a lot to absorb. I suggest going to bed. You'll feel better in the morning. Goodnight, Luke. Tell your mother I'm ready for bed now."

12

A NEW MISSION

Luke is on the floor, surrounded by toys and unable to walk. He sees his mother, but she appears younger, her hair is longer, and she looks slightly skinnier. Luke squints, and after closer inspection, spots him. The Masked Haunter is right behind his mother. What could he want with her? Luke is powerless to stop the demonic-looking figure, as he can't move at all.

"You did not heed my warning, boy. You reap what you sow."

Luke attempts to talk back, but no words come out. Nothing but incoherent babbles escape from his mouth. Looking down at his hands, he is shocked to see his once long, slender fingers resemble Vienna sausages. This confirms what he suspected all along. He is a mere toddler who can't walk or talk. Luke is trapped in his own vulnerable body, and he can't help his mother, let alone himself.

"I want you to remember this moment. Boy, if you go through with this journey, there will be hell to pay," the Masked Haunter says.

The Masked Haunter then does something that will stay

114

with Luke for a long time. He transforms himself into some sort of serpent. As Luke falls backward and crawls frantically, trying to put distance between himself and the snake, it lurks toward the young Courtney. Luke tries to warn her, but it is too late. He bites her on the back of the neck, and the venom affects her immediately. She falls down, and her motionless body lies there, to Luke's horror. Luke tries to stand up, but he cannot. The giant snake slithers over Courtney's body. It stops in front of the child and stares menacingly. Luke looks into the slits in his eyes that bare no goodness. The evil serpent coils its body around him, squeezing until no air can escape, and locks eyes with the frightened toddler. The reptilian creature sticks its forked tongue out, revealing its fangs before lunging at Luke, ready to impose its will on the terrified child.

Luke wakes up screaming at 3:12 in the morning. He gasps for breath as he clenches his throbbing chest. They're getting worse, Luke thinks to himself. He wipes his sweaty forehead with his shirt and forces himself to return to sleep.

Luke arises, breaking the crust as he opens his heavy eyelids. He feels as if he's hardly slept. Luke hopes that it was all just a nightmare —Natalie, the fight, the police station, and worst of all, his grandmother telling him that his father is not, in fact, deceased but rather hiding away somewhere near Memphis. It takes most of Luke's energy to lift himself out of bed, and he descends the stairs as if walking to his imminent death. Luke feels empty. The Masked Haunter wanted to terrify him. Why did he want him to remember that moment? He peeks his head into the kitchen; his grandmother and mother are both eating cereal for breakfast.

"Morning, sleepyhead. Now remember, you're grounded, so you are not leaving this house once this whole weekend," Courtney says.

"Yes, Mom, I recall last night clearly," Luke says.

"Don't be a smartass," Courtney snaps.

Luke's mother just confirmed that it wasn't a dream. He doesn't even have to ask his grandmother if she really spoke to him last night. Luke decides to just pull up a chair and eat some Cheerios. He eats so slowly that the plain oats cereal gets soggy when his bowl is still half- full.

"Honey, are you okay? You don't seem yourself," Courtney says.

"Yeah, I'm fine. It was just a tough day yesterday. My whole body hurts," Luke says, resting his head on the table.

"You'll be fine, dearie. You're strong, just like your mother," Sophie says.

After he finishes his unsatisfying breakfast, Luke takes some ibuprofen to alleviate the pain in his body. Sadly, it does absolutely nothing for his mental pain. Luke goes back upstairs to reflect on why these awful things are happening. Courtney follows to check on him. She knocks on his door. She opens the door to see Luke pacing back and forth in his bedroom.

"Honey, is everything all right?"

"Yesterday was a bad day. I'll be fine eventually," Luke says.

Before departing for the hospital, Courtney reminds Luke not to leave the house. After Luke is sure his mother's gone, he rushes downstairs to visit his grandmother, who is watching the morning news in her wheelchair, like most mornings.

"Bela, why did you tell me the truth?" Luke asks.

"I thought you were ready," Sophie says.

"I don't think I was. I thought I knew what had happened, but it was all a lie."

Luke feels enraged and upset. Like an innocent child who finds out that Santa Claus isn't real and discovers it was just their parents bringing them gifts all along. Sophie motions Luke to come closer so she can have a heart-to-heart conversation with him. Luke does as he's instructed, and he drags his feet toward his frail grandmother until he is right beside her.

"Luke, everything happens for a reason. I know it sounds vague, but it's true," Sophie says as she places her wrinkly hand on her grandson's shoulder.

"I'm just so angry at him, but you're right."

"You'll get through everything. The bullies are gone, the girl is gone, and your dirtbag of a father—who knows if he's even still there."

"Yeah. I suppose you're right. I wouldn't have been ready to hear that even if I was thirty years old. Better late than never I guess," Luke says.

"See dear, you just need time to process. Time heals all wounds," Sophie says softly.

"Thank you for the advice. I'm gonna go wash my face," Luke says.

"Okay dear, just be careful of your eye," Sophie says.

Luke goes upstairs to the bathroom and splashes cold water in his face. He looks up into the mirror. He barely recognizes himself. The area surrounding his eye is black and blue. He tries to touch it, and a raw pain arises from the pressure of his soft hands, making him flinch. Looking down, he remembers the vision of seeing his mother getting attacked by the serpent form of the Masked Haunter. He can only imagine what the actual experience must've felt like. The fist connecting with his mother's stomach, causing the death of his unborn sister. His father knocking his mother unconscious in front of a toddler Luke, and just leaving her to die. Luke wonders what he felt in that very moment. Did he feel scared? Possibly indifferent? He can't remember his emotions at that time no matter how hard he tries.

Luke looks up, his beaten face reminding him that he is a warrior and that he can fight and defend the people he loves.

Ideas begin to form inside Luke's head. If his father is close to Memphis, what would stop him from going after him? Luke believes his father doesn't deserve a peaceful life after what he has done. His fear begins festering into anger, and that anger turns into ideas. All that is left to do is to put those ideas into action. He decides to talk this out with Drew and Bonnie on Monday.

Remembering that he is grounded pushes Luke over the edge. He glowers at his mirror reflection and chucks a toothbrush at the wall before storming off to his room. The rest of the weekend consists of Luke doing chores around the house while still internally processing everything his grandmother has told him. His own father had abandoned him over something that he couldn't control. The only thing that keeps him distracted from this uncovered truth is the physical pain. Luke's whole body is sore. He feels like he got hit by a truck.

Luke isn't sure how he will, but he has to tell Bonnie and Drew this new information. It is taking everything in Luke not to go to his mom and tell her this and demand her reasoning for telling him a lie and letting him believe it for all of his young life. But from what his grandmother told him, even though this was hard for Luke, it must've been a hundred times worse for his mother. Luke tries to remember that whenever he has the thought of confronting her. Luke holds it in for two slow, painful, and grueling days.

The following Monday, while Luke is walking through the halls with Drew and Bonnie, they hear students whispering to each other and notice their stares. They are looking at the three students that caused Rob, Travis, and Brandon to not only be expelled but also arrested. The three friends aren't in any mood to answer rumors. Their bodies are sore, and their parents are irate with them.

"So, I got grounded for a month," Luke says, slamming his locker door.

"I got a week," Drew says.

"Wait, y'all got grounded for a scrap that we didn't even start? I just told Daddy we stood up to some bullies and won the fight. He said he was proud of me and that was that. No punishment, no warning, no nothing. Guess I got off scot-free," Bonnie says, touching her bruised cheek.

"Why can't we be that lucky?" Drew asks, shaking his head.

"It was less about the fight and more that I lied to my mom about my breakup and started arguing with her on the ride home," Luke says.

In English, Natalie sits in the same seat as the day before. As Luke is writing, he thinks that he catches her staring at him, but when he looks up, she is nose deep into her paper. Maybe she sensed Luke about to catch her gazing at him and retreated quickly. Perhaps Luke's mind is playing tricks on him. Mr. Alterman calls Luke over.

"Luke, I heard about what happened yesterday. Do you want to talk about it?" Mr. Alterman asks.

"Not right now, Mr. Alterman. I would like to just get through the day," Luke says, exhaling sharply.

"All right, Luke, but just remember, I'm here if you ever need me," Mr. Alterman says.

"I appreciate it, Mr. Alterman," Luke says, not looking directly at his teacher.

Mr. Calhoun seems to be the only person on earth angrier at Luke, Bonnie, and Drew than their parents. The bullies are practically saints in his eyes, since he's known Rob for years through his uncle. History was also the only subject Rob cared about, and his antics flew under the radar around Mr. Calhoun.

As they enter his classroom, the teenagers feel like they are walking to their deaths. Mr. Calhoun will no doubt make their lives more miserable than they already are. Today, whenever he yells at them, his mustache would start ruffling, like the feathers of an aggravated bird.

"Robert Jones was one of my favorite students, and you three troublemakers just had to poke the bear! I am giving you three extra homework. Just be grateful I don't give you detention," Mr. Calhoun bellows.

Drew grinds his teeth forcibly as Mr. Calhoun speaks about the bullies in such high esteem. Drew has had a deep-seated hatred for Mr. Calhoun since the first day of school, but the fact that he has just shown little concern or compassion for some of his own students pushes him over the edge.

"Why on earth would you give us detention for your KKK-ass- kissing self?!" Drew roars as he lifts himself from his desk.

The entire class flinches, and Mr. Calhoun raises his eyebrow. This is a rare occurrence, for Mr. Calhoun to be challenged by a student. The class is on the edge of their seats, all eyes moving back and forth between Mr. Calhoun and Drew. Drew's initial outburst startles Luke. He covers his ears to brace for further eruptions but continues looking on.

"Sit your Black ass down, before I . . ."

"What? Send me to the principal, who also has a Black ass?!"

Mr. Calhoun is now seething. Luke can tell he wants to do something very drastic, but Principal Jackson wouldn't tolerate a teacher doing what Mr. Calhoun is thinking about doing to a student. His mustache moves so forcefully it appears almost alive.

"Mr. Thompson, I'm assigning you a ten-page essay on the Civil War to write, and it's due by tomorrow," Mr. Calhoun says while thrusting his arms in the air, revealing the dark circles underneath his armpits before landing back into his chair.

"Yeah, that's what I thought," Drew says to himself.

"We should key his car or egg his house. This has gone too far," Bonnie says to Drew and Luke.

"Why? We would probably be suspended," Luke says.

"Man, this guy has been getting on my nerves for days. He

would lynch me given half the chance. I think he deserves what's coming to him. Bonnie, what do you think?" Drew says.

"I'd be happy to help. Look, I don't disagree. This school would be a much better place without Mr. Calhoun, but if the police catch us, we'll be joining the three stooges. How about we catch him calling Drew something horrible like he just did a minute ago?" Bonnie says.

"What do you mean, Bonnie?"

"I mean, I have a tape recorder in my backpack, and if we catch Mr. Calhoun saying something similar to what he just said, Principal Jackson would have no choice but to fire him."

"That's brilliant, Bonnie."

"Hell yeah it is," Drew says, as a mischievous grin spreads across his face.

"I'm going to separate you three if you don't shut your mouths!" Mr. Calhoun says.

"Now?" Drew whispers, placing his hand to the corner of his mouth.

"Sure, just give me a second to set it up," Bonnie whispers.

Bonnie reaches into her backpack and pulls out a small device and a couple of batteries to put in the back.

"Hurry, Bonnie, we have one shot at it."

Luke feels good, like exposing bad people for their actions is the right thing to do. This would be the second time in less than twenty-four hours they would deliver justice against a common enemy. Luke decides it is best to tell Bonnie and Drew about his father at lunch. Right now, their focus is directed at getting Mr. Calhoun terminated.

"Okay, Drew, now," Bonnie says.

"Hey, Mr. Calhoun!"

Mr. Calhoun turns away from the chalkboard, palming his pudgy face, and slowly drags his fat hand down. He locks eyes with Drew as if challenged to a duel.

"What could you possibly want now?"

"Tell me again, was it your sister or your cousin that you married?" Drew asks.

The class laughs with such force that the entire classroom erupts. Ryan O'Connell nearly falls out of his desk, while Harper Lavine has tears flowing from her eyes that she tries to wipe away. Even David Smith, a very serious and quiet kid, can't help but chuckle. Once Mr. Calhoun shifts his head to the direction of the class, they quickly cease their behavior for self-preservation.

"What did you just say, you . . . you . . ." Mr. Calhoun says as a vein pops on his forehead.

"What? What am I? You racist, inbred piece of garbage?!" Drew shouts.

Bonnie clicks the record button on the tape recorder. They all know a bomb is about to go off. Mr. Calhoun's chubby face is as red as a freshly picked apple.

"You little monkey! Oh, fifty years ago, the things I'd gladly do to you. You're just lucky we're in school, boy. Now, sit down or get the hell out of my classroom," Mr. Calhoun says, pointing his pudgy finger toward the door.

Drew sits down and digs his fists into his face. He looks at his friends so that he can be reassured they got what they needed. Drew, Bonnie, and Luke all smile gleefully. All they have to do is bring the evidence to Principal Jackson. The whole class has their mouths wide open in disbelief at what they just witnessed. Harper is still crying; however, the emotions behind the tears have drastically changed from earlier.

"Guys, I think I can handle it from here. Anyways, I always wanted to talk to Principal Jackson. I was always curious as to how a Black female became a principal in Tennessee," Bonnie says.

"Hopefully, when we see you again, you bring good news with you."

"Drew, are you okay?" Bonnie asks.

Luke turns around, taking in the strange sight. Drew hasn't said anything since standing up to Mr. Calhoun. He just looks down at his desk, hunched over, which is unusual for Drew. He would normally say something sarcastic right now or be pumped at the possibility of getting Mr. Calhoun fired.

"Yeah, I've been called names like that since I've gotten here. I'm glad I have you two, or else I would've left this god-awful place a long time ago," Drew says, burying his head in his arms.

"Drew, I think you should speak to someone," Bonnie says, tapping his shoulder.

"Like who?" Drew asks.

The bell is going to ring in about ten minutes. The way Luke sees it, Mr. Calhoun already had it with them, so they could just leave class, and he most likely won't even bother trying to stop them. Drew seems to be in a rough place and needs some guidance. Luckily, Luke knows just the right person to take Drew to.

"I know someone. Follow me. He's a nice guy."

"Meet you boys at lunch," Bonnie says as she briskly walks the opposite way, her two braids swaying back and forth between her shoulders and the air as she goes.

"Don't let the door hit you two on the way out," Mr. Calhoun yells at Luke and Drew.

Drew inhales sharply, tugging on the sides of his afro until it no longer presents in its usual bulbous shape. Appearing as if he were about to pull out clumps of hair, Luke taps on his shoulder, causing Drew to release his grip. When Drew lets go, he carelessly punches a locker, making a clanking echo through the halls. After a few seconds, seemingly calmer now, Luke beckons Drew in his direction.

"What a douchebag. Hey, where are you taking me?" Drew

asks, flexing his fingers outward, causing his hair to revert back to its curly nature.

"Mr. Yamamoto," Luke says.

"Wait, the old janitor you talked to last week?"

"The one and only," Luke says.

"I know you said he's wise and all, but how the hell is wisdom gonna help me now?" Drew asks.

"When Natalie broke my heart, I couldn't do anything but run away. He helped stop me and face my problem, and I could think again."

"You're not making a lot of sense."

Drew shoots a look at Luke as if he had just spoken in a different language.

"Okay, I'm not very good at explaining things like this. Just listen closely to him; you'll see what I mean."

Luke and Drew arrive at Mr. Yamamoto's closet. Before they can even knock, the monotone voice of Kai says, "You may enter."

They open the creaky wooden door slowly, peeking their heads inside. Luke smirks when he sees the face of Mr. Yamamoto, whose expression rarely changes. Drew seems puzzled, unsure what to feel in this situation.

"Ah, Mr. Ramirez, back again I see. So, what brings you boys here today?" Kai asks.

"Kai, my friend Drew here sometimes feels he doesn't belong." "Is that correct, Mr. Thompson?"

"Yeah, Mr. Yamamoto," Drew says.

"Please call me Kai. I'm not your teacher, just the school janitor," Kai says as he bows respectfully.

"Right, Kai, do you know Mr. Calhoun?"

"Unfortunately, all too well. When he was first hired here twenty years ago, he tried to make my life a living hell. Purposefully leaving garbage in his classroom, calling me *chopsticks* or *rice farmer*. Even one time tried to get physical with me. I assumed his goal was to get me to quit. Thankfully, he failed quite miserably.”

“Well, we recorded him calling Drew something not so nice. It was actually quite heinous. It might be enough to get him fired,” Luke says.

“Are you asking for my blessing? Because you have my permission to get him fired. He would not be missed,” Kai says.

“No, Bonnie is taking care of it,” Luke says.

“I just don’t feel like I belong here, you know?” Drew says.

Kai Yamamoto slowly nods in an understanding manner. Luke knows he will tell Drew the sad tale about his father and his upbringing in a place where folk reminded him constantly that he didn’t belong.

“All too well, kid,” Kai says.

“How?” Drew asks.

“My father was in an internment camp during World War II. It changed everything for him—couldn’t get the job opportunities he wanted.”

“Damn, that’s real rough,” Drew says, looking down.

“Indeed, it was, my friend.”

“So, what? I need to become a janitor to survive here?” Drew asks.

“No,” Kai says. “You find your purpose. My purpose isn’t keeping the building up to code. It’s to help kids like you get through the hardships of high school.”

“So, what is my purpose?” Drew asks.

“Right now, I think your purpose is to help your friend here. Think it will help you find yourself,” Kai says.

“With what?” Drew asks.

“I think he will tell you soon enough,” Kai says, shifting his gaze to Luke. “Unless he wants to share it now.”

“Drew, I need to tell you and Bonnie something important at lunch,” Luke says.

"Thank you, Kai, you really pulled through today," Drew says, appreciatively as he firmly shakes Mr. Yamamoto's hand.

"My pleasure, kids. Glad to be of service. Be safe now."

Drew and Luke exit the janitor's closet with their heads held high, and they walk briskly down the halls toward the cafeteria to wait for Bonnie to return with news. Her task is to convince the principal to fire Mr. Calhoun, so that the school has one less person to wreak havoc.

13

A WOMAN'S SCORN

Bonnie walks over to Principal Olivia Jackson's office. She starts twisting her braid with her fingers and stares at the plaque on the wooden door that reads Principal Olivia Jackson, School Principal. Bonnie has always admired Principal Jackson—her perseverance and dedication to this school is admirable, despite having faculty like Earl Calhoun try to pull her down simply for the fact that she is an African American woman with authority. Mr. Calhoun considers it shameful that he is the subordinate to someone like Principal Jackson. Bonnie feels it is time for Mr. Calhoun to get his comeuppance. Bonnie knocks on Principal Jackson's door.

"Who is it?" Principal Jackson asks.

"It's Bonnie Davis. I have a serious complaint with a faculty member."

"Come in, Ms. Davis."

Bonnie pushes the door open with what feels like all of her body and sees the small Principal Jackson at her desk reading a file.

"So, what complaint brings you to my office today?"

Principal Jackson asks as she closes the file to give Bonnie her full, undivided attention.

"I actually have a tape recording of Mr. Calhoun verbally abusing a student."

"Well, Mr. Calhoun has always had such a fine way with words," Principal Jackson says, rolling her eyes.

The tape plays, and as the events unfold, Bonnie notices the principal's eyes open wide and her hands clasp together with her index fingers pointed at her nostrils. Once the recording stops, Principal Jackson takes a deep breath and cleans the lenses on her glasses, so she has a moment of silence to take in everything she just heard.

"So, what will you do about it, Principal Jackson?" Bonnie asks, anticipating her answer.

"This is a very serious issue you've brought to my attention, Ms. Davis."

"I wouldn't have come forward if it wasn't."

"I will talk to Mr. Calhoun and see what I can do to make sure outbursts like these won't happen again."

Bonnie thrusts her arms into the air.

"So, that's it?! He treats his students worse than garbage, and he has absolutely no respect for you. So, why are you protecting him?" Bonnie asks.

"It's a complicated situation, Ms. Davis," Principal Jackson says.

"Try me," Bonnie says, folding her arms and crossing her legs.

Principal Jackson leans left and right, as if checking to make sure nobody is listening. She beckons Bonnie closer, who slides her chair to the edge of Principal Jackson's desk.

"I like you, Ms. Davis, and I remember you once telling me that I'm a role model to you. If you promise not to tell anyone what I'm about to tell you, I will explain myself."

"I promise Principal Jackson."

"So, I tried to fire Mr. Calhoun long ago, but he has friends in city council and on the school board. He called me the N-word to my face on my first day. I fired him on the spot, and he filed a lawsuit against the school and won."

"Oh my God," Bonnie says as she raises her eyebrows in shock.

"It was a tough pill to swallow. I wanted to quit right at that moment. Luckily, I remembered that if I quit, he gets this job, and I can't allow that."

"Can you fire him for this?"

Principal Jackson sits back in her chair, stroking her chin. Her eyes dart down and back up at Bonnie. The principal lets out a defeated sigh.

"The Board of Education will probably just say it's not enough evidence, but I will try."

"I have a question, Principal Jackson."

"Ask away, Ms. Davis."

"Why did you become the principal of this school in the first

place if you're not treated with respect?" Bonnie asks.

"I wanted to show the children that if you work hard enough, you can become anything you want. Even if a lot of people don't like you, for your skin, gender, or sexual orientation. If I have to take decades of bull crap from the staff, so just so one girl can look at me and say, 'I can do that too,' it would all be worth it," Principal Jackson says.

"I'm sorry, Principal Jackson, but I have an idea."

"What is it?"

Bonnie shudders and squeezes her thigh, trying to force the words out of her mouth.

"If . . . if we release this to the press, people all over the state will go to Princeton County High School and city hall to demand Mr. Calhoun be fired."

Principal Jackson's eyes bug out for a moment but quickly

sink back into their sockets after a few seconds. A slight grin spreads across her thin lips.

"A protest? That could very well work. Your thinking is impressive, Ms. Davis, but I'm afraid I can't do it myself. The superintendent will just think I'm staging something to get Mr. Calhoun fired. He knows how I feel about Mr. Calhoun."

"Thank you, Principal Jackson, for your time. In that case, I'll do it myself as an anonymous tip," Bonnie says.

"Thank you, but before you go, I have a question for you, Ms. Davis. Why would someone with your potential and intelligence hang out with the likes of Drew Thompson and Lucas Ramirez?"

"I'm not sure I understand the question, Principal Jackson."

"Mr. Thompson is chasing a pipe dream of getting into the NBA, and Mr. Ramirez is not even sure what he wants to pursue after high school. I just wonder why they're your friends."

Bonnie isn't shocked or angry at this question; it is quite understandable. This isn't the first time this question had come up. She remembers when her mother had asked this back in grade school when Luke and Drew visited her ranch for the first time.

"We don't have a ton in common, Principal Jackson, but I wouldn't trade those boys for anyone in the world. As much as I look up to women, I just don't have much in common with most. Those boys understand me, I understand them, and we understand each other," Bonnie says.

"I've heard that you saved Luke from Rob back in elementary school," Principal Jackson says.

Bonnie thinks about Natalie and how she had been envious of her when she was with Luke. The satisfaction she felt when she punched her was jealously boiling over. She thought Luke was being reckless, but in truth, Bonnie just wanted it to be her instead.

"Yes, that is correct," Bonnie says.

"Do you have feelings for him?" Principal Jackson asks as she claps her hands together.

Bonnie starts to play with her hair again. She hadn't expected this question to pop up. All these memories come flooding in; the day Luke accepted a hug from Bonnie after he was yelled at by one of his teachers, that fateful day she became the first person besides his mother and grandmother to touch him without him pushing back.

"I know when a girl likes a boy, even if the boy doesn't know himself. I understand, Ms. Davis, what it's like to like a boy when you're not sure if he returns your feelings."

"I . . . I just think he's so sweet. He trusts me and will even hug me occasionally. I've liked him for as long as I've known."

"How come you've never told him how you feel, Ms. Davis?"

"I just don't want to risk what we have. If I tell him how I feel, and he doesn't feel the same way, he might never speak to me again."

"Ms. Davis, if you don't tell him how you feel, you will regret it for the rest of your life. You said he's sweet. If you're right, and I think you are, Luke will remain your best friend whether he returns your feelings or not."

"You really think so?" Bonnie asks.

"I know so. He's a sweet kid. I know he's capable of more than most think," Principal Jackson says.

"He sure is, Principal Jackson, he definitely is."

"So, tell him, and soon, Ms. Davis."

"I will, Principal Jackson, I will," Bonnie says, nodding her head.

"So, are we going to bring Calhoun down, or what Ms. Davis?" Unable to contain her excitement, Bonnie claps her hands once and smiles, baring her teeth. She jumps up from her chair and reaches for Principal Jackson's hand.

"Go big or go home, Principal Jackson. This has been a long time coming."

"It sure has. Now make sure you bring that recording to the press right after school. Good luck, Ms. Davis," Principal Jackson says as she shakes Bonnie's hand.

"Thank you, I will, Principal Jackson."

Bonnie leaves the principal's office, closing the door behind her. She feels a newfound confidence. She walks to the cafeteria and joins her friends at lunch to discuss what their next move should be.

14

PREPARATIONS IN PLACE

At lunch, Luke, Bonnie, and Drew all meet up with rejuvenated spirit. Drew's head is in the right place again, and Bonnie has the perfect plan to get rid of Mr. Calhoun once and for all. Luke knows it is time to tell his friends the big secret. He feels that he has to acknowledge the elephant in the room. Luke sees the curiosity in both of his friends' eyes. In Luke's peripheral view, he spots Natalie sitting alone at the exact table where they had their first conversation. Why wasn't she with Sandy and Patricia?

The two girls are at their usual table, crying into their hands. Distraught at the news of their boyfriends in custody, a few other girls try comforting them. Those girls eye Luke, Bonnie, and Drew contemptuously. Luke feels some sympathy for Natalie, but he still can't bear to speak to her with his wounds so fresh.

"So, what is it you wanted to tell us, Luke?" Bonnie asks.

"Yeah, dawg, what's on your mind?" Drew asks.

"When I got home from the sheriff's office last night, my Bela told me that my father's not actually dead."

"What?!" Bonnie and Drew say simultaneously.

Their shouts are loud enough that students from a few tables over stare in their direction. Natalie looks up, curious to know what the commotion is all about. She stares at Luke, Bonnie, and Drew for several seconds. Luke places his index finger over his mouth and hushes his friends. They say nothing for a few moments until the students get bored of staring at them and resume eating their lunches.

"Yeah, apparently he couldn't bear the thought of his child being autistic," Luke says, his voice fading into a whisper.

"Hmm, so much for father of the year," Drew says, scoffing.

"It sent him into a downward spiral. He drank a lot, lost his job, and even started beating my mom."

"Wow, that's just sickening," Bonnie says, exposing her teeth like she had just smelled something revolting.

"That's not even the worst of it. My mom was pregnant with my little sister. One day, he hit her so hard that it caused a miscarriage."

"What the hell?" Drew gasps.

"I'm sorry, Luke," Bonnie says.

"Why'd she tell you this now?" Drew asks.

"How'd they keep it hidden for so long?" Bonnie asks.

Luke's lower lip protrudes, and he shrugs his shoulders.

"I don't know. They wanted to protect me, I guess."

"They were just looking out for you is all," Bonnie says.

"My Bela told me that she was proud of how we stood up to those bullies and said her dying wish was to see my father brought to justice."

"She wants you to track down your abusive dad and turn him in?" Bonnie asks.

"I don't think so, but I maybe I should. I don't know anymore," Luke says, shaking his head.

"What do you mean? You don't want to go after him?" Bonnie asks.

"Of course, some small part of me does. Another part thinks I should leave it alone. So, I'm not sure what to do," Luke says.

Luke lowers his head and rests it on his forearms on the table, letting out a deep exhale. He feels Bonnie's hand place down on his forearm, right in front of his nose.

"Why can't your mom just . . . you know . . . report it? Get that piece of shit locked up?" Drew asks.

"Bela said she's scared to face him again. For a long time, she was scared for me to find out the truth."

"That doesn't shock me. Most women that have been abused just try to survive, forget what happened, and move on. I doubt your mom would help us, especially since she didn't want you to know in the first place," Bonnie says.

"I think I should go after my dad, and I want you guys to help me. Us in it together, I suppose."

"I think you—*we* should," Bonnie says.

"Us? We?" Drew asks, pointing at himself and Bonnie.

Luke lifts his head up from the table. He licks his lip and looks down for a couple seconds, thinking carefully about what he could be walking into. Luke looks up and sees a grin across Bonnie's face, and somehow it encourages Luke to return it.

"Yes, Drew, we're gonna help Luke," Bonnie says sternly as she slaps the table and cuts her eyes at Drew. Her two braids wriggle around like snakes every time she jolts her head.

"We don't even know where he is. He could be across the country, for all we know," Drew says.

"Bela said that he's probably just outside of Memphis."

"That's over fifty miles away, over an hour by car," Bonnie says, scratching her chin.

"And guess what? None of us has a car or enough dough saved up to take a bus that far," Drew says.

"Not to mention how suspicious it'll look if three teenagers take a bus during the school day," Luke says.

"I have some horses on the ranch. Horses can travel thirty

miles a day. We can get there in less than two days," Bonnie says.

"That'll take too long. Unless they're racehorses from the Kentucky derby, I'm pretty sure our parents will send a search party out for us," Drew says.

"No, it's a good idea, Bonnie," Luke says.

"Drew, it's that or walking," Bonnie says.

"I mean . . . we could ask . . . you know who for a ride," Drew says while tilting his chin toward Natalie.

As Drew gazes over his shoulder in the direction of Natalie, Bonnie elbows him to get his attention. It is too late; Luke looks past Drew, noticing Natalie, his ex-girlfriend. Luke looks down at the table, remembering what has transpired. He sits there and shows his teeth, trying to contain his anger. Across from him, Drew and Bonnie start bickering at one another.

"Drew! I should smack you just for thinking about that," Bonnie whispers in a disciplinary voice.

"What? She has a car! Maybe Natalie's sorry? The witness was a girl, right? It could've been Natalie, I don't know. All I know is she ain't hanging out with those two anymore. Besides, she's kind of cute."

Bonnie punches Drew in the shoulder that had been injured in the fight. Drew winces in pain and rubs his shoulder. They berate each other, grumbling and pointing fingers at one another while Luke rolls his eyes at his two friends, hoping it will pass.

"What's her looks have to do with the fact—"

Luke feels like this is starting to get out of hand. While Natalie does have a vehicle that could buy them a whole night, the fact remains that he doesn't want to sit in a car for hours with Natalie. It is time for Luke to say his piece. He slams his hand down on the table to get his friends' attention.

"Guys, stop! Drew, it's a good idea, more efficient than

Bonnie's, but I'm afraid it's not an option. We can't trust her to not do something out of the ordinary," Luke says.

"After what she did to Luke, there's no world where we ask for that bitch's help," Bonnie says.

"It was just a suggestion, geez, get off my back," Drew says, throwing his arms in the air.

"An idiotic one. I think you just wanted a reaction out of me," Bonnie says, giving Drew a hostile glare.

"Boy did I get one," Drew says under his breath.

"Bonnie, get the horses ready. We're going with that plan," Luke says. "Sure thing, just need to get them rested and fed."

"We can't fool around y'all. We'll only have so much time before someone realizes we're gone, maybe a day. I say we go tomorrow. If you guys are with me, I'll tell my mom we're having a sleepover," Bonnie says.

"Sleepover on a school day? I don't think our parents will go for it, definitely not mine. You really think we should go for it tomorrow?" Drew asks.

"Bonnie's parents have let us stay over during the week before. So, why not?" Luke asks, raising his eyebrow.

"True, but I think we'll be better off waiting until Friday. Drew's still grounded 'til then; we can't have both of y'all sneaking off while grounded. Also, that way we'll have time to gather everything we need, and our parents don't notice us taking a bunch of food and supplies all in one afternoon. Besides, I'd still have to convince my parents I'm staying over at one of your houses too," Bonnie says.

"Hmm . . . you make an excellent point. Okay, we leave Friday. So, who's with me?" Luke asks.

Luke lays his hand in the middle of the table, hoping his friends will join in. Luke needs to know that he has his friends' support in this endeavor. As soon as he puts his hand in, Bonnie reaches in and places hers right on top of his.

"Count me in," Bonnie says.

"I don't know, man, seems crazy to me," Drew says.

"Drew I'm doing this with or without you, but it would be preferable that you're by my side, brother," Luke says.

Drew hesitates for a brief moment, but in the end, he reluctantly puts his hand in to signify unity in the party, coming to the conclusion that he can't let his friends do this by themselves after all they've been through together.

"I've always had your back, bro, so what the hell, I'm in too," Drew says.

"I'll get the horses clean and fed. They'll be ready for Friday. I'll make sure of it," Bonnie says.

"I'll bring plenty of food. I'll have to get someone else to take my shift at the burger joint that day though," Drew says.

"Bonnie, make sure you bring the tape recorder. We might need it," Luke says.

"I was thinking the same thing. Just have to handle the Mr. Calhoun situation first," Bonnie says.

"Just in case they lose the tape, or it gets damaged, I'll make a copy of Mr. Calhoun's outburst on a different one. I'm stopping by at the press to hand it over, on my way home," Bonnie says.

The rest of the school day goes by normally. Luke would occasionally look up from time to time to see Natalie giving him puppy dog eyes. However, Luke and his friends have more meaningful priorities than Natalie feeling sorry for herself at the moment.

"Is it okay if we go to your ranch after school Friday, Bonnie?" Luke asks.

"Wouldn't be an issue if y'all weren't grounded. If you could convince your parents otherwise, I'd just tell my mom y'all are gonna help out around the stables in the afternoon," Bonnie says.

"I'll be good by Friday; I only got a week. Can't say the same for Luke," Drew says.

It hits Luke like a ton of bricks. Amidst the chaos with Mr. Calhoun, it slipped his mind that he would still be grounded on Friday.

"We have a few days to figure it out. Just meet me at my house Friday morning," Luke says.

"All right," Bonnie says, nodding her head.

"You do know that our parents are gonna kill us when they find out we're gone, right?" Drew asks.

"They'll be angry, but one day they will understand, Drew," Luke says.

"Whatever you say, man," Drew says, rolling his eyes.

They all discuss what each person is responsible for. By the end of lunch, each person has an important assignment. Drew has to pack up food rations, Bonnie has to get the horses prepped, and Luke has to find his father's address.

"Okay, let's all go home and get what we need to get, all right, boys?" Bonnie says with passion in her tone.

"Sounds like a plan. I'll bring some grub," Drew says.

"Together, we can do this. I'll find out the address," Luke says, while intensely nodding his head.

The three friends fist bump each other before going their separate ways and heading home. When Luke arrives back, he checks the house to make sure his mother is still at work. Once he determines that the coast is clear, he goes into the basement and picks up three sleeping bags. He carries them up to his bedroom and stores them in his closet. Luke is confident his mother will not notice, since they have not gone camping in years. Since his mother isn't home and his grandmother is still asleep, Luke doesn't worry about being seen snooping through the phone book in the living room. Luke opens the phone book and searches for the name Benjamin Miller, but alas, there are nearly a dozen Ben Millers in Memphis alone. Luke grunts in frustration. He never asked before about his father's middle name. His only option is to ask his grandmother if she knows. Luke goes to the guest bedroom and slowly creaks the door open. The light creeps in, and Luke hears Sophie begin to wake up from her afternoon nap.

"L-Luke? What do you want?"

"Bela, I forgot. What's my father's middle name again?" Luke asks, attempting not to sound suspicious.

Sophie looks weak, her hands are shaking, and her breathing is raspy. Luke can instantly tell this is one of her bad days, which sadly, have been occurring more frequently these past couple of months.

"R-Ray . . . why do you ask?" Sophie whispers.

"Just curious to know a little more. Thank you, Bela," Luke says before running out of the room.

Luke looks in the phone book again. He races his finger across the dry, thin paper, searching through the Ben Millers. He finds a Benjamin Ray Miller that lives on 86 Birch Drive, in Cottonmouth, Tennessee. This is it. Luke now has his father's address, and his plans are gaining steam fast.

* * *

Back at 22 King St., Drew is packing up some provisions such as crackers, cookies, canned food, and multiple bottles of water in the privacy of his own room. The first thing Drew does when he gets home is call out of work, so his shift can be picked up tomorrow.

"Just in case, I'll bring some money too," Drew says to himself.

As Drew finishes packing up, he hears someone running outside his room. Drew rolls his eyes as he braces himself for what's about to happen next. Drew's little brother, Elijah, barges in unannounced and shouts, "I want to play some video games!"

"No, get out of here, I'm busy doing homework," Drew says, as he shoos his brother away.

"You're lying! I'm gonna tell mom!" Elijah says in a shrill voice.

"Go ahead, you little snitch; she'll side with me," Drew says, calling his bluff.

Elijah begins to take short, fast breaths; his eyes start to flood with tears. He throws his hands in the air and runs out of his older brother's room shouting, "Mom!"

"Spoiled little asshole, always running to mama when he doesn't get what he wants," Drew whispers to himself. Drew rapidly stuffs a few more cans of food into his backpack. He stops when it is a quarter of the way full. His goal is to pack it until it is not physically possible to fit any more cans into the bag.

"Okay, that's enough for today," Drew tells himself.

Drew hides his backpack by sliding it under his bed, as his mother could storm in at any second. He knows he has to hide his true intentions, or he will be severely punished. Drew hears heavy footsteps approaching fast. He prepares himself, expecting to receive a strong rebuke. Not even a moment later, Drew's mother, Tiffany, bursts the door wide open and says, "Why won't you let your brother play your games?!"

Tiffany Thompson is a heavyset woman with a curly weave and large earrings. She takes no nonsense from anyone, especially her own children. She is a receptionist for an insurance company but also provides for her two kids. Balancing work with family is one of her special skills. Stephen Thompson, Drew's father, works long hours and is seldom home during the day. So, Drew and Elijah rely mainly on their mother to take care of them.

"I'm doing homework, Mom," Drew says, crossing his arms.

"Drew Martin Thompson. Don't lie to me. It sure doesn't look like homework to me."

"Fine, Jesus . . . he can play."

"Yay!" Elijah screams ecstatically as he grabs a controller.

"Also, Mom, tell Dad he doesn't have to drop me off at school on Friday. I'm walking with Luke."

"Fine. Just don't let me catch you wearing one of your nice pairs of shoes on that dirty road."

"Yes, Mom," Drew says as he puts his hands behind his head.

Drew is still convinced the plan to ask Natalie for a ride would've been a better plan than the horses, but he was outnumbered two to one. Then again, Drew had been jealous that Natalie fell for Luke but didn't say anything to him out of respect. It doesn't matter now anyway since they were all heading out to the town of Cottonmouth tomorrow. Drew sits on his bed, crossing his arms, while his little brother blasts his video games.

* * *

At the Davis Ranch, Bonnie is grooming and feeding the horses. She had already brought the tape recording of Mr. Calhoun to the newspaper office on her way home. All there was left to do was wait for the press to do their thing and publish a story.

"In a few days, it will be a long journey, so rest up and eat. I want you at full strength," Bonnie tells the horses.

The three horses Bonnie has chosen are Red, Blacksmith, and her personal favorite, Lucky, as the ones they will take to Cottonmouth. Bonnie has packed up three bags of hay and vegetables for the horses to eat during the trip. More feed would've been ideal, but the horses can't handle the weight.

"I'm sure there'll be plenty of grass to graze on out there as well. Goodnight."

"Bonnie! Time for dinner!" Randall Davis yells.

Randall Davis, Bonnie's father, has lived on the Davis Ranch all of his life. He has a hunched back, tired green eyes, no hair or facial hair, and he wears a straw hat to protect his head from the harsh UV rays of the sun. He is a private individual and rarely leaves the ranch that he grew up on, only leaving weekly to attend church, and on special occasions, such as his kids' graduations. While his wife, Laura, takes care of everything outside the ranch, he takes care of the animals, crops, and machinery. Bonnie has told her friends that he does like Luke and Drew, though they are both skeptical because he rarely talks to them when they are on the ranch.

They all have to rely on each other to do their jobs. They have no other choice since none of them have cell phones. Luke's mother doesn't trust him with a cell phone. Bonnie's parents say there's no need since they live on a ranch. As for Drew, he had one until he dropped it in the toilet, so his parents refuse to buy him a new one. So, the three friends have no discreet way to contact each other after school.

They check on each other over the following days to provide updates on their efforts. Bonnie purchased a map of Tennessee for Luke to help guide them, so they don't get lost. All three sneak around their houses to get the supplies they need for the journey ahead.

Simultaneously, over the next few days, a protest slowly begins to form in front of Princeton County High School. Growing twice the size each day, on Wednesday, Mr. Calhoun doesn't come in for work, much to the delight of the students. Drew gives a pat on Bonnie's back to commend her on her efforts. Luke attempts to ignore Natalie throughout the week. He doesn't want to lose focus on his assignment. On the way out of school, Luke, Bonnie, and Drew meet up one final time before the big day.

"I think I swiped enough food and water for the trip," Drew says.

"The horses are refreshed and ready for the long ride. Also packed up their own food," Bonnie says.

"Good. I got the address and the sleeping bags ready," Luke says.

Luke, Bonnie, and Drew smile and depart. They know tomorrow will be a brand-new day, and it will change everything. Luke goes home and puts the map and the piece of paper that he wrote his father's address on in a small bag. Something springs into Luke's mind; therapy with Dr. Washington is today. He hasn't spoken with Dr. Washington since before his date with Natalie. So much has transpired in the span of a week. What will he tell him or not tell him? Luke paces back and forth, thinking of what he should share. He doesn't want to accidentally spill his plans to his therapist. A couple hours go by. While Luke is finishing getting dressed, he hears a rumbling voice from downstairs.

"Luke, it's time to go to therapy. I'm driving you today!" Courtney shouts.

Luke nearly trips from going downstairs; he stops halfway to see his mother with her hands on her hips, tapping her foot repeatedly.

"I usually walk there, Mom," Luke says.

"Well, I'm not taking any chances. Hurry up and get in the car."

Luke doesn't even bother arguing back. He walks down the rest of the stairs without uttering a word. He walks out the door and gets in the passenger seat.

"Don't be so hard on him. The boy can walk himself. It's not like he's an escaped convict," Sophie shouts from the living room.

"Ma, stay out of it."

Courtney leaves, shutting the door behind her. She enters her car. The drive is silent; Luke simply stares out the window. The car ride lasts only a few minutes before their red station wagon pulls into the doctor's parking lot.

"I'll be out here in an hour. Have a good time, honey," Courtney says.

"Thanks, I'll see you then, Mom," Luke says with his hands in his pockets.

"You know I love you," Courtney says.

Luke scoffs, not saying anything in return. He continues advancing toward the building without looking back. As he pushes the door open, Luke hears his mother drive off. Luke travels through the waiting area, waving to Mae.

"You're early today, Luke."

"I know. Is Dr. Washington ready for me?" Luke asks.

"He sure is. You can head right in," Mae says as she admires her nail polish.

Luke opens the door and heads down the hall, finding the office door of Dr. Washington. Luke knocks three times, as he normally does. He is immediately answered by the inviting tone of Dr. Washington.

"Come right on in."

Luke turns the knob and steps inside the room, where Dr. Washington already has his clipboard and his pen prepared for the session. His head is down, already writing something down. The natural light bounces off his forehead, making his scar glow.

"What are you writing down? I haven't said anything yet," Luke says, still standing up.

"Oh, Luke, your mother called and told me about what happened last week," Dr. Washington says.

Luke grumbles in anger. Now he has no choice but to speak on the topic of last week. Dr. Washington taps his hand on the seat across from him to tell Luke to sit. Luke gladly obeys and takes a seat across from his longtime therapist.

"It's to my understanding you had quite the situation after last week's session."

"That's putting it a little delicately," Luke says, clenching his jaw.

"Why don't you tell me what happened, and we can discuss it," Dr. Washington says.

"I don't really want to talk about it," Luke says as he squeezes the cushions underneath him.

"That's fine. You can take as long as you like until you're comfortable sharing," Dr. Washington says.

Dr. Washington gets up and walks to his desk to retrieve his cup of coffee. He returns to his seat and gazes in Luke's general direction, anticipating his next move as if he were in a chess game. Luke slumps over the side of the couch, frowning. He's still upset with his mother, his father, Natalie, and everyone around him. He is most disappointed in himself and his inability to control his reactions sometimes due to his disability. Luke and Dr. Washington sit there in silence, neither saying a word for half an hour.

"The date went good, but after that . . . it was awful," Luke says quietly.

"I'm sorry to hear that. What happened after that was awful?" Dr. Washington asks as he sits up.

"The day after, I overheard Natalie talking to not-so-pleasant girls. She said that I'd end up in a group home and our whole relationship was a lie."

"Oh, those are reprehensible actions on her part."

"After that, Rob and his friends surrounded us, and we fought back. Rob, he wanted to hurt us really bad. He brought a pocketknife and slashed Drew's face," Luke says, keeping his head down.

"I'm sorry that happened to you and your friends. This

world—it seems as though violence is around every corner. I heard he and his friends are in custody doing their time."

"That's correct. Thankfully, nobody got seriously hurt. We got grounded by the way. That's why I got here a little early."

"That's excellent to hear—not about you being grounded. Admittedly, I never understood the reasoning behind one's action to bully others, especially for something out of one's control, such as you with your autism. Until I studied psychiatry that is," Dr. Washington says, smiling.

"What's the reason, Dr. Washington?"

"Insecurities, my boy. When we're frustrated with a lack of ability to fit in, or we want to be liked, we often want to unleash our inner fury on a target. Most don't target someone they believe will fight back, so they go after the small, quiet kids. You know, I think you've earned some perspective. I had an encounter with a bully once a long time ago. Fellow walked up and stole my toy truck, and everyone laughed at me when I tried to jump up and grab it to no avail. He was much bigger than I. So, you know what I did?

"What?" Luke asks, patting his lap.

"I punched him in the stomach as hard as I could. He fell to the ground right there. He never bothered me again; he knew I wasn't intimidated. Next day, he went after someone else."

"That's cool, but I stood up to Rob, and it had the opposite effect. He wasn't even bullying me. Why's that?" Luke asks.

"You challenged him. Some people don't like it when they're stood up to. So, they just pursue you until they feel that they've won the war."

"Speaking of which, what was the Vietnam war—" Luke starts before being interrupted by Dr. Washington.

"Luke. Stay focused, please; our session is almost completed. I already told you a personal story. Is there anything else on your mind?"

Luke exhales. He got through the entire appointment

without mentioning finding out about his father. He wants to talk to Dr. Washington about it more than anything. The only obstacle preventing him from talking about it is the risk of him telling his mother.

"No, I think we went over plenty," Luke says.

"All right, Luke, next time we're discussing post-secondary education. College, no excuses. Have a good night."

"You too, Dr. Washington," Luke says as he shuts the door.

Luke exits the doctor's office, waving to Mae. Once outside, he scopes out the area and locates his mother's red station wagon across the street. He looks both ways before jogging across the road. He opens the car door, making Courtney jerk her body in surprise. She had been reading a book while waiting for him.

"How was therapy, honey?"

"Good. Very productive. Dr. Washington even rewarded me with a rare story."

"That's nice of him. What was the story about?" Courtney asks. "Bullies," Luke says.

"I see. Honey, I'm sorry for being so hard on you. I just want what's best for you, understand?"

"I know you do, Mom. I love you."

"Your Bela is worried that I've been a little too rough on you these past few days."

"Maybe. Can we talk about this another time? I'm tired," Luke says, resting his head against the window.

"Of course."

Courtney and Luke arrive home a few minutes later. There is already dinner on the table. Tonight's supper is yellow rice, beans, and pork chops. Everyone is quiet after saying grace, even Sophie, who normally chats the most. After Luke finishes his plate, he goes upstairs to take a shower. He immediately heads to bed after the shower. He stops and lowers himself to his knees, praying one final time before he heads off for Memphis tomorrow.

"Dear Lord, I hope you exist, because I'm gonna need all the help I can get. I was taught to believe everything happens for a reason. I think the reason for me learning the truth about my family is to confront my father. I just pray you watch over my friends and I tomorrow. Amen," Luke says to himself.

15

THE RUNAWAYS

As Luke is sleeping, he is dreaming about the quest he and his friends will embark on. Luke is with Drew and Bonnie. They are on the backs of their horses and on their way to Memphis when, in the middle of the road, Luke spots him, the Masked Haunter. The horses stop in their tracks. Bonnie and Drew are frightened, as they should be. Why is there an eyeless man engulfed in flames in the middle of the road?

"Luke, what the hell is that?!" Drew asks in a panic.

"Luke, maybe we should turn back," Bonnie says, her voice shaky.

"If you go through with this journey, you and your friends will perish," the Masked Haunter warns.

"How do you know that?" Luke asks.

"I know because I am everything you fear. I am you."

Before Luke can even open his mouth to respond, the Masked Haunter lunges at him and his friends. Luke shrieks, knowing they are done for.

As Luke revives, a black mass hops off his bed, and Luke wildly scrambles to turn on his lamp. He relaxes his shoulders and smiles when the snout of Pedro is at his bedside. Luke pats the dog's head and looks at his alarm clock. It is only 3:41 in the morning. Luke leads Pedro out of his room and shuts the door behind him. Pedro scratches the door for a few minutes until eventually giving up. He hears the pitter-patter of the German shepherd retreating downstairs. It dawns on Luke that he isn't tired anymore, so he just tosses and turns on his bed until morning.

Once the sun rises, Luke gets out of bed, raises his arms above his head, and stretches. He puts on his favorite gray T-shirt and a worn- out pair of jeans. He takes out the sleeping bags and fiercely packs them into a duffel bag, nearly prepared for what he and his friends have planned today, until the muffle of brisk footsteps downstairs diverts his attention. Courtney has not yet left for work. Luke feels awful and decides he has to say goodbye to his mother. She is completely oblivious to the fact that her son will disobey her and not only hang out with Bonnie and Drew but leave town. Luke has to do the very least and wish her goodbye. He thrusts the duffel bag into his closet and rushes downstairs. Luke catches his mother as she is halfway out the door.

"Honey, what are you doing up so early?" Courtney asks.

"Having a hard time sleeping. I just wanted to give you a hug and say I love you," Luke says.

"Oh, Lucas, that's sweet."

Luke and his mother hug each other tightly. Luke's nose bridge wrinkles as he catches a hefty whiff of vinegar that Courtney had used to clean a dry bloodstain off her scrubs that morning.

No one else can replicate the warmth and sense of security he feels with her. He doesn't want to let go of his mother, wishing he could stand there forever with his arms wrapped around her, but he knows that sooner or later he'd have to let go.

"I know these last few days have been tough on you. It will get better, sweetie," Courtney says as Luke releases his hold.

"I hope so, Mom. I hope so. So, are you having a date with Mike tonight?"

"We sure are, so I will be home later than usual," Courtney says.

"Okay, Mom, have fun," Luke says.

"I will bring dinner home."

"Sounds lovely, Mom."

"So, don't cause any trouble, Luke. You're still grounded, remember."

"I won't, Mom. I love you."

"Love you to the moon and back, sweetie."

Courtney blows a kiss and walks out. The door closes silently behind her. Moments later, Luke hears the old station wagon's engine turn on and slowly fade away into the distance. He remembers that he will be leaving his grandmother too. She doesn't know about his plans either. *I can't tell her. I have to lie*, he thinks to himself. Shivers run up his spine at just the thought of lying. Luke paces outside his Bela's bedroom for five minutes, practicing his tale of deception. Finally, he exhales deeply and opens the door.

"So, I'm going somewhere after school today, Bela."

"Good luck, dearie. Where to exactly?" Sophie says.

"To a friend's house for a sleepover," Luke says as he gulps nervously.

Sophie sits up so fast that her oxygen mask slips off her face. Luke notices her shoulders shaking as they try holding her frame up.

"But you're grounded, honey. I don't think you should go, Luke."

Luke has an uneasy feeling in the pit of his stomach churning as he lies to his grandmother. Never before has he done this, especially to his own family. Knowing Bela would try to stop him from going to Cottonmouth, Luke sticks to his guns.

"I shouldn't, but I am."

"Just . . . be safe, and don't worry. I won't tell your mother, Luke."

"You're not going to try and stop me?" Luke asks.

"I would have better luck trying to stop a moving train," Sophie says chuckling.

Luke sighs loudly and attempts to grin at her laugh.

"Just be back the following morning."

Luke nods, but he can't meet Sophie's gaze. He hopes the dark conceals this slipup from her.

"Will do. I just . . . need some time away after everything. But Bela, everything happens for a reason, right?"

"It always does, Luke. God has a plan for everyone," Sophie says. "Can you let me go back to sleep, sweetie?"

Without saying a word, he obliges and closes the door shut. Luke is now at ease after saying goodbye to both his mother and grandmother. Then Luke realizes he has almost forgotten about someone. He looks at the living room floor and sees Pedro napping. When Luke gets near, Pedro springs to life and gets up on his hind legs to give Luke affectionate kisses. Suddenly, Luke has an epiphany. If his father is not at the written address, then maybe Pedro could possibly help them track him down. After all, Pedro has a keen sense of smell and enjoys new experiences.

"You're excited to see me so early, huh boy? Want to go on an adventure, boy?"

Pedro barks excitedly at the question. Luke smiles as he pats Pedro's head. That was all he needed to hear to put his new plan into action. "You can assist us in tracking down Dad. Once we get there, just get a whiff of his scent," Luke says to his dog in a playful voice.

Why wait until school ends when we could just leave now? Luke wonders. It would buy them a few needed extra hours. Luke smiles, but then he hears a knock at the front door. He's not used to getting visitors this early. He marches to the door and looks through the peephole. Luke sighs in relief when he sees it's Bonnie and Drew at the front door. They have arrived to revise the plan one final time and make the call of when to leave.

"Ready to go to school?" Bonnie asks.

"Actually, the plans have changed. We're leaving right now," Luke says.

"Why?" Drew asks.

"Pedro is coming with us. He can help by tracking my dad down in case we lose him."

"What about school? Won't they call our parents or something?" Drew asks.

"I saw on the news that the protest is enormous now. They're even outside city hall. Mr. Calhoun's outburst going public is making the town famous. Good for the town, not for him," Bonnie says.

"They have their hands so full they won't even notice we're gone. It's Friday. Missing one day won't impact our grades."

"It's what the guy deserves. Hopefully he's canned by the time we get back," Drew says.

They stop at Drew's house to retrieve his backpack filled with provisions. Drew grunts as he lifts the bag up, using most of his effort to stay upright. They all decide to walk down the street to take the city bus, as Bonnie's ranch is nearly a thirty-minute walk from Drew's house. They stand at the bus stop for fifteen minutes. Luke and Bonnie admire the baby-blue sky while Drew plays fetch with Pedro on the field behind them to alleviate the boredom.

When Bonnie notices the gray bus looming in the distance,

Drew leads Pedro back to the bus stop. The sleek bus slows down, the brakes screeching as it pulls over. Before entering the bus, Drew spits on the ground next to Bonnie, narrowly missing her boots. Bonnie responds by side-eyeing him before spitting directly on his basketball shoes. As they enter the bus, Drew pays the fee for all three of them. The driver scowls when he sees Pedro. Pets are allowed as long as they behave themselves. Luke has no worries since Pedro has always been a remarkably behaved dog. Luke and Drew sit on one side, while Bonnie sits across from them. Pedro settles in the aisle between them, and the bus driver adjusts his mirror to keep tabs on the dog. The poorly maintained bus reeks of old garbage and rocks the passengers back and forth after hitting the smallest bumps.

The ride affords Luke the time to daydream. The voices of the other passengers blend together as the bus picks up speed and the passing pastures are reduced to hazy blurs. Bonnie yanks the cord when they're a block away from her ranch. The ride lasts seventeen minutes, and as the three teenagers get off, the driver's bloodshot eyes glance at Pedro one final time. The teenagers jog down the empty road, hidden by the tall cornfields.

"Good thinking having us stop a block away," Drew says.

"Shh . . . be quiet. We still have to sneak past my parents. My mom is still asleep, and my dad is probably feeding the chickens."

"Luckily, the stables are on the opposite side of the ranch. Right, Bonnie?" Luke whispers.

"Yeah, lucky us. Can we hurry up? This shit is heavy on my back," Drew murmurs under his breath.

"Maybe you should've packed less. Quickly, it's now or never," Bonnie says, beckoning Luke and Drew to follow her.

"Right behind you," Luke says.

"Okay, let's do this," Drew says with surprising enthusiasm.

The teenagers sneak past the main house, tiptoeing across the entire ranch. They manage to get to the stables without seeing anyone or being seen. Bonnie opens the stables, where the stench of barn animals permeates the air. Drew pulls his shirt over his nose, but Bonnie and Luke are used to the foul odor, since they've hung out here in the past. They open the creaky wooden door, peek inside, and lo and behold, three horses are there just waiting for them. Pedro growls, showing off his canine teeth. "Pedro, sit," Luke quickly says.

Pedro reluctantly obeys; he sits outside the stables. Luke gives him a treat, which the German shepherd voraciously eats. He is not sure how much longer he can keep Pedro quiet. Luke knows they have to get out fast, before Pedro blows their cover. Luke quietly enters the stables to mount their horses.

"Woah," Luke says in awe.

"Which one is mine?" Drew asks impatiently.

"Either Red or Blacksmith. Lucky is all mine," Bonnie says.

Lucky is a white horse; she looks like she could camouflage herself in a blizzard. She is the only female of the three and also the smallest in size. Blacksmith, like his name suggests, is a black horse. He has a mean look to him and is the largest of the three horses. Red is a chestnut-colored horse; he has a flowing mane that drapes over his neck that would blow elegantly in the wind.

"I'll take Blacksmith," Drew calls out like he is calling shotgun for the passenger seat.

"Doesn't surprise me," Bonnie whispers to Luke.

"Okay, I guess that means Red is mine," Luke says, weak in the knees.

Drew walks up to his horse, plants his left foot on the stirrup, and propels his right leg over the large horse's back. Bonnie pets Lucky's face before mounting the white horse on her first attempt. However, Luke stands there with his feet planted on the ground and a slight frown on his face. Bonnie raises her eyebrows while Drew scratches his head, confused as to why Luke isn't following their lead.

"Is everything okay, Luke?" Bonnie asks.

"I . . . um . . . I have to confess something. I've never ridden a horse," Luke says, rubbing the back of his head.

"Really, man?" Drew asks, struggling to smother a laugh.

"Drew, will you hush up? It's not hard, Luke. Want me to show you?" Bonnie asks as she dismounts Lucky.

"Please, Bonnie."

In the last week, Luke had fought bullies, almost been arrested, and is now sneaking off to Memphis to find his father. Despite all the things Luke had gone through recently, getting on this unfamiliar animal seems scariest at the moment. He starts fidgeting with his hands before Bonnie carefully separates them and guides Luke toward Red.

"So, first, you want to remain calm. If you're scared, he's scared. He can sense if you're afraid," Bonnie says.

"Okay, I'll try not to be afraid."

"Secondly, you want to walk up and give him a pat, to establish trust."

Luke warily approaches the horse. He reaches his hand out, but it starts shaking like a leaf. He can't put his hand on Red. Something inside Luke seems to prohibit it. Luke needs to ask the person he trusts more than anyone else to do this for him.

"Can you help me, please?" Luke asks.

"Sure, happy to oblige," Bonnie says.

Bonnie gently takes Luke's hand and places it on the horse. Luke caresses the horse's neck, which feels like touching a hairy, breathing wall. Luke can feel the massive muscles in the horse's neck. He peers back at Drew, who is watching silently, as if waiting to see how this will play out.

"It's that simple?" Luke asks.

"It's that simple. Lastly, you want to mount your horse."

Luke, feeling much bolder now, slowly puts his foot in the

stirrup. He breathes in deeply through his nose and out through his mouth.

"So, I put one leg over the saddle, like this?" Luke asks, making sure, he is doing it correctly.

"You got it now. See, you could've done that on your own."

"Now, remember, if you want to turn, you pull the rein the direction you want to go in. Now, we'll be trotting most of the way, so give Red here a kick every once in a while, to go faster. If you want him to slow down, take your heels out of his side, pull back on the reins, and say woah," Bonnie says to Luke.

Luke nods his head and repeats every word Bonnie had said back in his head a couple times, until the instructions are firmly embedded in his mind.

"This is amazing, thank you, Bonnie."

"You're welcome, Luke. I told you that you could do it."

"What do we do to get the horses to go full speed?" Luke asks.

"Oh, you want to know how to gallop? Okay, instead of a kick, you squeeze your legs in and keep squeezing until you don't need to gallop. You wanna stand up in your stirrups too. It takes some weight off the horse's backs. Now, only make the horse gallop for emergencies, or else you'll burn him out," Bonnie says, pointing at Luke.

"Okay, only for emergencies. Got it," Luke says.

"So, only like if we're getting chased or something?" Drew asks. "Yeah," Bonnie says.

Luke takes the reins and pulls to steer the horse to the left. He smiles feverishly when the horse follows the command. Bonnie's eyes crinkle at the corners, gazing at Luke like a knight in shining armor riding on his noble steed.

"Are you two ready to do this or not?" Drew asks.

Bonnie unlocks the gates to the stables, and she raises her fist to signal Luke and Drew to be silent. She checks outside to make sure her father isn't in sight. Bonnie breathes a sigh of relief when she realizes her father isn't in the vicinity. She gives Luke and Drew a thumbs up before effortlessly mounting Lucky once again.

"We're in the clear. All right, let's ride boys. Just in case, we're going full speed out of here. So, on the count of three, give your horses a good squeeze."

"You sure your father isn't out there?" Luke whispers.

"I'm positive. Now, make sure we stop once the ranch is out of sight," Bonnie says.

"Yeah, yeah. It'll tire out the horses. What we waiting for then? It reeks in here," Drew says, pinching his nose.

Bonnie raises three of her fingers in the air.

"All right. One. Two. Three . . ."

In unison, they all dig their heels into the sides of their horses.

Blacksmith, Lucky, and Red gallop so fast out of the stables that Luke nearly gets bucked off his horse. Pedro's ears shoot up straight into the air. He looks at the horses, barks, and sprints to catch up to Luke. The horses cause a big cloud of dust to rise on the dirt road, providing a cloak for them. The cloud disappears quickly from the breeze before it can draw attention to them. Luke feels a rush of adrenaline as the wind blows through his thick hair. As the horses begin to pick up speed, Bonnie's braids smack her face, and Drew's afro moves up and down and side to side. They ride until Bonnie's ranch is out of eyeshot.

"Hold up, let Pedro catch up! Woah," Luke says as he pulls the reins back.

Red eventually screeches to a halt, but Bonnie gets Lucky to stop with no problem. Drew struggles with Blacksmith and almost turns into a cornfield.

"Where are we heading?" Drew asks.

"East. Bonnie, do you still have the map?" Luke asks.

"I sure do," Bonnie says as she pulls it out of her saddlebag and examines it.

"I think we can make it to Cottonmouth by tomorrow morning," Bonnie says.

"If we ride through most of the night, maybe," Drew says.

"We ride until Pedro needs to rest. If we're too slow, the police might get to us before we get to my dad," Luke says.

"They have their hands full with the protests, Luke. I wouldn't worry about them right now," Bonnie says.

"I hope you're right. How's the horse, Drew?" Luke asks.

"Not too bad. It ain't that different from riding a bike," Drew says as he smiles.

"Except this bike eats, sleeps, and craps," Bonnie says.

"How long before your family notices three horses are gone?" Drew asks.

"I checked the stables this morning; they won't check for a while. Besides, we've had horses stolen before. They won't assume it was us. Also, do you ever stop asking questions?" Bonnie snaps.

"Hopefully, we can get halfway to Memphis. That would put us around Huckleberry Pasture or Shepherd's Creek before sunset. Our goal is to be there by midday tomorrow. What do you say we put some distance between us and Blackroot, guys?" Luke shouts.

"Let's do it!" Drew cheers.

"As you wish," Bonnie says.

"Hey Pedro, you ready?" Luke asks.

Luke hears Pedro's collar bells jingle behind him. The German Shepherd trots towards the horses, barking loudly. He starts wagging his tail rapidly, signaling that he is ready for the long road ahead.

"Okay then!" Luke screams as he kicks into Red's sides.

"Only kick him once," Bonnie says as she catches up to him.

"Wait for me, guys!" Drew calls out.

The three teenagers ride out of Blackroot, passing the town line within minutes. The wind picks up even with the horses moving at just a trot. Despite the gust ruffling Luke's hair, he doesn't take his eyes off the road ahead of him. It doesn't matter now. In Luke's mind, he had already left Princeton County days ago. All Luke cares about now is finding his father and uncovering the truth.

16

LIGHT AND DARKNESS

Protestors, many of whom have come from outside of town, surround Princeton County High School to protest Mr. Calhoun. The press had released the audio clip of Mr. Calhoun calling one of his students a "monkey" to the public four days ago. Now, people are exercising their right to protest to demand the termination of the history teacher. In class, Natalie wears a Band-Aid over her nose since it still felt achy. She notices a few empty desks in Mr. Alterman's class—no Luke and no Bonnie. This seems strange, as both of them have superb attendance. This worries Natalie, but maybe they couldn't get past the crowd. Natalie decides to go ask Mr. Alterman if he knows why two of his top students are absent.

"Excuse me, Mr. Alterman, did Luke and Bonnie call out?"

"I'm not sure. Many parents called out for their kids once they saw the crowds on television. Luke isn't a fan of crowds, so I naturally assumed he turned around and went home. His mother leaves early, so possibly he panicked and Bonnie is comforting him as we speak."

"Thank you for your guess. You're probably right."

"Glad I could help. Now carry on with your work, Natalie. Despite the disruption outside, this is still a place of learning."

"Right away, Mr. Alterman."

Natalie returns to her seat, her index finger and thumb across her chin, still questioning where the two of them could be. Mr. Alterman has to be right. The odds of Luke and Bonnie being sick at the same time are slim. Luke must have been discouraged by the protestors, and Bonnie must be by his side.

* * *

After about three hours on the road, the horses and Pedro are beat. They need to find a place to rest. Drew has been complaining for the past hour about being hot and hungry. The only person who knows where they are is Bonnie, since she has the map.

"Where the hell are we?" Drew asks.

"Near Beaverford, a small town. We're barely a quarter of the way there," Bonnie says, letting out a deep sigh.

"Oh, come on," Drew says, throwing his hands in the air.

"We have to keep going. My mom will be home in a couple hours. We have to create more distance if we have any hope of finding my father."

* * *

At Blackroot Hospital, Courtney is walking through the clinic to pick up medical supplies for the ER when she notices Mike sorting pills behind the counter. For the past week, Courtney had thought about the topics Mike brought up on their last date. Since they have been seeing each other for a while and he is a great guy, she wants Mike to move in with her. Courtney had planned on bringing this question up for a couple of days, but hadn't gotten the chance with all that has been going on in her life lately. Courtney needs a win, and Mike needs a suitable roof over his head, so she stuffs her jitters down her and approaches Mike. Courtney tries to conceal her excitement, but her blushing cheeks give it away. She feels like the nerdy girl asking out the jock in high school.

"Hey Court, what do you need?"

"Oh, just the basics, Dr. Montgomery—some bandages, hydrogen peroxide, and ibuprofen."

"Coming right up. Just so you know, you can call me Mike here."

Mike rummages through the medical supplies, his eyes shifting left and right to look for what Courtney has requested. Courtney struggles to look Mike in the eye. She feels awful about leaving him last week. She smacks her lips to prepare an apology to him.

"Hey, I'm sorry again about what happened last week. It was an emergency."

"It's all right, I understand. Is . . . is everything all right? Looks like you have something on your mind," Mike says.

Courtney swallows her saliva. She had rehearsed this question a hundred times in her head, but it never sounded right. She wants to take this relationship to the next level. She takes a deep inhale and exhales.

"Um . . . I was wondering if you would . . . want to move in . . . with me?" Courtney asks, rubbing her elbow.

"Oh, I wouldn't want to cause any trouble . . ."

"It's no trouble. You don't belong in an apartment."

"Tell you what, I'll think about it. We'll discuss it more at dinner. See you then."

"Okay, sounds good."

Courtney turns around, and a pleasant grin starts to spread across her face. Elated now that a great weight is removed from her shoulders, Courtney leaves the supply room. She glances over her shoulder at Mike one last time. His eyes quickly shift from her back to the medical supply rack. She laughs as she exits the clinic, not fooled by Mike's failed attempt to conceal his true emotions at work.

* * *

Back on the road, the teenagers decide to slow down their pace, so as not to exhaust the horses. At one o'clock, they hitch the horses on some tree trunks and take a lunch break on the side of the road.

"So, what makes you think your pops is still there?" Drew asks as he opens a can of baked beans.

"My Bela told me, and I have faith in her."

"I'm guessing your grandma has no idea we're doing this, right?" Drew asks.

Luke's gaze retreats to the ground. He cradles his knees to his chest and rocks.

"No, obviously. I told her I was going to Bonnie's for a sleepover," Luke says, shaking his head.

"Funny that you lied to someone you have faith in," Drew says.

"What's that supposed to mean?" Luke asks.

Drew sneers before shoving a spoonful of beans into his mouth. Bonnie gives Drew a side glance of contempt as she takes a bite out of a red apple.

"Well, if that's good enough for Luke, it's good enough for me. Because I trust him," Bonnie says.

"Thank you, Bonnie. You two didn't need to come, but you both did anyways. You are true friends. I hated lying to her, but it was the only way we could do this."

"That must've been hard. I don't think I've ever seen you lie," Bonnie says, gently placing her hand on Luke's shoulder, who chuckles and nods at her.

"Sure thing, but you still owe me big time for this, Luke," Drew says.

"Of course, but you know, Drew, I didn't force you to come along. So, on the one hand I appreciate your company here. On the other hand, I would very much appreciate it if you'd stop complaining every other second."

Drew drops his lunch and marches toward Luke with clenched fists. Something has snapped. Luke leans back as Drew jabs his finger deep into his chest.

"I will stop complaining when we actually find out if your dad is still there or even alive, for that matter," Drew yells.

"Don't touch me," Luke says as he pushes Drew away.

Bonnie sprints in between them, arms reaching out. Still chewing pieces of her apple, she turns her head at both of them as she swallows the last remnants of apple in her mouth.

"Boys, stop arguing! We're too far in now. There's no going back. So, stop acting like babies, and let's work together," Bonnie says, her glare shifting from Drew to Luke.

"My bad. I'm just a little on edge right now," Drew says, backing away.

Luke takes a deep breath and lowers his arms.

"Bonnie's right. We need to stick together. We can only get to Cottonmouth as a team. I'm . . . sorry," Luke says.

"Shake hands," Bonnie says.

Drew extends his hand out, and Luke does the same. Luke has to squeeze to match Drew's firm grip. Far from hearty, the handshake is short and dry. Luke releases his hold first and walks off to get a can of peaches. Drew turns away, thrusting his hands in his pocket.

Within seconds, he winces as he feels his afro cave in, followed by a brief, dull pain in the back of his head. He rubs the back of his head and turns back to the sight of Bonnie with her palm out. Drew's nose crinkles as she beckons him to come in her direction.

"Why did you slap the back of my head?"

Bonnie pulls Drew's ear and yanks him down like a mother about to scold her misbehaved child.

"Have you lost your damn sense? You know better than to touch him without permission," Bonnie whispers to Drew.

Drew sighs deeply and slowly nods, knowing he was in the wrong. Bonnie lets him go and picks up her unfinished apple, while Drew picks up his can of beans. They sit by Luke in the knee-high grass, eating canned food to satisfy their hunger and drinking bottled water to quench their thirst. Luke takes out the map and scans it intently, trying to find out where they are as the animals voraciously chow down their own food.

"Hand me the map. We gotta find a stream for the horses to get a drink. They already drank all the water I brought for them," Bonnie asks.

"There's one near where we're stopping tonight; I already checked," Luke says as he wipes his sticky hands on his shirt.

"Oh, wow. Good job checking on that," Bonnie says.

"Look at you, man, on top of it all. Again, I'm sorry about freaking out on you," Drew says.

Luke glances back with a pensive grin.

"No hard feelings. I think we were just hungry and tired."

* * *

At Princeton County High, Natalie stares at the vacant table where Luke, Bonnie, and Drew usually sit during lunch. It is awfully peculiar that all three of them are absent. Natalie bites her lip aggressively. Where could they be? Before she can think any further, a familiar fragrance invades her nostrils. Her face puckers as the billowy scent of lilacs grows stronger. Natalie's head swivels around as Sandy and Patricia approach her with scrunched faces, as if repelled by the smell of their own perfume too.

"Looking for someone, you lying bitch?" Sandy asks, tilting her chin.

"It's none of your concern," Natalie says, furrowing her eyebrows.

"Our concern? You put my boyfriend in cuffs, and it's none of our business? Sounds like our business, right Patricia?"

"Sure does, Sandy."

"Listen, you lied to me first. Your boyfriend got what was coming to him," Natalie says, pointing her finger at Sandy.

Something begins boiling inside Natalie; her entire body strains. Her muscles tense up with enough force that her arms judder intensely. All of her life she has felt powerless, but not this time. Not to these bullies, not anymore.

"You could've ruled this school with us, but you chose to hang with a bunch of losers," Sandy says.

"Shut up," Natalie mutters under her breath.

"Then again, why should I expect anything else from savage scum like your—"

Sandy hadn't seen it coming at all. Natalie had stood up and slapped her so hard that a red handprint had already begun forming on Sandy's face. Patricia grabs her friend and pulls her back. Sandy is almost rendered speechless that Natalie put her hand on her.

"You're gonna regret that one day. I'll find out where you live and send you back to Oklahoma, you savage," Sandy says as Patricia pulls her back by her waist.

Students observe the three girls intently. What Sandy just said jarred mixed reactions—some with open mouths, while others chuckle into their palms. Most of the cafeteria lean at the edge of their seats, wondering what Natalie will do in retaliation.

"Sandy, calm down. Just let it go. People are staring," Patricia says, still restraining her.

"I'd rather hang out with those 'losers' than you any day,

because at least they're real. I don't care about being popular. Also, have you looked in a mirror lately? You're the only one here who looks like a savage."

Natalie points at the red handprint embedded on Sandy's face. The blonde girl pushes the tousled bangs out of her eyes, grinds her teeth, and growls ferociously at the Native American girl. Patricia tugs Sandy away; her cheeks turn crimson when she recognizes the intent stares beaming down at them. After a few moments, Sandy backs up and marches away. Patricia drops her head down as they attempt to disappear through the crowd. Natalie remains standing tall and continues glaring at the empty table, pondering where the three teenagers could be.

"Stop right there! Where do you two think you're going?" Principal Jackson asks, pushing her way through the surrounding crowd.

"We-we were just—" Patricia says.

"Girls! Just because there is a protest outside does not give you permission to bring that anger inside. All three of you in my office now," Principal Jackson yells.

"But Principal Jackson—" Sandy pleads.

"I was told you two instigated the whole thing. For goodness' sake, I was prepared to stop watching over you kids during lunch when those three troublemakers were suspended, but it seems that I will have to continue babysitting. Now, follow me to my office," Principal Jackson says.

Natalie acquiesces without uttering a word. The three girls follow Principal Jackson to her office with clenched fists. Natalie detects the snickers and stares from her fellow classmates. She hides her face with her hand, ashamed, regretting what she has just done, knowing that her mother will scold and punish her for picking a fight at school.

* * *

Twenty-five minutes have passed by since the three adventurers pulled over for a lunch break. The teenagers and animals have finished eating their food in peace. Once their bellies digest their food, Luke picks himself up and decides it is time to get back on the road.

"I think it's time to move again, if we have any hope of getting to Shepherd's Creek before dark."

Bonnie narrows her eyes up at the fiery orb of light—its rays stretching like fingers across the blue sky. The sun brushes their faces with its balmy touch.

"I reckon we have maybe four or five hours of daylight left," Bonnie says.

"Where are we supposed to sleep?" Drew asks.

"I brought sleeping bags. It'll just be for a night," Luke says. "That's fine by me. I don't mind the outdoors," Bonnie says.

"Pfft . . . speak for yourself," Drew says.

The teenagers mount their horses, determined to ride out until the sun sets, trying to make ground toward Cottonmouth. When they arrive on the highway, people driving past them on the road blare their horns and give them gazes of confusion.

"What are you looking at? Take a picture! It will last longer!" Drew shouts to staring passengers in passing vehicles.

"Drew, relax. Folk just aren't used to seeing teenagers riding into town on horses with a dog by their side. I hope we're not drawing too much attention to ourselves," Bonnie says, looking back at the road.

"No one here knows us, guys. We'll be fine. We already passed Huckleberry Pasture. We have to get to Shepherd's Creek before nightfall if we have any chance of getting to Cottonmouth," Luke says.

"We should be coming up near it any minute now," Bonnie says.

Now a man on a mission, Luke, for the first time, doesn't care what people think of him. A fire he had not known has risen inside of him, and it cannot be doused by any normal method. This is something he has to do. Not even the Masked Haunter can deter him from getting to 86 Birch Drive.

"Look!" Bonnie says, pointing her finger.

A large wooden sign has the message, "Welcome, You Are Now Entering Shepherd's Creek", written in red paint. Placed beside an empty wheat field, it's easily visible from a great distance.

"Nice, finally halfway there," Drew says, wiping sweat off his forehead.

Suddenly, several booming caws burst their eardrums. A swarm of crows tear out of the tree canopy above their heads. The spooked horses rear up, and the teenagers hang on for dear life. Pedro barks and gives chase to any and all crows nearby. Dozens of dark blurs pass by, the wind from their flapping wings piercing the riders' faces like razor blades. Once the chaos subsides, Bonnie whistles loudly, calming down the horses. Luke opens his eyes, catching a glimpse of the black mass of birds as they fly toward the nearby field and the setting sun like a dark curtain eclipsing the waning light.

"What the hell was that?!" Drew screams, swiping at his hair.

"I think it was a herd of crows," Luke says, clutching his chest.

"Actually, a group of crows is called a murder. Jesus, I ain't ever seen one that size before," Bonnie says, watching the murder of crows disappear into the horizon.

"Okay, with that, I think it's time to call it a night," Luke says, looking up at the pinkish sky.

"I agree," Bonnie says before yawning.

"Thank you, God," Drew says as he wipes his forehead in relief.

The teenagers reach a consensus to set up camp on the side of the highway in a lush, wooded area by the creek. They would be out of sight from passing vehicles but close enough to get back on the road quickly if they needed to. Bonnie leads the horses toward the stream to get a refreshing drink, while Luke and Drew set up the sleeping bags. The teenagers set out to gather firewood, returning to the orange sunset piercing the pink sky. It is a sight to behold as the teenagers all admire it for a minute before opening up their canned dinner to consume.

As Luke feeds Pedro half a can of wet dog food, he looks back at the direction of his home. He knows that in an hour or so his mother will come home to the horrific fact that he isn't home. All he can do now is watch the sun disappear over the horizon.

* * *

An hour later, in Blackroot, at 47 Lincoln Avenue, Courtney arrives home from a fantastic date with Mike Montgomery. The sun has set, and the sky is now a mysterious shade of black. As Courtney unlocks the door, she mumbles to herself, "I can't believe I just asked Mike to come move in with us and he said yes. Hola, I'm home!"

No one answers. Courtney scratches her head but guesses that Luke and her mother turned in early. She takes pride in being a responsible and caring mother and decides she should still check on them. Courtney slowly walks to Sophie's bedroom, cautious not to make noise. She turns the doorknob and peeks into the bedroom, hearing the concentrator on and seeing her mother in bed.

"Ok, Ma is asleep," Courtney whispers to herself as she closes the door.

Courtney cautiously ascends the stairs, careful not to wake Luke. She tiptoes and creeps open the bedroom door. What she sees makes her drop her purse in absolute shock. She flicks on the light switch and rushes toward the empty bed. Courtney viciously tosses the blanket and pillow to the side. She starts hyperventilating and pulls her hair.

"*Dios mio*! Where the hell's my son?" Courtney says.

Courtney dashes down the stairs so fast she loses her footing and falls down. She shakes it off, hardly caring about her own well-being. The only thing that matters to her right now is finding out whether or not her son is okay.

"Ma! Wake up now!" Courtney says.

Assuming her bloodcurdling scream has woken her mother up, Courtney pries Sophie's bedroom door open. She turns on the light to Sophie already sitting up and wiping her eyes. Courtney sits on the edge of the bed. Sophie muffles something through her mask, but Courtney can't decipher the words. She reluctantly turns off the concentrator and helps remove Sophie's oxygen mask.

"What's wrong, *hija*? Why are you screaming?" Sophie asks.

"Luke's not in his bed!" Courtney says, fanning her face.

"Calm down, Courtney," Sophie says.

Sophie pauses for a moment to catch a breather. Courtney's patience is at the end of its rope. If it was anyone but her mother, she would've jumped on top of them and beat the knowledge of her son's whereabouts out of them.

"He told me he was sleeping over at his friend's house. Not sure which though," Sophie says, placing her bony hands over Courtney's.

"He knows he's grounded. Why would he . . . I'm calling Laura and Tiffany," Courtney says, pushing herself off the bed.

"No, you'll wake the parents. Wait until morning," Sophie says, reaching out and grabbing Courtney's arm.

"Are you sure he's at one of his friends'?"

"I've never known my grandson to lie to me, *hija*."

"Okay, Ma, sorry for waking you up."

Courtney puts Sophie's mask back on, turns on the concentrator, and leaves the room. She sees a soft smirk on

Sophie's face before the mask clouds up. She yawns, and the adrenaline wears off. She collapses on her mattress while still in her scrubs; her last thoughts are of her son. When the following morning comes, there will be no stopping her from bringing her son back home.

* * *

Back in the camp off the highway, the teenagers are getting in their sleeping bags. The first day is over. They should be able to get to Memphis by midday tomorrow.

"Okay, guys, I need you two to wake up by four o'clock in the morning," Luke says, covering his mouth to contain a yawn.

"I do that already," Bonnie says.

"Why?" Drew asks, nesting into his sleeping bag.

"If my mom doesn't already know that I'm not in Blackroot, she will by morning. So, we gotta get moving before our parents have a chance to catch us," Luke says.

"All right, that makes sense, I guess," Drew says. "Okay, let's get some shut-eye, boys," Bonnie says. "We fed and watered the horses, right?" Drew asks. "Yeah, I did," Bonnie says.

"Night, guys," Drew says, shutting his eyes.

Pedro trots towards Luke; he is taking the journey very well. He lies on top of Luke like a pillow. The stench of his dog's breath is overwhelming, but Luke thinks about other things to distract himself. Luke thinks about Rob, Natalie, and his father. He still hasn't grasped the events that have transpired over the last several days.

"We'll be there soon, boy," Luke says as he yawns.

Luke rubs Pedro's head until he finally dozes off.

People that care about him—Bonnie, Drew, Mom, Bela (and Pedro)—surround him. The sky is cloudy like the storm to end all storms is coming. The horses are struggling to fight through

174

the howling wind. Luke sees a silhouette in the distance; he smiles and waves his hand.

"Over here, can you help us?" Luke screams.

The man doesn't respond, so they march a little closer. The man comes into view, and he has his back turned to the teenagers. Luke squints to get a better look at the man. His face drops when he realizes it is not a man but the Masked Haunter. He turns around, no longer a cold-blooded reptile. An aura of flames shoots up around him and he points at Luke with his bony finger.

"Boy, I warned you, and you did not heed it. Now you will be at my mercy," the demonic voice of the Masked Haunter says.

Luke draws a sharp breath and trembles with anxiety. He grabs the reins as he nearly falls off his horse.

"Why . . . why won't you leave me alone?"

"Soon. All will be revealed soon," the Masked Haunter says. "What will be revealed? I have no idea what you're saying."

Luke could never deduce the Masked Haunter's emotions due to the empty eye sockets and blank expression. All around him, his loved ones are melting and screaming in agony for Luke to help them. Frozen with fear, Luke can't do anything. He can only watch helplessly as his friends suffer, and the Masked Haunter just stands there, admiring his work.

"You can't save them if you can't save yourself," the Masked Haunter says.

"Who are you? What do you want?" Luke asks.

"I am you, Luke. I want you to succeed, but you keep ignoring my words, and it keeps leading you right back to me."

"No, you can't be me. You're a monster," Luke says, shaking his head in denial.

"No, Luke, I'm not a monster. I'm everything you fear manifested in a physical form. You need to wise up fast, kid. Or you'll be seeing me every day for all eternity."

"No, no, *no!* You lie!" Luke yells.

Luke slaps himself in an attempt to wake up, but it doesn't work. He screams and charges at his "fears," refusing to believe it. In his mind, Luke is a good person and believes in God. How can this devil-like creature be in his head? The Masked Haunter merely laughs. "See you soon, boy."

The Masked Haunter vanishes before Luke's very eyes, and he is left alone in the black void.

Luke arises, but it is still dark. Only the waning embers of the campfire are left to illuminate the night. He springs up so fast that Pedro yelps and jumps off him. He leaves his sleeping bag and sits on the grass a few feet away. Luke rocks back and forth, taking short, deep breaths and keeping his eyes closed. The clamorous sounds of Pedro and Luke wake up Bonnie. She sits up and rubs her eyes, glancing at Luke's empty sleeping bag. Bonnie's ears pick up the crunching of tall weeds behind her. She looks past Pedro and notices a shadow in the clearing. She exits the comfort of her sleeping bag and tiptoes in the sound's direction.

"Luke? What are you doing out of your sleeping bag and away from the fire? There's copperheads out here; you know they're venomous."

Luke doesn't respond to Bonnie's warning. Whatever was going on in his head feels far more dangerous than any venomous snake. He sits in the grass, waiting for a sign, something to make sense of his nightmares. Bonnie kneels down beside him and puts her arm around him, gazing at the stars.

"They're beautiful, aren't they? If you open your eyes, you can see them for yourself."

Luke opens his eyes and looks up at the sky. He smiles brightly at the midnight blue sky speckled with white dots. He feels a calming tenderness gazing at the stars, like a critic admiring an artist's canvas. Now that Luke has soothed his anxiety, he prepares to open up to Bonnie.

"They are. I feel a little bit better now."

"What's wrong? I can tell you're not yourself."

"I had a horrible nightmare. I can't go back to sleep."

"I'm sorry about that. Do you wanna talk about it?"

Luke has never told anyone about these relentless nightmares that haunt him—not even his own mother or grandmother. He believes that if he tells anyone, they will get hurt. The Masked Haunter had been completely correct in his predictions. He said that Natalie wasn't who Luke thought she was, and he played the role of his father in another dream. Was the Masked Haunter correct in this latest prophecy of his friends getting hurt or dying if they continue on their journey? Luke decides to tell Bonnie since he knows she won't laugh at him. Luke thinks that if Bonnie knows, maybe she will go back and be spared.

"I've been having these crazy nightmares for a while now."

"How are they crazy?"

"This same creature, or man, I'm not sure what he is. He keeps reappearing, and every time he comes, I see myself or people I care about die."

"It's just a nightmare. Look, we're all fine; everything's gonna be fine."

"Just the other night he showed me a memory of my mom being knocked out, but I don't remember it at all."

Bonnie tilts her head, cradling it in her hand. She hums and taps her foot as Luke glances at her, waiting for her reaction.

"Wow, that's strange. Definitely not a coincidence. What did he say now?"

"There's more. The day before we found out about Natalie, he told me that 'she wasn't who I thought she was.' And 'that no one could ever love someone like me.' Let's face the facts: he's right."

"Luke, now that ain't true in the slightest. You're a great guy. There is a lucky gal out there who loves you." Bonnie wraps her arm around Luke.

"I didn't listen to his warning. If we go to Cottonmouth, we'll all die."

"Hey, I'm right here. Look, we ain't gonna die. These nightmares, they will pass," Bonnie says as she flings her other arm around Luke and squeezes him for a hug.

"Aren't you worried? Are you going to go back?"

This question makes Bonnie's forehead crinkle between her eyes, as if she has been personally insulted.

"Absolutely not! You should know me by now. A little nightmare won't scare me off."

"But everything he's said has come true so far."

"Which means if we prove him wrong, he'll go away for good."

Luke had never thought about that. What would happen if the Masked Haunter's prediction was inaccurate? Would he leave him alone? It makes sense to Luke. If the Masked Haunter is wrong, Luke can protect himself and the people he loves. Luke believes that if he can face his father, then he can finally be free of the Masked Haunter's grasp.

"Hey, I think I know something that'll cheer you up."

This catches Luke's attention, and he looks to the other side of her. To her right, amid the grass, lies a weed. Bonnie plucks it from the grass. The flower is now a puffball, white and wispy. The slightest breath could disperse the seeds across these plains.

"Hey, do you know what this is?"

Luke narrows his eyes. He's seen that plant many times but never cared for what it was called.

"Some weird flower," Luke shrugs.

Bonnie smiles gently, showing teeth. "It's a dandelion."

"No. Dandelions are yellow and have petals. That's white and looks almost dead."

Bonnie snickers slightly before bringing the dandelion closer to Luke's face.

"They are, but when they get older, they turn white. Before it dies, the seeds get blown by the wind, and then they grow somewhere else. A single dandelion can create a colony of dandelions, and the cycle keeps repeating."

Bonnie hands the flower to Luke. He narrows his eyes and rotates the stem in his hand as if looking for some secret chamber within the bulb.

"What do I do with it?" Luke asks.

"You're supposed to make a wish and blow."

Luke's eyes fixate on the little weed, but he turns toward Bonnie, and his face brightens up.

"So, like birthday candles?"

"Exactly."

"Do you want to make a wish with me?" Luke asks.

Luke holds out the dandelion, and Bonnie's eyes shift from the flower to Luke's soft brown eyes.

"I'd be delighted to."

Bonnie's hand clasps over Luke's. Her hand is warm like an oven mitt. They lean closer together, cheek to cheek. Both close their eyes for a moment, pondering their desires. They open their eyes and look at each other.

"On the count of three, blow. One . . . two . . . three."

Simultaneously, they both round their lips and huff, sending every seed away, fading into the night. They gaze down at the naked bulb, and then to each other. Luke chuckles and claps his hands. Bonnie wraps her arm around his shoulders; it's the first time he's smiled in days.

"That was great. What did you wish for?" Luke asks. "You're not supposed to say. Otherwise, it won't come true." Luke shakes his head, attempting in vain not to smile. "Thank you, Bonnie, for listening."

"Much obliged. I appreciate you opening up to me, Luke."

Bonnie is one of the few people who seem to know exactly what to say to Luke. Luke reaches in for a hug. They both smell like a mixture of the outdoors and horses, but it doesn't matter. As they release, they look at each other for a moment, waiting for the other to speak, but neither does. Bonnie gets up and starts walking back to the camp when Luke asks, "Are you mad at me?"

Bonnie stops and turns back.

"Why would you say something like that?"

"I noticed lately that your face turns red a lot around me. I remember watching a cartoon, and the characters turned red when they got angry."

Bonnie takes a drawn-out breath and sits back down in the grass. She gazes up at the stars once again.

"I don't know if you remember, but one day when we were little, you came up to me and said, 'The dots on your face look like stars,'" Bonnie says, pointing at her freckles.

"You poked one of the freckles on my cheek and then you dragged your finger across my nose and to my other cheek, making some imaginary path. My guess: the stars. My face turned so red you had trouble seeing the dots on my face, and then you turned and walked away like nothing happened."

"So, you got red because you were mad that I touched your face? Well, I'm sorry. I know I would've gotten angry if I was you."

Bonnie laughs and shakes her head at this, which causes Luke to raise his eyebrow.

"I got red because I was laughing. It was just so random, funny, and . . . you. I wasn't mad or embarrassed. You make me feel . . . warm and fuzzy on the inside. That's why sometimes I turn red around you, and if I seem mad, it ain't directed at you. You understand?"

"I think so . . . 'warm and fuzzy,' that's a good feeling, right?"

"One of the best. It's like having a blanket during a cold day. You can't describe it well, but you just know it's good."

"Well, you just made *me* feel warm and fuzzy."

Bonnie blushes and giggles as Luke pushes some of his hair off his forehead and places his hand on hers again. They stare at one another even longer.

"Um . . . we should head back to bed now. Long day ahead tomorrow," Bonnie says, tugging on her overall straps.

"Oh, yeah . . . right. That sounds like a good idea," Luke says, nodding his head.

Drew is still loudly snoring in the comfort of his sleeping bag, his protruding hair giving him the appearance of a tree on its side. While Bonnie goes back to sleep, Luke can't help but ponder what the Masked Haunter meant by, "Wise up." Did he mean he should abandon the mission? Listen to his mother? Or not fall for tricks? The Masked Haunter was very vague. Luke never wants to see that creature again. He has an inclination that Bonnie's plan to prove the Masked Haunter wrong is the only way to be rid of him.

Luke takes in the wilderness surrounding him. The noises of wildlife, from the chirping of crickets to the hoots of owls, echo in the eerie night. He had never really noticed the sounds of nature around him, but they are rather soothing in a way. Luke cannot go back to sleep, so he stares at the sky and listens to the animal calls, pretending to be asleep until he eventually drifts off around four o'clock.

17

THE CHASE IS ON

Despite having a rough time lying on the hard ground, unable to sleep most of the night, Luke picks himself up at dawn's light, splashing water in his tired eyes to wake up. Pedro and Drew are still fast asleep when it is time to go. Bonnie is already getting the horses ready. The left side of Luke's hair is sticking straight up from sleeping on his side. He tries pushing it down, but his thick mane won't comply, so Luke pours some leftover water on it to push it down.

"All right, get up!" Luke says to Drew.

"Hmph," Drew grunts.

Pedro barks repeatedly at Drew to speed the process along, as if he knows the mission as well as Luke does. Drew kicks his feet toward Pedro to get him to be quiet, with no success.

"Fine, I'm getting up," Drew snaps as he sits up, throwing the sleeping bag off himself.

Now that all three teenagers are awake, and for the most part ready, Luke mounts Red without a moment's hesitation. It feels as though the closer he gets to Cottonmouth; the more determined Luke becomes to get there.

"We have about two or three hours before our parents realize we're missing, so let's get to Cottonmouth, and fast," Luke says as he claps his hands like he just got out of a huddle during a football game.

"I think we should stay off the main roads," Bonnie says.

"Yeah, great idea, to avoid any cruisers that might be searching for us," Luke says.

"Will we get there today?" Drew asks.

"We should, but it will be in the evening if we don't hurry up," Luke says.

"All right, then we better get a move on!" Bonnie says, leading the way.

"I'm right behind you!" Luke says, following her.

"You guys are always in a rush!" Drew says, bringing up the rear.

After three hours of riding, they manage to get through most of Anderson County with no setbacks or delays. By noon, they take a break, as they are all dripping in sweat, with sweat stains visible on their clothes. They are worn out but already halfway to the capital. Pedro has calmed down, now that he is used to the horses. So far, he has kept pace with the group, only stopping to drink water and go to the bathroom. The dog's endurance had been a concern for the teenagers at first, because if he wasn't able to keep up, they would have had to slow down to accommodate him and possibly miss their window to get to Memphis.

"Only one more county before we arrive in Memphis," Bonnie says.

As Bonnie gazes carefully at the map of Tennessee, she smirks broadly, showing her dimples as she sees that they will get there sooner rather than later.

"We should get there by lunchtime," Bonnie says.

"Are you ready to meet your pops, Luke?" Drew asks.

"I'm nervous. What . . . what if he calls the cops on me or shoots me on sight? He . . . he abandoned me and nearly killed my mom," Luke says, his voice quivering.

"We have your back, Luke, don't worry," Bonnie says.

"Yeah, man, we got the tape recorder for backup. If he does try anything, we'll have photographic evidence too," Drew says as he pulls out a camera.

"Nice thinking, Drew," Luke says, nodding at Drew.

"Wow, Drew, you said a four-syllable word. I'm impressed," Bonnie says.

"Shut up, and you're welcome," Drew says.

* * *

On the outskirts of Blackroot at dawn, Laura Davis is lying in bed with her husband, Randall. Their landline rings, immediately waking up Laura. As Randall groans, she hastily picks up the phone before Randall fully awakens.

"Hello?" Laura says, groggily wiping her eyes.

"Laura, is Drew there with Bonnie?" Stephen Thompson asks, his words sputtering out.

"Huh . . . come again?" Laura asks.

Stephen had fired his words so rapidly that Laura didn't understand half of what he said. All Laura could decipher from his sentence is that something is terribly wrong. It is in the sound of his voice. Also, a call from one of his daughter's friends' parents so early in the morning is incredibly rare.

"Is. Drew. On. The. Ranch?" Stephen asks.

"No, I thought Bonnie was with you."

"Well, she's not! Neither is Drew."

Laura sits up so fast her back cracks, and her husband tosses and turns, almost waking up. Laura hadn't realized her daughter is missing. The Davis family never really spent time together during the week, as there is always work to be done around the ranch.

"What are you saying?" Laura asks.

"I'm saying our children are missing!" Stephen says.

"I'll . . . I'll call Courtney," Laura says, breathing heavily.

"She already called me. They're not with her either."

"We have to call the sheriff's office! Randy, wake up!" Laura says as she shakes his shoulder.

"Hmph!" Randall says, waking up.

"I don't know if they're gonna pick up. Looks like all the cops are dealing with the protests down at the school and city hall."

"Okay, well, I'll head down to the school right now."

"Okay, bye Laura. I'm halfway to work. Tiffany will meet you there," Stephen says.

"Wait, what the hell is going on?" Randall asks, sitting up in bed.

"Bonnie's missing, so are Courtney and Stephen's kids," Laura says, putting on her pants.

* * *

Courtney is already at Princeton County High School. She called out of work right after she called Stephen. The only thing on her mind is Luke, not work. When she pulls up to the school, her mouth drops. A hundred or so protestors are outside the school, demanding the termination of Earl Calhoun. The angry mob chants, "Hey, ho, Earl Calhoun has to go!" repeatedly. Courtney approaches a deputy that she recognizes from the sheriff's office.

"Excuse me, Deputy Johnson, right? Do you happen to know where Sheriff Berkowski is? I really need to speak with him," Courtney says.

"It's Ms. Ramirez, correct? He's over by the front entrance," Deputy Johnson says.

"Thank you," Courtney says, nodding her head.

"Just be safe, ma'am. A lot of folks on edge right now," Deputy Johnson says, tipping his hat at Courtney.

Courtney turns around. She scopes out Sheriff Berkowski at the base of the front steps of the school with a megaphone, inside a perimeter of half a dozen other officers fending off the rowdy protesters. She looks for a way around the crowd, with no success. Courtney inhales and begins walking through the group of people, finding the gaps between protestors where she can. Courtney swats away outstretched arms to make a clear path, and soon she finds the building through the picket signs. *Almost there*, she thinks to herself. Finally, Courtney manages to escape the crowd but is blocked by a wooden barricade. She cups her hands together and shouts out, "Sheriff! Paul!"

The screams of protestors drown her calls out. She can hardly hear herself. Courtney exposes her teeth and risks it, ducking under the wooden barrier. An officer tackles her to the ground, and she winces as both of her arms are yanked behind her.

"Lady, what the hell you doing? Protestors ain't allowed past the barricade," a young officer says.

"Wait, I'm not a protester, young man. I just need to speak with Paul. It's an emergency."

The young officer digs his knee into the back of Courtney's head, forcing her against the sidewalk.

Sheriff Paul Berkowski, catching the scene in his peripheral vision, drops the megaphone to the ground, clears his throat, and points his finger directly at the officer.

"Wright! Unhand that woman right now, or it'll be your ass, rookie," Sheriff Berkowski says.

The young officer immediately releases his hold without even talking back to the sheriff and backs away from Courtney.

Sheriff Berkowski grabs the megaphone once again, while Courtney pulls herself up and approaches the sheriff at the bottom of the concrete steps.

"Everyone, please back up so that faculty and students can enter the building," Sheriff Berkowski orders into his megaphone. "It may be Saturday, but some people still have to get inside for detention, custodial work, sport practices, tutoring sessions, and all that stuff. So, step back."

Courtney sees a scowl form on Sheriff Berkowski's face. His words fall on deaf ears, as the disorderly crowd doesn't budge an inch.

"Sheriff!" Courtney yells, waving her arms.

"Ms. Ramirez, I'll be with you in a minute. It's a little chaotic right now."

"But it's my—"

"If y'all don't back up this instant, I'll be forced to make some arrests for trespassing and disturbing the peace!" Sheriff Berkowski shouts.

With that direct order, most of the protestors back up, providing enough space for the officers to move the barricades so that faculty and students have an open path to enter. The chants of "We Want Calhoun Gone" are still prevalent. Courtney ignores them though, as she is not concerned about that right now. Sheriff Berkowski smiles at Courtney; he raises his eyebrow when he sees how unruly her hair is. She wasted no time brushing her hair this morning, which now resembles the appearance of a tumbleweed.

"Sorry for that, Ms. Ramirez, Private Wright is fresh out of Opal Academy, and he's a little stickler for the rules."

"Never mind that now Sheriff, I need—"

"Also, this god-almighty mess we got here. They all want an allegedly racist teacher fired. Based on the chants, my guess is Earl Calhoun, but nobody's seen him in two days. Honestly, he might as well quit now before he gets the boot, because he will. Calhoun made the school look bad. That won't stand with the superintendent. Hell, while he's at it, he might as well skip town," Sheriff Berkowski says as he chuckles.

"Sheriff, my son is missing, and so are Tiffany and Stephen's son, Drew Thompson. Also, Randall and Laura's daughter, Bonnie Davis."

Sheriff Berkowski stops chuckling instantly. Like a record player coming to a scratching halt. His eyebrows narrow and his scowl becomes so prominent that he looks like he could kill the next person that speaks to him.

"I remember those three from last week. How long have they been missing?" Sheriff Berkowski asks.

"Almost a day. I think the last any of us saw them was yesterday morning before they went to school."

"Okay. Well, if they've been missing for more than twenty-four hours, you can file a missing person's report."

"That's why I'm here. I-I haven't seen him since yesterday morning," Courtney says as she looks upward and fans her eyes.

"Do you have any idea where they could be, Ms. Ramirez?"

"No! My son has never even been outside of town, and I have no clue where on earth the three of them would go."

"Anyone besides you know where he might've gone?" Sheriff Berkowski asks.

"No. No one, I can think of . . ."

All of a sudden, someone comes to Courtney's mind. Her mother is the one who told her that Luke was sleeping over at his friend's house. Why would Ma lie to her? No! She couldn't, she wouldn't.

"Ms. Ramirez? Courtney? You there?" Sheriff Berkowski asks, waving his hand in front of her face.

"Y-yeah. What if they're outside of town? Maybe even outside the county?" Courtney asks.

Sheriff Berkowski removes his tan hat, pressing it to his hip. He caresses his beard and shakes his head.

"If they are, then I'm afraid there's not much I can do to help. That'd be out of my jurisdiction. Although, I could talk to the state police to be on the lookout for three teenagers, if that's the case," Sheriff Berkowski says.

"Thank you so much, Sheriff. I need to find out for sure. I'll call you in a few if I find out they're heading to Cottonmouth," Courtney says, turning around.

"Sorry I can't do more to help, Ms. Ramirez. Wait, did you say Cottonmouth? You don't think—"

Courtney sprints back in the direction of her car. She glances back at Sheriff Berkowski, who raises his eyebrow and places his hands on his hips as he watches her.

"Courtney, I'll make some calls. I reckon they can find them!" Sheriff Berkowski yells through his cupped hands.

Already halfway to her vehicle, Courtney is long out of earshot and can't make out what he says. She buckles herself up and steps on the gas. "Ma knows. She told him about Ben," Courtney says to herself. Before long, she's back home. When she opens the door, she now realizes Pedro is nowhere to be seen either.

"Where is he, Ma?!" Courtney asks, her fists clenched.

"Oh, hi sweetie," Sophie says.

"Where is my son? Cut the act now," Courtney says.

Sophie's face drops. She wheels herself closer to Courtney and raises a shaky finger to her.

"What do you mean? He's at Bonnie's," Sophie says.

"No, he isn't!" Courtney shouts.

Sophie's eyes fall to the floor, and they widen with panic at the realization of Luke's true whereabouts.

"You did not!"

"I . . . did. I didn't think . . . I told him not to go," Sophie says, crossing her arms.

Courtney screams in frustration and slams her purse to the ground, knocking contents from it across the floor. Taken aback by this, Sophie places her hand over her heart. She has never seen her daughter react like this.

"He . . . he said he was going to a sleepover at Bonnie's. I didn't think he'd lie. He never does."

"When and why?" Courtney asks, her voice shaking.

"After the sheriff's office. Your son deserved to know the truth because I thought he could handle it and learn what kind of man not to be."

"But why?" Courtney asks as water wells up in her eyes.

Tears stream down Courtney's face, unable to hold them back any longer. She can't believe her own mother aired her worst secret to her son. They had promised each other a long time ago that Luke could never know what really happened on that day.

"What Ben did to you wasn't right. He should've been put in jail years ago! I just wanted Luke to know his father wasn't dead, and more importantly, isn't a good man," Sophie says, slamming her chair arm.

"I was worried about Luke. I was protecting him."

"I was too. That's why I kept my mouth shut for thirteen years. When he stood up to that bully, I knew he was ready to know about him," Sophie says.

"This isn't over, Ma. Food's on the table if you're hungry," Courtney says as she walks to the kitchen.

"Where are you going?" Sophie asks.

"To protect my son," Courtney says, grabbing the landline.

"He's most likely already in Shelby County. I told him Ben's lives in the outskirts of Memphis and . . . *Dios mio.* I told him Ben's middle name too. He must've asked me to find the right Ben Miller's address in the phonebook," Sophie says.

"Shit! Well, if I can't protect him from the truth, I'll have to protect him from Ben. He's a sixteen-year-old boy with autism. You should've known better!"

Courtney dials Mike's phone number, as she does not want to do this alone. Also, his car is a Ford Mustang, which is much faster than her old station wagon.

"Hi, can you drive me to Memphis? It's an emergency. I'll tell you about it on the way."

"Um . . ."

"It's Luke. Please."

Courtney squeezes the cord, shuddering as she waits for a response.

"Sure, I'm on my way. Just need to get dressed and call out," Mike says before hanging up.

"Hold on, Luke, Mama's coming," Courtney says, stepping out of the house.

* * *

At Princeton County High School, Sheriff Berkowski is on the phone with a distressed Laura Davis, trying his best to soothe her temper. "Now, Mrs. Davis, I know you're worried, but I need you to calm down and talk slowly."

"Calm down?! My daughter is missing! And now my husband wakes up to see that three of our horses have been stolen! How in heavens do I calm down?"

"I am sending someone out there right now, and I am working on finding those three teenagers."

"I don't wanna hear it. The Thompsons and I are coming down to the station, and you better be there with some answers!"

"Mrs. Davis, I—"

Before he has a chance to finish his sentence, the line disconnects. Laura Davis has hung up on Sheriff Berkowski.

"Everyone thinks I'm a goddamn miracle worker," Sheriff Berkowski whispers to himself.

Paul Berkowski has been good friends with Courtney Ramirez for some time. In his first year on the force, he suffered a gunshot on duty, and Courtney was one of the nurses who helped him at the hospital. He only knew Benjamin Miller for a little while, but something about Ben had always made Paul's skin crawl. When Paul had received word that Courtney was in the hospital with serious injuries, he had an inclination that Ben had something to do with it. He offered to find him, however, Courtney begged him not to look for Ben. Initially, Paul was going to look for him anyway, but then he learned that Ben skipped town. There wasn't much Paul could do at the time, but now is his chance to make things right.

"Hello, this is Sheriff Paul Berkowski of the Princeton County Sheriff's Department. I'm calling because I have reason to believe that three teenagers are heading toward a Benjamin Miller's address in your city. One of the teens happens to be his son, who has autism."

A few seconds pass with nothing but static on the other end. Sheriff Berkowski sighs and prepares to turn the walkie talkie off. He halts when he hears a voice respond on the receiving end. It is choppy because of the long distance at first, but it begins to sound clearer after a couple seconds.

"Thank you, Sheriff, for bringing this to our attention. We'll contact all the Benjamin Millers in town and find out which of them is the boy's father. We'll call you back once we have any information," the operator says.

"Thank you for your help," Sheriff Berkowski says.

Sheriff Berkowski gets off the walkie and looks out into the distance. If there was one person who had gotten away that haunted Paul over the years, it was Benjamin Miller. He puts a cigarette in his mouth, nearly forgetting about the protest happening just feet away from him.

Paul's mind falls on his own two kids, twin girls named Chloe and Elena that are a couple years younger than Luke. Unfortunately, his ex-wife, Kinga, has custody of them. After the divorce was finalized, the judge ruled in favor of her, but at least he still gets to see his girls regularly. *What if it were Chloe and Elena who were missing?* he asks himself. If his girls ever disappeared, he would go to the ends of the world to find them, and there would be hell to pay for whoever responsible.

"We'll find you, and this time you won't escape, you bastard," the sheriff utters to himself as he lights the cigarette in his mouth.

18

ONE'S SACRIFICE

Luke and his friends are scaling a steep hill. The horses struggle to carry the combined weight of the teenagers and saddlebags up the slope. They have been riding for the past five hours, and everyone is tired. The horses fight and gallop up until they reach the peak along the road. Their jaws drop as they see it just beyond the horizon—the city of Memphis. The outlines of skyscrapers can be seen from miles away. Luke points out the metal sign above them, Shelby County, the area of land which houses the city of Memphis. Their stomachs growl loudly, and their eyelids are heavy. They have been riding all morning in hopes of getting there sooner rather than later since they are almost out of provisions. Drew had lost a few cans of food unknowingly along the way. Bonnie had scolded Drew for his reckless act of stupidity for most of the morning.

"I hope we get there soon. We're running low on food," Drew says as he searches through his bag.

"Horse, human, or dog?" Bonnie asks.

"All three," Drew says.

"Guys, we're almost there, but our parents can't be far behind. Let's move it," Luke says, clapping his hands.

194

The teenagers are on schedule to arrive at their destination in less than two hours. Luke can feel it. They are close, so close, to finding his father and confronting him. Luke and his friends haven't talked for what seems like years. He has an inclination that Bonnie and Drew sensed the quiet rage radiating from him, and that they understand that he just needs to get to Cottonmouth. Pedro, on the other hand, cannot contain his excitement. He wags his tail vigorously and pants heavily even though he has never met Luke's father. Dogs are interesting creatures. They're so loyal and loving; that's why they're called "man's best friend," Luke supposes.

"I think we should stop somewhere to eat before we go any further. Horses could use the break anyway," Bonnie says.

"Yeah, dawg, I'm starving too," Drew says.

Luke had hardly noticed it until now, but he is famished as well. Seeing a sign that says, Rest Stop 0.5 miles Ahead, his stomach growls loudly at the mere thought of food.

"All right, but let's hitch the horses somewhere no one will notice."

Luke, Bonnie, and Drew stop at a small diner called the Smokey Titan just off the main road to eat some breakfast. They hitch the horses in the nearby woods. Luke knows they need to be quick; he has a gut feeling that his mother is on her way to him at this moment. Drew and Bonnie both get coffee, while Luke orders an orange juice.

"Why don't you get a coffee, Luke? It'll keep you awake," Drew says.

"How do I put this delicately? Coffee tastes like liquid dirt, in my opinion."

Bonnie laughs so hard that some of her coffee comes out her nose, which Drew ridicules for a few minutes. A few moments later, an older server with a red kerchief covering most of her short white hair arrives at their table to take their orders.

"My name is Ginny, welcome to the Smokey Titan. What would you three like to order?"

"I'll have toast, eggs, and bacon, please," Luke says.

"An omelet with a side of sausage for me," Drew says, licking his lips.

"I'll have a bagel with a blueberry muffin, and a fruit bowl, please," Bonnie says.

"It'll be out in a few minutes," Ginny says, letting out a sigh.

"You're really missing out on meat, Bonnie," Drew says.

"I know about the high cholesterol and heart disease from eating the animals I raise. Yeah, I'm totally missing out," Bonnie says as she rolls her eyes.

* * *

Little do the teenagers know, Mike and Courtney are already halfway to Memphis, closing in on them quickly.

"Where are we going again? Memphis?" Mike asks.

"No, Cottonmouth, it's a small town just outside of Memphis. That's where my ex-husband is. Luke's going after him."

"Did the sheriff make the call yet?" Mike asks.

"He called all the departments from Madison to Shelby County about three teenagers on horses."

"Horses?" Mike asks as his voice rises in volume.

"Yeah, Randall and Laura called me and said that three of their horses are missing from their stables."

"Those kids are crazy. Did they not have enough money to take a city bus?"

"Probably not. Plus, they would risk running into familiar faces, and it would take numerous buses."

"Why not just take the train then?" Mike asks.

"I think they brought the dog; dogs aren't allowed on trains," Courtney says.

"Why on earth would they bring a do—"

All of a sudden, Courtney's phone rings—the shock of the blaring ringtone makes Courtney flinch a little. Mike attempts to place his hand on Courtney's shoulder to relax her. Courtney swats his hand away to snatch her phone and answer.

"Hello? Is this Courtney Ramirez?" the dispatcher asks.

"It is."

"We believe we've found your son in a diner in Shelby County. I asked the officer not to engage until backup arrives."

"Thank you so much, officer. We'll be there in about forty-five minutes. Please keep your distance, but if they try to leave, then you can stop them. Just be gentle with my son."

"Thank you, ma'am, will do. We'll see you there." "This is intense," Mike says, exhaling.

"Can't believe they've made it that far," Courtney says. "It sounds like he's fine though."

"He's just a boy. He has autism. He could be freaking out or worse," Courtney says.

"Courtney, everything's going to be fine. You told me he's a smart boy," Mike says.

* * *

In the diner, the teenagers are in the middle of their meal. Suddenly, Drew stops chewing his food and signals for his friends to lean in closer. He swallows his food and whispers, "Is it just me, or is that cop watching us?"

Bonnie and Luke turn and look over their shoulders to see behind them. Drew is right. A state trooper is watching them by the counter, but he turns away, noticing the three of them staring back at him. Luke sinks in the leather booth. He knows they are all thinking the same thing. They are being watched. The state police must have joined the search for the three missing teenagers from Blackroot.

"Yeah, we're being watched," Bonnie says.

"I'm afraid so, but what's he waiting for?" Luke asks. "Probably for backup," Bonnie says, pounding the table.

"What should we do?" Luke asks, his gaze switching from Bonnie to Drew.

"We didn't come this far to be caught now. We can't run for it. He'll chase after us," Drew says.

"I know we can't outrun them with horses, and I refuse to leave Pedro behind. The sirens will spook him though," Luke says.

'We need a new game plan right now," Drew says.

All three of them gaze down at the table in defeat. The hope has left them. Luke tries to think of a strategy, but nothing comes to him. Bonnie snaps her fingers, and the boys glance up at her.

"Boys . . . I think it's best I stay here," Bonnie says.

Luke's jaw drops and Drew looks at Bonnie with bug eyes. *Bonnie really doesn't expect us to just leave her, does she?* Luke wonders in disbelief.

"Bonnie, what are you talking about?" Luke asks.

"Yeah, have you lost your damn mind?" Drew asks.

"He'll never think we'd split up. You two should pretend to use the bathroom and sneak out the back," Bonnie says.

"What about you?"

"I'll be fine. He hasn't been here long enough to have backup come, and besides, Luke, this is your quest. We're here to help, right?" "I guess so, yeah, but—"

"But nothing! I'm doing my part. Hell, if my brother can serve our country, I can at the very least do this. Drew, here, take the tape recorder and leave Lucky hitched up at the tree."

"I'll tell them you're going down the main roads, but try to stick to the back roads. That will buy you a little more time."

"Drew, you get up first, so it doesn't look suspicious. Just wait for Luke by the horses. Luke, you'll get up in a few minutes."

"Thank you. You know, you're braver than most guys, Davis."

"Don't get sentimental on me, Thompson. Now get. Hightail it outta here."

Drew chuckles one last time before he gets up and heads toward the restrooms. Luke and Bonnie wait a couple of minutes. The officer stares at them intently, oblivious to their plans. Luke is holding in tears; he doesn't want to leave his best friend behind.

"Bonnie, I don't know if I can do this without you. What if this was part of the Masked Haunter's plan?"

"Luke, you can do this. You're the bravest, smartest, and kindest boy I know. I'll be fine. No nightmare is gonna hurt me or you. I guarantee it."

A single tear drips out of Luke's eye. He simply can't hold it in any longer. His best friend is sacrificing herself for his cause.

"Back in grade school, when Rob pushed me, you saved me when I couldn't save myself."

"You've grown so much since then. You beat Rob in a fight just days ago. You're one of a kind, Lucas Alexander Ramirez, and don't let anybody tell you different," Bonnie says to Luke.

"Bonnie, if it wasn't for you, I might've never learned to stand up for myself."

"It was in you all along, Luke. I knew it, your mother knew it, and everyone else who knows you knew it. You just needed a little push."

"I just have to know . . . why did you convince me to go along with this?"

"I was scared you'd try to go at it alone if I didn't come. That day you said that you weren't sure you'd go after him, but I know you. You knew you were going after him the moment your grandma told you. I care about you a lot, Luke, I always have. Here, take this map. I don't need it anymore," Bonnie says.

However, Luke refuses to reach for the map, instead placing his hand over Bonnie's outstretched arm. Suddenly, these feelings come over Luke. He gazes into Bonnie's green eyes and twirls her braid. He leans in closer until his lips meet Bonnie's. At first her lips are tight, but then, they slowly become delicate. Bonnie's lips are warm and moist from the coffee she has been drinking. The faint yet bitter taste of coffee isn't enough to deter Luke. This kiss is nothing like the one with Natalie. The biggest distinction is the enormous spark Luke feels with his kiss with Bonnie. It's otherworldly, like fireworks are going off in Luke's heart. His hands glide up her face, cupping her cheeks. Only just noticing Bonnie's hand cradling the back of his head, Luke opens his eyes and remembers what he has to do. He slowly separates his mouth from hers.

"Thank you so much, Bonnie Anne Davis. You're amazing, and I'll see you soon," Luke whispers into Bonnie's ear.

Luke grabs the map from Bonnie, whose grip has loosened due to what has just occurred. Luke leaves the booth and begins his trip to the back of the diner. He looks back. Bonnie is blushing red and smiling at him. All these years, the girl that Luke likes the most was right in front of him, and he hadn't realized it until she sacrificed herself for him. He won't let Bonnie down; he can't. He refocuses and pretends to walk to the restrooms, only to sneak out the back door. Luke sprints toward the wooded area where they hitched the horses. When he arrives, Drew is already waiting on his horse.

"Come on, let's go, homie. We gotta move," Drew says to Luke.

"Come here, Pedro," Luke whistles and slaps his thigh to get the German Shepherd's attention.

Luke rummages through his pocket for the bacon he had stowed away for Pedro before he left the diner. Luke gives the piece of bacon to his dog. Pedro gobbles it down quickly and wags his tail in appreciation.

"Full steam ahead to Cottonmouth!" Luke says as he climbs onto Red.

Luke grips the reins and glances at Drew, who nods back. He takes a deep breath in and out. At the same time, the two teenagers squeeze their legs into their horses and take off like a bolt of lightning.

Over the horizon, Luke notices a massive, black-tar cloud looming over the city of Memphis. That combined with the cool air and familiar earthy scent warns him that a storm is coming. The Masked Haunter pops into his mind again, but he can't let Bonnie's sacrifice be in vain. Luke recalls what Bonnie had said in the barn. He presses his heels into Red's side, and the horse speeds up. Drew does the same once he realizes he's falling behind, but he makes up ground rather fast. Side by side, they ride full speed to Cottonmouth while Bonnie stays behind at the diner. Luke doesn't look back, despite wanting to. If he does, he fears he will go back to her.

* * *

Bonnie hasn't moved an inch since Luke kissed her, remaining as still as a statue. She is so enthralled by the experience that she still isn't fully convinced that what just transpired wasn't a dream. Her best friend and crush for the past decade has just kissed her. Once she realizes it was real, she simply waits for the officer to inevitably approach her. She had done her part of the journey. It is now up to Drew and Luke to finish it.

"Go get him, Luke," Bonnie whispers to herself.

19

THE TIME HAS COME

At 86 Birch Drive in Cottonmouth, a middle-aged man dressed in a stained white tank top and worn-out jeans is on the couch watching TV with a can of beer in his left hand and a cigarette in his right. The man has brown, messy, mop-like hair and rosy cheeks from being tipsy. Benjamin Miller is watching the news about the protests breaking out in Princeton County, his old town.

"Thank God I got out of that shit hole when I did," Ben tells himself before taking a long drag of his cigarette.

Ben's ears prick up when he hears his phone ring upstairs, but it is quickly silenced when his pregnant girlfriend Emily picks it up.

"Who is it, woman?" Ben asks.

"It's for you," Emily says.

Ben puts out his cigarette in the ashtray, heaves his frame out of the recliner and chugs the rest of his beer. As Ben unhurriedly ascends the stairs, he taps his chest to expel a loud belch trapped in his body. Once Ben enters the bedroom, he snatches the phone from his girlfriend's outstretched hand.

"This is Ben Miller, what do you want?" Ben asks.

"Hello Ben Miller, I'm with the Memphis Police Department. We just wanted to ask if you have a son with autism."

Ben pulls the phone away from his ear and glances at Emily. He sweeps his hand through his damp hair, wiping the sweat on his pant leg. Did he mishear the caller? How did this question come up? *Did the police know about his past?* Ben wonders. He quickly brings the phone back to his mouth, attempting to gather his composure so that he doesn't seem suspicious.

"Um . . . why are you asking?" Ben asks as he clears his throat.

"We got a report of three teenagers leaving Princeton County, one of which is a son to a Ben Miller. So, we just wanted to know if he is yours."

"I don't have a son, but I'm expecting a daughter in a couple months," Ben says, giving Emily a scowl.

"Well, congratulations, sir. Thank you for your time. Have a good day."

"You too. Bye."

Ben slams the receiver down onto the base of the telephone, causing the entire end table to rattle. His race reddens even more, and he stomps toward his girlfriend, Emily. He stares at her, huffing like a predator stalking its prey. She puts her head down, not daring to look at him. He's furious at her for picking up when the police called.

"You picked up when it was the cops. You handed me the phone knowing full well they wanted to speak to me! Why didn't you just say I wasn't home?" Ben screams.

"I'm sorry, Ben. I wasn't thinking," Emily says, looking down.

"Yeah, clearly. Now you need to be disciplined," Ben says.

Ben grabs Emily by her arm violently, pulling and thrusting her against the wall. She rotates her body to shield her round belly, but Emily's head slams with a raucous thud. Emily massages her head to ease the pain; her bell had been rung. Ben stands over her, casting a shadow. He huffs as Emily attempts to make herself as small as possible. This is punishment for her stupidity. Ben had "disciplined" Emily enough times that she has lost track.

"Next time you do that, I won't be so gentle," Ben says, pointing his finger at Emily.

"Yes, sorry, Ben. I love you," Emily says, backing away skittishly.

"I love you too."

Ben returns to the comfort of his recliner. The police's question swirls in his head like a tornado. *Why come after him, and why now?* he asks himself. Some kids had apparently deserted Blackroot, but it had to be a coincidence, and it must be a different Ben Miller they're looking for. He lights up another cigarette and tries to clear his mind of the phone call.

* * *

At a small apartment complex in Blackroot, Natalie has just arrived home from finishing her shift at the clothing store. As expected, her mother is not home; she is working. Her mother, Sisika Brown, is not very involved with Natalie's personal life. While she appreciates the independence, she wishes her mother would talk with her more. Natalie trots toward her small television and turns on the news, curious to see any updates on the school protests.

"Come on, just fire that teacher already. He's a horrible man," Natalie says as she throws her backpack on the couch.

Natalie sits back and watches the news, anticipating the board terminating Earl Calhoun. Only the newsman isn't reporting the protests but rather three missing teenagers from

Blackroot. Natalie jumps up, and her eyes bulge out when she looks at the television screen.

"Three missing teenagers. They can't be . . ." Natalie says as her hands cover her mouth and she lets out a horrified gasp.

Trouble continues in small-town Tennessee. Three local teenagers— Luke Ramirez, Bonnie Davis, and Drew Thompson— are missing from their homes in the small town of Blackroot. They were last seen yesterday morning, heading off to school—the very same school where protests against high school history teacher Earl Calhoun are still prominent after he allegedly was recorded making racist remarks toward an African American student.

It is believed the teenagers are heading to the city of Memphis. Authorities are searching for these teenagers and hoping to return them to their families soon. If anyone sees three teenagers on horses in the Memphis area, they are encouraged to contact the police immediately. Next up are the sports . . .

Natalie turns off the television. She looks out the window, recalling the argument with her mother yesterday. She had her ear chewed out when her mother found out that she slapped Sandy. Natalie grimaced as the wooden spoon struck across her forearm. She was warned not to leave the apartment for anything besides work or school for the next month. She tosses the remote to the side and quickly returns to her room. While swiftly changing into the first set of clothes she finds, Natalie glowers at the bruise she received yesterday, not caring about disobeying her mother. She grabs the phonebook and her keys and leaves her apartment.

"Memphis. Memphis. Benjamin Miller. Benjamin Miller," Natalie says to herself.

Natalie races downstairs to her car, flings her door open, juggles her key, and inserts it to start the engine. She turns on the radio and begins fiddling with the knob. Natalie grunts strongly, trying to find a station that will provide more information on the story. Stomping her foot on the gas pedal, she heads in the direction of the capital to locate her friends.

* * *

It has been nearly an hour and a half since Bonnie decided to stay behind at the diner. It's strange because, before that event transpired, all Luke could think about was getting to Cottonmouth to meet his father, but now he can't get Bonnie off his mind. A heavy guilt has come over him; it hangs like an anchor. Is this what the Masked Haunter meant by consequences from Luke's actions?

"Luke, hey Luke! Snap out of it, man!" Drew shouts.

Luke looks up and squints; down the road there is a sign. They trot toward it until the words become readable. The black paint on the rugged, wooden sign reads, Welcome to Shelby County, Home to Tennessee's Music City of Memphis. Drew pounds his fist into the air excitedly, and Luke chuckles, realizing they are less than half an hour from Memphis.

"Let's go."

"Right behind you man," Drew says.

* * *

A few minutes later, the officer's backup finally arrives at the diner. A couple of officers surround the booth Bonnie is in. She looks down, as if she's being interrogated. She glances up to two towering figures with hands on their hips, waiting for her to crack.

"They're heading to Memphis, officers," Bonnie says.

They look at one another as if surprised Bonnie revealed that information with no probing.

"Which direction did they go in, girl?" one officer demands, looming over her shoulder.

"I told you already, Officer, Memphis."

"I know, I heard you the first time, but there's multiple routes to Memphis. Which one did they take? Also, which address are they heading toward?"

"I don't know. Those boys don't listen to me half the time anyways, but I told them to take Route 84."

"Thank you. Was that so hard to say?"

"Am I free to go, Officer? You can't arrest me unless you have evidence that I've committed a crime."

"We're here to make sure you get home, not take you to jail. And no, you're not going anywhere until Ms. Ramirez comes to pick you up. Apparently, she's in the area, and your father gave her permission to pick you up."

"Can you at least take my horse back to my farm?"

"Sure, I'll get someone on it," the disgruntled officer says before taking out his walkie talkie.

Bonnie sits there, stewing, while the officers patrol around her booth. After about ten minutes, Courtney Ramirez and Mike Montgomery run through the diner entrance with panic written all over their faces, gasping for air. They scout for any sign of Luke and the others. Their eyes finally settle on Bonnie, near two police officers.

"Oh, Bonnie, thank God you're all right. Where are Drew and Luke?" Courtney asks.

"Ma'am, everything's under control. We'll handle the rest. We know where they're going, so take Ms. Davis home, and we'll bring your boy home," the officer says.

"May I come with you? I need to see my son, please. I might know where he's heading," Courtney says, clasping her hands together.

"Sorry, ma'am, but we can't bring you along. We don't know if it'll be dangerous."

"He's sixteen. It'll only become dangerous if he reaches—"

Courtney says before stopping after Mike places his hand on her shoulder.

"Calm down," Mike whispers.

"Are you saying there's nothing we can help with?" Courtney asks.

"You've done plenty, ma'am," the officer says.

Courtney begins seething but stops speaking to the stubborn officer before she says something she may regret later. Mike steps forward and clears his throat.

"Officer, she just wants to help her boy. Let us help," Mike says.

"As I said before, we got it handled, sir, now go home. This is the police's business now," the angry officer says, extending one arm out defensively.

"Yes, I understand officer," Mike says as he sucks his teeth.

"Bonnie, let's go. We're taking you home now," Courtney says.

They all march out of the diner and head to Mike's car. Courtney and Mike are irate at the fact Luke isn't there and that the officers refuse to let them help. Bonnie is only disappointed that she's not with Luke and Drew right now.

"I lied to them, Ms. Ramirez. Luke and Drew are taking the back roads. They should be in Memphis by now," Bonnie says.

"Why would you lie to the police?" Courtney asks.

"For Luke. He needs to do this. For him and you. You already had your chance to set things right a long time ago."

"What does she mean by that?" Mike asks.

"It's complicated, Mike."

"Try me. I'm not moving this car until I know the truth. I wanna know exactly what is going on," Mike says.

"Okay, fine!" Courtney yells as she pulls her hair in frustration.

Both Bonnie and Mike are listening intently now. The only person that knows the full truth is Courtney.

"I was married to a man named Ben Miller. He seemed so sweet for years, but when he found out Luke was autistic, he went crazy, started drinking, and lost his job. When he tried to beat Luke, I wouldn't let him, so . . . he beat me instead. I thought having another kid would help things. I kept it a secret for a few weeks to surprise him," Courtney says, licking her lips. She shudders as the memory of what happened next comes flooding back.

"When I told him, he . . . he didn't even acknowledge it. Af-after about five months, he was having one of his really bad days. He punched me so hard in the midsection I started bleeding internally and they couldn't . . . save my daughter. I told him as I was on the floor barely conscious that . . . he had just killed his daughter."

Courtney sniffles in between sentences and blows her nose. She notices Mike as he squeezes the steering wheel until his knuckles turn white. She turns her attention to Bonnie, whose eyes well with tears. A single tear streams down her face, but Bonnie's gaze doesn't turn away from Courtney. Bonnie looks as if she's watching a car crash. It's tragic, but she can't bring herself to look away. Courtney takes a deep breath before finishing the story.

"I looked up and saw the shock on his face, like he had just realized what he had actually done. Then everything went black, and I woke up in the emergency room. Luke must've somehow dialed 911. The first thing they told me was that I lost the baby due to internal bleeding. I cried all night, but Lucas was there by my side the whole time. When we finally went home, most of Ben's things were gone. I knew he wasn't coming back. I couldn't bear the thought of telling Luke that his father abandoned him or was in jail, if I reported it to the police. So, I told him that . . . he died in a car crash."

Courtney buries her face in shame. She quickly reaches into the console and pulls out a napkin to wipe her tears and blow her nose furiously. The normally level-headed Mike grinds his teeth and balls his fists. He looks like he could kill the next person he sees. Bonnie taps his shoulder to calm him down. Mike draws his breath in and quickly expels it out from his lungs. He reaches toward Courtney's back and pats it gently, which helps both of them regain their composure—until Mike's eyes widen with realization.

"That's why you asked if I . . . wow. I'm so sorry, Courtney. I had no idea. Do you want me to bring you home?" Mike asks, his voice breaking.

"No, Bonnie's right. We have to help my son get that SOB. I can see why Luke admires you, Bonnie."

"I know. He actually kissed me before he left the diner."

Mike and Courtney look at Bonnie and then at each other, mouths agape.

"Did you like it?" Mike asks, looking at Bonnie through the rearview mirror.

"Mike! That's so unlike Luke. He's usually so shy, but that was sweet of him," Courtney says as she slaps Mike's shoulder.

"He's amazing. I've fancied him for years. But now we have to get to Memphis. Wait, what was the address Luke told me?" Bonnie asks herself, scratching her head.

"86 Birch Drive, Cottonmouth. That's where he is," Courtney says.

"Okay, I know exactly where to go," Mike says.

Mike stomps on the gas pedal. He grew up in Memphis, so he knows its roads like the back of his hand. He quickly takes a sharp turn; the tires screech as they fight against the road. This led to the back roads, devoid of any police presence. They are going against direct orders from the Shelby County Police Department, but they all know they have to try and save Luke and Drew from possibly getting hurt—or worse.

* * *

Just outside of Memphis, Luke and Drew cherish the view of the musical city, relieved that they have finally made it to their destination. Pedro pants but is still wagging his tail noticeably around Luke. Luke offers Pedro the last of the water, which he voraciously licks from Luke's cupped hand.

"We did it, Drew. We're finally in Memphis."

"Hell yeah, man, we did it. Never a doubt in my mind. Now, where does your pops live again?"

Luke takes out the map and unfolds it. He squints at the directions that he wrote down. Luke slowly guides his finger across the foldable paper, searching for his father's address.

"86 Birch Drive, which is about five minutes to the north. Let's ride!"

"Right behind you," Drew says.

After about five minutes of riding on the back roads, they see the town sign, You Are Now Leaving Memphis. Come Back Soon. The smooth, paved roads swiftly shift into pothole-filled roads. The houses are isolated from each other—each house spaced nearly two hundred yards apart from the next. After several minutes of intense searching, they finally locate the street, Birch Drive. Luke stares bleakly as Pedro gets excited; he barks a couple times and accelerates toward the house with great speed, almost as if he knows what is next to come. Two minutes pass by, and a mailbox with the number 86 comes into view.

"Let's hitch the horses near the woods. Do you have the camera and tape recorder?" Luke asks.

"I sure do!" Drew says as he takes it out of the bag.

"Pedro, go toward the shed. Drew will be right there."

Pedro barks in compliance with the order Luke has just given him. He trots toward a large bush by the decrepit shed and sits down, waiting for Drew.

"You ready, Luke?"

"As ready as I'll ever be, Drew."

"Nice. Glad to hear that."

The house is shrouded by forest on all sides, invisible from anywhere else but the main road. It looks to be in poor condition. It has chipped paint, rotting wood, and stained windows. An old, rusted pickup truck is in the driveway. His father has to be home, Luke decides.

"I'll walk up while you hide over there in that bush and get pictures. I'll give you a signal to turn on the tape recorder," Luke says.

"Okay, what's the signal?" Drew asks.

"I'll put my left hand behind my back and give you a thumbs up."

"You know, once you knock on that door, there's no going back?" Drew asks.

Luke grapples with this question, looking at the house and back at Drew.

"I know, but all the people he's hurt, and Bonnie giving herself up to the police. I . . . I can't go back."

An eruption of thunder echoes around them. They look up at the sky. The grayness in the clouds signals a huge storm on the horizon. Their hair blows, as the wind has picked up steam.

"I understand. Good luck, brother. Make this quick. It's gonna pour any second," Drew says.

"I'll try, and thank you."

As Drew runs toward the rusted shed with Pedro, another rumbling of thunder bombards the city, like the mighty roar of a lion.

Luke flinches at the noises, and his body stiffens when he feels the first frigid drops of rain. He recounts his nightmare, when the Masked Haunter had killed his friends in a vile storm. He stands in the yard, anchored to the ground, shivering in the heavy rain, eyes not moving from the door. Can he really do this? He's not sure he can. No, it can't be. He didn't come this far to stop now, Luke tells himself.

"Come on man, we're wasting time!" Drew yells. "Sorry, I'm just thinking," Luke says.

"Well, think and move at the same time." "Okay, will do."

Luke marches through the yard, the water-absorbed ground caving in under his mass. Once Luke arrives at the porch, he looks back at Drew once more. From behind a bush, he gives a thumbs up. Luke cautiously ascends the steps, the wooden floorboards creaking loudly under his body weight. Luke gulps as he gazes at the old, paint-chipped door. After a few seconds, he summons the courage to knock three times.

"Ben! S-someone's at the door. Can you get it, please?"

The voice is somewhat distant but no doubt feminine, so Luke furrows his brow at first. Does he have the right address? He thought Ben would have been alone in this old house, but it appears that he has company.

"Be right there!" a gruff voice bellows.

Luke backs up, taking a deep breath. That has to be him.

"Emily, did you order pizza or something?" the same voice asks.

Who is Emily? The old rickety door opens, and a slightly overweight, middle-aged man towers over Luke with dark, unkempt hair that falls just short of his broad shoulders and a five o'clock shadow. The man is wearing an old, dirty-white tank top and worn- out jeans. He looks down with his bushy eyebrows raised and asks, "Can I help you with something, kid?"

"Yes, you can, Dad," Luke says through clenched teeth.

20

___

THE EXILED KIN

Ben squints his eyes, sticking his pinky finger into his ear and digging around. He rubs his fingers together and flicks the earwax aside.

"What was that, kid?" Ben asks.

"I'm your son, Lucas."

"Holy shit," Ben says, his eyes widening.

Ben looks absolutely flabbergasted, like he has just been given a surprise party that he didn't want. However, his initial shock seemingly turns into a slight curiosity. He pinches the bridge of his nose and slides his hand down his prickly stubble. Ben admires Luke like a piece of abstract art, as if unsure what to make of him. His father's icy stare sends chills down Luke's back, but he holds eye contact. Luke clears his throat. He decides it is best to be straightforward so he can figure all this out.

"Yeah, Bela told me the story about how you abandoned me."

"So, what you want from me?"

A rage engulfs Luke's entire body. He can't control it any longer. This man, who almost destroyed his family, has the

214

audacity to ask what he wants from him. Luke pounces on his father, driving him to the floor, and starts punching him repeatedly. It catches Ben completely off guard. He tries to protect his face with his hands, but that leaves his body wide open. Luke takes full advantage and wails on his kidneys to cause the most pain possible.

"Get off me, you little runt! You done lost your mind!"

"Oh, I'm crazy? You abandoned your family!" Luke yells, still throwing punches like a madman.

"Screw you!" Ben snaps.

Ben uses his superior size and strength to push Luke off him with his legs. He scurries behind his couch, and Luke quickly pursues him.

"Get out of my house before I shoot you!"

"Not a chance!" Luke says.

"Ok then, you little asshole. I warned you!" Ben shouts.

Luke charges at his father, but Ben pulls out a revolver from underneath his couch and points it at Luke. Quickly realizing this, Luke puts his hands up. Face to face with the silver barrel, Ben has him dead in his sights. In his peripheral view, Luke notices Drew outside the side window with his camera. He can tell by Drew's furrowed eyebrows and unsteady hands that he's scared for his friend's life. Luke clenches his chest; his heart is hammering and lungs gasping for air. He attempts to calm down by taking a long, deep breath, to no avail.

"Get . . . out . . . *now*!" Ben shouts as he massages his jaw.

Luke stands his ground; despite shaking and being short of breath, he does not move. He does not hear Ben's commands. Luke stands frozen in shock. His entire world is turned upside down. All he can see is the barrel of the gun pointed straight at him.

"Are you deaf or something? I can shoot you, and it'll be self- defense since you invaded my home," Ben says.

"I . . . I can't . . . leave. I need to know," Luke stutters.

"Put your hands up," Ben says.

Luke nods his head and does as ordered. His arms feel heavy, like two anchors about to crush him. Luke's anxiety rears its ugly head as sweat drips from his forehead down to his nose, and his father grins, seemingly knowing it's not just residual rain. Ben lowers his gun slightly and removes his finger from the trigger, but still keeps the weapon ready. He waves his hand in Luke's general direction, noticing the teenager's wild-eyed look.

"Damn. You really are my kid, huh? No normal kid would walk up my doorstep, claim to be my son, attack me, and stand like a fricking statue," Ben says as he chuckles.

Luke does not find any humor in what his father just described. He notices his heartbeat begin to slow down slightly, and he slowly regains some of his motor skills.

"I couldn't control myself. I'm . . . sorry for attacking you," Luke says, squeezing the sofa cushions.

Ben hesitates for a moment, as though considering his son's apology. He holsters his gun and pulls his tank top over it to conceal it. Ben snorts and spits some mucus in his ashtray.

"Fine, I'll ask one last time. What do you want?"

Luke casually lowers his hands down and gives Drew a brief thumbs up from behind his back. He grimaces as he stares at Ben the entire time to make sure his father doesn't take notice of his hand. He keeps it out of his sight as a precaution. Luke feels his heartbeat accelerating once again. He takes a deep breath to gather the courage to answer Ben's question.

"All right, I want—" Luke says.

"Ben, is everything all right? What's going on?" Emily asks.

Ben pulls out his revolver swiftly and Luke immediately puts his hands in the air once again. Ben lifts his finger to his mouth. Luke nods, understanding he wants him to be quiet.

"Everything's fine sweetheart, just an . . . unexpected visitor! Don't come down yet!" Ben yells.

It takes Luke everything in him not to yell for the woman to get out while she still can. The only thing keeping him in his place is the gun pointing at his head. His knees are weak, and he feels like a fool for getting himself in this circumstance, yet he doesn't regret it. Confronting his father and bringing him to justice is his only objective.

"The reason why you left me. Just the truth. A few minutes of your time," Luke says, massaging his white knuckles.

"Luckily, we ain't got nothing but time, son," Ben says.

"Well, glad we agree on something."

"Sit down."

"Oh, that's all right, I . . ."

"This ain't a discussion. Sit down. I won't tell you again," Ben hisses.

Luke immediately obeys this command. Once he sits, his legs start trembling. The only comfort keeping him from shutting down is knowing Drew is right outside. Luke notices that the house possesses a putrid odor of smoke, and alcohol permeates the air. The stench is so nauseating that it triggers Luke's gag reflex. He immediately covers his face to avoid vomiting. How can anyone live in these conditions? Luke wonders.

"Oh, how rude of me. Can I get you anything to drink, son? Hey, never thought I'd hear that sentence come out of my mouth," Ben says with a bright smile.

Ben laughs so hard at his own joke that he nearly hacks up a lung from coughing. Luke spots an ashtray. Ben seems to be just as much of a smoker as he is a drinker. Luke doesn't like the two of those put together. He decides to play along, act friendly. He doesn't want to risk the fact that Ben may have an itchy trigger finger.

"Water is fine, D-Dad," Luke says.

"That's more like it. See? We can just talk. No need to get rough. Don't start no funny business while I'm up."

Ben tucks his handgun in his pants and walks to the sink to get a glass of water for his son. Luke feels his entire body sag in relief that the gun is no longer aimed in his direction. His tongue feels unclean after uttering the word, *Dad*. Luke looks around the place; it is pretty empty. A soiled couch, an old recliner, a small, out-of-date television, and an end table that holds a lamp, two empty beer cans, and a full ashtray is all that occupies the living room. No coffee table, bookshelves, or family photos in sight.

"Here you go," Ben says as he hands Luke a cup of water.

Luke takes a huge gulp of water. It is the first drink he has had since the diner, but he nearly spits it out. It tastes like rust; the old, neglected pipes are the culprit. Luke powers through it and swallows the unpalatable drink. By the look of things, it seems very likely that Ben is unemployed.

"So, shoot with your questions. What do you wanna know?" Ben asks.

"First off, who is the woman who lives with you?" Luke asks.

"Oh, that's my girlfriend, Emily, who's pregnant, by the way," Ben says, tilting his head upstairs.

"Oh, well . . . congratulations," Luke says.

Luke lowers his head. When he hears that Emily is pregnant, he can't help but think of his sister whom his father killed. He also isn't too fond of the idea of a child being raised in this type of environment, with an abusive and jobless drunk as a father, in a house that appears in desperate need of repairs.

"Shit . . . I guess you know that part too," Ben says, noticing Luke keeping his head down.

"Why did you leave my mom and me?" Luke asks, holding back tears.

"The quick answer: we weren't right for each other," Ben says. "You mean I wasn't right for you!" Luke says, stomping his foot.

"I thought you were gonna be a burden; I thought you were

never gonna amount to anything. I'm sorry, son. I know now I was wrong," Ben says, rubbing his hands together.

Luke's father is not at all what he expected him to be. His grandmother had said that he was sweet at first and then turned into a wrathful monster when he discovered that his son has a disability. Yet, the man sitting in front of Luke looks to be a sad, miserable, middle-aged man living in his own filth. Luke almost feels sorry for him but then reminds himself of the story his grandmother had told him. Who is his father truly, deep down? Luke wonders.

"Do you know that you killed your daughter when you hit Mom, the day you left?"

Ben frowns and scratches the back of his head, making his mop-like hair move.

"You gotta know, I-I was . . . drunk and forgot that she was pregnant. When I saw what I had done, I left and never came back."

"You never came back because you knew you'd rot in a cell if you stayed," Luke argues, pointing his finger at Ben.

"Maybe you're right, but I already lost my job and had a bottle in my hand all the time by then, so I didn't really have much else to lose," Ben says. "I exiled myself because I knew your life would've been hell if I was in it."

"My life hasn't been much better than that, if I'm being completely honest."

"How you mean?" Ben asks.

"All my life I've been bullied, my Bela's very sick, a girl broke my heart, and I found out my dad left me and nearly killed my mom."

Ben smacks his lips at this information. Luke narrows his eyes. He can't tell if Ben is empathetic or apathetic at what he has just told him. One moment he was smiling brightly, and then a second later he was frowning boldly.

"Well, I'm sorry about Sophie being sick. The bullying explains the black eye," Ben says.

Luke touches his left eye, feeling some pain from the pressure of his fingers. He had forgotten about his black eye, since a lot of the pain and bruising had faded. The fight with Rob, Travis, and Brandon seemed so long ago, but it was only last week.

"You should've seen the other guy," Luke says.

Ben laughs for several seconds, while Luke's gaze falls to the side. Luke has no idea why he made that comment. It was the first thing that sprang to mind when Ben mentioned his black eye. While his father is laughing, Luke attempts to think of a means of escape. Luke notices Drew capture pictures of Ben and is hopeful that his friend got Ben's confession. The only problem: Luke isn't sure how to get out without getting a bullet put in him.

"It's not all bad. I have two amazing friends, a loving mother, a grandma that's not afraid to tell the truth, and a passion for justice."

"That's something. Not bad, Lucas," Ben says.

"I prefer Luke, and you were wrong. My disability isn't a curse; it's a blessing. I have to work twice as hard as most folk to do some everyday tasks, like social interacting or getting a job. I do enjoy the challenge, and having a loving family helps me."

"Good for you. Even though you banged up my kidneys," Ben says.

"Thanks, but I didn't come for your approval or validation. I have that at home."

"No. You came for the truth, right? Why don't we go out? There's this great family place on the other side of Memphis. You'll love it," Ben implores, trying to sell his son on this offer.

"I don't really want to. We're fine right here."

"Oh, come on, you came all this way. It'd be rude of me not to bring you. Speaking of which, how did you get here?"

"Horseback. One of my friends lives on a ranch," Luke says.

Ben's eyes widen initially, and his mouth opens, perplexed, exposing his yellowing teeth. His shocked expression quickly turns into a slight smirk.

"Interesting. So, your mother isn't here with you?"

"No . . . no she isn't," Luke says, struggling to look Ben in the eye.

Luke has a strong inclination that by now his mother is on her way, but he feels that Ben shouldn't be aware of that. Luke knows he has to be careful with what information he shares with his father.

"Huh, okay, we'll have some father and son bonding time, and I'll get you home before dark," Ben says.

Luke looks at his father and is met with a slight grin. Ben's facial expression keeps changing; it is off-putting for Luke. He smiles and darts his eyes around the room quickly, hopeful that someone will arrive in the vicinity and interrupt them.

"Um . . . like I said, I'm good, but thank you for the offer," Luke says.

"I'm afraid I must insist that you go with me," Ben says as he pulls his gun out.

"O-okay."

"Emily, come down here and meet my son!" Ben yells.

"Okay, I'll be right down," Emily says.

Ben rapidly conceals the gun once again. They both notice the shadow appearing upstairs. A redheaded woman walks downstairs gingerly. Her belly is as large and round as a beach ball. Luke bites his tongue, recalling a time when his mom told him, 'Never ask or assume a woman is pregnant. They'll usually tell you. You don't want to hurt their feelings if they're just fat.' He doesn't fully comprehend how it's not polite, since pregnant women are fat.

"I heard some yelling. What happened?"

"Nothing. Emotions ran a little high. Oh, Emily, this is my son, Luke Miller."

"Actually, it's Luke Ramirez," Luke says.

"Nice to finally meet you, Luke. I'm Emily Sullivan. Ben has told me about you."

"Has he really?" Luke asks, tilting his head to the side.

"Yes, of course. Told me all about how tough it was for him that he didn't get custody from the divorce."

Luke attempts to look past Emily, but she tugs Luke into her and wraps her pale arms around him. She has to bend over due to the size of her belly. The hug makes Luke stiffen his body, since he is not used to receiving hugs from complete strangers. He keeps a level head to not scare her or give a reason for his father to pull the trigger. He catches a quick glance of his father. Luke thought that he saw Ben's face drop when he discovered that his son took his ex-wife's maiden name rather than his. Luke hopes it was just his eyes playing tricks on him again.

"Hopefully you get to meet your half-sister; her due date is in about three weeks," Emily says.

"Con-congratulations, I can't wait to meet her," Luke says.

"Yeah, her name will be Abigail. Abby for short," Emily says.

"That's a lovely name," Luke says.

Emily is perky, and she looks a decade or more younger than Ben, which creeps Luke out. Before he can dwell on this disturbing thought, Luke notices what looks to be a bruise on her arm. Emily quickly hides it from him, covering it with her sleeve.

"Oh, I fell down the stairs, but the baby is fine. I'm a klutz," Emily says.

"We're gonna head out and catch up a little," Ben says.

"Are you sure, Ben? It's getting nasty out there," Emily says.

"Yeah, we won't be long, right boy?" Ben says as he puts his arm around Luke.

Luke quickly wriggles away from his father's grip.

"Ri-right," Luke says while wearing a strained smile.

"Okay, I'll start making dinner for when you boys get back," Emily says.

"Sounds great, honey," Ben says.

Ben keeps the gun hidden from his girlfriend, pretending he doesn't have it, but Luke knows he does. It makes Luke sick to his stomach that he is Ben's prisoner. He can't stop thinking about the destination Ben plans on taking him to.

"We'll be back soon; come on Luke," Ben says as he wraps his large arm around Luke's neck.

"I would . . . okay, fine," Luke says.

Ben and Luke walk outside toward the pickup truck, and Luke feels a couple raindrops land on his skin. Out of the corner of his eye, Luke sees Drew with a confused expression on his face. Luke mouths, "Help me." Ben pushes Luke into the passenger seat of the truck. Luke buckles up, and Ben gets in and starts the engine.

"Off we go! You're gonna love this place, son, trust me," Ben says, smiling.

Suddenly, Ben lifts his son's head, catching a closer look at him, and Luke jerks away. His breath is shaky and body stiff as he stares at the floor, feeling violated.

"Wow . . . you got your mother's eyes. Big and brown," Ben says as he steps on the gas pedal.

* * *

Drew peers from around the side of the house, ducking for the bushes as the truck's headlights turn on.

"What the hell, Luke? What about the plan? Why'd you have to jump him?" Drew asks himself.

As the pickup truck starts backing out of the driveway, Drew realizes what's happening and springs into action.

"Wait, where's Ben taking him? Hold up, okay, I got you Luke," Drew says as he unhitches Blacksmith.

"Pedro, you have to stay here," Drew says to the German Shepherd as the pickup truck disappears into the fog.

He opens the last can of dog food and throws it inside the shed. Pedro rushes ahead and starts chowing down. Drew closes the door behind him, as he doesn't want Pedro getting soaked in the rain that is coming down with more force by the second.

"I got two pictures of that oversized Oompa Loompa pointing a gun at Luke. The first one is blurry, but the second one isn't. I got the tape recording, but the audio isn't the best. Crap. Hopefully the police can at least get him on kidnapping or something," Drew whispers quietly to himself as he mounts his horse.

"Okay, Blacksmith, follow that rusty pickup truck!" Drew says as he leaves the property.

21

DRIVE TO INSANITY

On the highway, Mike is in hot pursuit of the teenagers. He hasn't felt blood pumping through his veins like this since he found out his ex-wife cheated on him. The radio is on in case they hear an update on any of the stations. Nothing yet, only the lyrics of Toby Keith's "Does That Blue Moon Ever Shine on You" fill their ears.

"We're about forty-five minutes from Memphis. This is a hell of a storm. I can barely see the road," Mike says as he turns on the windshield wipers.

"Luke and Drew should be at Ben's by now. God have mercy."

"I'm sure they're fine, Ms. Ramirez. They have a tape recorder and camera to get the evidence."

"If Ben finds out they're trying to get him arrested, he'll go ballistic," Courtney says.

"Should I step on the gas?" Mike asks.

"Go as fast as you can without going over the speed limit. I don't want Luke being out there in that storm long," Courtney says while fanning tears from her eyes.

"Does Luke remember?" Bonnie asks.

"Pardon me? Mike, turn that off for now," Courtney says.

The music ceases so that Courtney can hear Bonnie clearly, while Mike quietly sulks at the fact one of his favorite songs is no longer playing.

"You said Luke was in front of you when Ben punched you, and that he was three years old," Bonnie says.

"I did say that," Courtney says.

"Luke told me he didn't have any memories of his father, but by that age, you're already forming your first memories," Bonnie says.

"You're right," Mike says.

Courtney places her hand on her forehead and shakes her head. A tear rolls down her cheek, the clarity of her son's suffering now revealed.

"Oh my God, I was dead set on him not knowing the truth, but he must've blocked it out because the experience traumatized him."

"Courtney, it's okay, you'll make it right in the end. I know you will," Mike says. "Funny how I ran after my wife after she was unfaithful to me. However, this son of a bitch beats you, and yet he ran away. Something ironic about that."

"Your ex-wife cheated on you?" Bonnie asks, leaning out of her seat.

"Vows meant nothing," Mike says, grumbling.

"Let's just focus on getting the kids back safe," Courtney pleads. "Absolutely," Mike says.

Bonnie gazes out the window; she can just make out the shadow of the city through the storm.

"Just hang in there, boys, we're on our way," Bonnie says.

* * *

The rain is no longer light or gentle; it has evolved into heavy sleet. As the rain pelts Drew powerfully, his hair starts to deflate, becoming flatter and flatter with each passing second. So, it won't impede his vision, Drew pulls his hair back. Drew wonders where Ben is taking Luke. Unfortunately, by the look of things, Luke had not gone with Ben willingly, though Drew wasn't exactly sure what Luke was thinking anymore.

* * *

Ben drives through the city while staring at the roads coldly, like the storm hasn't fazed him in the slightest. The fog obscures their vision; neither Luke nor Ben can see five feet in front of them. Luke rocks back and forth, attempting to distract himself by looking around the city.

He has never been to Memphis before, but he has heard stories about the attractions that lure people from all over the state. Given his circumstances, he would rather be anywhere but here. The scenery is something out of a nightmare: lightning races across the sky, while the anticipation of the unknown chills his bones.

"So, have you given any thought to your future career?" Ben asks.

"You really want to talk while you hold me hostage?" Luke asks.

"Yeah, we're gonna talk. I wanna know a little more about you before we get to where we're going. So, again, what you plan on doing with your life?"

Ben lifts his tank top, revealing the gun, reminding Luke who is in charge here. Sweat drips down Luke's forehead, but he clears his throat casually, not daring to raise suspicions. He decides it is best to go along and ignite a normal conversation.

"Um . . . not really. I don't know what I'm good at or what I like to do, but people keep telling me that I will know soon."

"I'm sure they do, and they're right, son. You'll find your purpose in this life. We all have one," Ben says.

"What's your purpose, exactly?"

"Before, I was a mechanic, a damn fine one at that."

"But what happened?" Luke asks.

Although Luke already knows the truth, he wants to hear it from Ben himself. He desires to take his mind off the situation.

"Well, like I said, I couldn't bear the thought of my son having a disability, and I drank so much that one day I nearly killed a coworker, so they fired me," Ben says.

"Have you found your new purpose?"

"Well, I spent years with my parents, and then they passed away. My father had lung cancer and my mom, well, let's just say she didn't take his death so well."

"Was it a broken heart that killed her?" Luke asks.

Ben pauses; his eyes shift toward his son and then back to the road.

"One can put it that way. I'll tell you another time. So, then I met Emily. Now we're gonna have a baby, and I will apply to this mechanic in town looking for a new employee," Ben says.

"That . . . sounds great."

"It sure is, son. Last question, been bugging me since you arrived. Why come find me now? When they tell you about me?"

"I only found out you were alive a couple days ago. Bela told me. Mom said you died."

Ben chuckles. He puts two fingers to the side of his neck, checking to make sure he still has a heartbeat. "Still got a pulse. We'll be at the place in two minutes, just relax," Ben says.

Luke swallows, his throat becoming increasingly dry. Luke jiggles the door handle, but the door doesn't budge. With each passing moment, he feels increasingly uncomfortable. They are no longer in the concrete jungle of Memphis. He looks out the water-covered window. The roads are abandoned, and forests circle the area on both sides.

Luke's brain starts moving a mile a minute. He begins

playing all the plausible scenarios in his head. He is positive that he is being taken to his death, as he moves his eyes toward the gun tucked in Ben's pocket. Luke wants to reach for it, but his instincts prevent him from risking his life. He decides to wait for an opening, if he is going to get out of this alive.

"We're not in the city anymore."

"No, we're not," Ben says flatly.

"Isn't the famous Mississippi River nearby?"

"Sure is. Can almost hear it." Ben says in the same emotionless tone.

* * *

Not far behind, Drew is pursuing the pickup truck. He can see the taillights, but the fog consumes the body of the truck. Invisible to his eyes, Drew squints to not lose sight of the vehicle.

"Not too close now, Blacksmith. We don't want Luke's pops knowing we're following him."

Drew squints down at the map of Tennessee. It is drenched, but he can still read it. He speculates on where Ben could be taking Luke. Drew notices there is a restaurant, but it's four in the afternoon; it's too early for dinner. No amusement park would be open in this weather. The only place in this direction is a mental hospital right on the outskirts of Memphis. No. He wouldn't, would he? The map disintegrates in his hands.

"I gotta stop him before Luke gets chucked into a nuthouse," Drew says.

* * *

"Well, here we are," Ben says.

Luke shakes like a leaf. On one side of him is nothing but dark secluded woods, and on the other is the Mississippi River.

Is he going to shoot me in the woods and dump my body in the river? Luke worries. He is relieved when he sees a building up ahead, the only one for miles. Luke looks back. He can hardly see the outline of the city behind him. Benjamin pulls over in front of the mysterious building.

"This is our stop," Ben says.

"What is this place?" Luke asks as he unbuckles his seatbelt.

Luke squints as he peers out the window to get a better look at the building through the ominous fog. The structure in front of Luke is unlike any he's ever seen before. It is massive and dark gray and looks almost haunted. There are metal bars on all the windows, a chain- link fence around the perimeter, and the structure is made of solid concrete. At first glance, Luke thinks it is a prison before noticing there are no guards or spotlights.

"It's a home where you can meet people like yourself. I'll bring you in, and then I can pick you up in a few hours."

"No thanks, I don't really want—"

Luke and Ben get out of the truck. As a flash of lightning momentarily lights up the area, Luke scans the building plaque in front of him. A dread weighs down on his shoulders, each passing word he reads making it heavier and heavier until the sentence is complete. The Redwoods Psychiatric Ward.

"Wait, this is an insane asylum! What is this?" Luke asks.

Luke turns around to face his father, squinting to see his face more clearly, hoping to hear something along the lines of, "Sorry, son, I took a wrong turn." Tragically, it isn't the case. Ben is making the same disdainful frown Luke is sure his father made briefly back at the house. His nostrils flare, eyes narrow, and teeth bare like a rabid dog.

"Oh, so you can read. You're just full of surprises, ain't you?" Ben says.

A look of pure rage engulfs Ben's face. This must have been

Ben's plan all along, to bring him here. All that talk was just that, talk.

"Come here, boy, this is for your own good!" Ben says.

Ben grabs Luke forcibly and starts dragging him toward the entrance by his arm. Ben grunts as Luke drags his heels on the wet concrete in an attempt to stay put.

"The more you fight, the more you'll prove my case, boy! They'll lock your stupid ass up forever for acting like a lunatic!"

"Let me go!" Luke says, swinging at the air above him.

"You shouldn't have ever come here! Should've left well enough alone. You already ruined my life once; you're not taking this second chance from me. Just be glad I didn't shoot you like a dog when I had the chance," Ben yells.

"You don't deserve a second chance, you sociopath!" Luke screams.

The rain makes it difficult for Ben to keep a firm grip on Luke at first, but he recovers and grabs Luke forcefully by his arm and shirt collar. The collar of Luke's shirt begins to tear as he resists; Luke kicks his legs back at Ben's shin, helplessly. Ben is much stronger, and Luke can't fight much longer. Ben's hands locked on Luke's forearm feel equivalent to a python constricting the life out of a mouse, secured tightly, with no intention of releasing its prey. The more Luke fights, the more insane he looks. Luke begins to hyperventilate, fearing that he will spend the rest of his life in this place.

"Got you now, boy," Ben says.

"Luke, behind you!" Drew calls out.

"What the hell is that?" Ben asks as he peers intently in the direction of the yell.

This is Luke's chance, perhaps his only one. He kicks Ben's shin as hard as he can. The force causes Ben to release his hold on his son and sink to the pavement. Ben places his hands over his shin and grimaces over the sharp pain he feels in his leg.

"Ow! Why, you little shit!" Ben howls.

"Quick, Luke, hop on!" Drew says as he lowers his hand for Luke to grab.

Luke attempts to jump onto Blacksmith, but he slips in a puddle. He falls face-first onto the cold, wet pavement. The horse neighs and raises his front legs. As they plummet back to the ground, Luke moves out of the way. He had been directly beneath the horse and was mere inches away from his head being trampled.

"Shit! You okay?" Drew asks.

"Yeah, I'll live," Luke says as he winces in pain.

Drew has to lap around again, due to the horse being frightened. Luke licks the inside of his mouth and discovers that his gums are bleeding. He also feels that his front tooth has been chipped. The metallic taste of iron saturates his mouth. He spits and a glob of red mucus plops on the ground. Just as he lifts himself off the sidewalk, Ben tackles him from behind like a football player, creating an enormous splash.

"No you don't, boy!" Ben bellows.

"Get . . . off . . . me . . . you murderer!" Luke says.

"Hey, ugly!" Drew shouts.

This distraction causes Ben to look up momentarily. Luke realizes Drew has provided an opening for him. Luke quickly chops Ben in the throat, feeling his hand drive back to Ben's Adam's apple. This causes Ben to fall backward and cough frantically as he gasps for air.

"Now, Luke!" Drew yells.

Luke scurries to his feet and dashes toward Drew. He grabs Drew's dripping, outstretched hand, pulls himself onto the horse, and throws his leg over the other side of the enormous, black horse. As Luke adjusts himself, he looks over his shoulder and sees Ben getting to his feet.

"I'm on!" Luke says to Drew.

"Get us out of here!" Drew orders Blacksmith.

"This isn't over . . . not by a long shot!" Ben screams as he reaches for his revolver.

With Drew and Luke mounted on his back, Blacksmith gallops out of there as fast as Drew can get him to go. Moments later, a sudden crack echoes past Luke's left ear. Ben fired a shot that was centimeters from hitting Luke. Adrenaline rushes through Luke's body as he feels his heart racing like he just ran a marathon. Luke doesn't look back. He wants to get as far away from the place as possible.

* * *

"Hello? Anybody out there?" A voice calls out.

"Shit," Ben whispers as he runs into his pickup truck.

A beam of light flashes from the institution's entrance, futilely attempting to penetrate the thick fog. The beam changes direction, as if trying to locate something or someone in the mist. A middle-aged man with short hair calls out.

"Hello? I'm Ed, an employee here. I thought I saw some headlights and heard some commotion. Is anybody out there?"

Ed anticipates a response but does not receive one, other than the powerful howl of thunder in the sky and heavy droplets of water pummeling the ground. Ed cautiously approaches the entrance gate.

"If you're out there, visiting hours are over. You need to leave. You can come back tomorrow."

Ed reaches the gate, only to find there is no one there. He shines his flashlight to the ground, and his eyes open wide as possible. On the ground are three fired bullet shells. He quickly shines the flashlight both left and right.

"If this is some kind of prank, it ain't funny. I'm . . . I'm gonna call the police if you don't show yourself!" Ed stutters.

He begins to back up slowly, not turning his back in case the person who fired is still in the area. In a few moments, he arrives at the door, reaches into his pocket, and tries to find his identification tag. He groans and pats himself frantically before realizing his tag isn't on him.

"Crap. Did I drop it out here? Or did I leave it inside?"

He doesn't risk searching for the tag. Ed pages the nurse, the only other employee on call right now. After a few minutes, when no one comes to the door, he begins knocking vigorously.

"Joanna! Open the door and call the damn police. Something ain't right out here!" Ed howls.

Ed's ears pick up something faint on the other side of the hospital. The chain-link fence rings as if someone is trying to climb it. He jogs to the other side and points his flashlight indiscriminately, not seeing anyone along the fence.

"Must have been the wind or something," Ed tells himself.

He takes one step before looking at the ground. He kneels down and picks up a plastic, rectangle card. Rotating it in his hand, he squints his eyes and realizes it's his ID tag.

"How ... the ..."

* * *

Drew and Luke run for their lives. The rain and wind pound their faces as they try to put distance between themselves, Ben, and the mental hospital. Luke puts pressure on his ear, in an attempt to stop the ringing.

"What the hell just happened?" Drew demands.

"I have no idea! It just came out of nowhere," Luke says.

"Shit, is he shooting at us?"

"Quick, take us into the woods," Luke says.

Drew pulls the reins to the right, leading the horse into the tree line.

"What kind of father tries to drag his own son into a nuthouse?" "The kind that abandons his son and nearly kills his mother. I should've seen it coming a mile away."

As water streams down his cheeks, Luke can't tell whether it's just rain pelting his face or tears. He really wanted to believe his father changed a little and regretted what he did. But he couldn't change just like Luke couldn't, he thought. Luke didn't know if anyone really could.

"I'm sorry, man, I would've stopped you sooner if I realized where he was taking you."

"No, it's my fault. I should've never got in the truck."

"It's all right, man, it's not your . . . crap, we gotta stop. It's too thick. The horse can't get through the brush."

Drew tugs back on the reins. Blacksmith snorts, raising his neck upward. The horse obeys, finally slowing down short of the dense forest.

"We can hide in the trees. The fog will cover the horse," Luke says.

"Woah," Drew says as he taps the side of the horse's massive neck.

Drew jumps off Blacksmith while Luke slides his foot into the stirrup, wheezing as he lifts his leg. Feeling unsteady, Luke reaches out his hand. Drew notices this and grabs Luke's hand, wrenching him off. Luke slips, collapsing to his hands and knees. Drew leads the horse to an oak tree and hitches it. Luke spots a dead tree, partly covered by bushes. He taps Drew's shoulder, pointing toward the rotted trunk. They sprint, diving behind the log. Gluey mud envelopes Luke's forearms and pant legs. Jagged breaths escape Luke's lungs; Drew raises his finger to his lips. Luke covers his mouth, silencing the heavy breathing. Seconds feel like an eternity before the sound of rustling tree branches and heavy footsteps attract their attention.

"Where are you?! I saw you head this way. I have a good thing going here, and I'm not about to let you or your mother take it away from me," Ben yells. "You can't hide. I know that big-ass animal can't make it far through here! You kick hard, boy! Bad news for you, I kick harder!" Ben screams.

Luke hears the sounds of heavy footsteps splashing through puddles coming closer and fast. He closes his eyes and nestles deeper behind the log.

"Why don't you come out?" Ben calls.

Luke twists his head toward Drew with his eyes open wide. Drew side-eyes him and sharply inhales, not uttering a word. Luke's entire body is trembling. He has to clench his jaw from making any sounds.

"No? Maybe this will help you change your mind," Ben says. "What do we do now?" Drew whispers.

"Do you have the tape recorder?" Luke whispers back. "Nah, I left it on the horse," Drew says.

"Last warning!" Ben bellows.

Seconds later, three rounds fire off into the forest—one is fired in the boys' general direction. Luke jerks his entire body and covers his ears, putting all his effort into not making a single sound. Drew's mouth drops when he hears his horse neigh loudly across from them. The animal bucks in a panic from the noise.

"Oh, look what we have here, your horse. Let's see how far you get without it," Ben says gleefully.

"What's going on, Drew?"

"He's gonna kill the horse unless we give ourselves up."

"We can't. He'll kill us next."

"If that horse dies, we have no way out," Drew says.

"Last chance," Ben says. "One Mississippi. Two Mississippi. Three Mississippi. Okay, this horse is history."

Luke's entire body begins to ache; he can feel his lungs begging for air. He fortifies himself, preparing for a bullet to be fired, followed by a humongous thud hitting the earth. Only he hears nothing, just the continuing sound of rain hitting the foliage.

"Son of a bitch!" Ben bellows.

"He's out of ammo," Drew whispers.

They hear footsteps squelching through the terrain heading in the opposite direction. The sound swiftly fades away into the distance. Luke and Drew poke their heads above the rotting wood and rise to their feet and run back to the horse. Luke pats the horse to calm him down before freeing him from the tree.

"I'm . . . a foul mess," Luke says, gazing at his drenched clothes and filthy hands.

"We have to get the hell out of here," Drew says.

"Cold. Wet. Dirty. Where . . . am I?" Luke says as his senses overload. His brain puts a stranglehold on all his actions.

"Luke?"

Drew turns around and observes Luke pacing back and forth, tugging on his wet hair. Luke collapses, and his breathing becomes erratic. He clasps his hands over his ears and starts groaning.

"All wrong!" Luke says.

"No . . . not now. Luke, stay with me!" Drew says, running toward Luke.

Drew reaches his hand out, but Luke slaps it away. He leans back against a tree, and rocks, hitting his head against the trunk. Loud moans emit from Luke's mouth, and he blinks his eyes rapidly. Drew tries approaching Luke again, who immediately starts screaming until he backs off.

* * *

"I can't touch him, and we can't stay here. What would Bonnie do?" Drew whispers to himself, looking back at Luke.

Drew scratches his square chin and exclaims. He trudges to the horse and rummages through the saddle bags, eventually finding what he's looking for, Bonnie's journal.

"Bingo," Drew says to himself as he looks back at Luke muttering unintelligible words.

He flicks some mud off his fingers before turning the pages rapidly, looking for any useful tips on how to calm down Luke when he's like this. At first, it's just poems and homework notes. Finally, he finds a quarter taped to a sheet that says, "Give to Luke if he's having a meltdown." Below, it also mentions to, "Count from one to ten and repeat until he comes back." Drew rips the quarter out and cautiously approaches Luke, who is still rocking. He drops the quarter in Luke's palm. Slowly, Luke rubs the shiny surface of the coin. He fidgets with it, spinning it between his fingers like a top. His moans turn to clicks, and his eyes turn to Drew.

"One. Two. Three. Four. Five . . ." Drew says.

* * *

It takes Drew three rotations of counting before Luke regains his composure. He hangs onto the now grimy quarter and continues stimming with it.

"We have to get out of here. Are you okay? We lost you there for a second."

Luke ignores the second sentence. He spins around, slowly remembering where he is. Luke pinches his nose and takes a couple deep breaths. Luke pats the horse to calm the animal and himself down.

"Right. How about we head east?" "What if we get lost?" Drew asks.

"We won't. East leads back to the city; we can get back to the house. Besides, we can't go any deeper into the woods, and back west is my crazy father. Our options are limited."

"I don't agree, man. We should go to the police!"

"Did you get anything we can use as evidence?" Luke asks.

Drew searches the saddlebags for the camera and tape

recorder to show Luke what he managed to capture back at the house. Luke stares at the photos, clutching the camera as he shudders.

"Yeah man, got one of him pointing the gun right at you and another of him pushing you into the truck. The rain made the pics blurry though. It might be enough to bust him, it might not."

"I still can't believe that happened back there," Luke says, shaking his head.

"Me neither. Give it here."

A thought forms in Luke's mind as he hands Drew back the tape recorder and camera. It is a risky plan, but this has become more personal than ever. Luke shuts his eyes, inhales slowly and lets out a deep breath. He opens his eyes again and says, "We have to go back."

"To where? The woods? Home?" Drew asks.

"No, to 86 Birch Drive."

"Maybe you *should* be in a nuthouse, because you're talking crazy right now!"

"Pedro and Red are still there. We can't turn back now; we've come too far."

"The police will get them for us, Luke. This is done. We did all we could. I got pictures of him pointing the gun at you. We can get him on assault and kidnapping."

"But not murder? Or domestic abuse?" Luke asks. "Besides you just said it might not be—"

"I know what I said! Listen Luke, I don't think . . . it won't happen, man. I tried, man, the audio sucks ass on this thing. I don't think it'll be enough to get him on the shit he did to your mom," Drew says.

"I attacked him first, and I was in his house. They can charge me with trespassing. I'm so stupid!" Luke says as he kicks a couple rocks.

"We tried, man. I would've done the same if I were in your shoes," Drew says.

"Listen, he has a girlfriend, pregnant, and I think he beats her. No, I know he does. It's my mom all over again,"

"What do you mean?" Drew asks.

"She has bruises. I saw them with my own eyes, and she is pretty timid around Ben. If we don't go back now, she and the baby could end up like my mom and sister did. I can't let that happen, Drew. I'm going back with or without you," Luke explains.

Drew shakes his head and places his hands on his hips. He sucks on his teeth and glares back at Luke. Luke folds his arms and stares back at Drew, not giving an inch. Drew lets out a long sigh and concedes defeat.

"Luke, you're both stubborn and cocky as hell, but that's what I like most about you. I'm in," Drew says.

Luke hands Drew the dirty coin back, who puts it in his pocket just in case.

"Not cocky, just concerned. But good. Now hurry, we don't have much time to waste. Let's go!"

Drew jumps on top of Blacksmith and reaches down. Luke hesitates but grabs onto Drew's outstretched hand and gets on.

"All right!" Drew shouts as he pushes his heels into Blacksmith's sides.

Blacksmith gallops through the trees, fighting through the branches. Before long they're out in the open, heading back toward the city.

22

NO TURNING BACK

The police have blocked off the main roads, so traffic is backed up for miles. Off the highway, on the back roads, Mike, Courtney, and Bonnie are driving through the storm, hustling to get to Memphis. "Come on, Mike, we should've been at Memphis half an hour ago," Courtney says.

"Finding a different route ain't easy. This fog is thick as hell. This damn storm came out of nowhere."

"We'll be at 86 Birch Drive in about ten minutes or so," Bonnie says as she presses her index fingers to her head, trying to remember map directions.

"How do you know that, sweetie?" Courtney asks.

"I looked at that map of Tennessee for nearly two days straight," Bonnie says.

"We're going straight to 86 Birch Drive? You sure about this, Court?" Mike asks.

"I've never been surer of anything in my life," Courtney says. "Police won't get there first I reckon, right?" Mike asks.

"There's far too many Ben Millers for them to get there before us," Bonnie says.

"Good, it has to be us that stops him. It has to," Courtney says.

"Is there a way to get past the traffic?" Mike asks.

"A right turn is coming up. After that, it should be smooth sailing from there. Then it will be about a ten-minute ride," Bonnie says.

"I like this girl, Courtney," Mike says, smiling as he slowly turns right to avoid hydroplaning.

"I do too," Courtney says.

"We will be there soon. Luke and Drew, please don't do anything foolish," Bonnie says to herself.

* * *

In the saturated outskirts of Memphis, Drew and Luke are racing against time. The roads are empty, it appears, as though the city has been completely abandoned. No one is foolish enough to drive in these conditions. The city differs vastly from the small town that Luke grew up in. The buildings are tall and numerous, like mountain ranges.

Earlier Luke was so focused on speaking with his father that he had not noticed the bright city around him initially. He reminisces about the small trees, fire hydrants, and billboard signs scattered along the city. On the side of the road, a tall, gray rectangle comes into view. When they're within ten feet of it, Luke sees that the rectangle is a phone booth.

Luke stares at the old phone booth, the cracked glass indicating that the booth had been neglected for years. It gives him an idea that he will call his grandmother. She can inform him how long ago his mother left and how close she might be. Luke has to know that if he is putting their lives on the line, there is the slimmest of hopes that the authorities or his mother will get to them before Ben.

"Wait, Drew. Stop!" Luke says.

"Huh, why?"

"I gotta make a phone call. Give me the quarter, please."

"Woah there," Drew says to the horse.

Blacksmith stops and Drew digs into his side pocket and pulls out the same quarter he gave Luke with back in the woods.

"Here you go, man. Hopefully you don't need this later," Drew says.

"Thank you, friend."

"Make it quick. We're soaked, and he could be right on our tail," Drew says.

Luke dismounts, nearly slipping over a puddle, and then he jogs toward the phonebooth. He has to talk with his grandmother; he needs to tell someone what has happened. His father had nearly dragged him into a mental institution. The truth is, Luke isn't sure if he should go back; he almost doesn't want to. So far, the Masked Haunter's warning seems to be coming to fruition.

Luke steps inside the glass booth and jams the quarter into the coin slot. As the phone rings, he hears his heartbeat accelerate and his breathing deepen. He can only hope that his grandmother picks up.

"Come on, Bela, pick up, please," Luke whispers to himself.

"Hello?" Sophie says, her voice frail but sweet.

"Hi, Bela!"

"Luke! Is it really you?" Sophie asks.

"Bela, I just wanted to say you were right for wanting him in jail. He literally just tried to drag me to an insane asylum," Luke says.

"The nerve of that man! Where are you now?! You need to go far away from him!"

"I am. But he has a pregnant girlfriend, and I think I should go back and help her."

"Luke, please don't. You've done plenty. I'll call the police. Just get somewhere safe."

"I have a feeling Mom is coming. She is, isn't she?" Luke asks, already knowing the answer.

Sophie grips the phone tighter, licking her lips and clearing her throat.

"She sure is. She left this morning," Sophie says.

"Thank you, Bela. I'll see you soon . . . I love you."

"Dearie, please don't go back to—"

Luke hangs up the phone and leans against the dusty glass. A shudder escapes his lungs. He can't bear to lie to his grandmother again. He has to finish what he started. After all he and his friends have been through, he can't stop now.

"Let's get back to it," Luke says. "Let's go, homie," Drew says.

* * *

At 47 Lincoln Avenue, Sophie Ramirez is all alone. Her grandson has just hung up on her. Dropping the phone on the floor, she takes frantic, shallow breaths that cause her to cough uncontrollably. She drinks her water through a straw until the liquid halts the hacking.

"What have I done?" Sophie asks herself.

The icy tone in Luke's voice tells her he was serious. No justice on Earth is worth Luke's life. She rolls herself to the phone, dialing the Memphis police to tell them Ben's address.

"Memphis Police Department, what's your emergency?" the operator says.

Sophie clears her throat and decides to tell a white lie to explain how she knows the teenagers' whereabouts.

"Hi, I just saw the three teenagers that are missing from Princeton County. They're heading toward 86 Birch Drive."

"86 Birch Drive. Thank you for your help, ma'am."

"You're welcome. Make sure you bring them kids home safe," Sophie pleads with the operator.

"We'll do everything we can. Have a good day, ma'am."

The operator hangs up, and all Sophie can do now is wait for her daughter to call her or watch the local news for any updates on the missing teenagers.

* * *

Meanwhile, in the rain, Ben is nursing his shin with one hand, while the other tightly grips his pistol. His eyes are narrowed, looking in the same spot where he had the black horse at gunpoint. He drove his truck off-road, into the woods. He grinds his teeth in frustration, angry that he had the teenagers in his grasp, only to foolishly waste his ammunition. So, he takes a minute to recover and plan his next move.

"I've made my last mistake," Ben says to himself.

Ben spits on the ground and gets back in his truck. He grabs the flask of whiskey he keeps in the glove box and takes a couple of swigs to numb the pain. He grabs some spare bullets and loads his revolver, tossing it into the passenger seat. Furrowing his eyebrows, he turns on the windshield wipers and floors it, heading full speed ahead, back in the direction of Memphis.

"I tried it the nice way; now you're gonna get it, boy. You will not ruin thirteen years of hard work! I hope you're going back to my house; you don't strike me as someone willing to just let it go after all that. One way or another, you and your friend are gonna pay for what you did to me. You both will wish you were never born!"

Not too far away, Luke and Drew are trying to put some distance between themselves and Ben, but the horse has no traction on the cement. His vision is affected by the storm, and he's exhausted.

"The horse is gassed, Luke. If we go back to the house, we ain't escaping on it," Drew says, his voice trembling.

Luke sucks on his lower lip; Drew is right. It is not possible for Drew, Luke, and potentially Emily to all fit on one horse.

"Listen, the police and my mom are closing in. Hopefully they can help us before he gets back."

"You're putting our lives on the line, based on what? Hope? Faith?" Drew asks.

"Yes, it's gotten us this far, hasn't it?"

"We got ourselves this far, and I'm starting to regret it," Drew says.

"Come on, Drew. Just this one last stop, and then we're home free."

Drew shakes his head and lets out a dragged-out sigh. Chewing on his lip, he glances in Luke's direction. Lifting his finger, he points right at him.

"Remember, you owe me big time, Luke. But we ain't dead yet, so I'll trust you," Drew says.

"I can't thank you enough, Drew," Luke says, breathing a sigh of relief.

"Ride or die, man. This cut on my face and that black eye on yours proves it. Don't forget Bonnie too. We got each other's backs no matter the odds," Drew says, pointing at the now scabbed-over cut across his cheek.

"We're coming up on the house in a few minutes. I'll go inside. You should keep a lookout," Luke says.

"What about the woman?" Drew asks.

Luke scratches his chin and hums.

"I'll talk with her; she'll probably be on our side."

"Why? You barely know her."

"It's the right thing to do. One day he'll kill her and maybe her baby. Think if this were Rob and us," Luke says.

Drew closes his eyes and nods his head aggressively.

"You're right. We gotta do something. That man is messed up in the head," Drew says, pointing at his own.

"He's a bad man. My mom said he was very sweet until I was born. Did . . . did I break him?"

"Luke, if there's anything I learned in this life, it's that people don't change. They just show their true colors when they have no reason to hide them anymore. Your dad was always a scumbag."

"You think so?"

"I know so. Now let's hurry up and do this thing," Drew says.

* * *

Back in the car, Mike, Courtney, and Bonnie have made it to the city of Memphis. While Mike and Courtney pay no attention to what the city has to offer, the foreign surroundings of the urban city put Bonnie at a slight unease, as if the skyscrapers are closing in and trapping her like a pack of wolves hunting a baby elk.

"How much further?" Mike asks.

"Oh, we're only ten minutes away, Mr. Montgomery and Ms. Ramirez, nearly there."

"I know where he lives," Courtney says. "Here, take a right. Doesn't surprise me that he went back to this mud hole to hide."

"How do we even know Luke's still there?" Mike asks. "He's there. I know he is. He has to be," Bonnie says.

* * *

Back at 86 Birch Drive, the storm has started settling down. The front yard is now a marshland. As Luke and Drew dismount

Blacksmith, the ground immediately gives way to their weight and makes a disturbing squishing sound.

"We're here," Luke says as he moves his drenched hair out of his eyes.

"This place is hella creepy," Drew says.

Luke's eyes dart to a dent in the grass. He walks toward it and spots a hammer on the ground outside the shed. Realizing this might be useful, Luke picks it out of the thick mud with some difficulty. It seems to have been there for some time. He taps the head of the hammer in his palm twice, getting a feel for it. As Luke examines it, he sees it is slightly rusted from weathering but still in decent condition.

"Here, you take this hammer just in case Ben comes back and sees you first. Please, just keep Pedro safe and stay hidden. I'll be in and out."

As Luke hands Drew the tool, he realizes that he has called his father by his first name. He knew Ben was not worthy of the title, Dad. Not sixteen years ago, and most certainly not now. Drew examines the hammer and swings at the air, gauging its effectiveness.

"Protect yourself and Pedro. I'll be fine."

"Thanks, man. Hey, be careful, Luke. I love you like a brother," Drew says.

"I will. Thanks, that means a lot coming from you. I'll be right back. Pedro, go follow Drew."

Drew guides Blacksmith as Pedro follows him. He hitches Blacksmith to the same tree that Red is tethered to. They hide in the bushes as Luke trudges to the front door. Luke bangs on the door with such force that his hand throbs and his knuckles turn a raw shade of pink. The scent of chili fills the air. Emily must be cooking dinner.

"Emily, are you still here?!" Luke asks.

Luke hears footsteps approaching from inside. His muscles

begin to strain as the doorknob clicks open. Luke heaves a sigh of relief as he's greeted by Emily in front of him.

"Oh, Luke, I made chili for dinner. You're soaked. Let me get you a towel," Emily says.

"No time, we have to leave right now," Luke says as he waves his arms frantically.

Emily's brow furrows and her lips purse. She gazes over Luke as if he is a thief hiding something behind his back.

"Wait, where's Ben?"

"He . . . tried to throw me into an insane asylum, so I ran," Luke says.

"Oh my God," Emily says while covering her mouth.

"My friend rescued me, so I'm here to rescue you."

"What do you mean?"

"I know he hits you; that's why you have bruises," Luke says.

"Oh, these little things? He doesn't mean anything by it. He loves me. He tells me that every day," Emily says.

"He said the exact thing to my mom. He beat her too and killed his own baby while my mom was still pregnant."

Emily's jaw drops. Tears well up, and she caresses her belly as if she understands the pain.

"Good heavens. Ben never told me anything like that. He said his ex-wife was selfish drug addict and never let him see his son," Emily says, shaking her head.

"I'm not shocked, but we gotta leave before he comes back."

Emily ponders, and goosebumps run down her arms as she cradles her belly. Emily turns her head around, wiping the tears from her eyes.

"I . . . okay, I will, just to get this all cleared up at the station," Emily says.

"That's perfect. Do you have a car?" Luke asks.

"No, it's in the shop," Emily says.

"Do you have a gun?"

"Yes, a pistol, underneath the couch, but we shouldn't bring a gun to the police station."

"Sorry, I didn't think of that. You're right."

"Okay, just give me a minute to use the bathroom."

"Okay, but please hurry. We might not have much time."

Emily goes upstairs to use the bathroom. Luke ponders how they are supposed to escape from there since they only have one horse with enough stamina to leave the area. All three of them aren't leaving on Red. Luke is willing to let Emily take Red since she's pregnant. He and Drew would run for the woods and wait for the authorities to come. A few minutes go by before Luke's ears pick up footsteps. He smiles slightly as Emily makes her way downstairs.

"Come on, let's go out the front. We have a horse that you can take," Luke says.

Luke grabs Emily's chilly, damp hand, attempting to coax her into moving faster. They walk toward the front door. Emily stops abruptly in the middle of the living room to talk to Luke.

"I just want to thank you for what you're doing. You're a brave young man, and I don't know how to thank—"

The front door swings open aggressively, and Emily's mouth opens in horror. Ben barges in and pistol-whips Emily in the back of the head. She falls with a loud thud on the wooden floor; her still body lies in front of the doorway. Is she dead? Is the baby dead? Luke worries.

Ben takes a few heavy breaths as he checks on the unconscious Emily while keeping his eyes and gun steady on his son. Luke had forgotten the revolver hadn't been underneath the couch since Ben pulled it on him when Luke had attacked him. It had been with Ben the whole time. Luke stands there frozen, looking at Emily as he feels the world spinning around him. It is happening again. He hadn't expected Ben to be back so soon. His father looks like an oversized, wet rat. His unkempt hair falls in all directions. After Ben has made sure Emily still has a strong pulse, he leers at Luke and slowly raises his weapon at Luke.

"So, where were we, son? You weren't really gonna leave without saying goodbye to your own dear father, were you?"

23

DAVID VS GOLIATH

Luke gawks at Emily's unconscious body for what feels like years, even though he has a gun aimed at his head. He can't believe it; not even he could have predicted this situation. Luke gathers the courage to muster a few words.

"Had a hunch you'd come back here," Ben says, wiping sweat off his brow. "Y'all should've gone to the police station when you had the chance."

"Why . . . why are you doing this?" Luke asks as he takes a step back.

"Time for questions is done. Time to hush up and listen," Ben says.

"But—"

"How about you have a seat, like you did earlier?"

Ben motions the gun toward the couch, signaling Luke to sit on the old, filthy piece of furniture as he sits in the recliner across from his son. Luke's body vibrates noticeably, and he stares wild-eyed at nothing. The realization hits him like a ton of bricks. Coming all this way intending to confront his father and turning him in. He feels like a fool for letting his guard down. Luke actually feels bad for this pathetic excuse for a man. Now Ben has a loaded gun pointed at his son's head, and Luke is at his mercy.

"She didn't need to see this," Ben says as he stares at Emily's unconscious body.

"She wasn't a part of this. This was supposed to be between you and me," Luke says.

"I'll just tell her she got hit by the door or something. I could tell that woman that I'm president, and she wouldn't doubt me."

"You beat her, that's why," Luke says.

"You're damn right I do. I guess I should explain myself."

"You think?" Luke asks.

"Watch that mouth of yours, boy. Remember, I'm the one holding the gun here," Ben says, brandishing the revolver. Luke doesn't know if Ben had more ammo in the truck, but he's not taking any chances.

The reality of a gun pointing at him makes the hairs on the back of Luke's neck stand up. Ben is right. The truth is that he has all the power, and his son has none. Luke has no choice but to do as he orders. For a moment, deadly silence fills the house, so quiet that they hear the birds chirping outside. The serenity in the creature's song briefly tames the rage inside of Luke. It reminds Luke of the months that have gone by since he took the opportunity to appreciate life around him. Now that Luke sees his father for who he really is, he is finally seeing things more clearly.

"I can see you're enjoying the birds. I thought I was saving you back then, I really did," Ben says.

"Saving me from what? You?" Luke asks, pointing at his father.

"All this fuss between us. I just wanted a normal kid," Ben says without hesitation.

Luke's muscles stiffen. He rocks back and forth, unable to think straight. What could compel someone to make such an outlandish justification? His body trembles, resisting his fight-or-flight instincts, Luke's gaze falls to the floor with bewilderment written across his face.

"I don't understand."

"Of course, you don't. You're as slow as the doctor said you'd be." Luke closes his eyes, trying not to cry.

He doesn't want to show weakness. He yearns to punch his father again, but he knows if he does, he risks being killed. Luke bites his tongue and doesn't respond to Ben's claim. He just keeps looking down.

"Look me in the goddamn eye when I'm talking to you, boy!"

Luke opens his mouth in protest, but Ben points the gun at Luke, signaling him to shut up, reminding Luke once again that he is in control of this situation. Luke rarely makes eye contact with people he doesn't know or like. Seeing as he has no choice in this instance, Luke slowly lifts his head up, battling himself until his brown eyes stare into his father's hazel eyes. From what he can tell, they don't show the slightest ounce of remorse.

"Aw, are you gonna cry? You scared? Grow a pair."

"N-no," Luke says, trying to put on a brave face.

"You should be. Did your mother not teach you manners? Don't interrupt. Then again, your mother was always a hot mess. You know, not long ago, parents who had kids like you locked their kids in the basement because they were ashamed. No one wanted to deal with that. You know what people like you are, son?"

"Wh-what?"

Ben leans forward, his face close enough so that the pungent odor of booze on his breath invades Luke's nostrils, and the yellowing on his teeth is obvious. "You're God's mistake," Ben says, staring straight into Luke's eyes.

"God doesn't make mistakes. Bela taught me that."

"She told you He doesn't. Ain't that just precious?" Ben chuckles. "Maybe you're my punishment then."

"Maybe I was your test, and it's clear that you failed."

"No! You shut up. You failed me! This is all your fault, you autistic idiot!" Ben shouts.

"I had no control over it. I still don't, and I'm sorry. Is that what you want from me?!" Luke asks as tears start flowing from his eyes.

"Don't cry! It's too late for amends. You should've stayed home or gone to the asylum, because now I have to kill you."

"You don't have to. We can go our separate ways and never see each other again," Luke says, trying to look anywhere that's not Ben or his gun.

With his free hand, Ben reaches out and seizes Luke by the jaw. Clutching Luke's cheeks with his strong fingers, he squeezes hard enough that Luke cannot speak. Placing the cold barrel onto Luke's temple, he tilts his son's head forcefully until their eyes meet. Luke wriggles in his father's grasp like a worm, sniffling and shutting his eyes as the hammer clicks. Ben breathes heavily, baring his teeth. Just as it seems he will pull the trigger; Ben lowers the revolver and thrusts Luke's head onto the sofa's back.

"Don't bullshit me, boy! We both know if I let you go, you'll rat me out to the cops. I spared you twice, I won't make that mistake a third time."

"You're absolutely right, I would," Luke says, still clutching his chest.

Ben's scowl turns into a wicked smile upon hearing Luke's answer. His grin exposes his yellow teeth, some of which have dark specks on them.

"Good. That's good. Courtney and Sophie taught you that you shouldn't lie. It's a sin after all."

"You've done a lot worse than lie," Luke says, his nostrils flaring.

"Can't argue that. Well, like they say, like father, like son. I guess the apple doesn't fall far from the tree. We're the same," Ben says.

"I'm nothing like you. I would never beat the one I loved or abandon my child and attempt to kill my wife."

"I told you to watch your mouth. You definitely inherited your mother's tongue."

He has had enough of the ongoing threats and insults. Finally, Luke looks up, but his eyes dart to the already opened door as it slowly swings farther outward. Drew's head peers through the open gap; he lifts his finger to his lips. Ben does not see him since the recliner he is occupying faces opposite the doorway.

"By the way, where's that friend of yours?" Ben asks.

"What friend?" Luke asks, buying time for Drew.

Ben chuckles. Luke looks beyond him, at his friend. Careful where to tread, Drew takes one step at a time, making sure his drenched sneakers don't slip and cause an alerting noise. Shock crosses his face as he tiptoes around the unconscious, pregnant woman.

"I can't tell if you're for real or not. That Black kid with the horse who saved you in front of the insane asylum."

"Oh, that friend. He left. Didn't want to risk his life again."

"Huh, smart kid. Smarter than you," Ben says.

Drew closes in methodically while Luke continues to distract Ben.

They have to stop Ben here and now, and they only have one chance to knock the gun out of his hand, or else. The thought of what the alternative would have in store makes Luke's stomach turn.

"Any last words . . . son?" Ben asks as he wears a haughty smirk at Luke.

"No, I don't. I have no plans to die for a long time."

"As you wish. Get ready for He—oof!"

Drew had swung the hammer with all his strength and struck Ben in his right arm. The shock causes Ben to drop the loaded gun. Ben is in intense pain and quickly covers his arm with his free hand. Ben removes his hand once he sees Drew, and a bruise is already beginning to form on his bicep.

"Luke, quick, get the gun!" Drew says.

Luke dives for the gun, but Ben kicks the weapon toward the door before he can get to it. Luke hits the floor, the old, chipped wood scratching his elbows. Ben kicks Luke across the face while he is on the floor.

"You little shits!" Ben yells.

Drew winds up the hammer for another blow, but Ben blocks it. He outmuscles Drew for the hammer and tosses it aside.

Ben punches Drew in the gut, which knocks him to his knees. Luke gets up and punches Ben on the bridge of his nose, breaking it. Ben winces in pain but then lets out a little chuckle as he shows off his now-crooked nose.

"Oh, hell, you got a fire in you, kid. This is gonna be fun," Ben says as he licks blood off his lips.

Luke goes for another punch, but Ben ducks out of the way. Ben knees Luke in the sternum and tosses him to the wall, reaggravating Luke's sore back. Ben bends over to get the gun, but Drew picks up the hammer again and strikes him in the back of his knee.

"Ow! So, you want some more?" Ben asks.

Ben punches Drew in the jaw, knocking him down. Drew is still conscious but shaken up. Drew spits on the floor as he picks himself up. Ben swiftly picks up the gun and points it at Drew. Ben turns to Luke and says, "You'll see your turd friend die first!"

All of a sudden, a loud bark echoes through the house. Luke can hear the pitter-patter of four feet climbing the creaky wooden steps. Ben looks up and squints to see what is coming.

"What the hell is that?! Oh shit!" Ben yells.

Pedro comes in charging like a heat-seeking missile. Ben raises his gun, but Pedro pounces on him before he can fire a shot, knocking Ben on his back.

"Grr," Ben grunts.

Ben raises his right arm to guard his face. Pedro bites Ben right on the same arm that Drew hit, causing him to drop the gun and scream in pain. Pedro thrashes his head back and forth, sinking his teeth farther into Ben's arm. Ben rolls over and spins around in circles, desperately trying to get Pedro to release his death grip.

"Ahh! Get off of me! You damn dirty dog!" Ben screams.

Luke reaches for the gun, but Ben regains his composure quickly and stomps on the gun with one foot and kicks Luke in his ribs. Luke writhes in pain, cradling his midsection. With his free arm, Ben punches Pedro's snout. The dog lets out a hitch-pitched cry of pain. Ben scrambles for the revolver and finally manages to grab hold of it. Before he can turn around, Pedro is on him once more, knocking him on his back again. Ben grimaces as Pedro bites down again—this time on the other arm. Ben fights off Pedro and points his gun in the dog's general direction. Luke gets on his hands and knees and stretches his arms out, fingertips away from the revolver.

Without even looking, Ben pulls the trigger, shooting Pedro in his hind leg. Pedro yelps in pain, and the German shepherd falls to the floor and starts shaking and crying in agony, as blood spills on the floor. Ben pushes the whimpering dog away from him before pulling himself to his feet. While cradling his forearm, he gawks at the shredded skin and punctures as blood drips from them.

"No! *Pedro!*" Luke cries out.

"So, this mutt belongs to you? Well, he's about to be nobody's now," Ben says, bursting into laughter.

Seeing nothing but red, Luke balls up his fists. He doesn't

care about his physical pain any longer. Even if he got shot and is killed in the process, he no longer cares. Ben shot his dog in cold blood and now must pay. Luke drives Ben back into the TV, and the screen breaks. The gun gets lost in the mayhem. Broken glass from the screen is everywhere. Lacerations cover Luke's arms from the shards. Once he is up, Luke uses all of his body weight to pin Ben against the wall and starts wailing on him.

"Argh! Enough!" Ben says.

Ben knees Luke in the stomach, and he drops to his hands and knees. Luke looks up. Ben is a bloody mess but still snickering maniacally. His nose has been broken, and Luke notices that he knocked some of his teeth out. Luke thinks Ben has to be drunk to be able to withstand all that pain; it is the only reasonable explanation. Ben coughs up a little blood and starts stomping on his son like he is nothing more than an insignificant insect. Luke braces, but the onslaught doesn't stop. With each kick he feels less pain. His vision becomes fuzzy, and everything around him begins to dwindle away to nothing. Luke hears a glass shatter above him, and the stomps, at last, cease.

"Ahh!" Ben screams.

"Is that all you got? You fat, drunk, tub of lard," Drew says, flipping Ben off.

Luke opens his eyes, holding his ribs as he coughs. Drew broke a glass bottle over Ben's head, knocking him to his knees and elbows. Ben crawls to the kitchen and uses the sink as support to pick himself up. He runs his fingers through his wet, messy hair and looks at his hand in shock when he sees blood on his fingertips.

"Luke . . . let's finish this," Drew says, trying to catch his breath.

Drew quickly grabs a large kitchen knife from the table. He grips it tightly and sprints toward Ben and drives the knife through his shoulder, stabbing him. Ben howls in pain, the knife making a squishy sound as it pierces flesh. Ben kicks Drew in the groin, knocking him to his knees. Drew lets out a drawn-out, high-pitched whimper and clamps down on Ben's belt to keep from falling over while weakly attempting to strike at Ben's legs.

"Time to sleep, afro boy," Ben says, snarling.

Ben grabs Drew by his hair and, with surprising strength, lifts Drew up and throws him through the kitchen window. Shards of glass spread all across the room, and a thump followed by a splash is heard outside. Luke, still on his hands and knees, looks up with his mouth open in horror. He isn't sure if Drew survived the impact. Luke can't give up. He has to keep going—for Drew, Bonnie, Mom, Bela, Emily, and himself.

Luke uses what is left of his stamina to pull himself up and charge at Ben. Luke kicks Ben in the midsection, but he does more damage to himself than Ben. Luke collapses due to the unbearable pain. Ben grabs Luke's collar and picks him up, pressing him against the counter. Ben pulls Luke's hair to look out the window. Drew is face down in the mud, unconscious or worse. His head is covered with blood. Pedro's cries of pain are now muffled and sporadic, and he would bleed out from the bullet eventually at this rate.

Bursting with adrenaline, Luke tries to push off the counter, but Ben grabs Luke's arm from under him, and he falls face-first onto the countertop. With his large hands, Ben yanks a handful of Luke's thick hair and smashes his head on the surface, twice.

"For good measure," Ben says as he straightens Luke's arm.

Ben latches onto Luke's arm like a vice, and Luke is helpless. He tries freeing himself, but Ben wraps one arm around Luke's wrist, trapping it. Then, with all his weight behind him, he plunges his bloodstained forearm directly on Luke's elbow, breaking it.

Luke screams.

The crunching sound of bone snapping can be heard throughout the house. Luke feels lightheaded, and he can no longer move his left arm at all. Ben tosses Luke back to the floor. Luke, lying on his stomach, attempts to drag himself toward the rusty hammer near the couch.

"Where . . . do you . . . think . . . you're going?" Ben asks as he stomps the back of Luke's knee, crushing it.

Luke grimaces and pounds his good hand into the wood to stop himself from shrieking. Ben loses his balance and drops to a knee but quickly recuperates. Luke can barely move. He struggles to flip himself onto his back with one arm, but he succeeds. His arm is limp like a noodle, detached from his forearm; somehow, it doesn't hurt. Oddly, he feels an odd sense of comfort in this position, like he could take a nap and all of his problems would fade from existence. Though he knows that this is not so, it feels like the end. The Masked Haunter has triumphed over him. He warned Luke, but he did not listen, and this was his punishment. Luke will never see Bonnie, his mother, or his grandmother again. Pedro is still moving, but his cries are becoming further apart. As for Drew, well, if he isn't dead already, Ben will go outside and finish the job after he is finished with Luke.

"I don't know where my gun is . . . but you know what? You would be a waste of ammo anyways," Ben says, licking his chops.

Ben stumbles over to Luke and stops once he's standing over him, casting a shadow. Ben begins pulling the kitchen knife out of his shoulder, grunting the whole time. The knife makes a squelching noise as the blade comes out slowly. Once the knife is out of Ben's shoulder, he sighs in relief. Blood spills out of the wound, dripping over Luke's face. Ben, with his good hand, raises the blood-covered knife above his head, getting ready to stab his beaten, autistic son.

"Fuck! When I'm done here . . . I'm gonna kill your mom next, and then your Bela. Your friend and mutt are already half-dead. I should've killed your mom back then, made you an orphan," Ben says.

Luke is sure this is it. No one is going to save him from this sociopath. His eyes meet Ben's. He knows there will be no mercy shown to him. Luke coughs heavily. Each one is painful, due to his cracked ribs. Luke brushes it off before managing to muster some strong words. Luke is sure they will be his last; his fate feels sealed. Luke isn't about to leave this world quietly; he winces as he lifts his head up off the floor.

"Do . . . your . . . worst."

With those words, the back of Luke's head meets the ground again. He doesn't have anything left in him. If he is going to die right here and now, Luke refuses to die a coward or beg for his life. All his life, even though he rarely showed it, Luke was afraid of people, being different, and death. The Masked Haunter's prophecy is about to be fulfilled.

"Good choice of last words, kid. I'll see you in hell!" Ben howls, lifting the knife above his head.

Luke closes his eyes, accepting his fate. Time slows down. A tear falls out of Luke's eye; he's ashamed he has failed the mission to bring his father to justice and avenge his unborn sister. Luke hears a loud gunshot, followed by a clatter and thud on the floor next to him. He opens one eye. The knife is just inches from his face. However, his father isn't standing over him. Luke opens the other eye and sees Ben on the floor, writhing in pain and clenching his stomach. He turns his head, and there, in the doorframe, he sees his mother is holding Ben's silver revolver in her hand, which is shaking. The barrel is releasing smoke from where the bullet fired out. Courtney had shot Ben in the stomach to save her son.

"Wh-what?" Luke says.

Courtney swallows, the gun still aiming at the writhing Ben. *Should I put him down?* Courtney wonders. Mike glances at Ben and back at Courtney, realizing what's going on. He slowly tiptoes toward Courtney from behind. On the verge of breaking down, Courtney sniffles, the revolver practically jumping from her grip. Her breath becomes more unsteady, much like the gun, contemplating what to do. Mike wraps one arm around her shoulder and places his hand over the barrel of the revolver and gently lowers it.

"You don't want to do this, Courtney. It's over. You got him. Your son needs you."

Courtney takes her finger off the trigger and releases the gun, giving it to Mike. She wipes her nose before sprinting toward Luke.

"Luke, honey, I'm here," Courtney says, kneeling at her son's side, kissing his forehead.

"Huh? *You*?! Kill me, you damn woman. I . . . know . . . you want to. So, just do it," Ben screams, struggling to lift his head up.

"You've taken too much from me. You won't take anything else from me," Courtney says while assessing Luke's injuries.

"Oh, Luke, what has he done to you?" Courtney asks.

Mike runs past Courtney and approaches the injured Ben, whose red-stained hand covers the bullet wound as blood keeps oozing out of it. Mike kneels down, shaking his head in utter disgust at the attempted killer.

"You don't deserve the easy way out, you piece of shit," Mike says.

"You're all . . . just as damned . . . as me," Ben says, blinking slowly.

Mike takes a lighter out of his pocket and flicks it on. He removes Ben's hands, lifts up his stained tank top, and presses the flame on Ben's flesh to cauterize the wound. Ben squirms in agony and screams like a banshee.

"Relax . . . this will help stop you from bleeding out. Not the best way, but then again, you don't deserve the best," Mike says as he removes the lighter from Ben's torso.

"You bastard . . ." Ben says weakly.

Ben barely keeps his eyes open, nearly passing out from the pain. Mike lifts the gun above his head and smashes it across Ben's skull with all his might, knocking him unconscious, ending his rampage once and for all.

"Dr-Drew and Pe-Pedro they . . . need help. Drew's . . . outside," Luke says as he gasps for air.

"Mike, check on Drew please!" Courtney pleads as she leans down by the dog.

"On it," Mike says.

Mike tosses the gun aside and darts through the back door to check on Drew outside. Luke sees Bonnie in the doorway, and she looks like an angel. The sky has cleared, and the sunset is casting a golden radiance around her hair.

"Luke! What happened to you?"

"Bon . . . Bon . . . Bonnie?" Luke asks, trying to stay conscious.

"Luke, it's okay, we're going to help you. Y-you did it. I knew you could," Bonnie says to him as she drops to her knees by Luke's side.

"We need to help this woman here, this must be his new lady," Courtney says. "Good, her pulse is still strong. I can't get the bullet out of Pedro's leg, but I'll do everything I can to stop an infection from spreading. Bonnie, get my first aid kit from the car."

"Yes, Ms. Ramirez," Bonnie says before sprinting out of the house.

Mike returns to the living room, shaking his head and

biting his lip. However, Drew isn't behind him or draped over his shoulder. Luke shudders, fearing the worst has happened.

"He definitely has at least a concussion. I called 911 and told them to bring an ambulance. I didn't want to move him and risk further damage," Mike says.

"That's good," Courtney says. "We're gonna need—"

"Oh . . . what happened?" Emily asks.

Emily stirs, lifting her head. She flips over to her back and slowly tries to get up. Her round belly prevents her from sitting up completely. There is a large gash on the side of her temple that is bleeding from the hit she took from Ben.

"Wh-what happened?" Emily asks as she places her hand over her wound.

"Don't get up. Let me check your wound, please," Mike says.

"Oh . . . okay."

"Who are you?" Courtney asks.

"I live here . . . with him," Emily says as she points at Ben's battered and unconscious body.

"Are you okay?" Courtney asks.

"Yeah, your boy's a hero. I was frightened of Ben, but he wasn't. I don't know what would've happened had he not come along," Emily says as she points at Luke on the floor.

Courtney looks over at Luke. She instinctively covers her mouth when she finally sees how battered he is. Turning away, she takes a moment to compose herself. A prideful smile emerges through her tears. She wishes she could hug him, but he's too injured. Knowing there is no time to waste, she begins to nurse their injuries until an ambulance arrives.

"Are you okay? I see that you're pregnant," Courtney says.

"My head hurts, but is my baby okay? I need to find out," Emily says in a shrill voice.

"We'll check at the hospital," Courtney says.

"Here's the first aid kit," Bonnie says as she runs to

Courtney. "Thank you. Just put it next to me so I can remove the bullet.

Mike's good. He'll clean your wound when I'm done, okay? My name's Courtney, by the way."

"Thank you so much. I'm Emily."

"Luke! Stay awake, okay? We're gonna help you," Bonnie says.

"Take care of him. I'll be fine," Emily says to Mike, pointing at Luke.

"Luke, I'm Mike. You, your friend, and your dog are gonna be just fine," Mike says as he examines the teenager's injuries.

Until today, Luke has never met Mike in person. He appears fuzzy, and he can't make much of his face out. Luke wishes they had met under better circumstances. Besides a broken arm and cracked ribs, Luke feels fine, thinking his family can be at peace now. Bonnie gets on her knees and looks down at Luke, futilely fighting back tears. She kisses Luke gently on the lips. Luke closes his eyes, returning the kiss. It feels like he is lying on a soft cloud. In the distance, he hears sirens, and then nothing. As the world fades to black, it feels like he has just tumbled off the soft cloud and plummeted into the abyss.

* * *

"Luke? Luke, wake up, they're on their way!" Bonnie begs, seeing Luke's eyes close.

"Court! I need your help over here!" Mike yells.

"Coming! Bonnie, look away," Courtney says as she pulls Bonnie away.

24

TYING UP LOOSE ENDS

Luke can't see or feel anything. A sense of weightlessness overtakes him. He opens his eyes and blinks rapidly, groggily pushing himself up. Luke balks; the first thing he sees is that his arm is fully healed. Then that familiar, deep voice hits his ears from behind. Luke slowly turns around, and there he is, the Masked Haunter, standing over him. Those empty eye sockets reveal nothing but darkness. Despite being engulfed in flames, he is still as a statue. What could he want at this moment? Luke isn't dead—at least he doesn't believe he is. The Masked Haunter stands in the vast oblivion, seemingly contemplating his next words carefully. After what feels like an eternity, the Masked Haunter reaches up behind his ears and casually removes his mask. Luke stands there perplexed; he hadn't known that it was merely a mask covering his face. Luke squints to get a better look; it is his father's face, but slightly different. His jawline appears more defined and his eyes livelier, as if he were much younger.

"It . . . it was you . . . all along?" Luke asks, his gaze fixated on the Masked Haunter.

Reality comes crashing in on Luke as he realizes that all this time the Masked Haunter represented the repressed memories of when his father abandoned him as a toddler. It all makes sense to him now. Luke holds back tears, not of fear but rather joy. He had conquered the demons that he had battled for years. The young Ben narrows his eyes and opens his mouth to speak.

"So, you survived, and here I thought you'd die horribly," the Masked Haunter says.

"Guess it wasn't my time," Luke says, shrugging his shoulders

"I Guess not. However, your day will come. Just like mine did."

"I know. But when that day does come, I won't be seeing you."

"You seem quite sure of yourself, boy. Pride and arrogance have led to many downfalls in human history," the Masked Haunter warns.

"It's confidence, not arrogance. God was with me today. You failed! You will never have me. I see now, this whole time, you've been a memory of fear. You're not fear itself after all," Luke says, pointing at his father.

The younger Ben seems to ponder Luke's statement. Luke stands there stiffly, staring him down, bracing himself for a lunge or a response.

"It seems our work together is just about done here . . . for now," the Masked Haunter says.

"So, it seems. You failed to turn me against love. Your attempt to let fear sway me fell short."

"I have, but it's never too late to change. This was only the beginning; we will see each other again. Goodbye, kid."

The young Ben vanishes, hopefully never to return to haunt Luke again. Luke doesn't understand why it took so long to find out who the Masked Haunter really was. Luke raises his hand

and drags it across his face, contemplating alone in the dark void.

Was his mind trying to warn him the entire time? Luke asks himself.

Luke slowly opens his eyes, but everything is blurry. He is lying in a bed that is not his own. He is surrounded by fuzzy silhouettes, and there is a needle inserted in his arm. Where was he?

"He's waking up!" an unfamiliar voice exclaims.

As Luke blinks rapidly to help his eyes start coming into focus, multiple figures become clearer and begin murmuring excitedly to each other. Mike, Courtney, Bonnie, Sophie, Emily, Stephen and Tiffany Thompson, Randall and Laura Davis, a doctor, and a female police officer are all circled around Luke. Looks of concern and curiosity are written all over their faces.

"Where . . . where am I?" Luke asks.

The doctor grabs the medical clipboard and walks up to Luke. The doctor has short, dirty-blonde hair and square glasses. He adjusts his spectacles before reading off the clipboard.

"You're in the hospital. You have a broken arm, a fractured knee, and cracked ribs."

"How long was I out for?" Luke asks.

"About three hours. You shifted in and out of consciousness on the way here, but I don't think you remember. The surgery to repair your arm was successful, and that took about two hours."

Luke looks at his left arm. He attempts to make a fist, but it is pointless, as he can't feel or move it one inch. His left arm is locked in a cast. He also winces in pain when he talks too much. He lifts up the blanket to the sight of his taped-up ribs.

"Please don't try to move. You need time to heal. I'll give you some privacy with your family. My name is Dr. Simon. Just call if you need anything," Dr. Simon says as he shuts the door behind him.

"Can I ask some questions first? I'm Sergeant Caitlin Brooks, a police officer in Memphis. I just need to get to the bottom of what happened," Sergeant Brooks says.

She is tall, brunette, and looks fearless. She slowly approaches Luke and takes out a pen and notepad. Luke's eyes widen, unsure if he is in trouble or not.

"It's okay, Sheriff Berkowski is an old friend of mine. He couldn't come, I'm afraid. It's not his jurisdiction, but it is mine."

Luke nods his head up and down slightly, signaling that he understands and is fine with answering her questions.

"First, I need . . . to know. What about him? Did he make it?" Luke asks, raising his one good arm.

Sergeant Brooks gazes at Luke and back at his visitors. They each look back and forth at one another as if wondering which one was going to step up and give him the answer. She looks down and sighs deeply.

"Benjamin Miller is down the hall recovering from surgery. They got the bullet out, and he'll live. Also, he's handcuffed to his bed, so he won't be going anywhere. He was pretty banged up when we got him," Sergeant Brooks says.

"So am I," Luke says with a slight smile.

"Honestly, if it wasn't for Mr. Montgomery here burning and sealing his gunshot wound, Ben Miller most likely would've bled out before we arrived on scene."

Luke lowers his head, pondering for a second if he would've preferred his father being dead. Sergeant Brooks whistles and Luke raises his head.

"I just need you to confirm one thing. Did Benjamin Miller assault you?" Officer Brooks asks.

"Look at me. That's putting it very mildly," Luke says.

"Can you tell me exactly what happened?" Sergeant Brooks asks as she continues to write down notes.

"He tried to put me inside an insane asylum, and then I tried to help Emily, and he knocked her out. Then he threatened to kill me and . . . he nearly killed me, my dog, and my friend," Luke struggles to say, whispering to minimize the pain. Wait a minute . . ."

"What's wrong?" Sergeant Brooks asks.

Luke turns to the right and then to the left. It dawns on him that he has no clue where Pedro and Drew are. He begins to fear the worst has happened. He remembers how horrified and angry he was when Drew got thrown through a window and Pedro got shot in the leg. Luke raises his eyebrows to the ceiling and attempts to look left and right, trying to spot a German shepherd or big afro in the vicinity. Luke takes short, deep breaths when he doesn't see them, and his skin begins to turn pale.

"Where's Drew and Pedro?" Luke asks, his voice trembling.

"On your right . . . man, behind the curtain," a weak but familiar voice says.

Bonnie pulls the curtain aside, and Drew is on the bed to Luke's left. His head is wrapped up and his face is cut up from the glass shards, but otherwise he seems in good spirits. He is looking at Luke with that look he has whenever they got out of a sticky situation. "I told you we would make it, Luke."

This is the first time Luke is grateful that he gave him that look. Remembering what happened at Ben's house, Luke looks down at the foot of his bed at Emily, who has a Band-Aid on her temple covering the wound that Ben created with the pistol. Thankfully, she seems all right otherwise.

"He'll be fine. Just a concussion and a few cuts and bruises," Bonnie says.

"Hey, it's a good thing that you want to play basketball and not football," Luke says.

They start rejoicing with laughter together, and their snickering rings off the walls, filling the entire room. Once the chuckles come to an end, enormous smiles begin to spread across all their faces. Luke feels genuinely happy and fulfilled. After all the terrible events that have happened over the past few days, he feels warm inside being surrounded by the people that love him. That is, until he remembers that Pedro had been shot, and he sees no sign of him anywhere.

"Wh-what about Pedro? Is he all right?" Luke asks nervously.

"I got the bullet out, and he's at the vet, but they might have to amputate his leg. He lost a lot of blood, Luke," Courtney answers.

Courtney notices the concerned frown developing on her son's face and sits on the edge of the hospital bed. She smiles and adds, "He's going to live."

Courtney kisses Luke's forehead, and Luke grabs his mother's hand. He squeezes it, as it's the closest thing to a hug he can give right now.

"Thank God. I was scared that I lost two friends in one day. I wouldn't have known what to do."

Luke's smile fades away, and the image of Ben standing over him comes flooding back. He shakes Courtney's hand and asks, "Mom, did you tell the police about what he did to you?"

"I did, Lucas. I did," Courtney says.

"I did too," Emily says.

"Your father has multiple charges against him. Domestic abuse, animal cruelty, negligent homicide, first-degree assault, attempted murder, and fetal homicide, just to name a few," Sergeant Brooks lists. "I need to know if y'all plan on pressing charges against Benjamin Miller."

"I do," Luke says.

"I do too," Drew says.

"Yes," Courtney says.

"Please, yes," Emily says.

"All right, y'all have a good day now. Get rested, you two," Sergeant Brooks says.

"Wait, Officer! What about the tape recorder and camera?" Drew asks.

"I gave them to the police already," Bonnie says.

"Good job by the way, kid. On getting evidence. Oh, I almost forgot. I have one more question for you, Luke."

"What is it?' Luke asks.

"Did you happen to see anyone leave the mental hospital?"

Luke stares vacantly back at the sergeant. His mind is still slightly cloudy. He tries to recall what happened. He does not remember seeing anyone exit the institution.

"Sorry, Sergeant. I just got out of there as soon as possible. I didn't see anyone go in or out. Why? What happened?"

Sergeant Brooks lets out a small sigh and removes her hands from her hips. She turns around, and Luke attempts to sit up once again and fails, succumbing to the pain.

"Nothing to worry about, kid. Y'all have a good day now," Sergeant Brooks says as she tips her cap.

Sergeant Brooks turns around, seeming to leave the room, but stops in the doorway.

"One last thing. Next time you feel like playing hero, just call the authorities. You could've gotten yourselves killed. Y'all are lucky you came out of this the way you did," Sergeant Brooks says before shutting the door.

Luke and Drew nod at each other, acknowledging this truth, though neither regretted their actions in the slightest.

"That's our boy. A hero," Stephen Thompson says as he tousles Drew's afro.

"I'm so proud of you," Tiffany Thompson says as she kisses Drew's head repeatedly.

"I'm sorry, Luke. I would've helped sooner, but I was recording his confession while he held you at gunpoint, for the evidence," Drew says. "No, you did the right thing. That's gonna land him in prison for the rest of his life," Luke says.

"You both did it! I'm proud of you two," Bonnie says.

Luke smiles and reaches for his ribs as a sharp pain runs through his body. Yet no amount of pain could take away the happiness he is feeling right now. Luke wants to preserve every moment of it. He can't stop smiling. Whether it is from the drugs in his system or his pure joy, he cannot tell.

His mother walks up to him slowly and places her hand gently on Luke's uninjured hand and says, "Luke, Mike is going to move in with us if that's okay."

Mike leans forward and places his elbows on the hospital bed. He gives Luke a pleasant smile and a gentle wave, as drips of sweat pour down his forehead.

Luke tries to sit up, unsuccessfully. The sharp pain shoots up his abdomen like a bolt of lightning, and he falls back. He glances back and forth between Mike and Courtney. A few days ago, Luke would have said "No" without a moment's hesitation. Luke thinks about the question. He's still somewhat uncomfortable with the idea of someone he doesn't really know living under his family's roof. However, had it not been for Mike, Luke more than likely would have perished. Luke doesn't have it in him to say no to him.

"Of course, it will be okay, Mom," Luke says.

"Thanks, buddy. That means a lot," Mike says, wiping his brow.

"What about her?" Luke asks, pointing at Emily.

Emily takes the icepack off her forehead, revealing a purple bruise. She sits back in her chair with her hands on her belly, grateful that her baby is fine. The doctors had done an ultrasound to make sure the baby is still healthy. Emily stares at Luke with tear streaks still on her face.

"Bless your heart, Luke Ramirez. I'm gonna be fine. I'm moving back with my Ma and Da in Nashville. Please feel free to visit your sister anytime when she comes," Emily says, patting her stomach.

Sophie had not yet uttered a single word; she has had her rosary clasped tightly in her hand for the past hour. She is sitting in her wheelchair, silently weeping at the sight of her grandson. Seeing Luke hurt, battered, and broken, she wishes she had stopped him from going on that quest.

"Bela, are you okay?"

"I'm so sorry. If I knew that you would try to find him, I never would have told you."

"Bela, it's not your fault. I wanted to do it. If it wasn't for you, who knows what would've happened to Emily and Abigail. I'm sorry for lying to you."

"Ma, I don't agree with the way you did it, but you did what you thought was right. You couldn't have known what he would do," Courtney says, rubbing Sophie's back.

"Oh, *hija*, I just wanted Luke to know the truth. I never thought he would lie to me," Sophie says.

Sophie breaks down and hugs her daughter tightly. She can't hold back the tears any longer. Courtney rubs the back of Sophie's head. Luke looks on at the scene. Bela must feel bad for not knowing where he had gone. With the mission over, the guilt finally starts eating him up for lying to his Bela.

"Ma, it's okay," Courtney says. "We're getting justice now. It's okay."

The door creaks open, and the nurse peeks her head inside. She clears her throat and says, "Excuse me."

"Yes?" Courtney asks.

The nurse looks behind her and back at the people in the room. "There's a young lady who would like to come in and visit for a second, said her name is Natalie Brown."

"No way!" Bonnie says, crossing her arms and wildly swinging them apart.

Conflicting thoughts sweep through Luke's mind. On the

one hand he wants to make amends, but on the other, this doesn't seem like the right time or place. Before Luke can deliver his say, Drew speaks up. "Hold up! Let her in. Please."

"Drew, I know you hit your head, but you can't really be—" Bonnie says.

Luke reaches his shaking hand over to touch Bonnie's arm since she is right next to him. She looks down at Luke in a surprised expression, and he just smiles back. Luke beckons Bonnie to lean in closer. He cups his hand and whispers into her ear, "It's okay. I don't feel anything for her anymore. But I think Drew does. Let him have this. Besides, I'm ready to hear her reason."

Bonnie nods, but her eyes focus on Natalie as she walks into the packed room. Her foot stumbles, making a screech across the tiled floor. Everyone's eyes lie on her—some of the parents gawking with puzzled expressions. Luke recalls not telling his mother the cause of their breakup. He didn't tell her then because he was heartbroken, but now it no longer mattered.

"I remember you. You're the young lady from the sheriff's office! The witness who saved our kids," Courtney says. "Wait, your name's Natalie Brown? The one my son dated?"

"So that's what your face looks like," Laura says.

However, she doesn't utter a word in reply; she approaches Luke and mouths the words "I'm sorry" to him.

"Nat, is this true? Did you really call the police?" Luke asks. Bonnie blinks and places her hands on her hips.

"Wait . . . you did that? You helped us?" Bonnie asks.

Natalie nods and turns around to leave, but Drew waves her over in his direction. She sits by his bedside, and they strike up a conversation, quietly whispering to each other.

Hours pass, but they feel brief. The families begin to leave, as visiting hours are just about over. Within minutes, Luke and Drew are the only people left in the room. Luke closes his eyes and attempts to fall asleep.

"Psst . . . Luke. You up?"

"Yeah. What's up?" Luke says as he opens his eyes.

"Taking down your pops today gave me a rush I ain't felt in some time. I'm thinking maybe I should be a cop instead of a basketball player."

"Did Natalie put that idea in your head?"

"Nah, man. Hope it's not awkward or anything but—"

"You like her. I remember. I'm over it. Can't say the same for Bonnie."

Luke and Drew burst into laughter like they would never get the opportunity again. In that moment, all Luke's memories of envying those with fathers begin to pop up. Like when he was six years old and playing in the park, he saw fathers and sons pitching to each other. Luke shakes his head and smiles, now realizing that he never needed his father; everyone he needs is right here beside him. For the first time in years, a sense of clarity overcomes Luke. It dawns on him how blessed he's been all along.

25

A HERO'S WELCOME

The doctors discharged Drew after three days, however, Luke remained in the hospital for the entire week. Once released, Luke would have a cast on his left arm for six weeks. Every day after school, Bonnie visits him in the hospital, along with his mother, to remind him of how brave he was. However, Luke doesn't feel very brave; he just did what he felt he needed to do.

"So, did the nightmares finally end?" Bonnie asks.

Luke gently nods his head, grinning from ear to ear. His nightmares have ended. The Masked Haunter no longer haunts Luke's dreams, finally allowing serenity in his sleep.

"I think so. While I was passed out, I saw him, and then he vanished."

"That's good, but you know, if I was there, all these injuries wouldn't have happened," Bonnie says, chuckling.

"Probably Ben would've been massacred with all three of us fighting. You're the best fighter I know that's not trained in martial arts. One day, maybe you could . . . show me the ropes."

Bonnie runs her hand gently across Luke's cheek. He had thanked her nearly every day for what she did for Drew and him back at the diner.

"It would be my pleasure. You and I could see Sensei Tom Lee together. It's been some time since I've—"

"Hurry up, honey. Visiting hours are nearly done!" Randall Davis says as he looks at the clock.

"That sounds amazing," Bonnie whispers. "Tell Pedro he's a good boy for me. See you at school tomorrow, hero."

Bonnie kisses Luke softly on his forehead before she leaves.

"Don't forget young lady, you're still grounded," Randall Davis reminds her as they walk out of the room.

All the parents are relieved to have their kids back home, but they still hand out punishments to the teenagers for running away, with Luke's sentence being tripled from the one originally assigned after the fight with Rob. Asking any of them, it is a light sentence, considering the fact that they all could have been arrested or killed.

Tomorrow, Luke will be heading back to school. He decides to take a nap before his mother arrives to have him discharged from the hospital. When Courtney picks her son up, they don't speak for a while, as they are both exhausted, mentally and physically. They stop by the veterinarian's office to bring Pedro home, as he has finally recovered from his horrific injury. They enter the clinic, which reeks of dog fur and cat urine. To Luke's surprise, Drew and Mike are waiting in the lobby. They rise up out of their seats to the sight of Luke limping through, both swarming Luke, who quickly swats them away with his one good arm. They quickly back off. Courtney hugs Luke, careful not to cause pain, while Mike sneaks a gentle tap on the shoulder. Drew hands Luke a manila envelope, which he hands to Courtney to open up.

"Here you go, man. The sheriff was here a while ago, and he wanted me to give this to you."

Courtney opens the letter and hands it to Luke. His eyes scan down the white paper.

Dear Luke,

I commend the bravery of you, your friends, and even your dog. If Pedro had kept all four legs, I would've asked if we can make him a police dog. Really, though, it takes guts to do what y'all did, and I respect that. I feel bad for what your family and friends went through to get your dad into cuffs. Sorry for being an asshole during that interrogation a while back. I think you more than earned this. Just do me a favor and stay out of trouble, listen to your mom, and please, next time, just let the police do their job. Sincerely, Sheriff Paul Berkowski.

Taped to the bottom is a deputy badge, the bronze shimmering against the white background. Luke takes it off and smiles, admiring the engraved lettering against the background. He approaches Drew and puts the sheriff badge in his hand.

"It's all yours, Drew, you earned it," Luke says, closing Drew's fingers over it.

Drew smiles and shows it off to Mike as they wait anxiously in the lobby for twenty minutes before being called in by a female, slim, brunette veterinarian.

"Ms. Ramirez? I'm Dr. Adams. We have Pedro ready."

"Okay," Courtney says.

"I think he'll be very excited to see you," Dr. Adams says to Luke as they enter the room.

Drew places his hand on Luke's good shoulder to comfort him. The veterinarian opens the door; inside the room is Pedro, who is alive and well. His long tongue is out, and he is panting excitedly. Luke counts only three legs. Pedro's hind leg that had been shot is no longer there. The nurse has him on some sort of specialized mobility machine made for dogs. As Luke stares at the once- maimed leg of Pedro, the emotions are indescribable for Luke. Regret mixes with everlasting gratefulness for his dog's bravery and sacrifice.

"We had to remove the leg since it got infected. I'm sorry

that we couldn't save it. I recommend physical therapy to help Pedro adjust to walking with three legs," Dr. Adams says.

"You saved our dog's life, thank you," Courtney says.

"He seems perfectly healthy, very energetic and happy. I'll let you have a moment," Dr. Adams says, smiling.

"Pedro, you're a hero!" Luke shouts as he hugs the hobbling canine.

"Yes, but I think his hero days are over. Now he can go back to just being our companion," Courtney says as she looks from Pedro to the two teenage boys.

"Drew and I wouldn't be here if Pedro didn't bite Ben on the arm," Luke says.

Pedro's attention shifts from Luke to Courtney, and he limps toward her.

"I remember you telling me, hon. Such a brave boy!" Courtney says as she rubs Pedro's head.

"You're an all right dog," Mike says.

"Hey, you're the best dog, dawg," Drew says.

"I knew it was a good decision bringing him along," Luke says.

Luke bends down, reaching his arm to pet Pedro. Luke doesn't even have time to say anything before his dog starts licking his hand repeatedly. Yet, despite the dog's happiness, Luke is aware that there is little he can do to repay Pedro other than to look after him.

* * *

The night is dark, with no stars out to shine the sky. Sophie is sleeping in the guest bedroom, while Mike and Courtney share a bedroom. Luke still has all the upstairs to himself, which is lonesome yet comforting. Luke takes these quiet moments to remember all the blessings he has in his life.

The following morning, Luke tries to use his left arm to

silence his alarm, only to be stopped by the arm sling he is trapped in for the next month. Luke's knee still is not fully healed, so he goes downstairs cautiously. He heads to the kitchen, where he is met by the sight of his mother making French toast, and it smells divine. She mentioned last night that Ben would force her to cook whatever breakfast he wanted. Today, she is able to make what she wants.

"Morning, honey, glad to see you up and about."

"I am too. Is that French toast?" Luke asks.

Courtney insists on offering Luke some French toast, but Luke just wants to eat a bowl of cereal. He isn't feeling very hungry today. The anxiety of going back to school stalls his appetite. Courtney lays two pieces of French toast on a plate in front of Luke. The scent of cinnamon fills Luke's nostrils, and he begins to second guess the offer. Luke finally caves in when his mom looks at him with her brown eyes and then continues cooking more for the rest of the family to eat. Luke takes a few bites, and the French toast is simply delectable. He feels a slight ounce of guilt when he's unable to finish his plate.

Moments later, Mike comes in with a bad case of bedhead. He doesn't let it crumple his spirits; instead, he gladly volunteers to finish Luke's plate. Luke lets out a chuckle and goes to the guest bedroom to visit his grandmother before he has to leave for school.

"Hi, sweetie. Good to see you home. How are you feeling? Is your arm better?"

"Better, I guess. It's getting there, I think," Luke says as he scratches the top of his head.

"Really? You don't seem yourself."

"I just wonder if people at school are gonna treat me like I did something important. I just want to be treated like Luke Ramirez."

"Well, you *are* a hero and a survivor. There's no changing

that, but keep your head up. All that matters is that you know who you are, Luke."

"Bela, thank you. You showed me something I can't put into words but can put into action. I'm gonna start going to church again."

Sophie's tired eyes sparkle. She reaches out and touches Luke's cheek with her unsteady wrinkly hand. Her thin lips curl at each end, making a small yet beaming smile on her aged face.

"That sounds lovely, dearie. Thank you. Have a wonderful day at school."

"Thank you, Bela. I will."

"Wait, Luke," Sophie says, grabbing Luke's hand. Her grip is weak as her cold hand slowly slips off his wrist.

"Yes, Bela?"

"I want you to not let the past get in your head, and if it does, just think of the future. You have a lot to live for, *nieto*. I shouldn't have let you do that. I let the past get in my head, and I'm sorry," Sophie says.

"It's okay Bela. It's not your fault. After you told me everything, I had to make things right."

"I know, sweetie, but remember, no amount of vengeance is worth your life."

"Thank you, I'll try to remember that."

"You're welcome. Now get to school before you're late, and again, I'm very proud of you."

Luke steps out, and he picks up the local newspaper. He gawks at it, seeing his name plastered on the headline with a mugshot of his father beside it. He examines it but can't bring himself to read the article and tosses it aside on the doorstep.

The protests at the school have settled down in the past few days. The board was ready to give into the protesters' demand. However, after receiving several threats in his mail, Mr. Calhoun sensed the direction the wind was blowing and apparently quit on his own, not giving Principal Jackson or the board the satisfaction of firing him. None of the students have heard from him since. Principal Jackson expelled Rob—who is serving eight to ten years in prison for assault and attempted murder—as well as Brandon and Travis after they were both sentenced to two years in juvenile detention for assault.

Luke goes around the dozen or so stragglers from the protests to meet Bonnie and Drew at the front entrance. Bonnie and Luke hold hands as they walk inside. As expected, everyone looks at them, whispering loudly to each other as they pass them in the hall. The teenagers ignore the stares and head to Mr. Alterman's class for first period.

"Luke, it's nice to see you again. How are you doing?" Mr. Alterman asks.

"Good. Well, getting better. It's been kind of crazy," Luke says, pointing at his sling.

"I see. I hope you heal well. Did I catch you and Bonnie holding hands when you walked in? What's that about?"

Luke looks back at Bonnie—who smiles down at her journal as she writes in it—and back at Mr. Alterman.

"I . . . um . . . took your advice on girls. I'll just leave it at that. I'm just happy to be back. I did miss writing a lot."

"Marvelous. Take a seat. We're writing poems again, just for you."

Yet something different happens in class today. Natalie Brown takes a seat right beside Luke. He glances at her, unsure what to make of it. Luke has been thinking a lot about Natalie ever since she visited them at the hospital. Learning that it was her who called the police on Rob, it seems she really regretted her actions from a couple weeks back. Luke still hates what Natalie did to him, but he remembers that his father held a grudge against him for years and poisoned himself. Luke doesn't want the same to happen to him. He takes a deep breath to calm down and shimmies himself to face Natalie, careful not to hit his bad arm on the desk.

"Hi, Natalie. How are you doing?" Luke asks, not looking at Natalie.

"I'm supposed to ask you that, Luke," Natalie says, staring at Luke's sling.

"Well, I already know I'm gonna be asked that question repeatedly today. I'm fine. It's Drew I would be concerned about. Anyways, are you okay though?"

"I'm glad to hear that. I could be better. I've become close with Harper, so I'm not all alone against Sandy and Patricia. I'm sorry for what I did to you. I feel like I started this whole thing," Natalie says.

Luke looks over his shoulder just to be safe, as he is sure his girlfriend would not approve of him talking with Natalie. Bonnie is too occupied writing her poem to notice the two of them.

"I would've learned about my father sooner or later. Also, Rob would've done what he did, regardless of your involvement. By the way, you . . . you do know I'm dating Bonnie now, right?"

"Word travels around. I've heard that, and I'm happy for you. I sensed some sort of chemistry when I first met you two. I'm not looking for us to be together. I just want to be friends."

"Natalie, you broke my heart. It really hurt me," Luke says.

"Sandy and Patricia lied to me," Natalie says. "Told me you guys started the whole thing with Rob and that you were just 'getting a taste of your own medicine.' I knew they were full of it, but then they started threatening me, saying if I didn't convince you to come along, they would find out where I live and make my life 'a living hell.' She planned a triple date so I would lead you to Rob. The way Bonnie spoke so passionately about you, that sealed the deal. I knew those were the words of someone telling the truth."

Luke ponders the betrayal he experienced and how it felt, but also what Natalie did for him. He repeatedly taps his foot as he thinks. He never wants to lie again, so he has to be honest with Natalie about his feelings toward her.

"Luke, if I could take back everything, I would in a heartbeat," Natalie says. "Sorry for leading you on and the group home comment. Can you ever forgive me?"

Luke takes a long, drawn-out breath, nervous of what his next words will be.

"Sadly, you can't take it back, but I sort of understand why you did what you did. Since Sandy and Patricia tricked you and threatened you, I can't stay mad at you. You were backed into a corner. Most people would've done the same thing. Anyways, my dad stayed angry, and look what he became."

"Hey, you're not him. Remember that."

"I appreciate you saying that. How did you find out so fast?" "When I got home from work, I saw the news headline, 'Three teenagers from Princeton County Missing.' I knew it had to be you three. So, I sat in front of my TV until the newsman confirmed my suspicions. Then I drove all the way to Memphis as fast as I could. Soon the radio had an update that you all were at the hospital, and that's when I made my way over there."

"Well, thank you. Drew and I are grateful for that. How about you have lunch with us today? Maybe we can start over."

"Absolutely. I would love nothing more," Natalie says, reaching her hand out.

Luke hesitates, glaring at her hand like it's a trap. He slowly reaches out his free arm and shakes Natalie's hand, calling a truce. After class ends, Mr. Alterman hands everyone their poems back. Natalie is the first to leave. Once he gets his poem back, Luke walks over to Bonnie packing her folder away. He taps her on the shoulder.

"Bonnie, Natalie's going to have lunch with us, okay?" Luke says.

"Luke, why would you go and do that?" Bonnie asks, her arms falling to her sides.

"She deserves a second chance. She's not my dad; she won't mess it up. At least I hope not."

"If you think she deserves it, then it's fine by me. But if we're gonna be dating, you need to talk to me first about things like this."

"I will, beautiful. My mom already told me to make sure I communicate with you about important stuff."

Bonnie places her hand to her chest and rapidly blinks. Luke's cheeks turn rosy as Bonnie leans toward him.

"Aw, did you just call me beautiful?" Bonnie asks before giggling.

"I sure did," Luke says, scratching behind his ear. He flashes a bright smile as his eyes retreat to his lap.

"You're adorable, Luke Ramirez." "Let me see your poem."

"Okay, but promise not to laugh."

You are my ray of sunshine
Together completely intertwined
I wouldn't trade you for anyone
Our journey together has just begun
Hopefully you return my strong feelings
So, one day in front of me you're kneeling

"I love it!" Luke says.

26

DUST SETTLES

Nearly nine months have passed since Luke tracked down and fought his father, Benjamin Miller. A lot has changed since then. Luke, Bonnie, Drew, and Natalie are almost halfway through their junior year of high school.

While Luke's physical wounds have fully healed, the imprint of his father standing over him with a knife remains stamped in his brain.

In Memphis, as he sits in the courtroom, mere feet away from his father, Luke's stomach twists into knots. He watches his mother on the stand testifying against Ben, who stares a hole through her. As the trial goes on, a dull pain arises in Luke's elbow and runs up to his shoulder. This happens every now and then since the surgery. He clenches his jaw, trying not to wince.

Emily had given birth to Luke's half-sister, Abigail Sullivan. The baby is beautiful beyond measure, her hair red just like her mother's. Emily hands Abigail over to Sophie as she is called to the stand. The jury gasps when she rolls up her sleeves. While her bruises have healed, some scars are still visible.

Once closing statements conclude, the jury leaves. As the

jury deliberates, Ben glances back at Luke, who is pulled away by Bonnie.

Less than an hour later, the jury enters the courtroom once again. The jury foreman hands the judge the verdict and returns to his seat.

"Will the defendant please rise?"

Ben and his lawyer stand up. Ben's shackles rattle on the floor and against his legs. He licks his lips as the old judge clears his throat.

"In the case of the State of Tennessee versus Benjamin Miller, we, the jury, unanimously find the defendant, Benjamin Miller, guilty on all charges."

As the judge declares him guilty, Ben slams the table and knocks papers to the floor. The once seemingly levelheaded man reveals his true colors to the world as a belligerent man. The bailiffs quickly restrain him, as the judge bangs his gavel.

"Benjamin Miller, I hereby sentence you to fifty years in prison without the possibility of parole for thirty years. Get him out of here!" the judge says as he bangs his gavel.

"Looks like you got what you wanted, you old bag! Courtney and Luke, y'all ain't seen the last of me," Ben screams as he is dragged away by the bailiffs.

After the verdict is read, Luke collapses to the floor, his bad arm buckling under his weight. He groans as his forehead rubs against the courtroom carpet. Both Courtney and Bonnie pick him up. Once back on his feet, Luke gazes at Sophie behind him. His grandmother cries tears of joy and relief as she watches the man who nearly killed her daughter and grandson sentenced to prison at last. By the time he'd be released, Ben would be in his mid-eighties.

"We did it, *mi familia*," Sophie says, as she embraces Courtney and Luke for a family hug.

The joy is brief, as less than a month after the trial, Luke's grandmother, Sophie Theresa Ramirez, passes away peacefully in her sleep. The family all knew it would happen eventually, but Luke just wishes they had more time together. Luke was honored to have granted her dying wish. The family started going back to church, as it's what Sophie would have wanted. Luke had also promised her, and he never breaks his word.

The disdain Luke's father had for him helped Luke realize that life is too short to hold grudges against people who don't deserve it. While Drew had forgiven Natalie back at the hospital, it would be a long road before she earned Bonnie's trust.

Being thrown into a glass window finally knocked some sense into Drew. He continued talking with Natalie, more often than Bonnie or Luke. They started dating after a while, which was awkward at first, but eventually Natalie was accepted into their group again. They're still dating to this day, which is Drew's record for a committed relationship by far.

Drew's dreams take a turn as well. He plans to enroll in the police academy and attend college for criminal justice to become a police officer. Luke believes he played a part in Drew's sudden career change. Helping put Ben behind bars had lit a fire in his belly, leaving him desiring more. Although it wasn't Luke's intention whatsoever, Bonnie appreciated Luke helping Drew achieve a more reachable goal.

It took some time to adjust, but Luke eventually warmed up to Mike and learned that he is a very nice guy. While Mike does tell a lot of dad jokes that Luke doesn't find amusing, he can tell that he cares deeply for his mother, and that's all that matters in the end.

Luke often goes down to the ranch to help Bonnie. The horses they journeyed on—Red, Blacksmith, and Lucky—were brought back to the ranch safely. Feeding them is Luke's favorite chore to do, making sure they are happy and healthy. At the end of most days, they sit and watch the sunset together, sometimes staying out until the moon lights up the sky.

Now that Bonnie and Luke are dating, she told him that she's liked him since the fourth grade. It embarrassed Luke of how unaware he was all those years, but he knows he can't change the past. Luke can't imagine his life with anyone but Bonnie now. He thinks about how much he'll miss her when she heads off to New York for law school. While Bonnie has her career figured out, Luke still isn't sure what lies ahead for him.

"Thank you for your help today, Luke. Sucks that we can't watch the stars tonight."

"No problem, Bonnie. It's okay. There will be other times for that," Luke says.

Luke and Bonnie wrap their arms around each other before Luke has to leave for his afternoon therapy session. Despite sweat dripping down their noses, they squeeze tighter together, feeling safe in each other's embrace.

"I should call my mom," Luke says as he releases Bonnie and reaches in his pocket for his new cell phone.

After weeks of begging, Courtney caved and agreed to buy Luke a cell phone for his birthday last month. He was ecstatic opening the small box to a flip phone. She gave it to Luke on the condition that he would be responsible with it. Luke obliged and only used it to call his friends, thankful to have it for emergencies too.

"It's fine. I can drop you off. It's your late birthday present from me," Bonnie says, twirling her car keys across her finger.

"Oh, thank you. By the way, is Drew really taking Natalie on a date where he works because he gets an employee discount?"

"Yes, he sure is. Some things never change I guess," Bonnie says.

Bonnie had gotten her driver's license some time ago. Since then, she started driving Luke home from school and to the ranch. Their rides are often filled with flirting and laughter as they travel through the countryside just on the outskirts of town.

"Well, here we are. Enjoy your session," Bonnie says, parking the truck.

"I'll walk home after therapy," Luke says, opening the door. "Okay. Oh, wait, you forgot something!" Bonnie says.

Luke glances back, seeing what he forgot. He looks at Bonnie, with her eyes closed, and her lips pursed. He chuckles and leans forward; he carefully lands his lips on hers like an airplane on a runway. His eyes close, and moments later he feels her warm hand touch his cheek. While her hands are calloused, her lips are soft, almost pillowy against his own. When they separate, Luke gets out, grinning ear to ear. He turns around when the truck starts up, waving goodbye to Bonnie as she drives off.

As Luke sits in the waiting room, he fiddles with his jewelry. When Luke turned seventeen, he received a special gift. On his birthday, when Luke's mother handed him a tiny wooden box. Luke raised his brow, as he had already gotten a cell phone as his present that morning, and he hadn't asked for anything else. Courtney coaxed him to open it, which he obliged. Inside the box sat a gold crucifix necklace. Luke's jaw dropped; he couldn't find the words to express his gratitude. Courtney revealed afterward that his grandmother had been saving it for years as a final gift to her grandson. Luke choked up when he heard this and hugged his mother. He has had an empty void in his heart ever since his grandmother died. When he first put it on, it felt like a part of her was with him again. Since the crucifix holds great sentimental value to Luke, he has worn it every day since receiving it.

"How are you today, Luke?" Dr. Washington asks as Luke enters his office.

"I'm pretty good. Still with Bonnie, and it's going well, so I can't complain."

"That's swell, Luke. I'm very happy for you. Oh, what a wonderful necklace by the way," Dr. Washington says, pointing at Luke's crucifix. "Thank you. Hey, Dr. Washington, how did you know that you wanted to be a therapist?"

"Well, after the war, I knew I did not like taking lives. So, I decided to help heal them."

"What happened in the war that made you want to heal people?" Luke asks.

Dr. Washington sets his clipboard to the side and starts licking his dry lips. Douglas has told very few people about his past. He leans forward and looks at Luke with a slight smile.

"I suppose you're mature enough to know a story or two now. In 1967, four years after I was drafted, my platoon came across a village. We had intel that a few guerrillas were hiding amongst the villagers.

My sergeant ordered me to torture the children until someone fessed up," Dr. Washington says.

"Did you do it?" Luke asks, sitting on the edge of his seat.

"No. I refused to harm children and civilians in this war that, honestly, I wasn't even convinced we should've been fighting in the first place," Dr. Washington says.

"What happened to you?"

Dr. Washington runs his free hand down his face, which allows an exhale to escape.

"Well, there were no guerrillas in that village we soon learned. But, due to disobeying a direct order from my commander, I was dishonorably discharged from the military. Which I'm actually thankful for. I went to school for psychiatry soon after I learned my friend in Vietnam suffered from PTSD from the war."

"How did you know being a therapist was your purpose?"

"I wanted to help people the way I knew how, by talking things out. Why are you asking this?"

"It's all coming to me. Mr. Alterman said I am a talented writer, my mom says I was always truthful, and my friends say I have a strong thirst for justice."

Luke starts connecting the dots. Things seem to be making sense to him now. Luke believes there is an occupation perfect for his set of skills. Dr. Washington writes as he witnesses the gears in his client's head turning.

"I know what I want to do, Dr. Washington."

"What's that, Luke?"

"I want to become a journalist," Luke says.

Douglas Washington looks up from his clipboard, and his pen stops in its tracks. He rubs his scar. A smile slowly spreads across his aged face.

"I think that's a fantastic idea, Luke. I bet you'll make a great journalist."

"I appreciate the support, Dr. Washington. Thank you so much."

"My pleasure. Now, I want you to do some research, and in a couple weeks we can discuss which colleges you think suit you best."

"Will do."

"Splendid, have a good evening, Luke."

As Luke walks home from therapy, he has a gut feeling that he's discovered his purpose in life, and he is more than ready for the challenge ahead. Luke sees the benefits of journalism, uncovering the truth and exposing bad people for their terrible deeds. Luke could even have the opportunity to travel the world. The only con is the fact that he isn't comfortable being far from home. However, in his mind, the good far outweighs the bad. He will have to figure out how to get past his fear of being completely on his own.

Luke is thankful to have family and friends for help along the journey if he ever needs it. Luke hopes one day to be fully independent, but he has learned that seeking out help doesn't make him weak. It actually makes him stronger and smarter. Luke grabs his crucifix and rotates it in his hand, reminiscing about what his late grandmother had told him: *Look forward in order to move forward, so that you can succeed with your family right by your side."*

Luke glances at the sunset, still holding his crucifix tightly. Noticing his shadow cast behind him by the sun, he pulls his shoulders back. He places his fists on his waist and plants his feet to the earth, like superheroes do in comic books. Luke clears his throat, ready to make a silent declaration.

"I can and I *will* conquer any obstacles I face, because I am Luke Ramirez."

27

UNLEASHED CRAZINESS

More than eight months ago, a rugged man with a blind eye sat back against a tree with his eyes closed, waiting. He breathed into his dirt- covered palms, trying to warm up on a breezy night. He had grown accustomed to the moist stench of the outdoors, lying low in the woods north of Memphis for the past couple of days.

"Almost there," he told himself.

The man pulled himself up; the painful growl of his empty stomach nearly brought him to his knees. He brushed his greasy, jet- black hair back out of his eyes and limped through the woods. His eyes observed his leg and the cut he suffered.

I gotta hurry before it gets infected, he realized.

The man noticed a bare branch and ripped it off the tree trunk. He used it to lift himself up and employ it as a walking stick. The injured man crossed a small ravine. He squatted along the water's edge and cupped his hand to get a drink. The man grimaced and spat out the filthy water. He coughed violently, gripping his stomach as he tried to hold it down.

"It needs to be boiled."

The man groaned and forced himself up off the ground,

abandoning the ravine. After five minutes, the man struggled to keep his eyes open until a black shape came into vision. The man slapped his face to convince himself that he was not hallucinating. An old, isolated cabin, almost as filthy and rugged as himself, came into view. A slight smile spread across the man's face.

"Hope she's home," the man told himself.

The man lightly knocked on the door three times. No one answered, yet the light was on. The man raised his arm to knock again but was taken aback when the door swung open. He was met by a woman with dark hair, high cheekbones, and voluptuous breasts, pointing a shotgun at his face. The man's slight sensation of fear quickly turned into glee; he let out a howl of laughter. The woman lowered the shotgun, her jaw dropping. She lunged forward, wrapped her arms around the dirty man, and kissed him passionately.

"I thought you were coming, been waiting, but I . . . how did you escape?" the woman asked.

"Give me a sec," the man said.

The man went inside, and the woman poked her head out and looked right and left before closing the door. The man immediately approached the sink and downed a couple glasses of water. He sat down in a chair, and the woman handed him a plate of venison she had prepared earlier. The man took big and voracious bites and sighed as the cooked deer slowly satisfied his hunger.

"So?" the woman asked as she watched him.

"Right," the man said as he swallowed his food and wiped his face.

"I saw an opening, and I took it. This new employee was about to give me my medication when he noticed some headlights. A couple minutes later, he heard some gunshots outside. Sent him into a frenzy, and when he went to check it out, he left his ID behind."

"Wait . . ."

"I took the ID and a tray. Hit the nurse over the head with the tray, used the ID to get out through the back, and climbed the fence. It was perfect. No one saw me through the fog, and there were only two workers in the building at the time. Hell, I thought it was you at first that caused that."

"I think I know what happened," the woman said as she stood up.

The woman opened a drawer by her bedside and slammed down a newspaper in front of the man. He admired the front cover that featured a stubbly, middle-aged man. He read each paragraph carefully, trying to digest all the information it provided. His eyes widened when it mentioned the mental hospital that he had escaped from.

"So, that guy brought his son to the hospital and apparently tried to shoot him dead. Can't believe that asshole is the reason you got out."

"He wasn't the reason. His son was," the man reiterated.

"It says right there he tried to shoot the kid. The same gunshots that scared that employee."

"He was only there to commit the kid. Besides, had the kid not escaped, the guy wouldn't have shot."

The man continued to read the news story and eat as the woman cleaned the dishes. He nodded his head and smiled bigger as he finished the story.

"This kid, Luke Ramirez, is special. Kinda reminds me of a young me."

"Yeah, he apparently tracked down his father and helped put him behind bars. Yeah, that kid has guts," the woman responded.

"Has autism too . . . interesting. Might have to meet this kid one day. Also helped get a notorious racist teacher fired," the man said as he itched his prickly, unkempt stubble.

"Maybe when you're not being hunted."

The woman's eyes looked up and down the man, scanning every mark on the man's body. She got up and unpacked a makeshift medical kit. The woman sat next to the man as he stuffed the last of his venison in his mouth.

"Let me clean you up." "Finally. My leg is messed up."

"I'm buying you new clothes first thing in the morning. Burn these crazy clothes," the woman said as she lifted up the man's pant leg.

"Absolutely."

The woman took out a bottle of hydrogen peroxide, doused an old rag, and applied pressure to the wound on the man's calf. The man squeezed his own knee and winced slightly. The woman wrapped some bandages around the man's leg.

"I need to lie low for a while. Then we make them pay," the man said.

"Excuse me? Who are you referring to?" the woman asked.

The man side-eyed the woman and sucked his teeth intensely. The woman nodded slowly, understanding exactly who he meant.

"The things they did to us. No parents . . . we were children, orphans. They probably still do it."

"What can we do about it? Happens everywhere," the woman answered.

"Take action into our own hands, like that kid did."

The man leaned over and picked up the wrinkled newspaper. He held it out to the woman's face and pointed at the article. The woman tilted her head and pursed her lips, contemplating.

"You and I are pariahs. No one likes us, and no one will help us. Except our own. We must find some angry, like-minded people like us, oppressed and held down by this world."

"Where do we find people like us?"

The man stood up slowly and approached the woman,

slightly hunched to place his hands on her shoulders, and sharply inhaled.

"The enemy of my enemy is my friend. Sacrifices have to be made, and they will. We'll find decent people like that kid. First, find your brother. We need someone like him with us."

"He's a little unstable. Ever since . . . you know."

"He has weapons, and he's like us."

The man released the woman and opened the door, looking up at the pale crescent moon illuminating the sky. The man took a deep breath and closed his eyes, listening to the sounds of the crows calling in the night. The mystic cawing caused an odd sense of tranquility within the man's mind.

"One thing that's been bugging me. Did you really kill her?" the woman asked his back.

"Whether I did or I didn't doesn't matter anymore," he replied without turning around.

The man removed his filthy, torn, gray shirt. He stared at it in his hands with contempt. Besides the layer of dried mud and tattered shreds, it was blank. No picture, no name tag, not even a number. He had been robbed completely of his individuality. This painful fact that he had been reduced to just another face made his hands tremble in a rage. He ripped the shirt in half and threw the shreds into a clearing. He picked up a gasoline canister and doused the fabric. The woman handed him a box of matches, and he lit one up.

"Never again," the man whispered as he dropped it on the remnants of the shirt.

The torn fabric lit up like a candle; the fire brightened up the man's face, making his discolored pupil more obvious as he narrowed his eyes to the flame. The woman scanned the man's naked torso, covered with scars and bruises. She hugged him tightly and stroked his cheek. The man sighed and settled down.

"I have an idea," the man said.

"I'm with you all the way, like I've always been," the woman reassured.

The man and the woman stared at the fire until it became nothing more than embers. Now that the torn top was only cinders and memories, the man limped back to the cabin with the woman's aid. They lay in bed together with the woman eventually going to sleep. The man sat up, grinned, and looked down at the floor. Each minute that passed by, more and more memories that were once faded came back to him; bits and pieces of his life that prescribed medication repressed had begun flooding back.

"No more medication. I'm . . . free," he whispered.

The man got up and took the same newspaper to read the article over once again. He was so fascinated by the story that he simply could not put it down. He began rehearsing the names he saw in the story over in his head until he remembered them. After reading the story for the fourth time, he let out a yawn and set it aside. He chuckled slightly and let out a sigh of relief before finally, slowly, drifting off into an undisturbed slumber.

CALL TO ACTION

Thank you for reading *Looked Down Upon: The Exiled Kin.* I hope you enjoyed the book.

A sequel is currently in the works. For news on upcoming books, please sign up for Jordan Lopez's Newsletter at jordanalopez.com

Luke Ramirez will return . . .

ACKNOWLEDGMENTS

Thank you to my editor, Sara DeGonia, for your impact on this book. Your approach and suggestions helped guide me through the storytelling process.

To Stacey Longo, who visited my college and graciously read the first draft of my manuscript. I hope to be half as talented as an author as you some day.

To the designer team at Miblart for the spectacular book cover they created. They nailed my vision perfectly, and I couldn't have asked for a better cover.

To Mrs. Brooks, my second grade teacher, who taught me how to read when others had given up hope. These words wouldn't have been possible without your famous hermit crab book bribe.

To Dr. Lucier, who taught me to tell jokes (even though I didn't say them right) and helped improve my speech and behavior. I wouldn't have found my sense of humor without you!

To Professor Hickox, who awoke a sleeping giant, your words of encouragement on my college essay lead to the creation of this project. Thank you for igniting my passion for writing again.

To my mother, Kelly Lopez, who never doubted for a second that I would get this book published. She just said, "Awesome, looking

forward to reading it." You've always been my number one supporter, and thank you for putting up with me whenever I asked for your opinion on a scene or sentence during the editing process. Love you, Mom.

To my grandmother, Debbie Sacherek, you were the first to read my book in its entirety. I know it was an early draft and looked much rougher and slightly different from the final product, but it made you cry, and you adored it. You urged me to continue writing, so I will grant your request. I hope you enjoy reading the finished version in heaven. I miss you every day, Grammy.

To my Autism, while at times you feel like a liability, randomly conjuring up this story one day made you my greatest asset. Without you, this particular story wouldn't exist, and more importantly I wouldn't be me.

ABOUT THE AUTHOR

JORDAN LOPEZ is on the autism spectrum. While growing up, he struggled with building social relationships, learning, and 'fitting in.' He expressed himself through the creative arts to cope. Soon Jordan embraced his disability and all the challenges that come with it. As a young adult in 2017, he developed a passion for writing. Eventually, some of his work got published.

In 2019, Jordan decided to write a novel. He has been a Special Olympics athlete for more than a decade and is an advocate for those on the spectrum. He was born and raised in Connecticut. For more information on Jordan Lopez, please visit jordanalopez.com

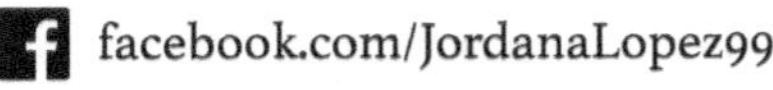 facebook.com/JordanaLopez99

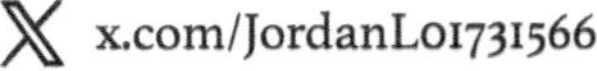 x.com/JordanLo1731566

instagram.com/J.lo_pez